COUNTERCLOCKWISE

A FICTION-ATLAS TIME TRAVEL ANTHOLOGY

C.L. CANNON   MATTHEW STEVENS

BREE MOORE   SARAH BUHRMAN

REBEKAH DODSON   DAMIAN CONNOLLY

K. MATT   BOB JAMES   MELODY ASH

NANEA KNOTT

FICTION-ATLAS PRESS LLC

COUNTERCLOCKWISE

A FICTION-ATLAS TIME TRAVEL ANTHOLOGY

FICTION-ATLAS
PRESS LLC

ISBN-13: 978-1-7323406-2-6

First Edition: August 2018

10 9 8 7 6 5 4 3 2 1

CONTENTS

ALL THE BROKEN PIECES OF ME (FRAGMENTS)

BY C.L. CANNON

The steady beep of a heart monitor echoed off the walls of the ward. Every click of his footsteps on the tiled linoleum floors and every breath of sanitizer Elijah had inhaled on his way up here left his stomach in a lurch.

The auburn-haired woman was back, or had she left at all? She had tired, puffy eyes and her mother's fire.

"Why are you here? I've told you to stop coming. You only upset her!"

"I'm sorry, I can't do that," he said, inching closer to the hospital bed.

When he'd tracked down Maddy's location a few days ago, he'd come in without a plan. He'd arrived without expectation of the consequences of his latest trip. He was not prepared for what he found.

"My mother... doesn't... know you," the woman said slowly as if explaining something complicated to a child.

"She did. Once upon a time, we used to travel together."

"You must have her mixed up with someone else. There's tons of

Madeline Smith's out there. My mother's never traveled in her life! Never even been outside the state that I can remember."

Yes, that is who she used to be. Scared of adventure, cautious of trying anything new, but time, ironically, had changed her.

"Your mother was magnificent. She just doesn't remember, and it's my fault."

"I think you're mistaken."

He chose to ignore her denial. There was no way she could understand. Instead, he strode the final few steps to the unconscious woman's bed. He gently took his hand in hers, rubbing his thumb over her palm.

"It's okay, Maddy. I'm going to fix this. I'm going to go back, back to 1965, and I promise we'll be together again." He brought Maddy's hand to his lips, placing a chaste kiss upon it.

"Sir, do you have anyone I can call for you?" the daughter asked.

Great, now she thought he was mental. Her stance was tense, and she'd advanced a few steps toward him when he touched her mother.

"I'm sorry," he whispered, letting go of Maddy's hand and meeting her daughter's eyes. There was so much pain there, stirring beneath the surface of those green orbs.

"It's okay. I just want to make sure you're all right." She'd loosened up a bit, her forehead creasing with concern.

She really was like her mother, worried over a stranger.

"Not for that," he said, glancing one last time at Maddy before closing the door behind him.

It wasn't an easy decision to blink someone out of existence, especially the daughter of his beloved Maddy, but this was the wrong timeline. None of this should have happened, so he had to wonder, was it really murder? Was he killing millions of innocents if they should have never been born? Perhaps not, but it did little to ease his conscience.

A familiar voice whispered suddenly from the right hallway. "What are you doing here? Cyrus will have your head if he finds out about this."

Elijah looked the man in the eye, then smiled. "He's not going to find out. I can't leave her like this, Kev. You know I can't. So, are you going to help me or not?"

Kevin pushed his glasses further up his nose before inhaling deeply. "Why do I let you drag me into these things?" he asked.

"Because you're a good friend," Elijah said, clapping Kevin on the back.

"And don't forget it. So, what's the plan?"

"I'm going back into my own timeline. I have to warn her."

Kevin shook his head back and forth, clearly not as on board with this plan as Elijah had hoped.

"Are you insane or have you forgotten how attached at the hip you two were? What if you run into your past self?"

"Don't worry. I'm going to keep my distance. The last thing we need is a paradox. You forget, I know past me's movements, hell, I lived them."

Kev did not look convinced.

"Elijah, you can't even remember what you had for breakfast this morning. How are you going to remember every single thing you did on any particular day in your past?"

"I have to try. Now c'mon. We need to get out of here before we're discovered."

"You didn't think of that on the way up here?" Kev asked, a sarcastic tang to his words.

***

Kevin was looking at the now half-uncovered time machine in horror. "Seriously, you hid the time machine in the trash pile? What if it was trash day?"

Elijah continued to drag large pieces of soggy cardboard off the top of the machine while defending his choice.

"I checked with the janitor. I'm not a complete idiot."

The edges of Kevin's lips turned up in a smirk.

"No, don't say a word," Elijah warned, pointing his finger at his best friend. "Just get in."

"Oh, whoo. No, that is disgusting," Kevin complained, dry heaving a few times before managing to pry the passenger door open. "Smells like someone died in here."

When Cyrus Industries had entrusted the triangular box to Elijah, this was definitely not how he imagined seeing the mysteries of the world. The temporal veil which disguised the ship in foreign times had gone out a few weeks ago, in the middle of a fight with a pair of HE 111s while escaping the London Blitz. Being on the run from Cyrus didn't really leave Elijah many choices when it came to repairs. For now, it was stash it, and hope no one notices.

"Next time, I'll let you park the pyramid, oh great one," Elijah said, flicking the preflight switches and checking the pressure gauges. Beside him, Maddy's jump seat remained empty. Something he needed to rectify.

"We'll get her back," Kev said, connecting the dots.

Elijah nodded, swallowing the doubt that had welled into a tight ball in his throat.

With a deep breath, he pushed the throttle forward and disengaged the grounding equipment.

The machine lurched to life, yanking the two men forward in their seats before the force of takeoff pushed them back against the leather headrests again.

When the whirling of the machine finally stopped, Elijah threw his belt off and turned the door cog.

Detroit, Michigan 1965, where it had all gone wrong. He'd climbed out of the machine a week ago with the love of his life at his side, excited to see the Beatles and fascinated by the heroics of the civil rights movement. He'd left empty-handed, with no intel, and no Maddy. He'd arrived back at the machine to find an older man in a dark business suit entering the driver's side door. They'd tussled, but the man was much quicker than he looked, especially for his age.

"Okay, man, where do we start?" Kevin asked, stepping into place beside Elijah.

"We need to find, Maddy. She was assigned to check out Viola Liuzzo, while I met with one of my contacts," Elijah turned, noting the time on the large clockface of city hall. "We've got about two hours before it all goes to hell again."

"Viola worked at a grocery store down on the other end of town. That's where Maddy said she was headed when I left."

"The way I see it," Kev began, "We've got two ways we can stop this. We can find Maddy and try to convince her to return to the machine early, or we can try to locate the man who started this in the first place. We should split up."

"No way. That's what got us in this mess in the first place. Plus, we have no idea who this guy is or what he wants."

"Shopping it is then," Kev said, admitting defeat. "What do you think he wants?"

"I really don't know. It doesn't make sense. He could have killed me, but he didn't."

A few blocks of walking and they'd arrived at the small grocery store where Maddy should have been, but she was nowhere to be seen. Kev entered the store, chatting with Viola and her friend Sarah. According to the ladies, they had not seen a woman matching Maddy's description come through the store. So where could she be? They began walking back toward the middle of the city, closer to the machine in case she'd doubled back for some reason.

One thing was certain, Kevin was the problem solver and he was the worrier. He'd never been much of a cool and calm in the face of insurmountable obstacles kind of guy. "Maybe she went to find you. Did she know where you were headed?" Kevin reasoned.

"No, I didn't even know until a few minutes after she left for the grocer. I got a text on my handheld."

"What about the guy you met with? Did he seem suspicious?" Kevin asked.

"Just a regular guy, as far as I could tell."

Elijah's hands went to his hair pulling and smoothing it back in anxious frustration.

"Elijah?"

And then, there she was.

"Hey, what are you doing here?"

He couldn't help himself. He scooped her up in his arms, twirling her around a few times before finally setting her feet back on the ground.

"Well, what was all that about? Are you okay?" She asked.

Elijah's eyes took in every last detail of her, and he exhaled a breath he didn't realize he'd been holding. "Better than I've been in so long. I love you."

She chuckled, wrapping her arms around him for a quick hug. "I love you too."

Her arms tensed around his neck before falling away abruptly.

"Wait, is that Kevin? Since when did they start sending two teams to intel gatherings?" He could hear the irritation in her voice. She never did like unannounced changes to our mission plans.

"They didn't send him. I did." Elijah said, nodding in Kevin's direction.

"Hey, Mad!" Kevin greeted her, throwing up one hand in a lazy wave.

Maddy shook her head, still surprised by Elijah's last words. "I don't understand."

"Listen to me carefully, Maddy," Elijah said, holding her arms at the elbow and leveling himself to her height. "Our timelines, they fragmented. We lost each other. But I'm here to make it right."

"Elijah, what do you mean?" Her forehead crinkled as she tried to decipher his words. "You're right here. I just saw you not thirty minutes ago."

"You saw past me. I've crossed my own timeline, Maddy. You know I would never do that unless it was important. So, will you please listen to me? You need to get back to the machine."

"Oh, God. You're not joking are you," she gasped, throwing her hand over her mouth.

"No. You have to get back, or it's going to take off without you. You'll be stuck here. We have to go now."

"Well, what about my Elijah? We can't just leave him."

"He has his own machine. He'll eventually become me. He'll travel to the future, see what a mess he's made and come back here to get you," Elijah explained.

Maddy bit her lip as he knew she often did when nervous. "I feel like I'm betraying him in some way," she confessed. He couldn't keep the grin from spreading over his face. "Trust me, he forgives you. Now let's go."

He took her hand in his, and the three of them raced for the machine. "Where did you go? We looked for you at the grocery," Elijah asked, his voice thumping as his feet hit the ground at such a quick pace.

"It's stupid," Maddy called back to him.

"Nothing you do is stupid."

"Gee, I wish… he'd talk to me… as nicely as he does you," Kevin huffed, trying to catch his breath.

Elijah could see the amusement on Maddy's face. There was that shy giggle again and the smile he'd missed so much. He'd been separated from her for a week, but it felt like an eternity of endless longing.

"Do you really want to know where I was?" she asked?

"Absolutely."

"There was a dress that caught my eye a couple of blocks from the grocery store. I wasn't exactly in a rush to interview a woman who was about to die."

"Only you," Elijah pretended to scold her.

A surprise awaited them back at the site of the machine. The businessman who'd fought with Elijah the first time was waiting for them. He was leaned back against the side door; his legs crossed at the ankles. "No, no. You're not supposed to get here until later," Elijah said, jabbing a finger in the man's direction.

"I could say the same for yourself."

"Well, what is it, old man? What is so important that you feel the need to kidnap me and steal my machine?"

"Her," the man replied, pointing to Maddy. "She's the reason for it all. For everything that goes wrong in our lives."

Elijah instinctively placed himself between Maddy and the old man. He would not touch her.

"Our lives?"

"Yes, our. Haven't you figured it out yet? How did I know when and where you would be? Where you'd park the machine on your second trip. How I could anticipate every move you were going to make the first time we met?"

"Oh, my god," Elijah gasped. "You're me."

"Yes, and I'm you. We're in a time loop, you idiot."

"That's not possible. Is it?" young Elijah questioned.

"God, was I really this naive?" Older Elijah muttered under his breath. "Of course it's possible. We've been doing this over and over for God knows how long and it has to end."

There was desperation in the man's graveled voice. How many times *had* he lived this moment?

"All along I thought the solution was helping you leave when I should have been doing the opposite," the man jibed, pulling a small tube from his pocket.

"Hey, isn't that the geo-temporal core?" Kevin spoke up.

"No, no." the younger Elijah began, waving his arms wildly in front of him. "You can't destroy the machine. What will that accomplish?"

"No time machine, no time travel," older Elijah reasoned.

"And what makes you think Cyrus won't track us down here and kill us?" Kevin asked?

"Oh, he will kill you, I've already tipped him off," he admitted. "But I'll be long gone by then."

"You don't need to do this, Elijah," Maddy called from her position behind the man's younger self.

"I do. You have no idea, Mads. I tried to save you. I tried to save you thousands of times, hundreds of ways and they all fail. This is the only way. I have to eliminate the time variables, and that includes you."

Maddy shook her head, denying him her understanding. "My

Elijah would find a different way. He wouldn't want to hurt anyone. He could never hurt me."

"You don't know or understand this version of me. You have no idea what I'm capable of or what I've done in your absence."

"No, I don't, and I'm sorry for that. I'm sorry I caused you pain." Tears welled in her eyes, and her voice was beginning to break.

"I waited and waited for you. And you never came back. I waited forty years in the past, growing old without you, and you just disappeared. Where were you?" the older man asked?

"I just wanted to look at a dress, that's all."

"And then you met us," Kevin interjected. "We kept you from going back to the original machine and the original Elijah.

"I stole you away from myself," Elijah realized out loud. He looked to his older self, broken by the time loop that he'd created.

"Is anyone else hella confused right now?" Kevin asked awkwardly raising his hand. "I mean I kinda understand, but still, it's seriously messed up."

"It's Quantum Superposition," the elder version of himself explained. "Two timelines occurring in parallel."

"If it can't be broken. We'll just continue to loop," the younger Elijah theorized, moving his finger through the air in a figure eight.

"Now do you see? I can't do this anymore?"

"There has to be a way to break it," Kev theorized.

"Elijah," Maddy began, stepping away from his younger self and walking closer to the older one. "Do you trust me?" "I don't know. I don't know who to trust anymore," the older man said.

Elijah could still see the tender look his older version gave Maddy. No matter what he said or how desperate he became, there was no way to forget this woman. No way to get over her. Every Fragment of his being was under her thrall.

"Please, I know what to do. I know how to end this. Let me."

"Maddy, what are you doing?" Elijah asked, suddenly feeling sick in his gut.

"Give me the core, Elijah." Her eyes never left the old man. Her hand gently reached out to him, and ever so slowly he let go. The core fell into her waiting palm, and she spared one last glance toward his younger self before unlatching the side door and barricading herself inside.

She was leaving them. She was leaving them all.

The hum of the replaced core sounded, and despite their pleas for entrance, the machine disappeared.

The steady beep of a heart monitor echoed off the walls of the ward. Every click of his footsteps on the tiled linoleum floors and every breath of sanitizer Elijah had inhaled on his way up here left his stomach in a lurch.

He made his way into the hospital room, anxious of what he would find there.

"So, what did they say?"

"I'm all good. I should be released tomorrow," Kev answered, smiling back at his best friend.

"Well, don't ever do that to me again, okay?"

"It's kind of hard to have appendicitis twice, bro. After they take it out, it's kinda done."

"You know what I mean," Elijah said.

"Oh, by the way, dude, you have got to see my nurse. She's exactly your type," Kev joked.

A sharp rap on the door made both men turn.

"Hello, gentlemen."

Kevin was right. The nurse was a knockout. Elijah read her name badge, noting it for later. Madeline Smith. Cute name.

ABOUT C.L. CANNON

C.L. Cannon is a publisher, publicist, editor, author, designer, and lots of other occupations with the -er sound at the end!

She is a woman of many talents who never gives up or stops improving. She enjoys writing about love and friendship. She loves it even more when she can add fantasy and science fiction aspects to those themes!

She's a self-proclaimed Harry Potter freak (Slytherin Pride people), lover of anything Joss Whedon (Spuffy forever), Tolkien fiend (who enjoys second breakfast), and addict of classic literature (Social class struggles turn me on... literally ;) yah see what I did there?)

She spends her days trying to #bookstagram (and probably failing), helping other authors grow and succeed (I love my job), and loving on her two babes (velociraptors), Seth and Petey.

She's also sort of a social media enthusiast! You can find her basically everywhere on the net (man I just aged myself) below!

Or, you can visit her website for more content!
http://clcannon.net

 facebook.com/clcannonauthor

 twitter.com/clcannonauthor

instagram.com/cl_cannon

FORTUNE FATED

BY MATTHEW STEVENS

"Horace, I'm sorry, but your recent actions have crossed a line that we cannot forgive. And, as such, we are going to have to let you go." Julia reached forward to adjust the nameplate on the front of her desk. In large regal letters, it read "Julia Michaels" and underneath, in the same font, but smaller, "NextEdge Head of Research and Development." All the while, her eyes mimicked her stone-gray suit.

"You have to give me a chance to explain. I deserve that much," Horace begged.

"Technically, I don't. Your actions have cost both companies," she motioned behind her where Damon Grimly, the President of Star-Tech, rival to NextEdge, stood perched, "the grant this year and a chance at it for the next five."

Horace quivered with anxious energy. He swallowed to keep his breakfast down.

"I know it's cliché, Julia, but it takes two to tango. If Steve hadn't approached me from StarTech, then my idea for time travel might have died in the proposal meeting."

"Throwing Steve from StarTech to the wolves won't save you. It's too late for that."

Horace didn't answer. They knew more than he realized.

"Don't worry. Steve has been fired for his role in this, too." Grimly emerged from the shadows to speak before stepping back and vanishing in silence.

"And while you may be correct about him finding you, you didn't have to take the deal. *That* is on you. Hence, the reason we're here." Julia continued, "The heart of the problem is your blatant breach of the NDA. You knew full well, anything proposed to the group falls under that umbrella.

"Not to mention your agreement to receive funds funneled through StarTech if the Foundation awarded them the grant based on your idea," said Skip Hanson, Chairman of the Hawking Foundation and member of the Hawking Research Grant for Advanced Physics. Until now he had remained lumped in the chair next to Horace. Even sitting up his blue pinstripe suit was so wrinkled it appeared as if a child had scribbled the stripes, and the dark blue bags under his eyes matched his clothing.

He mumbled something as his chin sunk to his chest. Horace glanced down at his tweed sports coat and burnt orange tie, which he just now realized boasted a sizable whitish splotch of dried tooth-paste. He grabbed his tie, licked his thumb, and vigorously scrubbed at the stain.

"I'm sorry, I didn't catch that." Horace sensed Julia leaning toward him.

Horace raised his head enough to enunciate his words but remained subdued and forlorn. "Please don't fire me. I don't have anything else. This job is my life. The hope of exploring micro-worm-holes and time travel is all I have left." The last thing he wanted to do was beg, but the prospect of not coming to work tomorrow made him miserable.

"Admirable as it may be, your persistence that time travel isn't theoretical verges on blasphemy. I wish I could do something, Horace, but you've forced my hand. *My* bosses have made the decision. Not to mention they are adamant about maintaining transparency with Star-Tech and the Hawking Foundation. This is truly our only option."

He rose to make a more impassioned plea, but one of NextEdge's multitude of black-clad ex-military security guards hands held him in place.

"Believe me when I say that I didn't want it to go like this. I fought for you and for your job. I did. But, what you've done, well, it makes people ask questions. Questions about your past work. About your publications. Your areas of expertise." Julia ticked off the points on her fingers.

"What are you saying, Julia? You know that all my work has always been legitimate. I led numerous projects. I brought forward ideas that the others thought were ludicrous, and we made them reality." The truth of Julia's words was sinking in, and Horace's fight or flight response drove him to obstinately defend himself even though he knew the effort would be wasted.

In his fervor, he stepped forward. The hand on his shoulder tightened its grip, forcing him back into his chair. When he first arrived in the room, he had been jittery with nervous energy. He still shook, but now it was from frustration, bordering on anger.

"I'm well aware of your CV, but that's also because I've known you for so long. Others in the industry know you by reputation and this …" Julia searched for the right word, "debacle, has tainted that."

The security guard slid himself between Horace and Julia's desk. Nearly six inches taller than Horace, the guard blocked Julia from view. He shuffled a step to his right. The guard matched him. Left. Same result.

From behind, the security guard, Julia said, "Horace, I think it's time you left."

"Are you kicking me out?" He howled with indignity.

"Of course not. But if you aren't going to leave the building of your own volition, I will have to make this security guard kindly remove you."

"This is ridiculous!" Horace had reached the point of no return. He was yelling.

The security guard, without audible instruction from Julia, swiveled Horace toward the door, and as gently as a freight train pushing a cow ushered him out the door.

Horace kicked and jostled once. The result was a hand on his collar and another on his waistband, and the security guard "walking" him to the front gate.

"What about the stuff from my desk? Aren't I allowed to gather my things?"

The security guard spoke, the baritone of his voice rattling Horace's soul, "Your items will be gathered for you and delivered to your place of residence."

They had reached the front gate. Another of the gang of black-clad security guards and Horace's captor shared an obligatory nod. At the curb, Horace was released. The security guard smoothed out the collar and shoulders of Horace's lab coat like a father straightening his son's tuxedo before prom, then took two steps back, crossed his arms over his burly chest, and waited for Horace to take the hint and continue off the property.

Horace remained inebriated and secluded in his apartment waiting for his personal effects to arrive until three days later, when still drunk and slurring his words, he phoned his former boss to inquire about their whereabouts.

"Ms. Michael's office, how can I help you?" Julia's assistant answered the phone.

"Where's Julia?" Horace demanded. "She fired me and had my ass dragged out of the building a few days ago. The meathead that kicked me to the curb said I'd get the things from my desk delivered. So far, I got nothin'."

"Ms. Michaels is in a meeting. If you leave me your name and number, I can pass on a message." She was courteous but had clearly been warned about this call.

"I'm Dr. Horace Wallen, and I needed to find out where my stuff went. I know she knows." Horace was on the verge of being belligerent.

"Whether she knows or not, Dr. Wallen, she is currently

unavailable."

"Put me on hold. I'll wait." He almost knocked over a side table with his shin before stumbling into his worn easy chair.

Hearing the stubbornness in his voice Julia's assistant attempted to defuse the situation another way. "Just a moment, sir, I will see what I can find out."

The tinny, choppy hold music started; some horribly-produced keyboard version of a Beethoven symphony. Horace lost track of how many movements he'd heard by the time the assistant returned.

"Thank you for holding. It seems that there is no record of what became of the personal items stored in your desk at the time of your termination." Her words held no empathy or remorse.

Horace, typically a quiet drunk, snapped. "What the hell? What do you mean they don't know where my stuff went? Someone cleaned out my desk. They did something with it! You need to find out where and how! Those are my things!"

"Please calm down, Dr. Wallen. I understand this is upsetting but yelling won't solve the problem."

Her continued cool served to infuriate Horace even more. He exploded with a string of expletives.

"I will tell you what I can do." She paused, waiting for an audible cue that Horace had calmed down.

Through a few heavy breaths, Horace grunted, "Ok."

"Now, what I can do is put in a request. Generate a work order. See if security can track down your belongings. The process may take some time, but at the end, we should have a definitive result. Either your items will be returned to you, or you will receive an answer as to what happened to them." She had slowed her speech, giving Horace time to focus on her words and slow his heart and breathing. "Does that sound like an acceptable solution, Dr. Wallen?"

By the time she asked her question, the hulking monster that had screamed into the phone moments before was back under wraps, leaving Horace slumped in his chair.

He wanted to disagree and barge into the building to demand his things, but he knew that was likely to get him arrested. This was his lone option. "Yes. That will have to do."

"Thank you, Dr. Wallen. As soon as we hang up, I will input the request and keep a copy here on my desk. The moment I hear anything I can give you a call."

Subdued, Horace agreed and hung up the phone.

With the hope of recovering the remnants of his past all but extinguished and knowing deep down that his things had been "filed" into the garbage, he had no choice but to move forward.

He tweaked and polished his resume. Pickings were slim. Few companies researched cutting-edge technology, and even fewer had open positions for theoretical physicists.

In a twenty-four-hour period, Horace found and applied to any job that mentioned advanced physics or research science.

The expediency of the replies made Horace question the shape of the space-time continuum, regardless of his background. One by one Horace scrolled through the email responses. Many were pleasant enough, thanking him for his interest, but informing that he wasn't a suitable candidate for the job opening. In the last one, the company insisted that he remove their information from his records and never contact them again.

Devoid of any confidence of finding a new job and fearing a fall back into a slump, Horace dressed and went to wander the city in hopes of finding, if not answers, at least inspiration. He had no direction and no commitments, so he wandered a path of abandon. He traipsed down streets he never knew existed and found himself in a part of the city where he had never ventured.

The sounds of old-fashioned manual labor rang between the old brick and mortar buildings. Hammers pounded, saws sang, and engines roared. Horace had no idea where he was. With his phone conveniently left charging on the kitchen counter and, unable to find familiar landmarks on the horizon, he couldn't fathom which direction to go even if he wanted to head home.

Guessing wrong, Horace turned a corner and found himself staring at a twelve-foot chain-link gate topped with barbed wire.

Resting atop the fence was a hand-made rusted sign: Fortune Faded Junk and Sales. Secured haphazardly to the sign was another offering: the business for sale and painted in a crooked line at the bottom was a number to call with a note: "Serious inquiries only."

He dug around in his pockets for paper and a pen to scribble the number down. Out of options, no job, and having always been one to tinker when the opportunity arose, purchasing and running a junkyard seemed a perfect solution to remedy the entire breadth of his issues. Pockets empty, Horace searched around. In his hasty scrounging, he nearly knocked over an old man who had appeared at his side.

"Oh, my. I'm so sorry, sir. I didn't hear you."

The man chuckled, which turned into a series of coughs that wracked his body. Out of impulse, he grabbed hold of Horace's arms to steady himself. Recovering, he patted Horace's chest and returned to leaning on his cane. "No worries, son. I have been known to sneak up on people from time to time. And you looked like you were deep in thought. Can I help you find something?"

Reminded of what he was doing when the old man startled him Horace responded, "Oh, I was trying to find a pen or pencil and paper. I want to call the number on the sign," he pointed above them, "about buying this junkyard."

"Well, lucky for you, I just happen to know the guy selling it," said the old man with a wink.

"Excellent. Is there another way that I can contact him? To be honest, I'm lost. I was out wandering around and not sure, if I leave, I can ever find this spot again."

"My, my, that is quite the dilemma." He reached up and stroked the few scraggly white hairs suspended from his chin as he pondered Horace's question.

Horace inquired again. "Any suggestions? Because I am very interested."

The old man shuffled past Horace and removed a small key ring from his belt. With one old, wrinkled hand, he jingled and jangled the keys until he found the one he wanted. He extended the hand and, in one swift motion—one out of place with the appearance and previous speed of his digits—he unlocked the gate.

Horace stood, eyes wide, mouth slightly agape. "You're the owner?"

"Yep." The old man grinned a wide, crooked, toothy grin. "Follow me in, son, and we can discuss numbers."

Over a cup of tea, Horace and Edgar hammered out the details for the sale. Formalities concluded, the two set aside the paperwork and lost themselves in conversation. Edgar, lonely and longing for dialogue since his wife passed, was forthcoming with the particulars about why he was selling his life's work and livelihood. A call from Edgar's son drew their chat to a close. Horace walked with Edgar to the entrance of the junkyard, where they wished each other well before parting ways. Horace watched as Edgar ambled down the street and out of sight before he locked the gate and wandered back home to celebrate the beginning of his new adventure.

The day after the completion of the sale—Horace's first as owner—was spent combing through the personal space, where Edgar and his family had lived, and the business office. He knew that he would have to alter his lifestyle. Junkyard owners earned significantly less than a theoretical research physicist, but, with living space included, he was confident he could make it work. The mountain of paperwork he needed to sort through to bring the books current took him the majority of his first day.

Horace made the trip back to his apartment after the sun had fallen behind the buildings, ending that first day. His assessment of the living space and the accounting books made moving out of his expensive apartment and freeing up those funds crucial.

When he arrived at the junkyard on the second day, Horace had one goal for the day–to make a complete circuit of the grounds and take a cursory inventory. He was pleased with his progress when he stopped for lunch. The items he had discovered so far were exciting and held promise. As a child, he took apart radios and other gadgets, putting them back together in better shape. The time he spent searching the junkyard for the first time was like a treasure hunt. But he found the real jackpot after lunch.

Horace picked his way across the top of a pile toward the corner of the property. At the apex of his climb, he gingerly put a foot down, testing the stability of the debris. It appeared as if it would hold his weight, so he eyed his next footfall and made his move. But the spot he thought secure shifted the moment he lifted his back foot. In an instant, Horace was surfing down the junk pile, heading straight for the hard ground and a large, ragged, and dangerous stack of miscellany. He flailed and wobbled, trying to control his descent. With no luck, he braced for the worst as the ground rushed up to meet him.

The collision with the ground was like something out of a cartoon —the screech to a halt, sparks from the grinding of metal on metal (which he momentarily thought were stars), and the giant crash as piles came crashing down on each other. Horace curled into a ball as he hit the ground, making himself as small as possible in hopes of avoiding significant injury.

When the cacophony subsided, and Horace pried his eyes open, he brushed his hands over his body, checking for protruding chunks of metal. Finding none, he released an audible sigh. No extra metallic appendages.

Horace picked his way carefully and deliberately from underneath the mountain of junk. Emerging back into the sunlight, Horace shielded his eyes and took stock of what had collapsed, what remained in place, and where he was. As he turned and took in the piles surrounding him, he caught sight of a snippet of a familiar bright red logo.

With the same care and precision he applied to his experiments, Horace began shifting pieces of junk one by one to reveal the full logo. Tucked neatly into a stack of half-finished rockets was a box bearing the angular "NE" mark of his former employer, NextEdge. Horace gave the box a gentle tug, testing to see if he could remove it without dismantling the surrounding pile. The box slid out with a slight tug.

The name scribbled on the box top almost sent him tumbling backward.

Staring back at him in bold black letters was his own name.

"Those bastards!" He exclaimed, unable to contain his shock and anger. "They trashed my stuff!"

Horace clawed the box open. Shoved unceremoniously into the box were all the trinkets and knickknacks he'd kept on his desk. Piece by piece he removed them. Toward the bottom, he found his awards and plaques. At least one of the glass awards was cracked, another was broken into numerous pieces, and yet another, which once bore a scientist holding up a test tube in one hand and a rocket in the other, was missing both his arms. Horace collapsed to the ground in tears, ears and eyes burning with anger and sadness.

As he sat surrounded by literal pieces of his old life and the debris constituting his new life, he couldn't help but wonder if this was his destiny, collecting junk and tinkering for the rest of his life. All his education and research were wasted because his coworkers laughed his time travel proposal out of the room. It was "wacky," they said. They feared lost grant money and possible lost jobs. But Horace was aiming higher. Yes, he wanted the prestige that would come with the legitimate discovery and application of time travel, but, more importantly, he wanted the knowledge that could be amassed from it. That hope, his dream, was gone and now lying in a pile of rubbish at his feet. Using his sleeve to dry his eyes, Horace was drawn back to the box. He needed to finish digging through his stuff.

Horace unearthed a shattered framed photograph of his former friend and college roommate, Dr. Wade Magellan, famous marine biologist. Former—he passed not long ago. Picking past the shards of broken glass, he found just what he didn't know he needed: motivation, in the form of the gift Wade's assistant Simon had sent after his passing. It was a sealed opaque plastic container. Horace shook it gently, and the saltwater sloshed inside, making the chunk of "exotic matter" bump against the sides. The note Simon included with the gift was explicitly clear. The unknown sample had been obtained less than a kilometer from the entrance to the undersea cave that mysteriously claimed Wade's life. Wade's desire to uncover the origin or usage of this gift had become all-encompassing.

Horace threw every test and experiment he knew of at the chunk of rock tucked safely inside that container. He was unable to determine the chemical composition, the atomic structure or the material makeup of the substance. Each inconclusive result pointed him closer and closer to one conclusion: this substance was the "exotic matter" was necessary to solve the equation of time travel. Now, his shot at answering that question had been tossed out of NextEdge along with his lab coat.

Horace had raised the container to inspect it, turning it end over end to make sure the seal hadn't been broken when, in the background, he noticed a familiar panel of knobs and switches pressed into the wall of junk. A closer look revealed his initial model for his time travel device.

He spent the rest of the afternoon uncovering pieces of projects he'd worked on over the years at NextEdge. By the time the sun set, Horace had uncovered dozens of his former devices. Having the "exotic matter" and his creations back under his control, Horace's whole body tingled with excitement and a revitalized itch to start experimenting. As dusk began to fall, giant sodium lights clicked on all over the junkyard, bathing Horace and his treasures in a golden aura. His fingers twitched, wanting nothing more than to start taking things apart and putting them back together, but he knew he would be best served to wait until the morning. It took three trips to the get the most essential pieces inside his living space where he felt they would be safest from the elements.

Many pieces were found at the bottom of a large pile from NextEdge, leading him to wonder how long they'd been there. Regardless, he had them back, along with his motivation. Tomorrow, he would fashion an indoor workspace. Then he would prove that NextEdge laughing at his theoretical time travel proposal was the biggest mistake they had ever made.

Horace awoke with the sun the next morning. He was halfway out the door to collect more of the pieces he'd left outside when his stomach groaned indignantly. He had gotten so wrapped up in his discovery from last night that he'd forgotten dinner. Cracking open the fridge reminded him that he'd been so preoccupied with the acclimation of his new home that he hadn't bought any groceries. He was filthy and wearing wrinkled, non-matching clothes. He lived and worked in a junkyard, but he couldn't introduce himself to the neighborhood looking like he'd rolled out from under a junk pile. He had the day before, but that wasn't something he needed to share.

Changing into something more presentable and headed out of the junkyard and down the street in search of breakfast and a grocery. He'd gone a couple of blocks when he found a greasy spoon café that was already open for breakfast. Horace settled down at the counter. The red and white speckled countertop was edged in the chrome banding that was so popular in the 1950's. Each booth seat and stool shined with red vinyl that squeaked with every minuscule shift. Behind the counter, a waitress in a red and white checkered shirt with a food-stained black apron lackadaisically carrying a half-full pot of coffee in one hand strolled down to where Horace had chosen to sit.

She reached down and flipped over the coffee cup Horace hadn't realized was in front of him. "Coffee, hon?"

Wide-eyed at the nostalgia of the place, his solitary response was to nod.

"Ya wanna eat too?"

Horace nodded again.

She slapped a menu down on the counter. "I'll give ya a tick." And she walked away.

By the time she returned, he had regained his composure and decided on breakfast.

Candace, as her name tag proclaimed, scribbled it all down. "Ya sure ya want all it?"

His stomach growled, answering her question.

"Ok, then!" Candace called the order out to the kitchen as she checked on other customers.

The smells of sizzling sausage and bacon and the scrape of the spatula on the flattop as pancakes were flipped and eggs were turned made Horace salivate. After what seemed like an eternity, breakfast arrived. The plates were barely on the counter before he dug in. A few minutes later, his fork clattered to his empty plate.

"Anything else I can get ya?" Candace asked as she scooped up all the empty dishes and stacked them expertly on one arm.

"Nope. Thank you," Horace said, stifling a belch. Candace laid down a bill and headed to the register, where she took his money. "You new 'round here? Or just passin' through?"

"Just bought the Fortune Faded junkyard down the way. So, I guess I'm a new neighbor." Horace offered a cheesy grin.

"All right then," Candace mumbled, nodding. "We'll see ya soon."

"Yep." Horace turned to leave. "Oh, is there a grocery close by? I'm not familiar with the area yet."

"Head 'nother block that way," Candace gestured, pointing away from the junkyard.

"Thanks."

Horace made his way down to the grocery, gathered a few things to keep him from starving, and headed back home to begin the work of piecing together history.

Before going to bed the night before, Horace had removed the container with his "time-fuel" and set it on the kitchen table. He wanted to know right where to find it the next morning. At least then he would know where *something* was. The stack of papers that his employer included in the miscellaneous items from his desk was another story. Shuffling through the pile, Horace found that most of what remained was inconsequential to his current time travel infatuation, but he did find his original memo with the general outline of his Hawking Foundation Grant application. He reread it while shoveling down his lunch.

The details about how the project would be constructed and how (theoretically) his time travel machine would work were not part of the memo, but, understanding the possible historical implications and the secrecy of his dealings with Steve from StarTech, Horace had personal copies of those explicit details tucked away where only he knew how to get to them.

His meal finished and pushed to the side, Horace began a checklist. His original proposal included a timeline, as required by the Foundation Grant guidelines—a timeline he would now have to extrapolate. He had planned for the assistance of coworkers and a team of assistants, which he clearly no longer had at his disposal. While the length of time required to complete this project was a serious concern for Horace at first, he ran across another as he ran down the checklist.

There were two integral parts to the theoretical time travel process, not counting the obvious hurdle of constructing the actual machine. The first was the time-fuel, which he was certain lay tucked inside the dimples and crevices of that hunk of unknown rock. The second, which occupied the largest area of worry in his brain, was how to activate the pieces of time-fuel.

Horace anticipated that a significant amount of power would be necessary to charge the time-fuel particles, activating them to allow for time travel to occur. He theorized that, given enough power, he could induce a positive or negative charge into the particles. Once combined with the machine and additional circuitry, they would accelerate, creating miniature wormholes to a specified point in the space-time of the universe.

He tried to focus on the other aspects of the project and impending construction, but he couldn't push past the worry about not having enough of a localized power supply. Horace left the container with his time-fuel, the assorted papers, and a few other small circuit boards and electronics scattered around his lunch dishes and wandered outside to find where the junkyard connected to the city power grid.

Horace lost most of his afternoon traipsing through the junkyard, following wires and attempting to determine those that carried power and those that represented previous failed attempts to bring power to the most remote corners of the yard. At the outset of his excursion, he was pessimistic that the power supply, despite the size of the junk-yard, would be insufficient. If that were the case, he would have to rethink his own strategy and extend the timeline even more as he manipulated ways to amplify power to the required levels.

Much to his excitement, he discovered that the power lines leading into the junkyard, once routed and funneled, would be more than adequate to service his project. Horace practically skipped back to his workspace to make the enormous red checkmark next to "Power Supply???" on his list.

Stopping for a bite, he reorganized the items on the table in prepa-ration for assembly. Looking at the pieces lying on the table, Horace couldn't help but chuckle to himself. His end goal was currently a theoretical functioning time travel device, and yet he was character-izing what he was about to do as puttering. Truth be told, what he was about to attempt was as far from tinkering as one could get. And he couldn't wait to get started.

Over the course of the next week, Horace worked from the orange and red predawn hours of the morning into the deep blues and black of the night calculating, finagling, adjusting, erasing incorrect projec-tions, piecing together hunks of disjointed metal and circuits, and repeating the process *ad nauseum*.

By the beginning of the second week, he forced himself to push back from the project to avoid burning out and allow for more sleep in hopes of negating critical (and possibly life-threatening) mistakes. He knew he needed to slow down, but his brain fought to keep working on the device even when he had intentionally stepped away to decompress, most often at the café where he'd first had breakfast. He could sit and have meaningless conversations with Candace while people-watching, which provided a welcome distraction from the magnitude of his project.

Horace closed in on the third full week of piecing together his time travel device made from remnants of his old projects along with other miscellaneous pieces he scrounged up from other corners of his livelihood. He was satisfied that he had completed the physical device as best as his theoretical knowledge would allow. Horace then turned his attention to beginning the long and tedious mathematical calculations he would need to solve to test his device.

His work on the equations took weeks. By the time he computed all the necessary answers, the walls of his living and work spaces were plastered with reams of paper. Sheets of numeric sentences flapped as he opened cabinets to retrieve dishware or food. He'd left himself one sheet-sized corner of the kitchen table on which to eat his meals. Even his bed crunched with paper when he forced himself to sleep.

The last step was, with extreme caution, to chip a pebble off the exotic matter of an exact size and imbue it, with the utmost care, with a precise electric charge, activating the inherent properties of the matter. Once connected with the machine, it would generate the micro-wormhole necessary for travel faster than light.

Horace's stomach grumbled, and he glanced down at his watch. As badly as he itched to run the initial test, he knew that, if the results didn't match his expectations, then sleep wouldn't come. He would sit and ruminate all night. Instead, he headed to the café, space out while having some dinner and inane conversation with Candace, after which he could return home, to double-check everything before getting a good night's rest in anticipation of his first experiment in the morning.

All the early mornings and long nights focused exclusively on the prospects of time travel had jeopardized the operations of the junk-yard as well as taking a toll on Horace's constitution. Yet, neither mattered in the least as he awoke the morning of his first experiment, well after the sun had risen.

In a vial on his bedside table was the time-fuel for the morning's test run. He tucked it into a shirt pocket and made his way to the kitchen. The night before, he laid out a quick, easy breakfast, which he ate as he quadruple-checked his calculations. Done with breakfast and number crunching, Horace moved to fine-tuning and inspecting the machine. He absent-mindedly poked his finger into his shirt pocket every few minutes to reassure himself the time-fuel was still there. Satisfied all his pre-test inspections were in order, Horace removed the vial from his pocket and placed it in the receptacle he'd fashioned as a charging station.

After one more examination of all the switches and buttons, power supply, and numbers, with a flick of a switch, Horace sent a short burst of energy through the power coupler into the charger. A giant cyan-tinged flare erupted from the time-fuel trapped inside the vial. Horace jerked his head away from the light, throwing his arm over his eyes. He hadn't predicted the burst of brightness from the exotic matter. The intensity made safety glasses inconsequential. With a gloved hand, Horace removed the vial and set it on the scale. Verifying that the weight hadn't changed was crucial. Determining the unequiv-ocal correspondence between the intensity of the charge and the mass, while unpredicted, made Horace overjoyed. An exorbitant amount of his calculations depended on the exact weight of the time-fuel.

Horace grabbed his modified multimeter and brought the probes to the sides of the vial. The digital readout fluctuated, then settled with the positive charge measured to the hundred-thousandths decimal place, just as he had predicted. With step one complete, Horace reversed the charging process with a second same-sized piece of time-fuel. As he flipped the switch, he turned away, shielding his face.

He repeated the process with the multimeter. The digital readout flickered, then blinked a negative number. Horace jumped, releasing a loud, uncontrolled exclamation. Everything was going according to plan. He took the second piece of time-fuel, packaged it along with his "reverse" calculations, and secured the bundle below the time travel device's control panel.

With the utmost care, Horace took the first piece of charged time-fuel and placed it in the power module on the control panel. He made one last inspection of all the necessary switches and knobs before closing his eyes and inspiring himself a wish of luck. He opened his eyes, depressed the button initializing the machine for time travel, and took two giant steps back.

Horace stood back from the pile of pieces he assumed he would need to allow a person-sized passenger on the time travel device. The junk mostly consisted of an old ratty chair and brackets to mount it to the control panel. The assembly wasn't his greatest concern at present. If he couldn't reconfigure the calculations for his own added mass and the required electric charge to the time-fuel, the installation of the chair was superfluous.

Horace scrunched his brow and rubbed his chin with ink-stained fingers. He was buried in thought when less than three feet behind him, a pop as if a child stomped on a giant balloon, snapped him out of his mental fog. The noise would have startled him more were he not expecting the arrival of his time travel device.

Horace checked his watch, reached up to flip over a paper attached to the wall, and grinned. "Right on time."

His calculations had been spot-on. He was thankful that he'd moved his version of the machine to avoid any sort of paradox or even a simple spatial displacement issue. Horace walked over to the device and retrieved the insulated pack from the base of the control panel. Inside the pack were the items exactly as he knew they would be. He'd packed them himself a few days before.

Horace chuckled when he unfolded the letter cordially addressed to "Future Horace." He skimmed to the bottom, having not forgotten a word of what he had written, but he still laughed aloud at seeing his previous self's signature, "Past Horace." The pages tucked and folded behind the letter were the computations necessary and the directions required to adjust the polarity of the time-fuel, in case, for some unknown reason, the negative charge had changed during its short trip through the micro-wormhole.

"Future Horace" spent the next two days inspecting and recalibrating the machine as per the instructions sent from "Past Horace." After completing all the necessary checks and verifying, much to his excitement, that the time-fuel's polarity and electric charge were both the same as when "Past Horace" packaged it, "Future Horace" inserted the time-fuel into the power module, adjusted the appropriate dials, knobs, and flipped the switch indicating direction of travel. With everything in order, "Future Horace" tucked a single slip of paper into the empty bundle at the base of the control panel and pressed the button to return his time travel device back to himself, successfully instigating the first-ever instance of backward time travel.

After initially shipping his time travel device off to the future Horace spent hours wandering aimlessly around the junkyard. He searched for something, anything, to keep him occupied and his mind off the possibility that his experiment was a grand failure and that he would never see it again. Based on his calculations and the perfect repetition of that number crunching, he knew that if his device was to return he had time to waste. Assuming the instructions were followed to the letter, which they would be because Horace was a perfectionist, his device would reappear in forty-eight hours.

Attempting to be optimistic about the reappearance, he scoured the junkyard for whatever he might need to add a seat. Presuming the machine arrived back when and how the computations predicted, Horace wanted very badly to make his next experiment include a human test subject—himself. Materials gathered, he began work on the adjustments to the equations allowing the machine to travel with additional weight.

Horace lost track of time and became engrossed in reworking the math for what he continued to hope would be his next experiment. From the other side of the room, Horace heard a loud pop. He twisted around fast enough to cause the papers he was working on to flutter in the resulting breeze. One hand slammed the paper back against the wall as the other shot up toward his face to check the time.

"Ah-ha!" Horace exclaimed, feeling like a mad scientist, but with less hair. "He did it! I mean, I did it! We did it!" He paused, trying to logic out who exactly had succeeded. "Nevermind! Reverse time travel has just been proven. Forward was the easy part, but now that you're back," Horace patted the control panel, "the work can continue! I can prove to those morons who cost me my job that I'm not crazy."

Horace spent the next few minutes dancing around the time travel device grinning. Coming down from his emotional high, he realized there was a small square of white poking out of the bundle attached to the control panel.

In the bundle, Horace found a piece of paper with his own handwriting on it.

"Congratulations! Keep up the good work! -F.H."

He burst out laughing. Horace hadn't realized until now how stupid "Future Horace" and "Past Horace" sounded. Too late now. He just hoped that F.H. had gotten as much of a kick out of it as he was now.

Having gotten all the excitement out of his system, Horace settled down and began focusing more diligently on his next task. If he was going to send himself into the future, he should make the trip worthwhile. He needed to generate proof to his ex-boss and former colleagues of what he had done.

While Horace worked out the details of the revised calculations, adjusted weights, and sizes necessary for the time-fuel, and installed the jump seat, he formulated ideas on how to gather incontrovertible evidence of his trip. A newspaper clipping or picture could be too easily faked or manipulated with ease. One possibility he'd pondered was a "cookbook" of sorts currently being assembled in the scientific community. The book contained a list of materials that could be produced and the corresponding "recipes." A futuristic version would contain items his former coworkers could only dream of. He was messing with the numbers drastically by including his own weight.

Transporting anything else of substantial size or mass was a task he would rather avoid.

Over dinner, as Horace approached the end of his calculations, an idea struck him. He remembered that, even though he'd been fired and escorted out of the building, they let him keep his name badge. Each badge was coded to the individual and fitted with a tiny hard drive that recorded extensive logs when swiped to get in and out of rooms and sections of the labs. Even the lunchroom and bathrooms were secured, and required badge swipes for entry.

Horace was planning to jump twenty years into the future. Not far, but to a time when the difference would be appreciable. He was banking on some form of the badge system remaining in place at NextEdge and hoped they wouldn't have moved to biomonitors or subdermal tracking. If he could get security to let him into the building, he could scan his badge somewhere, anywhere, and it would be recorded. And, while Horace had picked up some remedial computer skills, the security incorporated into that system was impressive. His abilities were far from adequate to perform such a hack, and his former colleagues knew it. That would be the proof he needed. For them, at least. He might bring back a newspaper too, for kicks.

The details of his evidence now worked out, Horace's full attention was back on the computations. Based on experience with other intense, complicated mathematics, he hypothesized that he would be finished before the week was out.

The closer Horace got to the answers he needed for his trip the more skittish he became about the whole prospect. He'd successfully sent the machine into the future, and it came back just the same, but he'd run one test. Just one experiment. The scientist in him knew that once was not enough to prove that results could be duplicated. Not to mention that he didn't have anyone checking his work. No one to verify his calculations. Horace broke into a cold sweat at the thought.

Horace dropped his pencil and ran to the kitchen. He flailed his arms across the table, briefly lifting arbitrary pieces of paper, then flicking them aside and checking others. The space was nearly clear when he raised a sheet up in celebration.

In the bottom right corner, circled with a thick red marker, were a few numbers Horace calculated while he waited for the device to return from its first trip. The numbers were similar to his first answers, but they would send the machine further in time—a few months instead of a couple of days.

Armed with the knowledge that he was close to finishing calculations for his own trip into the future and now equipped with the numbers for an extended trip with the machine, he made his way down the street to the café for some dinner and the atmosphere of the noisy restaurant. Over a double cheeseburger and chili cheese fries, Horace reaffirmed his thoughts since the danger posed by a one-time trial run had set him on edge.

If he sent the device forward a couple of months and again included instructions for the exact time for it to be sent back, and the return trip was successful, he would be reassured. He could be confident in his ability to manipulate the math, but it would mean that F.H. still existed. And, if that was the case, it would verify that P.H. had successfully sent himself forward *and* was able to return whole.

Not wanting to waste any time, he flagged down Candace, paid his bill, and ran back to the junkyard to charge the necessary pieces of time-fuel. The sooner the machine completed its extended trip, the sooner he could have it back. And, once that happened, his personal trip could get underway.

Horace was thrilled when he woke up a few days later to find that the time travel device had popped back into existence in the corner of his workshop. He had used the few days to double-check everything, make sure the yard was in order, and pack the appropriately sized chunks of time-fuel for the return trip.

He spent the morning securing his jump seat to the time travel device. He hoped that doing so would distract his stomach and brain from the lurching of incessant worry. It didn't. Lunchtime came and went, but Horace couldn't eat. He was too focused. He'd started the final preparations for the first manned time jump.

That solid thought was all his stomach needed to complete its coup. Horace barely turned fast enough, doubling over to retch into the corner of his workshop all over a stack of computations and figures. Minutes went by as he continued to dry heave, unable to stand as his stomach repeatedly contracted, forcing him into an unnatural crouch.

When the worst had passed, Horace made his way to the closest chair, which happened to be his jump seat for the time travel device. The realization struck him when he moved to rest his head and accidentally shifted a dial and depressed a button. His head shot up, and he twisted his body the rest of the way to face the control panel, inspecting what he had adjusted accidentally.

A gigantic sigh escaped Horace's lips when he saw that nothing he moved generated any substantial effect. He adjusted the dial back where had been set and unclicked the button. Everything stayed where it belonged, including himself. As a failsafe, Horace had designed the machine so that position of all the knobs, dials, and buttons, was significant at the moment the ignition was pressed. He had just unwittingly tested that.

Horace paced around his workshop. He was killing time until he could bring himself to return to the jump seat and begin final preparations. With the machine back, his confidence in his ability to complete the trip skyrocketed, but it also made the truth so much more real.

Calculations complete and with no other reason to stall, Horace forced a few long, deep breaths, retrieved the pieces of time-fuel he needed to charge, and set to work on final preparations.

All the pieces were in place (minus Horace in the chair) to make his dream a reality. As long as he'd waited for this moment, he was worlds beyond nervous. He stepped back one last time to take in the physical presence of what he accomplished. And all on his own. A smile spread across his entire face with that thought.

Horace straightened his shirt and ever-present lab coat before sitting down in the jump seat facing the control panel. He allowed himself one more look around the workshop and inserted the time-fuel into the power module, giving the control knob a hair adjustment. He secured the five-point harness, tugged the straps an extra time, and clicked the button propelling him into the future.

As if he was moving through a sludge pit Horace lifted his head and peeled his eyes open. His head and appendages weighed hundreds of pounds each. He blinked. Or at least he thought he did. Everything was beyond black. The complete absence of color. Distinctions about distance or surfaces were impossible. Minutes went by before he tried moving his arms. His next attempt was more successful, as he dragged them from his sides into his lap. He resisted the urge to try moving his legs, but settled for wiggling his toes around inside his shoes.

Horace waited a few more minutes. He could sense the heaviness dissipating from his limbs as time ticked by. If not for the harness he could have spent the last however long sprawled awkwardly in the dark of some unknown location.

He unbuckled the harness and leaned forward to check the bundle at the base of the console, sending a quiet prayer that he packed a flashlight he didn't remember. His forehead connected with the edge of the console. Stars exploded across his vision, but sadly, they didn't shine any light on the physical space he occupied. The blinking lights faded, and Horace massaged his head, wishing away the sharp pain. Using his hand as a cushion, he leaned back over to rummage in the bundle. He found no flashlight. It might be better that way since he hadn't speculated how alkaline batteries would, or could, survive micro-wormhole displacement.

Horace rose and shuffled across the floor, hands extended until they pressed against the cool uniform surface of a concrete wall. He worked his way around the exterior of the room until he located a doorway. It opened into a dark stairwell. Step by step, deliberately and carefully, he made his way up. A few steps up, he saw light emanating from a doorway atop the staircase.

Emerging from the darkness, Horace found himself in the lobby of a building exactly as he'd always dreamed the future would look—sleek, full of glass, and technology beyond anything he dreamed. Robots walked among people who were indifferent to the robots' existence. There were no signs or markings on the desks or walls to indicate the business name. Confident he looked out of place, Horace did his best to appear inconspicuous as he made his way for the exit.

He reached the street without drawing unwanted attention and scanned the roadway. Cars zoomed past, hovering inches from the road, seemingly nothing between. Overhead, more cars traveled in the opposite direction. The smile on Horace's face cracked into a laugh. He couldn't believe what he was seeing.

He pulled up a sleeve and pinched his arm. "Ow!"

Horace questioned whether that age-old trick worked. Regardless, now that he'd arrived, he had a goal. He needed his proof. Horace wanted to explore this future world, but he reasoned that, once he returned to his time and delivered his evidence to his ex-boss and former colleagues, he'd have the time and resources available to come and visit any time. He snickered at his own unintentional pun.

He needed to figure out his exact point in time and then make his way to the NextEdge headquarters. Horace scanned the shops, giving cursory looks to the passersby, searching for someone who might have a friendly face and point him in the right direction. He had just raised a hand to stop a woman who appeared she might be willing to help when, over her shoulder, he saw the best thing since the sunlight greeted him from the top of the stairs: his greasy spoon café, tucked in the bottom of an enormous skyscraper.

"Candace!" he exclaimed unintentionally as he froggered his way through traffic to the other side of the street.

Horace bounded into the café and right to the counter, to a seat that didn't squeak as he sat down. He flipped his coffee cup over and waited for Candace to amble over and fill him up. When she didn't appear, Horace leaned over the counter searching for her. He didn't see her. Instead, with the speed of a snail, a young woman made her way out of the kitchen to Horace.

"Can I get you something?" she asked dryly. Her attitude was reflected in her lips, chapped and cracked.

"Some coffee, black. And, is Candace around?"

"Who?" the waitress questioned him, perturbed he would make her think this early in the morning.

"Candace. She's a waitress here."

The young waitress twisted at the waist, angling a call back toward the kitchen, "Hey! Paulie, we got a Candace that works here?"

As she turned, he caught a glimpse of her nametag: Fiona. As she waited for a response, Horace noticed the state of disrepair around the café. Hardly a seat that used to be coated in gleaming red vinyl wasn't dingy and cracked. Even the countertop showed extensive wear and tear, reminding him, as familiar as the café was, how quickly things that seemed stable could change and be lost.

He attempted to get Fiona's attention back and apologize for bothering her, but the response was already being yelled from the kitchen.

"Not since forever. Who wants to know?" Paulie replied.

Fiona gave a judging stare in Horace's direction. "Just some guy."

Horace waved his hands, begging Fiona to drop the whole thing. He mouthed an apology, sorry he hadn't thought when he had first asked.

He pulled his coffee cup toward his body, deciding he would rather not stick around any longer. "Honestly, all I need to know is if Next-Edge Corp is still down at the end of Technology Row?"

Fiona crossed her arms in front of her and glared down her nose. Horace was all too cognizant of the fact that he stuck out like a sore thumb. "Yeah, they pretty much run the whole row. Why?"

"Oh, um, I'm from out of town, and my friend works there. Wanted me to meet him after work."

The intensity of her stare didn't change. "The main building is at the end of Technology Row."

"Thanks." Horace waved inelegantly and scooted out the door.

He made his way through the city to the NextEdge buildings, his hand clutching his old ID badge tightly in the pocket of his lab coat. Arriving at the NextEdge property, he stopped at the curb. It was the same curb he'd been ushered to weeks ago. Well, weeks for him. It was over twenty years in this place.

Horace shook his head to clear the confusing thoughts. He was here for one thing. He had to get the security guard to allow him to swipe his badge, generating a log on his card. Then he could retrace his steps back to the time travel device and head home, hopefully, to get his job back.

Walking up to the security gate, Horace studied the guard relaxing at his station, enclosed in his see-through box. From a glance, he suspected the guard was still toddling around in diapers when he'd been canned.

The guard greeted Horace. "Afternoon, sir. Welcome to NextEdge Technologies, how can I help you?"

The corner of Horace's mouth turned up in a half-smile. As many years as it had been, the greeting NextEdge employees were expected to use remained the same.

"Good afternoon …" he said, pausing to squint at the security guard's name badge through the glass, "Stanley. My name is Dr. Horace Wallen, and I was employed here many years ago."

"Glad you could stop by after so long. What can I do for you?" Stanley inquired again, maintaining professional courtesy.

Realizing he didn't answer the young man's question the first time, Horace began formulating his response, one that would relay the importance of his request without sounding like he belonged in a straitjacket.

"I just returned, having been out of the country for quite a few years, and I was hoping I could reconnect with a few of my old coworkers." Horace withdrew his badge from his pocket, holding it up for Stanley to see. "May I venture inside to visit with them?"

Stanley squinted as he leaned forward to inspect the badge, the bill of his navy blue NextEdge hat brushing the glass. "Sorry, Dr. Wallen. Those badges are no longer valid, and the building is on lockdown for the day. Something about highly classified experiments going on today. No one that isn't a current NextEdge employee is allowed past the gate."

Horace lowered the badge and his shoulders in disappointment. He had no Plan B, and now he needed one. The piece of time-fuel he brought with him for the return trip was slightly larger than the one he used to get himself into the future. He had prepared for a trip that lasted a maximum of twelve hours. His idea from the beginning of his personal excursion was to return to the approximate point at which he left the past, give or take a couple of hours. His goal was to not be officially absent from the past for more than half a day. He couldn't help but worry about what changes might occur in his own time the longer he was away, or what might happen if his disappearance was discovered.

This was a new venture, and he wasn't sure if there would be any lasting effects to himself or his physiology, or if that might influence the space-time continuum. This first trip was meant to be quick, therefore limiting the possible repercussions.

Every minute he stood chatting with Stanley or concocting a backup plan was more time for something to go wrong. Contingency plans had never been his forte. Auggie was always the one who was able to speculate around the initial idea and plan for hiccups.

"Dr. Milton!" Horace blurted out.

Stanley's brow scrunched. "I'm sorry. Who?"

"If I can't go inside, can you make a call inside to see if one of my former coworkers would be willing to come outside?"

Acquiring proof would be a problem his coworkers would help him solve. In fact, they would know the correct path to take because he would have already returned and informed them how they helped him help them. Brilliant!

"I'll try, but I can't make any promises. Like I said, the building is under lockdown." Stanley clicked a few keys on the computer panel in front of him. "Let me check the directory. Who did you want me to call?"

As far as backup plans, August Milton was his first choice. But, hopefully, he could contact all of them. "Can you try Dr. August Milton first, please?"

There was tapping, as Stanley searched the system. A brief pause. A confused look. More tapping followed by silence.

"I'm sorry, Dr. Wallen. I don't see a Dr. Milton in the system."

"Well, what about Dr. Luciana Dominguez?" No different than in the past, her name rolled off his tongue.

A few more moments passed, and a concerned look passed across Stanley's face. "No luck, sir."

Concern crept into Horace's mind. If he ended up with three strikes with no former colleagues still employed at NextEdge, the trip would be a bust.

Horace's final option was the one he was least excited to try. They worked well together, but, even after years of interaction, they were never friendly, per se. Horace always liked to think it was the cultural part of Badenhoff's personality and nothing against Horace personally.

He sighed, "Last chance. Try Gustav Badenhoff, please."

Stanley turned back to the terminal. A few moments passed before the same bothered squint returned to his face. "Dr. Wallen, are you certain you have the right tech firm?"

Horace did his best not to be offended. He turned his badge over in his hand, the angular red NextEdge logo as clear as the day it was printed and encased in plastic.

"Is it possible they left the company?" Stanley questioned.

"No, I can't see that happening. Can you search by department? We were in theoretical and research physics."

It didn't take long for Stanley's search to, again, return an empty set.

"Something isn't right about this." Horace pondered aloud, more to himself than asking Stanley for ideas.

Stanley stroked his beardless chin absent-mindedly. "You know…" he trailed off, disappearing in thought.

He stayed that way for several seconds before Horace rapped gently on the glass.

"What were you thinking?"

"I'm not sure. But about ten years ago, there was a horrible accident. I heard they shut down a whole wing of the facility for weeks. Police and feds were investigating alongside the NextEdge security emergency response unit. If I remember correctly, a few scientists died. I can't think of the names off the top of my head, but I want to say that their names were kind of foreign sounding. Like your friends."

Horace drew closer to the glass enclosure. "Is there any way you can search some records and see?"

Stanley's attention fixated on the screen in front of him, fingers moving over the keys. "I think I found it. Yeah, it says here in a company-wide press release that … eleven years ago … today," Stanley's eyes widened in shock. "Three lead scientists in the research and development branch of theoretical physics department lost their lives during a round of experiments." Stanley began to mumble as he skimmed over the rest of the information.

"Can you print a copy?" Stanley could read the pertinent information to Horace, but, if the names of his former colleagues were in there, he wanted to see it for himself.

He watched as Stanley tapped a few more keys then reached under the desk, retrieving a single sheet of paper. He passed the press release through the small slot meant for tickets.

Horace scanned the page, picking out the details Stanley hadn't yet covered, including the names of his three deceased cohorts. His knees gave way, and Horace crumbled to the curb.

"I'm very sorry you had to find out like this, Dr. Wallen. Now that I'm reading this, I remember hearing about the incident. It made national headlines. Especially with the feds coming in to investigate. Kind of surprised with all that coverage you didn't have any idea your friends were involved."

Horace was on the verge of tears. Where he sat, it may have been over a decade since their passing, but as far as Horace was concerned, he had been with them less than a month previous. "Dammit, Milton. You're supposed to foresee those complications."

Horace took a moment and reread the entire page, top to bottom. When he finished, he wrinkled his nose organizing his own thoughts.

Their experiments consisted of creating microscopic black holes, ones that would collapse in upon themselves very quickly. But, each black hole emits radiation, and they failed to consider the radiation each generated being amplified because of its proximity to others. In turn, they suffered from radiation poisoning. The area was contaminated like dealing with a very small nuclear bomb fallout. Hence, they shut things down. The press release indicated that it happened quickly, so they didn't suffer much. Horace's hand covered his mouth hiding the bulk of his shock and dread.

Horace knew the paper he held in his hand was laughable as evidence. Such a document was so easily forged that, even in the present if he brought it back as his only proof of time travel, he could forget being taken seriously. If they hadn't laughed at his time travel idea enough before, this would add insult to injury. His former colleagues dead and no way to get into the building, even the thought of tracking down one of those scientific materials "cookbooks," as they were called, had become much more difficult. He needed more. And, try as he might, he could think of one way to get that done.

Horace rose. "I'm going to tell you something, and you're going to think I'm crazy, but I don't know what else to do at the moment."

Stanley raised his eyebrows and scooted his chair back from the glass.

"Technically, I saw those coworkers no more than a month ago." Horace paused, waiting for Stanley to react, who appeared mildly confused.

Either Stanley was more seasoned in hearing people spout craziness than he'd let on, or he hadn't understood what Horace meant. "How?"

"There's only one way to say this, Stanley. I arrived here in a time machine. In the past I came from, I was fired for proposing this same time travel I've recently experienced."

Stanley's jaw dropped.

"If you don't believe me, scan my badge. It should pull up my file."

Horace handed Stanley his ID badge. Stanley took it with a skeptical look and pressed it against the scanner next to his computer. The terminal clicked and whirred as it accessed data buried deep in the recesses of its network.

The computer screen that popped up was packed with information. If Horace squinted, he could have read the screen, but he was confident he knew what it said. On the top left was Horace's picture, the exact one that was on the ID Stanley held. Studying the image on the screen, he compared it to the badge, then raised it for a side by side comparison with Horace, who still stood outside the booth looking identical to the computer file.

The words didn't faze Stanley until he scrolled down and reached the section about Horace's termination; of which a video file was included. The video ended, and Stanley turned, his eyes begging for an explanation.

"I'm lost, Dr. Wallen. What do you want me to do?"

Horace made a brief explanation about this plan to secure proof of his time travel via a badge swipe recorded in the system. He could then return and show his former colleagues what he had accomplished. He imagined them cheering and hooting with excitement as they pushed Julia to get his job back so the discovery could be shared by NextEdge.

"Needless to say, the fact that they aren't here, that they've all died, forced me to change my plan. Returning with proof isn't enough. And now that I know, and I can move successfully through time, I need to find a way to stop their deaths."

Stanley didn't respond immediately. He scratched the back of his head, pondering Horace's story. "I don't know how I can help, Dr. Wallen. The whole place is on lockdown. I can't even walk your badge in there and swipe it if I wanted to."

Horace couldn't hold back a chuckle. "I know you've already crossed the line, but I need a little more, Stanley. I need specific information about the event that led to their deaths. The more we discover, the closer I can get to the tipping point and hopefully warn them before they lose their lives."

Stanley took a long, deep breath and nodded. He spun his chair back around to the computer and began combing through files and documents for more detailed information from eleven years ago. The search was quick.

The next part was harder. And it relied solely on Horace. He would have to reconfigure his return trip to go a little more than eleven years into the past instead of the full twenty he'd originally anticipated.

Stanley printed out everything he could find for Horace, anything that would help to pinpoint the moment in time that Horace's arrival was essential to alter the future.

"For what it's worth, when you swiped my ID badge to bring up my file, we unintentionally succeeded in creating a record, undeniable, that I have traveled into the future. So, assuming I can return and save my former coworkers and then finish traveling home to my present day, I will still be able to prove to them I was here when I shouldn't have been. So, thank you."

Stanley's head fell into his hands.

"Honestly, I didn't realize what you had done until my information sprang up on the computer. So, if there is anyone to blame, it should be me," Horace said.

He could see Stanley's frame relax, minimally at least.

"For what it's worth, Dr. Wallen, I'm sorry about your friends and that I couldn't get you into the building. I hope you find what you're looking for."

"Thank you. What's your last name, Stanley? Presuming I get back where I belong, I'll be sure to tuck a letter of recommendation away for you for when the time comes. I feel like it's the least I can do for your assistance."

Stanley smiled a great big smile that spread across his face. "Thank you, and you're welcome, Dr. Wallen."

Having accomplished both more and less than he intended, but without the ability to achieve more, Horace left Stanley in his little security enclosure and made his way back to the unfamiliar basement and his time travel device. He needed to begin work on calculations for his modified return trip, to the point in time where he could save his friends and former colleagues.

He made a quick stop to get a flashlight-like contraption, so he would have light to work. Once he arrived back in the secluded basement, Horace set to work on adjusting his math. In preparation and as an effort to save time, he had completed most of the computations before he made the jump forward. Now he just needed to sort through the paperwork and find the instances of time or weight and charge of the time-fuel and adjust accordingly.

The most challenging task was going to be decreasing the size and reducing the negative charge carried by the time-fuel. If his hypothesis was correct and if he could chip off the proper sized chunk, the two pieces together would still equal enough to return him home, within a matter of hours, at least. Horace removed the stack of papers he'd tucked into the bundle at the bottom of the console, spread them out across the floor, set the light in the middle, and got to work refiguring.

He stood up a few hours later, confident in his numerical solutions. Once he got the charged time-fuel down to the right size and verified its charge, he'd be set. This basement wasn't as helpful as being in his junkyard, but he still managed to track down some tools and decrease the size of the time-fuel.

A check with the multimeter on both pieces confirmed that the weight was also correct. Content with the readings and weights, Horace twisted knobs, flipped switches, and adjusted gauges for his journey. Everything corrected, Horace double-checked that he had replaced the pile of computations and the remaining time-fuel in the bundle and strapped himself into the jump seat. One last long, deep breath and he flicked the switch, launching him back in time grasping onto the hope that he could save his friends.

Horace awoke to the same fatigued feeling he had after his first trip. He had hoped it was a one-time occurrence, a side effect related to his first trip. He wanted to think gathering himself this second time was faster, that he was less paranoid his limbs would never recover, but that would have been a lie. Horace kept himself calm and maintained measured breathing while the leaden feeling drained from his appendages into the floor. The junkyard came into focus around him, a sight he was thrilled to see. He wouldn't have to puzzle his way out of some foreign building.

When he regained control of his body, Horace unbuckled. He fought his desire to run. Inevitably, that would result in injury and would delay his rescue operation. Horace bounced a few times on each foot to test his legs. Once he felt that he wouldn't fall over if he walked more than ten steps, Horace felt in his pocket for his Next-Edge ID badge and headed toward the front gate of the junkyard.

Walking down the street toward the NextEdge campus, a red, white, and black checkered sign caught his attention. It was the café he'd made into a respite for his tired, wandering brain. It would be a perfect place to check and make sure he'd traveled back far enough. He found himself hoping that Candace was still patrolling the counter.

He wasn't disappointed, but her reaction caught him off guard.

"What're you doin' back in here so soon?" Candace strolled down the counter the moment Horace crossed the threshold.

"So soon?" Horace puzzled.

"Ya left not fi-teen minutes ago. An' I hope ya ain't hungry. Not sure we got enuff batter back der for another stack a' cakes like you just demolished."

The version of him that existed in this current time must have just left. His eyes went wide at the thought of what kind of paradox might occur if he ran across another version of himself. The saving grace might be that this F.H. would be familiar with time travel. Either way, it was not a theory he wished to test.

Horace tried to play it off. "Oh, no way." He rubbed his belly, pretending he was stuffed even though he wanted nothing more than some bacon and eggs. "I've just been buried under projects for a while. Remind me, what's today?"

Candace spun around to check the calendar posted behind the cash register. She rattled off the date. Exactly the day Horace needed it to be.

"Thanks." And with that, he bolted out the door, running down the street, toward the NextEdge campus.

Between the buildings on his right, Horace could make out a few of the buildings on the outer edge of the campus. At the end of the block and he turned right. He did a little sweet talking of the security guard was able to gain access to the landscaped walkway leading to the lobby of the main building. Once he got inside, he knew right where he needed to go. It was early, so they'd all still be gathered around one of their desks, speculating and pontificating about one thing or another. Horace checked behind him to be sure the guard wasn't looking, then veered off the path to the right, heading for the corner of the building that housed his old office space.

With one last check of his pockets for his ID badge and the papers Stanley printed off, Horace rounded the corner. The barbed wire fences, small security enclosure, and an impending yellow and black ringed security barrier greeted him. He slowed to a walk to slow down his breathing. Convincing the security guard to let him into a restricted entrance would be harder if he was huffing and puffing like he was running from the law.

Horace was no more than ten feet from the gate when a two-story tall fireball erupted from the side of the main building. The thunderous boom paired with a concussive blast of wind shoved Horace back, the corners of his lab coat snapping at his legs. Reflexively, he ducked down, wrapping his arms over his head and neck. Tiny bits of glass and debris blown out from the side of the building peppered him. When the raining debris halted, he dared to uncover.

The place where his office had been, the exact spot where his colleagues would have been congregating, was gone.

The entire right side of the building was scorched. Flames whipped out of a gaping hole in the structure, licking the roof, trying to grow and explore. Past the muted thrum of his heart beating in his ears, Horace could hear the sounds of sirens bouncing off the other campus buildings.

Horace collapsed to the curb. He buried his head in his hands. The tears streamed between his fingers. The chain link fence rattled against his heaving back.

How was this possible? Horace had perfected the calculations. According to the information compiled by Stanley, the critical radiation exposure point hadn't been until after lunch. He'd arrived the morning of the incident. He should have had plenty of time to warn them. But somehow, he'd failed. There was no way anyone in that corner of the building survived. Horace's mind raced. He could go back further. He still had time-fuel attached to the device. He could chip off another smaller piece, allowing him to go back to yesterday. Maybe he could stop Gustav or Luciana before they entered the building. He knew where August lived. Horace could warn him before he left the house.

His eyes burned, and his chest was sore from the intense sobbing. *What good is that stupid machine if I can't fix this?*

Horace leaned his head back against the fence. He tried to take a deep breath to give him a chance to think. Work through possible solutions. A small butterfly flitted and fluttered above him, oblivious to the despair and destruction of the surrounding area. The butterfly flapped its tiny paper-thin wings close enough to his face to cause a small breeze to dry a lone tear from his cheek. It bobbed and floated in front of Horace for a moment before catching a draft and disappearing up above the trees.

Deep in the recesses of his brain, synapses fired, and the reality of the situation ignited his mind. At that moment, Horace instinctively knew that no matter how many times he went backward or forward in time, or how precisely he figured his trips, attempting to save his colleagues would always end in disaster. There was nothing he could do to change that, and if he did, fate would intervene somewhere down the road refuting him.

Horace watched, helpless, as fire trucks soaked the building while emergency workers treated survivors. He gathered himself, realizing that he would soon be approached as a witness. Not wanting to endure the ensuing complications or cause any further disruption, Horace slipped away from the scene in the mass of people that had congregated and were now being ushered away from the buildings. He walked as if in a daze, finally arriving back at the junkyard and his time travel device.

Working on autopilot, he performed the calculations necessary to return him to his time before collapsing into the jump seat. When he awoke, back in the present day, he lay there unable to gather the energy even to attempt leaving the machine. Dragging himself from the device, he slumped over to the door of his workspace and surrendered himself into a kitchen chair. The container with the remaining time-fuel rested on the table and papers still covered everything.

ABOUT MATTHEW STEVENS

Matthew Stevens spent years dreaming about being a writer before he found time late at night after the house was asleep to create characters and worlds and the stories for them to inhabit. During the daylight hours, he balances many jobs; husband, stay-at-home dad, server at a local brew pub, and all-encompassing geek. His current projects find him dabbling in a wide range of genres from his drafted novel, a para-normal thriller, to numerous fantasy and sci-fi shorts, along with an occasional blog post examining his perspective on his own writing journey and any intriguing geeky topic that catches his attention.

He can be found online at:
theedgeofeverything.wordpress.com

f facebook.com/matthewstevensauthor
🐦 twitter.com/matt_the_writer
 instagram.com/matt_the_writer

SHIFTED

BY BREE MOORE

Every girl dreams of the day they get engaged to the love of their life; most only see it once. When it first happened to me, it was a scene I had experienced a hundred times in my dreams, but never like I was seeing it today.

The dock's sodden boards reached out over the foaming ocean. Thick rain clouds retreated towards the horizon, reflecting the sun's dying red-orange light in a spectacular display of nature's most vivid color.

My red hair blew in my face, and I drew it away with a finger, not really noticing the inconvenience. Not with Grant kneeling there, hand reaching into his pocket, a hopeful, confident look gleaming in his soft brown eyes.

It was happening. How hadn't I seen this coming? Yes, there it was, the little blue velvet box, his fingers on it, opening to reveal a large diamond ring.

My hand drifted up to my chest, heart throbbing so hard I almost didn't hear what he said.

"Evie Charleston, will you marry me?"

My heart dropped. I swallowed, reaching for that ring box and the gleaming diamond within.

Then, I Shifted.

Better see how this turns out, I thought to myself. The scene froze for a moment, and then, as if someone had hit fast-forward, everything blurred. Me accepting the proposal, hugging Grant's neck, kissing. It took getting used to, the fast movement, the zinging in my heart and across my skin as each sensation passed a million seconds at a time.

———

They call it Shifting. Not everyone can do it, or so Pappy told me. Pappy, my dad's father, came to me when Dad disappeared. I was twelve. Mom was already gone, taken by the cancer.

"Your dad is dead, Evie." He said it with a blunt finality.

"What?"

He sighed, rubbing the thin hair on his nearly-bald head. "He Shifted one too many times. Got himself into a situation he couldn't get out of. I tried to help, but...sorry, kid."

I remember sitting there, stunned. I remember falling into his arms and crying. It wasn't until after my body emptied itself of tears that I registered what he had said enough to ask questions.

"What is Shifting? Like driving a car?"

"Oh no, kid. It's a special gift we Charlestons have. A gene not very many people get. Shifting is...aw, hell. Never really had to explain it to a kid." He eyed me, then knelt beside me, pointing to the shadows under the maple tree in our front yard. The breeze was strong on that March day, and the sun bright, making the shadows dance and flicker on the green grass.

"See them shadows, how they move? We're like that, Evie. We can Shift from one point to the next through time, traveling anywhere in the blink of an eye."

My eyes widened. It was just like one of my sci-fi books. "Time travel?" I whispered.

"Sort of," Pappy said, rubbing the back of his neck. "You can only travel in your own timeline, as far as it possibly extends either way.

Can't go back past your birth, can't go forward past the latest possible point of your death."

"So, no dinosaurs?"

"No dinosaurs." He smiled and ruffled my hair. "When you Shift, you always enter any time-stream point in your own body, wherever it would be and whatever you're doing at the time you enter. Is this making any sense, kid?"

I wasn't entirely sure, but I bobbed my head up and down eagerly. That day, my life became like something out of a story. I practiced with Pappy, going forward minutes at a time, a few hours, working up to a day. He and Gran took me in, caring for me until I was old enough to go out on my own. They both died a few years later.

"A few things you must remember, Evie." Pappy's eyes had seemed so stern, I watched his face with my heart racing in my chest. What had I done wrong? His hand landed on my shoulder, and his gaze softened a little as if he could tell he had scared me. "Shifting is a wonderful gift—the ability to go forward to see what's unfolding, what different paths hold, then return to your present and made different decisions. We get to live many lives this way. But beware skipping through the difficult stuff. It's tempting to jump ahead, past the hurt and the pain, but remember that when you Shift to the future, you're still the same you. The damage doesn't go away, and it lasts longer when you're not present to process it. Only Shift when you really need it, kid. And, you can't always change someone else's decisions, so don't waste your energy trying. Sometimes people just make bad choices; you can't always be the hero.

"Third, watch out for the Shacklers."

"Shacklers?" I asked.

"Yeah. They Shift, like us, only they don't like that we can do it. They're some sort of government knockoff, keeping tabs on time-travelers. No Shackler is good news, Evie. It was Shacklers what killed your dad."

My blood ran cold. "What did he do?"

"Some people abuse Shifting, Evie. Some use it to commit crime. Your dad was a good man who got mixed up in something he shouldn't have. You ain't gonna be like that, you hear? Live a normal life. You just have a little advantage over most folk...like being a bit smarter in math or a bit faster on the track. It's a small thing that can help you live a good life. If you play your cards right, them time-travel cops will never catch you."

I still remember how it felt for him to ruffle my hair. I had gone back to replay that memory hundreds of times, to make sure I hadn't missed anything when I finally started Shifting months, then years at a time.

Today, I was Shifting through years.

I paused for a moment at our wedding, myself arrayed in a white dress that fit snugly in the hips, a veil flowing around my head. I smiled, holding an armful of flowers, walking through the hall of that white-walled church, a modest crowd of people looking on. Grant stood before me, handsome in his gray tux and purple vest, grinning at me. Who held my arm? I looked up into the beaming face of my uncle Craig. I smiled back at him. Everything felt so right, but you know what they say, when the honeymoon's over...I Shifted, and time blurred again.

The screen door banged behind me as I stepped through to the porch. I was already sweating, so the heat didn't bother me too much. The humidity was awful though.

"I don't need a bath no more, Pappy. Mother Nature got me covered." I grinned, lifting my arms to show off my pit stains, and Pappy laughed.

"I think your Gran'll disagree, with church tomorrow." He gestured to the empty spot beside him on the porch swing, and I obliged, crossing one leg beneath me, the other dangling over the edge.

"Evie, I've been thinking you should know something."

My hands pressed into the wood of the bench as I leaned over a bit, watching a beetle scuttle underneath. "Yeah?"

"Yeah. You're young and maybe ain't thought of this too much, about what you're going to do when you're older."

"Firefighter, Pappy." I reminded him, tossing my bangs out of my eyes as I looked up at him.

"Okay, firefighter. You could become a firefighter, an Olympian, a mob member, a billionaire, anything you want to be if you just go back enough times and fix every little mistake or obstacle that gets in the way. But if you Shift too many times, if you go down too many paths, you'll lose yourself, Evie. "

"Did that happen to Dad?"

"You could say that, kid. He wanted to get something right, but it went very wrong. Remember that, when you feel the urge to try a dozen paths. See something through to the end before committing. It's how I won your Gran over."

"It is?" I replied with wonder.

"Yep, sure thing. Now, I want you to try Shifting to find out what happens if you were to climb that maple right now."

I eyed the tall tree in the yard, then Shifted.

The wind blew a strand of hair into my mouth, and I spat it out, adjusting my grip on the two rough branches above. My foot slipped a little on the bark, but I caught my footing again and braced myself. This was the hardest part of the climb, that "y" in the branches where I had to get a leg hooked forward over one of the branches and push myself up. I licked my lips and Shifted.

My scream was cut off as I landed hard on a pair of muscled, hairy arms. Pappy's beard snagged my hair as I snuggled into him, breathing fast until the hiccups started.

He didn't say a word but carried me back to the porch and set me on the swing next to him, arm still around me. I was shaking.

"You knew I would fall, didn't you?" I accused, glancing up towards him.

"Of course. But I won't always be here to protect you, kid. You've got to learn to check a path before you go down it. It's the only thing'll keep you from a devastating mistake. And even then...well, life is life, even for us Shifters. You can't stop all the bad stuff from happening all the time. So, use your gift, but don't obsess. And remember: sometimes it's better not to know."

I nodded the first time I heard him say that, but I didn't really understand until the eleventh. Like so many things he taught me. I was lucky to have this chance to go back and hear him again, even if it changed a little each time I went back. The words might have changed a little bit, but Pappy never did. Who else got that chance? It was a special gift, Shifting. I hadn't used it for anything significant since deciding to go to college instead of volunteer at the fire station. Firefighter Evie became accountant Evie. I was a damn good accountant. I had Shifting to thank for everything in my life. There was no way it would let me down now.

I discovered after Shifting for a few years that I could feel the snag of significant events in my future, like a wave of emotion washing over me in the time stream. Discovering this ability prevented me from getting beat up on several occasions, by bullies. It stopped someone from stealing my car and even spared me getting raped at a college party. So, I could feel when Grant and I had our first fight.

I settled into that scene with a little time-travel vertigo swirling around my head. By my estimation, we had been married three years, had our first years, and...oh God.

My belly swelled beneath my tent-like clothes, taut and enormous, hiding my sandaled feet from view. Grant was yelling, and I was crying. I didn't even know what we were fighting about, but the emotion in my body was overwhelming, and I kept crying, and Grant kept yelling.

And then my water broke, splashing across the wooden floor in a great, unmistakable gush.

Grant stopped mid-rant and stared, blinking. He looked up at me. "Did you pee yourself, Evie?"

"What? No!" I replied, indignant. Honestly. "It's my water, dumbass. Get some towels." I sort of wondered what labor would feel like, but when that first real contraction hit, doubling me over, I Shifted my butt out of there. I could wait to experience that particular event. No one wanted to give birth to the same baby twice.

I found myself in the hospital bed, that tiny bundle in my arms, Grant peering down at the red, pudge-nosed face of our new baby boy. My heart swelled, and I smiled up at Grant, our earlier fight forgotten.

"Hi, Henry," I whisper softly, giving that sweet baby the name my father had.

Grant leaned down close and whispered in my ear, as if not wanting to disturb the sleeping baby I cradled. "What are you doing here, Evie?"

A chill ran up my spine, and out of instinct, I Shifted, backward this time, to that time in the cave, when all the lights went out, and my hiking group was listening to the guide talk about total darkness and nocturnal critters. I breathed deeply, knowing I had at least fifteen minutes of the drab discussion and complete dark to gather my nerves.

Was Grant...had he—?

"How will I know if someone is a Shackler, Pappy?" My fifteen-year-old self, perched on the bed, watching Pappy play cards with himself. He'd had a stroke, and was lucky to be alive, according to the doctor. I was old enough to know that meant I had to ask him every question I could think of because he might be dead soon.

"They break the time-stream, Evie. They'll look right at you when they should be doing something else. They'll approach you, sometimes, say things to jar you out of the timeline, make you Shift. The best thing you can do is act naturally. Train yourself not to look up when someone says something shocking, out of the ordinary. That's how they catch you, is when you Shift in front of them."

"What if I Shift without knowing there's a Shackler nearby?"

"Sometimes they'll notice, other times they won't. Here, see if you can feel this." Pappy blinked. I felt something, almost like wind, except it moved through my insides.

"You just Shifted!" I exclaimed.

Pappy nodded. "Easy to feel, when you're looking for it. Some Shacklers have been training for years, and inexperienced Shifters like you make bigger waves, more noticeable. You practice, Evie. Practice when no one is around, go to uncrowded places, the in-between memories. Get good enough no Shackler will ever catch you."

My breath came in quick little gasps; my head felt as if it had been caught in a riptide and dragged underwater. I began tapping my wrist, counting to ten until my breath came back. The lights in the cave turned on, and the tour continued. I stayed in the timeline, nerves ragged from that minute encounter with Grant. I must not have heard him right; he could have said, "What are we doing here, Evie?" Maybe as an apology for the fight earlier, maybe to re-evaluate our purpose being together. I set my jaw. I would not give up just because I was a little scared. The odds of Grant being a Shackler were so low as to be ridiculous. I just had to go forward a little further, but I would have to be more careful this time, not jump away like a frightened rabbit. I had to use my head, use my training.

I Shifted, watching the world around me melt like the clocks in that weird painting. I went past that scene where I held our baby, forward to that baby's eighth birthday. Singing to him, heart swelling with pride, Grant set the cake and its flickering candles down on the table in front of him. I watched Grant, eyes flicking from him to the boy, trying not to draw suspicion. The boy, my son, took a deep breath and blew, forcing the candles out nearly all at once. Just before they went out, Grant looked up, eyes gleaming in the last second of candlelight, staring at me. The lights turned on, and everyone was cheering; several boys ran up for the cake that Grant dished up. Family members milled around us, but all of them got settled, and no one seemed to notice the standoff between me and Grant.

I shook my head as if I had been staring into the distance at nothing, the way people sometimes do, smiling at the people around me, asking our son what he had wished for when he blew out those candles. His muffled answer came through a mouthful of cake, and I laughed, then glanced at Grant, who was still staring at me. I cocked my head and mouthed, "Are you okay?" He nodded, a small smile flicking onto his face, then he came alive, moving around the room and talking with people.

I escaped to the bathroom and splashed water on my face, then took a deep, calming breath. "See Evie? Nothing to worry about. You both just got caught up in the moment. He's no Shackler. He's not like the ones who killed Dad." My voice choked in my throat. I covered my mouth with the back of my hand, blocking the sound of the sobs that welled up and spilled out despite my attempts to get them under control. The water kept running, and the party was loud enough no one would hear me.

A knock came at the door.

"Evie, you in there?" It was Grant. I breathed in, then blew out slowly.

"Yeah, out in a minute."

I waited a split second, then Shifted the hell out of there.

Where to go? I felt trapped in time. I was Shifting forward, letting time stream around me, not noticing or caring where I ended up. I didn't have any proof, not really, and the tension was starting to get to me, no doubt making things seem far worse than they were. I changed my momentum, heading back through time, past the wedding, past the proposal, and stopped on a rainy day, running across campus with one hand full of books and term papers, the other desperately trying to get my umbrella down as the wind tried to rip it from my hands. Three, two, one...I tripped on a lip in the sidewalk and fell, scattering papers and textbooks, the still-open umbrella clattering across the sidewalk as the wind dragged it. Someone in a long black coat picked it up and handed it to me. I kept my head down, too embarrassed to look the stranger in the face, but when I finally glanced at him, my heart stopped.

I stammered my thanks. It was that cute, tall guy from my literature class, curly brown hair, and dreamy brown eyes. I had spent the better part of the semester staring at the back of his head from a few seats back; he was probably why my grade in that class never got up past a C+.   Grant Hansen, a college senior, straight As. That was the day he asked for my number, and, hands numb and wet from the rain, I scribbled it on a piece of paper and watched as he tucked it in his pocket, apologizing for leaving, as he had to get to class.

"I love you," I said into the rain, watching him go, heart aching after him. There were a dozen different decisions I could make here. I could miss the call that would come later that night. I could stand him up for our first date to that horrid play we laughed through. I could pretend to be sick. I could make-out with his roommate, a decent-looking guy who had eyes for me through most of our courtship; I know he wouldn't object, and it would break Grant's heart. Then we would never fall in love, never get to the point where he stood on that dock and knelt on the ground and pulled out that ring and—I was hyperventilating again, so focused on breathing as I stood getting soaked in the rain that I didn't notice when Grant turned around and started back towards me, eyes hard-set and glaring. My own eyes widened, and I froze, every muscle in my body screaming at me to run, only I couldn't.

He walked right up to me and kissed me hard on the mouth. We came away, panting, then met again, lips smashed together, his arms around me and my umbrella and my books, pressing me into him. When we parted, his eyes searched mine, as if looking for something. I licked my lips, not sure what to say. I had never seen this future before.

He smiled, released me, and ran off, jogging towards whatever class he said he had next. I knew he had liked me, but God, had it really been that much? Every other time I was in this memory I had just walked off, wanting to get out of the rain and away from the embarrassment of my crush seeing my sprawl out across the cement. Had I always just missed him turning around to come back and kiss me?

My mind was whirling. I waited a split-second longer, then Shifted. It wasn't good to Shift when your emotions were high; it could warp where you end up, besides making the Shift more notice-able because of the bigger waves it would make through time. My heart was trembling as if it had been through an earthquake, my mind spinning. Perhaps this was one of those times I should stop Shifting and just live it, consequences be damned. Was it worth the pain of finding out?

One more Shift. If I went far enough, it might tell me what I wanted to know. If anything had changed based on what I learned, the time-stream would tell me.

Black hats soared into the air and fell on the stage around the graduates. A curly-haired youth, the spitting image of his father, grinned at me and waved, making his way through the handshaking and the congratulations. Henry, my son, graduating from college. I beamed up at him, then lost sight of him in the sea of black gowns. I took the opportunity to glance around for Grant—where is he? Shouldn't he be here? A hand grabbed my arm from behind, turning me around.

"You shouldn't be here, Evie."

"What are you talking about? This is our son's graduation." I reply, putting on a confused expression.

Grant rubs his chin, hand lingering on the stubble there. "I want to believe you, Evie, I do. But you have to stop doing this. They're asking me to bring you in. I don't want to do it, but it's my job. You don't know how dangerous this is."

I snorted. "Dangerous? I've been doing it since I was twelve. It's not dangerous."

"To you, maybe. But to the rest of us? Think of the implications. Someone could really cause harm, Shifting like you do. Ripping through the time-stream like it's tissue paper, causing fractures that must be repaired before the world unravels. Every time you Shift, it rips. Did you know that?" He adjusts his position as someone jostles past, hugging a relative.

I shook my head. "No, I don't believe you. You're doing it too; it can't be that dangerous." My mind was reeling, looking for an escape, trying to find a way out. Where should I Shift to next? Could he follow me?

"The difference is that I'm licensed. I know what I am doing, how to make more controlled jumps, to rip in the right places." He licked his lip, looking down at me. I look away, unable to meet those brown eyes I've fallen in love with. "Come with me. We'll get you taken care of. I can talk to them, get them to lessen your sentence."

My mouth was dry. "My sentence? How exactly do you imprison a Shifter, Grant?"

"Gene splicing. They've been doing it for a couple decades now." He looked uncomfortable. I gaped at him.

"You...you want to take it away from me?"

"It's for your own good, Evie."

I shoved him, stumbling back into a group of people behind us. Henry finally pushed through, breathless.

"Mom, Dad, you're here!" He stopped, staring from Grant to me, at the space between us, the hard expressions on our faces.

"What's going on?" he asked.

I pointed my finger at Grant. "You're a Shackler; you work for the government. You want to control it, to control me like you did my dad. I'm sure our son has it. Would you cripple him too?"

"It's not what you think. Look, I don't know what happened with your dad, I wasn't part of that. I'm sorry he was killed, but I'm not a monster, Evie."

"Leave me alone!" I yelled. My skin burned this time; I Shifted so fast I didn't think about my destination. It was dark again. The cave. My breath heaved in my chest, like sucking air through a coffee straw. My entire body trembled.

"Are you scared?" Someone to my right asked. A friend whose name I couldn't recall. I made a strained sound. "I can ask them to turn the lights back on." She sounded concerned. I turned and ran from her, back toward the entrance of the cave, but it was several turns back, and I stopped running, suddenly afraid I've gotten lost. I could hear the voices murmuring in the distance. I slid down the cave wall to the ground, putting my head between my knees. What had I done? Had my Shifting at the proposal allowed him to find me? I could confront him, could ask. We could work this out. I didn't have to give in, to let him take Shifting from me. The only other option was disappearing, Shift until I entered a time stream without him, but I wasn't sure I could even do that. He knew my face, now. He would be looking for me, wherever I went.

Shacklers were relentless; Shacklers had killed Dad. Anger coursed through me, my hands clenched into fists. I had to know if Grant played a part in that. Had he known they would kill my father? Had he done it himself? The logical part of me said it wasn't possible, Grant was only a boy when Dad died, but I still had to know.

I Shifted, stepping from the darkness of that cave to the too-bright scene of a graveside service in a cemetery.

Something was wrong. One of the dark-coated men turned and, seeing it was me, walked over. Grant stopped in front of me, glancing back towards the small group of people clustered around an open grave, casket ready to drop inside.

"This is your funeral, Evie." He seemed saddened, but I knew it was all an act.

My fists clenched at my sides. "What have you done?"

"It wasn't me, Evie. It was you. You chose to run."

"And you just did your job, is that it?" My eyes blinked furiously, my lungs gasping for a full breath of air. Henry stood with another woman, Grant's mother, I think, gazing sightlessly at my casket.

"I did what I had to. You forced my hand."

"You don't have to do this." Could I even change it? Become a Shackler? Then they wouldn't hunt me down; then we could be happy. But even as I thought it, my insides clenched and I knew.

I couldn't betray Pappy or my father that way. "Shacklers killed my father." I choked out.

"I know. It's in the record. I thought that might convince you to surrender, rather than face his same fate."

"How did you bring me here? I'm dead in this time-stream. It shouldn't be possible."

"Special permission to make this trip. I did it for you."

My bottom lips trembled. "Did you ever love me? Or was it all a ruse to catch another rogue Shifter?"

"I loved you, Evie," he replied.

It was his wording that made me Shift. I loved you. *Loved*, not love. Not present tense, but past.

Against my better judgment and every bit of advice Pappy would have given if he were alive, I went back to that moment. I couldn't leave without saying goodbye. So, I went back to a moment before either of us knew anything. I went back to the picturesque sunset, the smell of the ocean on the wind blowing hair into my mouth. I sputtered and pulled out the intruding strand, not wanting to waste a single moment of watching the man kneeling on the damp wooden slats in front of me.

"—ry me?" His lips smiled up at me, a smile that, now I see, doesn't seem to reach his eyes.

Limbs and heart trembling, I reached for that blue velvet box and the gleaming ring inside and clapped it shut. My eyes blinked away the moisture invading my eyes, trying to clear the last view I would ever get of the love of my life.

"No, Grant." I swallowed.

"I was afraid you'd say that." He dropped the ring box and stood, pulling out a black-barreled handgun and leveling it at me.

Before I can think, before I can protest, before I can even Shift, he fires.

I felt the wave of someone Shifting; it wasn't me. A figure popped up in front of me with an audible sound, like paper ripping. It was a mirror image of Grant. For a moment I thought it was Grant, only shorter, thinner. Grant's aim wavered, and the bullet struck low, in the boy's gut.

"No!" I screamed as Henry dropped. He was gasping, hands shaking as they held his stomach, coming away crimson. I fell beside him, holding my hands over his own, trying to put pressure it, to stop the flow.

"Get help!" I yelled at Grant, who stood there, staring, mouth agape. My arm came up under Henry's shoulders, pulling him into my lap, holding him upright against him, blood seeping into my dress.

"How is this possible?" I whispered. "Pappy said you couldn't travel outside your timeline."

"Pappy...lied." Henry shuddered. "I figured...it out."

"Hush, now," I said, the words flat and inadequate. I looked at Grant again. "What have we done?"

He closed his mouth and shook his head but said nothing.

"How do we fix this, son? Just"—my voice broke—"just tell me, and I'll do it. I'll do anything."

He whispered something, voice nearly gone. I leaned in, catching the last of it. "Not supposed to...I can't..." he sighed, body slumping against mine. His eyes closed. I clutched at him, shaking him.

"Henry? Henry!" I glanced at Grant, then down at our dead boy, eyes blinking to clear away the moisture that obscured my last view of the love of my life. Then, I Shifted.

The dying sun was a blood-orange disc in the sky. I let my hair whip across my face and stared into a pair of brown eyes without really seeing them. "—ry me?"

I reached for that blue velvet box with one hand, the other grabbing the pistol stashed in the handbag at my side. We drew at the same time, but I shot first.

"That's for the son we'll never have," I growled. Grant gasped, clutching at the red that blossomed from his chest, then fell forward, dead. I stepped over his body, tucking the pistol away in my bag, leaning against the railing as I watched the sunset blur.

It is a scene I've seen a hundred times, in dreams and in nightmares. That shot shatters the air, and I see blood on the deck reflecting the blood-red sun in the sky. Maybe next time will be different. I let the wind tangle my hair as my skin begins to tingle.

Then, I Shift.

ABOUT BREE MOORE

Bree Moore has been writing fantasy since the fourth grade. She lives in Ogden, is wife to an amazing husband, and the mother of four children. She writes fantasy novels between doling out cheerios and folding laundry.

In real-life, Bree works as a birth doula, attending women in pregnancy and labor, which is a huge inspiration for her writing. Bree loves shopping for groceries like other women like shopping for shoes (no, seriously), movies that make her cry, and Celtic music. She likes both her chocolate and her novels dark.

facebook.com/AuthorBreeMoore

twitter.com/AuthorBreeMoore

instagram.com/author_breemoore

A TIME, A PLACE

BY SARAH BUHRMAN

Feb 26th, 1884

Tianna hitched her chin up and pasted a small smile on her lightly rouged lips. Despite the blinding lights inside the ballroom, she glided over the carpet runner, taking small steps to keep from stumbling over the sapphire blue skirt of her gown.

She lowered her eyelids in a modest-looking expression and drifted to a halt where she estimated the short entry hall ended. Looking down and blinking her eyes several times, she was able to adjust her vision to the sudden change from the dark entry to the crystal and gold enhanced lighting. The serving man next to her bellowed out her introduction.

Appearing graceful in the face of the many discomforts that came with rubbing elbows with the Dons and Donnas in Verona was a virtual act of willpower, and Tianna had learned that having willpower wasn't so much a choice as a survival tactic.

Men lined up to greet her, wearing tight breeches and coats fitted to the waist with tails hanging to the backs of their knees. Even though the customs had begun to loosen in recent years, Tianna still felt the insult from their audacity in not waiting for a proper introduction.

She knew it was because she was an entertainer, therefore, not a proper lady. Never mind that she had a perfectly modest upbringing. Never mind that her vocal talents were proper enough for any musicale. Never mind that she was only a few weeks past her sixteenth year.

She sang in front of an audience and was paid for it. Therefore, only her popularity with the upper levels of nobility kept her from being a whore.

Tianna pressed her lips together, ignoring the men as much as she dared. An outright snub would not be tolerated by one of her station, but she could refrain from responding directly to their veiled innuendos. She clenched her fingers together at her waist, putting on the mask of a perfect, virginal debutante, her only defense unless some matron would come to her rescue.

Fortunately, her wide blue eyes and pale skin gave her a delicate, fragile look. Though some felt her vibrant red hair was a sign of moral failings, her overall appearance was that of an innocent, and Tianna cultivated that appearance carefully.

Sure enough, a severe throat cleared at the back of the pack, and the men flinched away from the woman who strode towards Tianna like a force of nature.

Her dark brown gown was elegant in its simplicity, with only a few ruffles and a modest bustle. The woman was perhaps in her forties. She had brown hair with strands of bright silvery-gray running through it. Her eyes were a dark steel gray, and her expression alone put the men in their place.

As she approached Tianna, her face lit up with a pleasant smile, and she reached out a gloved hand to the singer.

"My dear," she said in a smooth alto, pitched to carry across the thick murmur of conversation. "So good of you to grace us with your presence. I am Contessa Lucia Priuli. Welcome to my home and allow me to make your introductions."

Tianna smiled, gratitude in her eyes as she murmured her thanks. With a few sentences, this grand woman had honored her as a special guest and reprimanded the men surrounding her for treating her so commonly.

Surprisingly, the Contessa was not finished with the public rebuke. She grasped Tianna's hand firmly and pulled her away from the pack towards more a more respectful young man before beginning her introductions, effectively snubbing the more aggressive men in a way that Tianna would never have dared to do herself.

The whirlwind of social niceties interspersed with being guided around the dance floor blurred in Tianna's head. After several hours, she found herself dropped onto a bench next to a plump matron in dove gray wearing a kind smile.

The Contessa winked at Tianna and stood partially in front of her, speaking to the matron about some charity board they were involved in. Tianna took advantage of the breather and let herself slump into the seat.

A red-faced young man brought her a glass of punch, stammering out a few words before ducking away. Tianna smiled, grateful for her hostess' body blocking her from view. She tucked the gown's train behind her feet and stretched out her legs. She wiggled her toes within the tight but fashionable slippers.

"So, you are the visiting soprano, damigella?"

Tianna turned to the matron in gray. "Si, Signora, a mezzo-soprano."

The matron waved a hand. "I'm sure that means more to you than it does to me," she said. "A luxury that I am well aware of. I only must attend the opera. I don't have to know anything about it."

Tianna caught a gleam of humor in the woman's eye and smiled softly. "As you say, Signora."

The matron smiled. "Now, what say you-"

An explosion shook the ballroom, as half of the outer wall collapsed with some kind of impact. Ladies shrieked, and a few cowardly gentlemen pushed their way through the crowd.

The Contessa staggered as the floor shuddered, then stood tall, surveying the damage. Tianna and the matron clung to each other to stay on the bench. Tianna stared up at the Contessa, shocked that the noblewoman was unfazed by the chaos around her.

"Signora Torelli," the Contessa said, raising her voice over the screams of her guests. "Would you be so kind as to escort Signorina Udovin to a safe room?"

She reached out and grasped a middle-aged serving man and spoke in his ear. Despite his obvious fear, he nodded and offered both hands to the matron and Tianna. The women grasped his gloved fingers and let him help them balance as he guided them to a small servant's door behind the stairs.

Tianna glanced back at the Contessa and froze, staring. The woman stood tall and waved her hands at the broken wall. The curtains seemed to come alive, wrapping themselves around a man who was climbing over the rubble. Three other people moved across the unlit balcony behind him. Tianna caught a glimpse of familiar, shockingly red hair, and she reached up to touch her own tresses.

The servant pulled Tianna through the door, and she shook her head, trying to clear her mind and make sense of what she'd seen. The three of them rushed through the narrow hallways to a staircase going down to the cellars. Signora Torelli hesitated, but the servant insisted they go down.

"It is the safest room in the house," he assured her.

Another blast shook the house, and Tianna cried out. "Just go!"

The woman hurried down the stairs behind the servant, while Tianna brought up the rear, bouncing on her toes when the older woman didn't move fast enough.

They moved through the buttery, and the servant grabbed a candle that had been lit to aid any servants needing to refresh the foods for the ball. He opened a large metal-wrapped door hidden in the corner of the subterranean room. He pushed the women inside with the candle and closed the door behind them with an order to lock it from the inside.

Tianna locked the door, and the matron immediately began to panic.

"Oh, mio Dio! Mio Dio! We shall die in this house, buried in the cellar like rats!"

"No, Signora," Tianna said, guiding the woman to a wooden crate and pushing her down to sit on it. "We will not die."

The woman rocked back and forth, weeping and moaning until Tianna began to sing. It was a song about a woman hoping for love, soft and sweet and calming. After a moment, the woman's crying faded as she listened to the music.

They spent nearly an hour huddled together in the dim light while Tianna sang to drown out the muted cries from above, reminding her of her early life, with the Russian liberation of the Balkans creating nearly constant fighting in the small villages caught in the crossfire.

Tianna had never had an easy life, though her trials recently were those of a woman with no title moving in circles of nobility. Her voice had saved her from a life of drudgery, and her striking looks assured her a place in the interest, if not the acceptance, of those wealthy enough to attend the social events where she performed. She'd learned the proprieties of being a lady with as much conviction as she'd practiced her singing, knowing without the one, the other would be a passing grace.

Her path was set for her, as a woman of her position could only hope to earn enough to be comfortable once her voice failed her. She could perhaps become a lord's mistress, trading her body for jewelry and a grand home, hoping for love that was unlikely, but she would never be considered as a wife.

Tianna's secret hope was to retire to America, where money mattered more than titles, and the wide-open spaces meant a sprawling estate or ranch. She might even find love there, away from the strict propriety of European nobility.

It was the freedom of living life on her own terms that drew her the most, though. She chafed under the yoke of constant social pressure and expectations, a powerless player in a game not of her choosing. In America, she could have her own way.

Tianna let the last notes of the song fade away. The silence around them was deafening and oppressive, but she couldn't bring herself to start another piece. She sat on the dirt floor next to the crate, holding Signora Torelli's hand as they stared at the candle flame slowly burning the wax down.

The women jumped at the sudden heavy banging at the door. Tianna picked herself up off the floor and shook out her skirts, a delaying tactic to gather her courage. She stepped over to the door and reached for the lock with a shaky hand.

"Signorina Tianna? Signora Torelli?"

Tianna nearly collapsed with relief at hearing the Contessa's voice. She unlocked the door quickly and pulled it open.

"Grazie Dio, you are both safe," the Contessa said, helping Tianna step out of the room before reaching back to help the matron. "The disaster is passed. Signora Torelli, I have a carriage waiting to take you home immediately. I'm sure you will want time to recover from your shock."

The matron nodded and burst into tears again. Tianna trudged behind the ladies as the Contessa shuffled the other woman out the door. Tianna waited to be dismissed as well, but the Contessa instead led her to a small sitting room.

The room was lovely, with cushioned chairs and settees, a small fireplace filled with dancing flames, a table loaded with small sandwiches, cakes and tea, and a decanter of Eau-de-vie, a brandy made with fruits. The Contessa gestured Tianna to sit in one of the chairs next to the table while she sat in the other.

Tianna glanced down at her gown, dirtied and mussed by the flight from the ballroom and from sitting on the cellar floor. She glanced at the Contessa, but the older woman just smiled and gestured to the chair again.

"Don't worry about the mess," she said. "I've been meaning to redecorate this room for some time."

Tianna sat and gratefully accepted a plate of food piled improperly high and a snifter of the brandy, smelling strongly of blackberries. She took a rather large drink of the brandy and nibbled delicately but steadily at the food.

"I realize you would rather be on your way back to your rooms," the Contessa admitted. "But I could not let you leave without discussing something with you first."

"Is it to do with that awful attack?" Tianna asked, swallowing a bite of Torrone, an almond nougat. "What happened, Contessa? Please, tell me."

The older woman nodded. "In many ways, it does have to do with what happened, though I am forbidden to tell you much. Instead, we shall have to discuss it in a more roundabout fashion." She leaned forward, her eyes flashing with intensity. "What do you know of the gente fata, the fairy folk?"

Tianna flinched. "Feya? I-I don't know. All countries have stories about them, but... What does that have to do with-?"

The Contessa slashed her hand between them, cutting off Tianna's words. "Do you believe me to be a fool or one easily manipulated?"

"No!"

"Good," the Contessa said. "I am telling you, as a learned woman of status and experience, the fae are real. Or at least, they were once. And you are a descendant of one."

Tianna sat with her mouth hanging open. The Contessa reached over and grabbed a baicoli and popped it into Tianna's mouth with a chuckle.

"Drink some tea before you choke, girl," the Contessa said. "And let me tell you our history, for I am descended from the fae as well."

Tianna slurped her tea, but she was too shocked to be embarrassed by that. Instead, she went back to nibbling at the sandwiches and cakes as the Contessa spoke.

"Thousands of years ago, the fae walked the world with us. Eventually, they found mates and their children were magical beings. These half-fae held the magic far better than they held the appearance of the fae, though there is a certain look that they often had."

The Contessa gestured to Tianna. "Hair of red or gold or sable, or even striated colors. Eyes of shining gold, bright green or impossible blue. Skin of cream or amber or sable, pure in color and without blemish. These were the signs of the fae-born."

Tianna swallowed hard and gulped down another mouthful of tea.

"More importantly, the magic stayed strong, giving the fae-born powers. The first few generations were called Mage, using their gifts as wizards and wise-women. But they are long gone from this world. They left us with only fairy tales and their children."

Tianna frowned. "You are saying that I, and you, are among these children?"

The Contessa nodded. "We call ourselves Magecrafters. The blood has diluted enough that we can only call forth one kind of magic each, but we can be immensely powerful with that magic."

Tianna bit her lip, considering. "Can you make things move?" she asked, thinking of the strange way the curtains had wrapped around the man in the ballroom.

The Contessa laughed. "Very clever! I am a Golemmer, which means I can make objects animate. I'm very good at puppetry, but I can do simple things with objects that are not shaped into an animal form."

"Oh, I see."

The Contessa smirked. "You don't believe me? Then watch the statue upon the mantel."

Tianna blinked and turned to the fireplace. On the marble mantel, a small horse figurine stood, poised with one leg raised as if stepping. Its mane was carved to flow back as though a wind was blowing into the animal's face.

As she watched, the horse shook its head, releasing the mane from its waves. It took two prancing steps, then reared up on its back legs. When it dropped down to all fours again, it froze like the ceramic it was formed from.

Tianna gasped. "Oh!" She pointed at the horse, looking over at the Contessa. "You did that! You made it move!"

The woman chuckled. "Yes, I did."

"Can I do that?" Tianna asked, her fear quickly giving way to excitement. "Can I be a... what was it? A Golemmer?"

The Contessa shook her head. "No, dear," she said. "You have a different gift. A rare gift, and a subtle one. You must spend many years doing very little with your powers, but when you are needed, you will do what no other Magecrafter can do."

Tianna turned to the Contessa. "You know what my gift is, then?"

The woman nodded. "You are a Timesinker."

Tianna frowned. "What is a Timesinker?"

The Contessa took a deep breath, gathering her thoughts. "You have a power within you to turn back the clock. I know, it sounds unbeliev-able. And it isn't quite so simple as that." The woman leaned forward in her chair. "You can put your power into a location. If you do this once every year, you will be able to travel through time at that location."

She sat back and waved her hand dismissively as Tianna gaped at her.

"Oh, there are limits to how far back you can travel, how long you can stay in the past, and such. But fear not, I will put you in contact with an experienced Timesinker who will teach you all you need to know."

Tianna frowned. "That's... well, not very useful."

The Contessa smiled. "You would have preferred a more exciting gift," she guessed. "As I said, you will spend much time doing very little with your power. But you will live for several centuries. Many Timesinkers become leaders within the Magecrafter community, having the benefit of more years of experience than others."

Tianna touched her face. At sixteen, she already felt so old, so tired. She wondered if she could stand living several times longer than most. "Will I be old for so long?"

The Contessa smiled. "You will stay young and fit, aging much more slowly once you reach twenty-five or thirty years. It seems daunting now, but you will do well, my dear."

"I'm not sure about that."

The Contessa reached over to pat Tianna's hand. "Worry not. I will take care of you and set you on the path of your destiny."

Tianna frowned. "Why? Why would you do that for me?"

The Contessa watched her with a small smile. "Just know that I promised you I would do so, and I will keep my promise."

Feb 9th, 1906

Tianna blinked up into the bright sunshine. How appropriate that she was blinded by the unseasonable glare. When she had met the Contessa, it had been the lights of the ballroom. Now, at the gallant woman's funeral, it was the flame of the sun that pierced her eyes.

She raised her chin, just as she had done more than two decades earlier, and watched as the elegant coffin was lowered into the rich-smelling dirt. A single tear fell from her eye.

Tianna smiled, tight-lipped and merely polite, while the rest of the attendants greeted her. As the heir to the dowager's estates, she had the social clout to demand manners, though she would never have the same respect as the blooded rich.

After the last mourner took her hand and murmured something appropriate, and a coin from her purse was pressed into Father Vincent's palm, she turned to the eclectic but well-dressed group gathered behind her. A small frown passed over her face when she noticed who was missing, but she tried to be generous. Fletcher didn't like goodbyes.

The six others straightened under her gaze. This was her group, her Magecrafters, now. Her inheritance included more than just money and a house. It included leadership of the local branch of M.A.G.E., the Magecrafter's Alliance Guild of Europe, as well as the Fountain in the Priuli Villa.

The Fountain had been bound to the Priuli family for seven generations, ending with the childless Contessa's death. Now, Tianna's thoughts kept returning to the problem of finding a new family to bind to the font of pure power.

"Madame Udovin." Vince Bussard stepped forward, offering his arm to her. He had the dark hair of Greece, though his eyes were a startling emerald green. His sharp suit was perfectly appropriate for the setting, with a charcoal gray coat over slightly lighter gray trousers. "We will need to return to the house to receive callers."

Tianna rolled her eyes. "I know," she said, taking the arm. "I just wish they would wait a bit first."

They made their way to the automobile, a 1906 Gearless Touring, fresh off the boat from the United States. The new machine was perfect for their needs, seating between six and eight people, depending on how many skirts they had to deal with.

Shoyebi reached the automobile first. The African man's nearly pitch-black skin stood out against the steel-gray and dark blue of his clothing. He pulled out the footstool and set it on the ground, his white teeth flashing brightly as he smiled.

Tianna suppressed a grin. Shoyebi was a Golemmer, and a powerful one, too. However, because of the society they were moving through, he played the role of a manservant in public. He would leap around to serve them, but he was more than willing to stand up to any of them in private. And he was just as likely to fake an accident to knock one of them down a peg if his lighter-skinned contemporaries went too far with the illusion.

Tianna settled her skirts in the middle seat, with Vince wedged in beside her. Lottie, Lorna, and Serina shoved their skirts together in the back.

Shoyebi handed a short young woman with pure yellow ringlets up into the front seat next to him. Her bright blue eyes, heart-shaped face and Cupid's bow lips gave her the look of the most feminine thing in the history of mankind, but all of them knew that Evia was violently protective of her new family. Her life before the Mage-crafters had not been kind, and she was not the type to be forgiving of injury to her friends.

Evia settled her skirts and reached out her gloved hands to touch the front of the automobile for a moment. Then, she nodded to Shoyebi and sat back.

The man had already retrieved the footstool and jumped into the driver's seat. He released the handbrake and hummed the little chant that let him control the vehicle without using the motor. The engine backfired, and Lorna let out a little shriek. Evia glanced back with a smug smile.

Tianna chuckled. "Perhaps, Evia, dear, a little less realism in your Glamouring?"

"Yes, Madame," Evia said in her perfectly proper voice. Much like her ability, her appearance was an illusion, crafted to ease her way through the life she'd made in Verona and the rigid hierarchy of European aristocracy.

Shoyebi maneuvered the vehicle through the streets quickly, and they reached the Priuli villa before the first visitors could arrive. Tianna changed into a dark gray morning gown and checked in with the kitchens about having tea ready.

The rest of the day was spent in a whirlwind of callers, each "terribly sorry" for the loss of the Contessa and certain that Tianna would handle the estates "with propriety and decorum." Twice, a dowager let slip that Tianna should pass on her inheritance to an "appropriate" family.

It wasn't until after the afternoon tea that Tianna heard Fletcher come in. His heavy footfalls echoed through the foyer and into the sitting room where she and the other ladies had settled. He strode in, dashing in his dove gray and navy, with a head of silky brown waves under his tall hat.

He sketched a bow and straightened with a grin. "Ladies. Tianna."

The way he spoke her name sent a shiver down her spine. She shook herself and frowned, thinking she was acting like a girl instead of a woman of nearly forty years.

"You missed the funeral," she said.

Fletcher chuckled. "Not as much as I missed you." He grabbed her hand and laid a gentle kiss on her knuckles. "Perhaps I should have attended, but I do hate being around so much sorrow. Promise you'll forgive me?"

Tianna gasped, pulling her hand from his. She stood up, backing away from him quickly. The other three women did the same, staring at the man.

"How dare you!" she hissed at him.

An odd look flashed over his face. Then his features settled into a flush of shame as he dropped his eyes down to the rug.

"Aw, Tianna, I'm sorry," he muttered. "I didn't mean it like that. It was just... a bad turn of phrase."

Tianna pressed her lips together, considering. Fletcher was an Oather, a rare type of Magecrafter who could use his power to bind people to their vows and promises. They were good for ensuring honesty and staying faithful to duty, and they were necessary for binding a family line to a Fountain, so Fletcher was likely feeling the impending pressure of creating the powerful bond that would stretch through generations of Magecrafters.

She let the tension drain from her body, her shoulders sagging a little. "It's alright, Fletcher. Just, please, watch your tongue. We are all a bit tense with the upcoming transition."

He nodded. "I just don't understand why one of us can't be bonded to the Fountain. It would make sense to get it done quickly, so the Unseelie Magecrafters don't have the chance to snatch it up."

Tianna shrugged. "It would seem that way, but it is important to have an already established family be bonded. It ensures a greater chance that we won't be back in the same situation in a few decades."

He opened his mouth to protest, but Tianna put up her hand. "Please, Fletcher, we've been over this before. I have considered the situation carefully, and I am satisfied with M.A.G.E.'s standard procedure for transitioning a Fountain."

Vince stepped into the room. "Madam Udovin, ladies, Fletcher. Dinner is served."

As was his habit, Vince stepped aside, letting the others go before him. He had been raised by his mother, a head housekeeper in a British nobleman's Grecian estate, and he had been trained to the behaviors of a high-class butler before the gifts from his father's lineage had brought him to M.A.G.E.

Tianna straightened her skirts and stepped forward after the other ladies had passed. Vince held out his arm to her, ever conscious of her place as the lady of the household. Tianna accepted his arm with a grateful smile.

After the household had gone to bed, Tianna paced in her rooms. She was too anxious about the rapid changes of the last few weeks, and she needed an outlet.

She let out an unladylike curse. What she needed was someone who she could talk to, someone to - not shoulder the burden with her, not even someone to advise her. She needed someone to talk out her thoughts and ask the questions she needed to be asked so she could get her thoughts in order.

She considered the other Magecrafters. Evia was young and impetuous and had no patience to allow someone space to simply talk things out. Fletcher was brash and, despite being an Oather, she felt he had an opportunistic streak in him.

Lorna, their Mattermaker, was a solid, sturdy woman with a personality to match. However, she, like her powers, focused on the physical, making her ill-suited for a lively debate on maybes and what-ifs.

Tianna smiled as she came to Lottie. The young Jewish woman was just as practical as Lorna. The Sniffer had used her gift of finding things to keep her family fed when they fled the anti-Jewish pogroms in Romania. When her family was safely on the boat to the U.S., Lottie had taken a position with M.A.G.E. to ensure a stream of income which she forwarded to her parents every few months with a letter.

She dismissed Serina immediately. The young Irish redhead lived up to every stereotype regarding temper and impulsive action. While that made her a good Boomer, allowing her to channel her anger into explosive bursts, talking to her about the nuances of leadership would be an exercise in frustration.

Shoyebi might be good for a deep discussion, though. The African was extremely intelligent and always seemed to enjoy talking with her about politics and ethical philosophy.

With a sharp nod, Tianna strode out of her room, intent on finding the man.

She stepped out the door into the back garden, unsurprised by the chill in the air. Shoyebi hadn't been in his rooms, so she had decided to check the small workshop he kept up in a small room off the stables. She huddled into the thick shawl she wore as the damp cold seeped through her cotton dress and stepped quickly across the cobblestone path underneath the bare trees.

It had been some weeks since the last snowfall, but the biting cold still cut her to the bone. She shivered as her breath clouded in front of her face and her cheeks flushed.

She wondered if her thought to find the African man had been such a good one. It hadn't crossed her mind that the evasive Golemmer would be so difficult to find. She shook her head and kept walking. It wasn't as if she would have been able to sleep instead.

"Madam Udovin, whatever are you doing?"

Tianna gasped and turned to face Vince. The dark-haired man stood up from his perch on one of the iron garden benches. She could just make out his face in the light of the full moon overhead. The concern on his face quickly fell away as he resumed his usual, neutral expression.

"Oh, Vince, I- You surprised me!" Tianna let out a little chuckle as her heart slowed now that there was no danger. "What are you doing here?"

Vince hesitated, then a smile quirked his lips. "I asked you first," he pointed out.

Tianna blinked at his response. He'd never shown her a playful side before, but she was certain he was teasing her. "So you did," she murmured. "I was looking for someone to talk to, and I had the idea that Shoyebi might be in his workshop."

Vince nodded. "Perhaps," he said. "Perhaps I could..." His voice trailed off, and he cleared his throat. "Our friend is usually... indisposed this time of night."

"Indisposed?"

Vince shifted his weight. "Er, yes."

Tianna pursed her lips. She hadn't considered that Shoyebi might dally with one of the young women who worked in and around the estates, but it wasn't exactly her place to pass judgment on him for it. It was just annoying that she'd been thwarted in her quest for a conversation.

Her eyes settled on Vince, and she suddenly realized what he had said. She wondered why she hadn't considered him. He was calm and intelligent, always aware of what was going on and anticipating what she and others in the household might need. He had never wholly embraced being one who was served rather than one who served, but she could appreciate the difficulty of that. Even after twenty years in the Contessa's household, she still felt like a low-class fraud.

Tianna nodded and smiled at him. "Vince, perhaps you could help me."

Vince nodded and held out his arm to her. "Anything," he murmured. "But let's get you back into the warmth of the house."

Aug. 8th, 1906

Tianna stood tall next to the automobile in front of the train station. She clutched her hands together at her waist and glanced back at the wagon she had rented for the occasion. Shoyebi lounged against the auto's front fender, while Evia paced nearby.

Tianna spotted Vince emerging from the doors to the train station, his arms loaded down with a steamer trunk and a young couple following close behind. They wore the elegant but straightforward traveling clothes of gentry, and the woman held a baby in a white frothy gown and bonnet. A very young woman dressed as a maid followed on their heels.

Tianna pasted on a smile as they approached. "Monsieur and Madame Boudreaux? Such a pleasure to finally meet you!"

She held out her hand when the young golden-haired man set down the large suitcase and pair of hat boxes he was carrying. He took Tianna's hand and bowed over it while Vince and Shoyebi loaded the luggage into the wagon and headed around the back of the station to get the rest.

"I am Madam Udovin, Tianna," she said, turning to greet the woman with a nod of her head. "I hope you will find your new home comfortable."

The man nodded. "I am sure we will get used to it," he said with a French accent. "We have not lived so lavishly before."

Tianna nodded as the two Magecrafters returned with another load of trunks. They made quick work of packing them away, then helped the young family and Evia and Tianna into the automobile. With a puff of Glammour-smoke, the auto glided down the street. Vince followed in the horse-pulled wagon.

The Boudreaux's quickly settled into the master suite of rooms, choosing to keep their young son with them rather than in the nursery on the next floor up. Tianna had the kitchens make a light but satisfying luncheon for the travel-weary family and served it in the sunroom rather than the large dining room. She wanted the family to become comfortable in their new home quickly.

Andre was a plant Totemist, giving him an advantage in his career as a chemist, analyzing plants for medicinal uses. His wife of two years, Lisette, had met her husband while working as a nurse-missionary in the Niger territory of France. The Anglo-Aro War had been brief but bloody. Andre's skills with medicine and Lisette's ability as a bone Mender meant that they had bonded over healing the wounded.

Tianna had read the M.A.G.E. report on the family several times and knew it by heart. Now, she wanted to get to know them, though it was unlikely she would veto the decision to bind them to the Fountain.

Tianna's pen made a light scratching sound on the thick linen paper as she finished her letter to the M.A.G.E. council. She had been quite impressed by the honesty and dedication of the Boudreaux's. They would make a wonderful bonded family, and she had expressed her opinion of that in her letter.

She stood and stretched out her arms, walking to her window, which overlooked the back gardens. She heard a loud voice and a ruckus coming from the stable, and she watched with a frown as

Fletcher's horse raced onto the grounds and reared as the man pulled the stallion up short. The stable hands rushed to calm the animal as Fletcher jumped off and walked away, weaving as if drunk.

It wouldn't surprise her if he were drunk. The Oather had been unwavering in his position that one of the current residents of the estate take up the binding. He'd even hinted that a pairing between two of her group should be encouraged. Add on that he hadn't yet made an appearance to greet the selected family, and he was treading dangerously close to mutiny.

Tianna sighed as he disappeared from her line of sight. If only she didn't need him to bind the Boudreaux family. She glanced at her letter to the M.A.G.E. council. Perhaps she should make a note of his behavior in her report.

With a nod, she quickly added a postscript. She was just finishing when a soft knock sounded at her door. She left the page to air dry and opened to find Vince smiling at her. Her lips curved up in response as she pulled him into her room and into her arms.

Since the night in the garden, when she'd sought out someone to talk with, Vince had become a steadying force in her life. He understood the nuances of her position and had no desire to draw attention to himself because of her reliance on his advice.

When they had become lovers, it had been a natural growth of their friendship, and she hoped he felt as she did. The reality was that she would watch him grow old and die, while she would continue to age slowly, making any formal and public relationship unsustainable.

Tianna smiled up at the man, certain she had found someone to spend decades with, and sure they would overcome the intrinsic issues of their relationship.

Aug 10th, 1906

"And thus do we swear, on behalf of ourselves and for our descendants, that we shall safeguard the Fountain at the Priuli Villa, share its power with those who need it, and prevent any abuse of that power to the best of our abilities, for so long as our bloodline continues and remains bound. We shall raise our children and our children's children with the knowledge of this honor and onus of responsibility. We swear to honor the code of the Seelie Magecrafters, to use power to better and safeguard and provide hope to all of humankind within the limits of safeguarding the secret of the Magecrafters and safeguarding the Fountain from abuse. By the power of the Faeblood within our veins, by the blood of our family, so do we make this oath."

In the salon, Tianna stared with wide eyes as the Boudreaux's tensed in unison, their bodies arcing with a shimmering silver power that flowed over their skin in waves. Even baby Antoine curved his little back, eyes wide and mouth agape, as the power tangled into their souls, creating a bond that could last for centuries.

Fletcher stood in front of the young family, the power surging from his outstretched hands. His mouth was set in a disapproving line, his eyes cold. He had been abrupt all day, not like his usual jocular self.

Tianna knew he was upset with her, and that he didn't appreciate her decision. She was, quite frankly, more than a little annoyed with him. It wasn't his place to question or challenge the decision of the council, or her choice to abide by it.

Fortunately, outside of outright refusal, he had no choice but to empower the bond using the ritual words that had been established centuries before and were revised and translated to each modern language as needed. Tianna was confident, however, that he would continue to protest the situation. She only hoped the M.A.G.E. council would take actions to remove him from this situation. He was obviously unwilling to follow her leadership.

The short celebration after the ceremony was pleasant, with lively conversation and good food. Tianna enjoyed spending time with each of her group members, and she appreciated what each brought. Even surly Evia took pride in using her power to project a vivid imagining of several of *Grimm's Fairy Tales*.

The Boudreaux family retired early, driven by baby Antoine's adorable yawns. The rest of the Magecrafters drifted away, either retiring to their bedchambers or heading out to indulge in the nightlife of the thriving Italian city.

Tianna soon found herself sitting with Vince on a wine-and-gold, Jacquard-upholstered sofa in the far corner of the room, in animated conversation about one of her first operatic performances. She trailed off with a laugh as her story ended, realizing they'd been left alone, and Vince leaned forward to capture her lips with his. His hands moved along her waist, pulling her closer to him. She leaned into the kiss with a soft moan and let herself get lost in the feel of his hands and lips.

"I should have known!" The harsh voice cut through the spacious room.

Tianna jumped with surprise at the sudden sound, and Vince leapt to his feet as if to defend her.

Fletcher strode in from the doorway, a sneer on his handsome face. "At least you have the decency to behave with the shame you should feel," he snarled. "This certainly explains everything."

Tianna flushed with anger and pushed to her feet. "What are you talking about?" she snapped.

"You never listened to me, did you?" Fletcher jabbed his finger at Tianna. "This destroyer has undoubtedly been working on you for some time."

Tianna gasped, her eyes going wide. Vince shook his head slowly, wavering as if he'd been struck a blow. In a sense, he had. As an Unraveller, Vince lived with the fear and distrust of most Mage-crafters. His power was to undo. Anything.

Unseelie Unravellers often burrowed into people's heads, undoing their will, their sense of ethics, even undoing specific thoughts. Others would literally unmake objects, turning them to dust without a care. A few would go so far as to expend a more substantial amount of energy to unmake living things, including people.

As such, Unravellers had long had a reputation as destroyers. Such an accusation could turn a M.A.G.E. branch upside down if they thought she'd been compromised by an Unraveller.

Tianna hesitated a moment, reviewing her relationship with

Vince. Then she shook her head. She could still feel her will at work, and she didn't have gaps of knowledge that would indicate he had wiped out thoughts. There was simply no reason to suspect him other than that he was what he was.

She stepped forward, raising her chin. "Fletcher, you will not make such an accusation lightly. You have no evidence of such a thing, for there is no Unravelling in my mind. You have been sowing the seeds of discord in this group for some time and, you should know, I have relayed my concerns to the council." Her eyes flashed at him as she saw panic flash over his face. "I suggest you pack your bags. You are no longer needed here."

"And if I don't?" he snapped. He was calling her bluff, but she wasn't bluffing.

Tianna raised her hands, drawing in the power of time. A distortion of reality wavered around her body, undulating the floor like ocean waves. "Then I shall return to the time when you were assigned here and reject your assignment to this location."

Fletcher gaped. His eyes darted around as if searching for a solution in the ornate room.

Tianna let the power fade from her hands. So long as she lived, she would be able to carry out her threat, and he knew it. With an Unraveller at her side, his ability to kill her was virtually nothing.

"Fine," he said, his body sagging as the bravado left him. "I'll be gone by morning."

He moved towards the door, then stopped and turned back to Tianna.

"I don't know where it went wrong," he said. "I would have loved you forever, sharing my power with you freely. I should never have expected so much from someone with your history."

Tianna frowned. "I beg your pardon? What history?"

Fletcher's lip curled. "A singer, a performer. You were destined to be a light skirt and a pretender to your station from the beginning."

Tianna felt the blood drain from her face at the insult. She knew it wasn't true, but the words cut her just the same. Before she or Vince could react, Fletcher was out the door, his boots clomping up the stairs to his chambers.

Tianna stepped back, and Vince was there to catch her in his arms. He guided her to sit on the sofa once more, murmuring reassurances in her ear. She stared at the door, fighting through her emotional turmoil until the pounding of those boots sounded down the stairs and out the garden entrance. Moments later, a horse screamed a whinny and hoof beats faded into the night.

"He's gone, love," Vince said.

She nodded, tears falling down her cheeks as she closed her eyes. "May he never return, the cad!"

Vince kissed the drops from her face and pulled her to her feet, leading her to her chamber.

Apr 14th, 1921

Tianna watched Vince step out of the 1919 Isotta Fraschini Tipo 8. She smiled at him as he turned to hand her out of the vehicle. Her smile widened when he pressed a kiss to her gloved hand. Her gaze lingered on the silver streaking the temples of his dark hair. He noticed her gaze and his smile faltered. She squeezed his hand, reassuringly.

Now in his forties, Vince was becoming more aware of how fast he was aging, and how she was not. She knew he was concerned that she would tire of him, but she loved him dearly. She only hoped he knew it. His smile returned, and they turned to look up at the Priuli Villa.

After the Great War, M.A.G.E. had decided to expand to the western hemisphere, creating the daughter organization M.A.G.U.S. in what was ostensibly the seat of civilization for that part of the world. Tianna had taken Vince and the others across the ocean, leaving only Serina with the Boudreaux's.

The Magecrafters Alliance Guild of the United States had successfully settled in New York. With Shoyebi in charge in the great city of New York, Tianna was in the midst of her annual tour, recharging each of her Timesinks during a three-month sweep of Europe and the East Coast of the U.S.

The Priuli Villa was a special stop for her and Vince, given their history with the large house. Tianna couldn't wait to see the Boudreaux's and exclaim over how big Antoine and his younger siblings, Yvette and Philippe, had gotten over the last year. As the door opened to reveal the rambunctious family, Tianna squeezed Vince's hand again.

Apr 14th, 1921 - morning

Tianna nuzzled Vince's chest once more before pulling herself away. She let her hands drag across his lean body, and she smiled before putting on her wrapper.

"I have a few notes to make in my diary," she murmured. "But I'm going to fetch some breakfast before getting to work. Do you want me to bring you anything?"

Vince lunged for her and caught her hand, pressing a kiss to her palm before responding. "I'm good. Maybe send up some coffee in a half-hour or so."

Tianna nodded and moved into the dressing room. She freshened up and dressed in a low-waisted, sapphire-blue silk frock. She pulled her long red hair into a chignon and topped it with a navy straw-braid hat with an upturned brim accessorized with navy fabric rosettes.

She made her way down to the kitchens, marveling at how things had changed in the last three decades. While before, an entire staff of servants would have seen to their every need, now, the family had only a chef, a pair of maids, and a gardener to help with the huge house. Two men kept the stables in good repair, renting stalls out to people with only one or two horses.

Tianna poked her head into the kitchen and smiled at the cook. She placed her order for toasted brioche with butter, a poached egg with a sprinkling of sheep's cheese, and sliced salami with a latte. She also asked for the woman to take up a pot of strong coffee to Vince.

Tianna made her way to the sunroom and smiled at the woman seated there already.

"Serina! How lovely to see you!" She moved forward to greet the Boomer with a peck on each cheek. "How are you?"

Serina smiled. "Oh, well enough. It seems you were just here, but I suppose it has been a year already. How is America?"

Tianna sat at the small table and grinned. "Oh, it's keen but so different. Those Americans just never seem to stop for one minute. Not like here. On the Continent, we know how to enjoy a moment."

They caught up for more than an hour, with Tianna telling Serina story after story about the reactions to the new Prohibition laws, which nobody seemed to want. Serina laughed out loud when Tianna ran through a long list of the slang people had started using to talk about alcohol.

"Oh, my," Serina said. "I don't know that I could live without a glass of wine with supper. How gauche!"

"So what news from you? How is that suitor you were telling me about last year?"

Serina frowned. "I don't- Oh, I have met someone, and you simply must meet him. He's a poor lost soul who needs our help, and I just know you can help him. Say you will come with me to meet him, please say you will."

Tianna frowned, overwhelmed by Serina's odd change of topic. "Of course, Serina. If you say I should help, I'll certainly try."

Serina grabbed her hand and pulled her to her feet. "I told him to come by today. He waits for me in the garden. Let's see if he's there now!"

Tianna let the woman pull her along. She couldn't put her finger on what was wrong, but something was rubbing her senses the wrong way. Serina wasn't the type to be scatterbrained, but she was undoubtedly acting the fool now.

They burst out into the garden, and Serina pulled Tianna along the cobblestone walk. Tianna smiled briefly, remembering when she'd come across Vince that night so long ago.

She spotted a shape perched on one of the iron benches, little more than a pile of worn and ragged clothes. The bearded face was smudged with dirt, and the man didn't meet her eyes as she approached.

Serina's face brightened. "Stephan, I brought her. Just like I said."

The man nodded and shrunk into the rags as the women came to a stop in front of him.

Serina turned to Tianna, her face full of hope and fear. "Please, Tianna, tell him you'll help him. He's so ashamed of his situation. Tell him you'll help him however you can."

Tianna frowned, the hairs on the back of her neck prickling. She was uncomfortable with the situation simply because it seemed so out of character for Serina. Eager to get the encounter over with, she nodded.

Serina clutched her hand, shaking it a little. "He won't look at your face, Tianna," she whispered. "You have to tell him."

Tianna swallowed. "Of course, I'll help. Stephan, I promise, I will do whatever I can to help you."

Tianna felt the waves of power flow over her as the man raised his hand to her. Her back arched and her eyes went wide. She could feel the words she'd spoken settle into her bones, her blood, her soul.

The ragged man lifted his head and met her eyes, those sharp hazel eyes beneath a swath of wavy brown hair. The man's mouth quirked into a smile.

"Hello, Tianna," he said. "I'm sure you remember me, though I went by Fletcher then." He grinned as her face contorted under the Oath binding he laid on her. "You can help me by not screaming."

Tianna's throat clamped down on the cry that had been forming, and tears streamed from her eyes.

Tianna stared at Serina in the anteroom of the other woman's bedchamber while Stephan Fletcher got cleaned up and changed. He'd made sure to let Tianna know that it would be "a help" for her to stay and sit quietly before he'd disappeared into the dressing room for his bath.

Her mind raced through the possibilities. Serina had been acting oddly, so it was very likely that Fletcher had locked her into an Oath-bond as well. It would also be very like his personality, to ensure her cooperation. At least, it had been before he'd disappeared 15 years ago.

Tianna wasn't sure what he wanted from her, but it seemed that he'd achieved a big goal by binding her. He wanted something from her, and that could only be a few things.

He might want to control M.A.G.U.S., but that assumed he was familiar with the nascent organization. He might also want someone trusted by the M.A.G.E. council, but there were other, more easily accessed people, including Andre Boudreaux, right here in this very house.

Fletcher had behaved as though he was attracted to her before he'd left, so he might be trying to force her to be with him. She frowned, not certain how she would handle the kind of violation that a power-forced relationship would be. She took some consolation that, if that were his goal, at least she wouldn't be involved in harming others, and her longer lifespan meant that she would win in the end.

A tear fell from her eye, and she brushed at it with annoyance. Self-pity wouldn't solve this issue. She needed to think.

Vince. Vince would notice any change in her behavior towards him, but he would likely think that his fears had come to pass, and she was simply leaving him as he aged. He would expect her to drift away from him.

He wouldn't expect her to be cruel about it, though. She had never given him reason to think she would cut him angrily. Such behavior might be enough to trigger his suspicions.

Tianna frowned. There was another possible reason that Fletcher had caught her in an Oath-bond. Her power. What if he forced her to change the past? Could she fight him? How would she prevent it?

She jumped when Fletcher strode back into the room. He glared at her for a moment, then turned to Serina.

"Dear Serina, tell the kitchens to serve us lunch up here. I need some time to phrase my request for Tianna's... help."

Serina jumped up to obey. Tianna also stood.

When Fletcher raised an eyebrow, she spoke. "I, er... I need to use the lavatory. And should I change my clothing?"

He glared at her, looking over the fragile fabric of her very modern dress. Finally, he nodded. "Go ahead. You'll want something more travel-friendly. But, remember, it would help if you didn't speak of me being here, or of the Oath-bond, to anyone."

Tianna fought the urge to bolt from the room. His presence made her skin crawl. She wasn't sure if his reference to traveling meant that they were leaving the Villa or moving through time... or both.

She hurried to her bedchambers, hoping that Vince hadn't left yet. He usually waited for her, having become used to working with her full schedule, even when they were ostensibly on holiday. However, being so familiar with this area, it was just as likely that he'd gone out for the morning by himself.

Tianna opened the door, and her shoulders sagged for a moment when she saw the room was empty. Then, Vince came striding through from the dressing room.

She rushed over to him and kissed him with every bit of passion she could muster. She ran her hands over his chest in the way she knew he liked and smiled up at him. As he stared down at her, she blinked slowly. She heaved a large breath.

"I'm leaving you," she said. "Today."

Vince staggered back a step. He caught her hands when they moved over his shirt again. "I beg your pardon?"

"You heard me." She choked on the words. "There is no other choice."

He shook his head, trying to understand through his shock. Tianna wracked her head. Now that she had his attention, she had to direct him to what was really going on without mentioning Fletcher or the Oath-bond he put on her.

Nothing came to her.

Vince pushed her hands down and ran his fingers through his hair, a sure sign he was upset. Oh, Dio, she knew him so well. If only he could read her behavior as well.

"How long have you been planning this?" he bit out.

Tianna felt her shoulders sag. His fear about her leaving him because of the aging difference was too strong. She opened her mouth to answer with the truth - that it had happened all this morning - when she was struck with inspiration.

She raised her head to stare into his eyes, willing him to see what she was really saying. "Since the night the Boudreaux family completed the ritual," she said, clearly. "After Serina caught us together, I started thinking about how much time we had." She emphasized the word "time" to give him a hint.

Vince frowned, and he opened his mouth to speak.

"No," she said. "Don't say anything. You can't change the past." She stressed "past," hoping he would start thinking about her power.

Vince gave her a sideways look, the one he always had when he wasn't quite sure when she was teasing.

Tianna clasped her hands together and pleaded with her eyes, assuming the universal pose for begging. "Whatever spell I have been under with you, your time has run out. What's been done cannot be unraveled."

Vince's eyes narrowed. "This isn't- This is wrong. You are wrong." He rubbed his chin. "Serina didn't catch us that night. Fletcher did."

He stepped back and dropped his hands. He paced back and forth, muttering. Tianna realized he was going over what she'd said, and her heart leapt with hope.

Vince didn't have a perfect long-term recall, but he could quote things people had said only a few moments ago. It was one of the little things that annoyed her, since he used it against her on the rare occasion they'd argued.

He stopped pacing and stared at her. "Can you smile and frown freely?"

Tianna nodded.

"Smile if I'm right; frown if I'm wrong," he said, locking his hands behind his back. "Fletcher showed up, enacted some plan he'd started in on the night he caught us, and used his power to Oath-bind you so he could control your Timesinking ability, probably today."

Tianna grinned.

Vince nodded and stepped forward, holding her head in his hands. "Hold still, love." He frowned down at her. "And don't ever say that stuff to me again. I'll never survive it."

Tears leaked from her eyes as she closed them, feeling the cool, slippery invasion of Vince's power-seeking out the Oath-bond. She did her best to keep her mind clear to make it as easy as possible for him to Unravel the power entwined in her mind. There was a chance he wouldn't be able to free her, or that freeing her would damage her mind beyond repair.

The panic curled in her belly as she felt the first tendril of pain in her temple.

Apr 15th, 1921 - noon

Tianna walked back into Serina's bedchamber and sat in the chair she'd vacated nearly an hour earlier. Serina watched her with a blank expression, then turned back to Fletcher. They were eating sand-wiches at a small table at the side of the room.

Fletcher slurped his tea and eyed her change of clothes. She'd changed into a more time-neutral skirt and blouse combination in shades of gray. She wore a broad-brimmed straw hat and a navy shirtwaist.

"Good god, woman, what took you so long?" the Oather growled.

Tianna picked up her sandwich and considered choking down a few bites. "I... ran into some people," she murmured.

Fletcher froze. "Who?"

Tianna shrugged. "The upstairs maid, Lisette, young Yvette-"

Fletcher waved his hand. "Fine, fine. Be a helpful bit and hurry up and eat. We leave in five minutes. And no questions."

Tianna choked on the words that had been forming in her throat. She crammed a large bite of the sliced ham on thin, heavy wheat bread into her mouth. She gulped her tea to help moisten the dry mouthful.

After a few minutes, Fletcher tossed back the last of his tea and pushed his plate away. Serina had mechanically worked through her luncheon and sat staring at the table.

"Serina," Fletcher snapped. "When we travel, you will be my tool. Tianna, you will help me get back to August of 1906. Serina, you will destroy the Boudreaux family, and I will instate another family."

The door opened to reveal a couple dressed in an eclectic combination of styles. The effect was that of collecting discarded finery from the past decade and wearing them with no care for fashion or fit. The colors tended towards black and gray, but bits of color showed through lace and a few tears in the fabrics.

Tianna froze, staring at them. The barely natural bands of silver-gray and golden-yellow in their dark hair and their eye colors - she had irises as black as pitch while his eyes were nearly white with a black ring around the outer edge - gave away the corruption of their power. The man had a strange metal brace on his left arm, ending in a metal-banded glove. His bare arm appeared withered within the metal and leather wrapped around it.

Fletcher. He grinned. "Oh, fine, I'll tell you. It's a family of Unseelie Magecrafters. Please say hello to Reta and Markus Hinshaw, Shadow-Walker and Golemmer."

Serina smiled and extended her hand out to the couple. Tianna barely managed to nod in their direction. The waves of their tainted power sicken her, like the scent of rotting flesh in the air.

Fletcher clapped his hands with a grin. "And then I'll just have a word with me, and we'll be set for life." He turned to Tianna, and the smile fell from his face, replaced with a sneer. "This time around, I won't be turned out like a dog into the streets."

Tianna bit her tongue on the protest that rose in her throat.

"Everyone ready?" He waited for the couple to nod, then gestured for Serina to move closer and grabbed Tianna's arm. "Serina, be ready to destroy anyone who tries to stop us. Tianna, be a helpful dear and get us to our destiny."

Tianna hesitated, staring at the Unseelie couple. Between them and Fletcher's control of the Boomer, she knew that anything she tried to do to stop them here would end in disaster.

Her eyes burned with tears of hate and frustration, and she squeezed them shut as she gathered her power, reaching for the tendrils of the Timesink she'd maintained each year for nearly forty years.

As the power gathered around her, she pulled in the people gathered around her, locking them into the vortex that would propel them into the past. The Oather, the Unseelie couple, the Boomer...

Behind her eyes, she saw the flicker of events near the Timesink, flashing behind her eyes like a moving picture played too fast. She caught a glimpse of dresses swirling, and she remembered the first time she'd entered the Villa.

Contessa Priuli's ball. The one that ended with her learning about her power. The one that had been interrupted-

Tianna's eyes flew open, and she let out a laugh. She pulled five Magecrafters with her into the vortex and, with a pop of displaced air, they were gone.

Feb 26th, 1884

Tianna strained to pull the vortex, allowing her to change their location in space as well as time, but only by a few yards. They appeared in the garden, several feet higher than the ground, and fell in a heap.

Tianna rolled immediately away from the group, towards, she hoped, the Magecrafter that the others weren't expecting. Fletcher cursed as the women's dresses tangled their feet, keeping them off-guard a few more minutes.

Firm hands grasped Tianna's shoulders and sat her up. She flung her arm up, throwing off the hat that clung to her chignon with long pins. Vince's face looked down at her.

"Two Unseelie," she gasped in a whisper. "ShadowWalker and Golemmer. Take care of them first."

Vince nodded and stretched out a hand with a grim look on his face. She knew it killed him to harm people with his power, but the Unseelie were addicted to using their power for their own ends. No one had ever brought an Unseelie back from the corruption. The couple was a lost cause.

"What about Serina?" he asked through gritted teeth.

Tianna scrambled to her feet, crouching next to him. "She has a part to play before we take her out."

A shriek pierced the air, and Tianna swallowed hard. In the glow of the gaslights spilling from the ballroom, she watched Reta Hinshaw simply dissolve into the air, her black eyes bulging as she screamed.

Tianna glanced around and realized that she and Vince were in the flowerbeds, flush against the wall of the house. The huge windows nearby told her that it was the ballroom on the other side.

She grabbed Vince and guided him as he turned his attention to the Golemmer. They would be safer when Serina attacked if they kept moving. She could see the three searching for them in the darkness, hindered by the lights shining into their eyes.

Vince tripped on a loose stone and let out a muffled curse. Tianna felt the power drain from him abruptly, and she pulled him down just as Fletcher cried out.

There was a series of flashes, and several objects struck the wall near them. As they hit the solid surface, they exploded in a quick boom-boom-boom that made Tianna's ears ring. The wall behind them crumbled, sprays of rock and debris raining down on their heads.

Vince grabbed her arm and pulled her up onto the broken steps of the balcony outside where the enormous glass doors of the ballroom had stood open to the night. Their shoes crunched on the glass that was all that remained of them, save for the shattered upper frames that swung in the air.

Tianna shook her head to clear the full, muffled feeling from her ears. She could hear a muted scream from inside the ballroom, and she pulled Vince back before he could step in front of the doorway.

On the other side of the balcony, Tianna spotted Serina and Fletcher scrambling up the ruined steps.

"We have to help the people in there," Vince yelled into her ear.

She shook her head. "Take out the Golemmer. The Contessa will handle Serina."

Vince shot her a confused look and glanced into the ballroom. His eyes widened, and he flinched back. He shot another glance at Tianna, then turned his attention to Markus.

The Unseelie man had grasped the edge of the balcony with his bracered arm and flung himself up over the railing with inhuman strength. He reached out with the contraption, stretching the covered fingers towards Vince's face.

Tianna shot a look at Serina and Fletcher. As she had thought, the heavy curtains around the doors had wrapped themselves around the pair. Fletcher had pulled out a knife and was hacking at the thick brocade fabric, screaming at Serina to destroy it.

Serina struggled within the bands of the curtain and managed to get a hand free. The glow at the end of it told Tianna that she was about to loose another explosive charge.

A scream drew Tianna's attention back to the Unseelie man. Vince had finally gotten his power strong enough to latch onto the Golemmer, and Markus' body was crumbling into dust before her eyes.

Tianna shot her gaze back to Serina and Fletcher just as the woman shot out a blast. Tianna flinched, but the thing didn't come at her and Vince.

Her eyes went wide as she watched the explosion land on the curtain wrapped around Fletcher's chest. He screamed "No!" a split second before the impact, then went silent as the blast and flames consumed him.

Vince turned just in time to see the Oather's destruction. He turned away, and his eyes fell on Tianna. He gathered her up, and they held each other as the reality of what they'd had to do struck them hard.

"Tianna?"

Tianna lifted her head at the sound of the beloved voice from the past. She pushed herself up and rushed over to the Contessa, still as young as the day they'd met. Tianna smiled to herself, realizing it actually was the day they'd met.

"Contessa," she said. "Oh, how I've missed you!"

The older woman frowned for a moment, then nodded. "So, you are a Timesinker?"

Tianna nodded. Vince moved up behind her, and she turned to him. "See if Serina is still caught in Fletcher's Oath-bind. Unravel anything that was left behind, if you can."

Vince nodded and walked over to the still-trapped Boomer. The Contessa glanced at Serina, and the curtains loosened to let Vince pull her free.

Tianna stared at the face of her mentor. "I guess I should explain what happened-"

The Contessa lifted a hand to stop her. "No," she said. "I can figure out enough, and more could cause ripples. Just tell me two things. Is this done?"

Tianna nodded. "Yes, all the threats are gone." She shivered at the memory.

The older woman nodded. "And secondly..." She hesitated, searching Tianna's face as if she could read her answers there. "Are we friends?"

Tianna swallowed. If she were to answer with absolute truth, she would have to admit to the woman that she was dead. But, then, did that really change how they'd felt about each other right up until the end?

"Oh, yes," Tianna whispered, forcing her words around the lump that had formed in her throat. "Great friends, doing great things, together."

The Contessa's face relaxed into a smile. "I'd hoped so," she murmured. "I liked you from the first, you know."

Tianna nodded. "And I, you."

The woman nodded, blinking rapidly. She glanced around at the destroyed wall. "I suppose this is a portent of things to come, but in the meantime, you had best return to your proper time, and I have a young Timesinker to befriend."

Vince came up dragging a dazed-looking Serina with him. "She was very much under his power," he said. "Fought it the whole time, though. Even the end was her choice."

Tianna glanced at Serina, letting the question show on her face.

The Boomer gave her a weak grin. "He demanded that I do something to free him," she said. Her expression turned hard and her voice, bitter. "He didn't tell me not to kill him in the process."

Tianna nodded and reached out to the woman. "He underestimated you," she said. "He underestimated us both."

She turned to the Contessa and hesitated before rushing forward to kiss both of the woman's cheeks. "Know I love and respect you every single day."

Tianna pulled back and reached out to Vince and Serina. She stared at her mentor as she gathered the power, filling her eyes with the sight of her friend for the last time. She pulled the two Magecrafters into the vortex and, with a pop, they disappeared.

ABOUT SARAH BUHRMAN

Sarah has been writing for more than twenty years. She lives in a magical land with two monsters (the kids), an ogre (the hubby), and whatever drama-llama is coming to visit this week. Sarah is the author of Too Wyrd and Fluffy Bunny, books one and two of the Runespells series. She has short stories and essays in several anthologies, including Visions IV: Space Between Stars, London Calling, Whispers of Hope, A Twist of Fate, and Chasing Fireflies: A Summer Romance Anthology.

facebook.com/AuthorSarahB

twitter.com/AuthorGoddess

instagram.com/authorsarahbuhrman

THYME FOR FIRE: A CURSE OF LANVAL SHORT STORY

BY REBEKAH DODSON

"We are time's subjects, and time bids be gone."
William Shakespeare, *King Henry V*

MARIE

"The gods must be crazy."

I stared at Gill. "What do the gods have to do with this, my love?"

"Look around you."

The daft fool; I had been looking. Gaping, even, at the squalor around us in this ancient version of London. I only knew London in two times—1156, where I had met the love of my life who stood next to me, and again in 1431, when my grandfather Merlin and I had the unfortunate pleasure of stumbling into Joan of Arc on the eve of her execution, where he had been foolish enough to save her life and help her escape. My grandfather's meddling with time then often had dangerous repercussions. France had found independence and peace from the English a century too soon, and as a result, in Gill's modern time they were now a part of the GBE—the Great British Empire.

Gill had told me the empire fell after something called World War II, which of course never happened in my timeline because England absorbed Germany in the nineteenth century. Or so Gill had told me. History was confusing, and for both of our time travels, I had a dozen different timelines in my head. I had no idea how Gill kept them straight.

Especially since we kept changing them.

"We are in London," I said lamely, still marveling how little the city had changed in the last two hundred years since my visit. St. Paul's Cathedral loomed on the other side of the bridge we'd just crossed. In Gill's time, it was a bustling steel structure known as the London Bridge. Now, however, it was just flimsy wood that could barely handle a hundred peasants traversing it every day to sell their wares. Nevertheless, London was still filled with peasant squalor, poverty, and dangerously un-fireproof thatch-roofed houses laden with tar. "When do you think we are?" I added.

"Sometime in the seventeenth century, I would suppose," Gill whispered to me as a peasant woman with two children in rags towed behind her passed us. "It's all rather Shakespearean in a way, right?"

"Who's Shakespeare?" I asked innocently.

He gaped at me. "Woman, I love you, but God, you are the daft one sometimes."

I kicked him in the shin. "I traveled through five different centuries to find you, asshole. I married your sorry ass. I brought your son back to you. Why do you always think I'm an idiot?" I pulled my hand from his and crossed my arms over my chest. "You are the history major, Guillaume Lanval. You tell me what year it is."

"You forget, Marie Lanval, I only minored in history. I majored in medicine. And that's Dr. Lanval to you."

"Jesus," I breathed. "You're never going to let that go, are you?"

Gill pecked me on the cheek. "No. But if the gods are crazy, making me fall for you was the craziest thing they have ever done." He grinned, shaking his head, and reached for my hand. "Now let's figure out why Mog sent us to this time. What do we have to fix now that your grandfather fucked up?"

"Now there's the Gill I know." I squeezed his hand and dropped it as more peasants eyed us strangely as they pushed by. "You assume the gods had a hand in that."

"They brought you back to me, didn't they?"

I didn't have a response to that. "Come on. We have to find out what year we are in."

"And how do we do that?" He objected though he let me pull him forward on the muddy street.

"Haven't you ever watched a moving picture?" I called behind me. "The main characters always meet in a tavern."

He groaned, but I ignored him. Even if we were in the seventeenth century, the wooden signs above the tattered doors hadn't changed much since the fifteenth. Like the silly songs I sang to Gill's son, Richard, there was literally a cook, a baker, and a candlestick maker all on this alley.

The Boar's Head was easy to find - if judging by the acrid smell of alcohol and death was any indication.

Unfortunately, I was a stranger to neither.

Maybe Gill was right about the gods. They had seen fit to send us to something less modern, and I felt more in my element than ever before.

"Marie, are you forgetting something?" Gill urged behind me. I turned to look at him, and he motioned down his front. "We should probably blend in more before we…"

"I know, I know," I told him. I spotted a tailor, marked only by a needle and a spool of thread above the door, two spots before the Boar's. I yanked Gill's hand as we ducked low over the threshold.

We were wearing what Gill called our "universal time travel uniforms," or plain clothes fit for almost any time period. We never had any idea where my great-uncle and Druid king, Mog, would send us in search of my grandfather, Merlin, who was wreaking havoc all over history.

Back in Gill's twenty-first century time, we had made outfits that made sure we wouldn't stand out in any period—him a Robin Hood-esque drawstring shirt with long, flowing sleeves, simple hand-sewn britches, and a simple corset covering my white cotton shift underneath. Depending on the time and culture, we usually needed to stop and purchase something to throw over our clothes just to blend in normally.

That was also why Gill had spent a small fortune of his doctor's wages on collecting ancient coins. The small pockets we had both sewn into our clothes held a variety of gold coins from Roman all the way to nineteenth-century currency.

Needless to say, we were extremely prepared time travelers.

Except for the part where we never knew where my rosary beads would take us.

"Hide that!" Gill whispered harshly, pointing to my neck as we stepped into the tailor's shop.

"Why?" I asked but tucked our time travel device in my collar just in case. I looked around, glad to see the shop was empty.

"England is fundamentally anti-Catholic in the seventeenth century."

I gaped at him. "Really? What happened?"

"Henry the Eighth happened, that's what."

"Who?"

"Never mind."

"What endues thee to mine own store, traveleth'rs?" A voice interrupted our urgent whispers. I turned to see a short, thin man, his long, thinning hair clinging to his head, and pockmarks dotting his long face, standing behind a counter. Which I suppose was honestly no more than a few pieces of wood shoved together. Before I could answer, he continued in his strange language, staring at us with wide eyes. "Forsooth what strange robes thee weareth!"

I blinked at him, wondering what strange type of English this was. "Est-ce que tu parles français?" I inquired about my native language. Everyone in England spoke French, right?

Gill nudged me in the ribs and stepped forward. He bowed with a flourish. "Mine own jointress and I art not restful, and seeketh thy wears," he said.

"Ah!" The man's face lit up. "Alloweth me to showeth thee what I has't!" He joyfully turned and pulled a stack of what looked like rustic sacks from behind him. "M'lady," he motioned me and held up a garish orange dress with shiny silver bows attached to the bodice, and a jacket in the same fashion. I threw Gill a look but didn't want to argue with the tailor. I bit my tongue and nodded, thanking him in French.

To Gill he nodded, producing shorter pants and a vest. Gill pushed two silver coins across the counter, and the tailor picked them up and bit them between his teeth. "Thanketh thee, m'lord," he said happily. I was sure from his face Gill had overpaid that man, but we had much, much more where it came from.

We nodded our thanks and ducked out of the store, finding a dingy and sewer-run alley between the Boar's Head and the tailor to change. As Gill tucked his purse back into his sleeve, I passed my hand over it, casting a light invisibility spell.

"I had forgotten about that," Gill said.

"Luckily, you are traveling with a sorceress," I grinned.

"Don't go broadcasting it," he winked.

"I never do. Where did you learn to speak that strange form of English?"

"Romeo and Juliet. I was Romeo in twelfth grade."

"Who?"

He laughed and shook his head, quickly slipping on the vest and new pants. I dressed quickly as well, pulling the dress and jacket over my head. "I have some things to teach you when we get back to my time," he chuckled.

I just laughed.

"Pin your hair up," he commanded but smiled all the same. "Women in this time don't wear it down. We should have got a hat … but no matter. Let's find out what year it is, shall we?" He offered me his arm, and we emerged from the alley, blending perfectly in with the other peasants and richly adorned folks on the street.

GILL

I stared as Marie pinned her brown curls behind her. I hated it when she put her hair up, but I had to remind myself when in Rome, do what the Romans do. Or in this case, what they do in the 1600s. I racked my brain for more Shakespearean language. I wasn't sure I had enough to convince people we were from this time, but if the time came, we could find someone who spoke French. In all of London, there had to be one.

As we entered the Boar's Head, it was a mild relief to see not much had changed by way of the mead houses from the twelfth century. *Alehouse,* I remembered and felt the excitement that beer had finally evolved from the disgusting brew of 1156. It was a crowded midday with men and women alike, and in the corner, a couple of passed out patrons lay sprawled over tables. *This is nothing like the bar down from the hospital serving the finest Guinness in Bay City,* I reminded myself. But it did remind me of another tavern, across the sea in France.

"Do you remember Calais?" I whispered to Marie, wiggling my eyebrows.

She frowned at me. "Where you almost died of the plague?"

"And when I recovered..."

She blushed, her cheeks a dark pink. "Of course I remember."

I winked at her, and she blushed even harder. "Not here," she whispered, "you disgusting fool."

"But shan't I inform this crowd I knoweth what lies yon under thine orange dress you're wearing?"

"Gill?"

"Yes, Marie?"

"Shut the fuck up."

I grinned. Though she was still the same poet I met in 1156, and time traveling hadn't changed her much, she was picking up some of my bad habits. Granted, I swore much less than I did in those days; becoming a doctor had seen to that. But Marie? She never changed. She was still just as bossy and confident as the first day I saw her in King Henry's, err... rather my, court.

We took a seat at one of the rough-hewn tables in the corner, and a barmaid approached us, her arms laden with lead mugs. "What shall thee has't?" she asked.

"Mincemeat and coffee, thanketh thee," I beamed at her, turning on the ol' Gill charm. She had a bit of a butter face, with a long, pointed chin and bushy brows over dull gray eyes, but that corset ... oh fuck ... that revealed too much of her breasts. What? Don't look at me like that. My wife may be sitting across from me, but I'm not dead. I can wonder what is under the barmaid outfit all I want. I'm not going to bone her, after all, unless by the gods' grace Marie was into that sort of thing. I still hoped, anyway. Get off my back.

Nevertheless, my smile worked with everyone, ladies especially, and this lass was no different. "As thee wisheth, m'lord." She ducked her head and scurried away from us.

"Do you have to flirt with everyone in front of me?" Marie leaned forward and whispered.

I grinned. She knew me well. "I'll flirt with you, mistress, if you'd like."

She rolled her eyes and leaned back.

"We still don't know what year this is. What's your plan, Gill?"

I shrugged. "I don't yet."

Marie just shrugged. "More importantly, how do we find my grandfather? He's here, somewhere, or Mog wouldn't have sent us."

I didn't answer her. While thoughts in my head rolled around about newspapers and where to find them, a commotion started across the room.

"I has't toldeth thee, nay more wine for thee, Thomas!" The same barmaid who juggled our steaming pies yelled at a customer four tables down. The man she yelled at was gangly and thin with hollow cheeks and wore a brown, sleeveless jerkin under a dirty white apron. He pointed a drunken finger at the barmaid and demanded more wine.

"Thomas?" I whispered to Marie and motioned to the table. She turned and looked.

"Lots of people named Thomas. It's a grand British name."

"But look at his apron. It's smattered with flour."

"And?"

Could it be... I frowned at Marie. "Could it be Thomas Ferriner?"

"Who?"

The excitement welled up in me, and I forgot to tease her this time. "Thomas Ferriner! He started, well, partially started, the Great London Fire of 1666! We must be in that year!"

"Well, why don't we ask?"

"You can't just ask, Gill."

"Well, why the hell not?"

"Shh, she's headed over!"

The barmaid approached us, shaking her head. "That gent be lily-livered!" She exploded, and the patrons around us laughed. "He'll get no more, or his head will roll."

Marie stifled a giggle.

"Thanketh thee," I told the barmaid as she sat down our plates. "My own nameth be Guillaume. Mine jointress, Marie. What is thy nameth?"

"Thea," she said, grinning at me. "I dost apologize for yon Thomas's behavior. Where are thee from, m'lord? M'lady?"

"France," Marie answered quickly. "Mine, uh, jointress and I hast traveled the silk road for many days. Prithee, bid us the date?"

I stared at her. My Marie knew more than I thought she did, as usual.

Thea's smiled disappeared when she looked at her. "Jointress?" She frowned.

"Husband," I whispered. "Not wife."

Marie glared at me but turned to Thea. "The date?" She asked again.

"M'lady it is September fourth, year of our lord sixteen-sixty-six. How doth thee not know'est this?"

"We has't traveled for a long time," I added truthfully, "it has't been easy to loseth the days."

She nodded. "I traveled from France when was't I was an issue."

"France?" Marie lit up. Rapidly she spoke to Thea in her native tongue, which Thea frowned at, but nodded and replied. I was fluent in modern French, so I only caught a few phrases in Marie's ancient tongue. Thomas, ale, and the frequency of his visits.

"*Merci beaucoup*, Thea," Marie nodded. The girl smiled at us, ducked her head, and went to her next table.

"What did she say?" I asked, sipping the coffee she brought us. It was grainy, strong, and tasted more like bark than coffee, but still better than ale.

"Thomas is a bit of a troublemaker," she said, digging into her pie. "The baker he works for, Thomas Dodson, leaves him unattended, and he often ends up here, instead of baking."

I nearly choked on my bite of mincemeat. "Dodson? Like the famous romance author in my time?"

"Never heard of him."

"Her. And I've never read her, but Jules loved her fiction."

"Oh, so your sister reads…"

"Shhh," I cautioned before she uttered the word lesbian, something likely no one would understand, but still better to err on the side of caution. "Something like that."

"You must buy me one of these romances when we get back," she said.

"I just might."

"So, what will we do with this Thomas?" Marie whispered, changing the subject abruptly as she finished her plate. "And what does my grandfather have to with him?"

"For starters," I whispered, looking around to make sure no one was listening in, "I'd wager Merlin has a mind to stop the Great London Fire."

MARIE

"The what?" I asked Gill, setting my two-pronged fork aside and pushing my plate away. I sipped the coffee Thea had brought us. I had a small addiction to these things called lattes in Gill's time, coffee mixed with rich milk and caramelized sugars. This coffee was significantly worse. I nearly choked and set it aside.

"Do you remember the song *London Bridge is Falling Down?*"

"I think so, why?"

"It's mostly based on the worst fire London has ever seen. I don't remember much about it, other than a baker, a painter, and a priest were involved in starting it. It levels most of London, including the bridge, and most of St. Paul's. About thirteen-thousand die, but history says it was probably more."

"Wow," I breathed, "but what does my grandfather want with the fire? And even worse, if he wants to stop it, won't he be *saving* lives?"

"Hmm," Gill mused for a minute, downing the rest of the awful fluid, "France is no longer the strong powerhouse it used to be before...well, you know. England is still at war with the Dutch, and maybe preventing the fire will help England defeat them. After the fire, the crown lacked the funds to continue their war."

"Why would my grandfather want England to defeat the Dutch?"

"That, I have no idea," he said. "There is another thing, however. The plague is ripping through London right now. It kills about twenty-thousand people, maybe even more. If the fire hadn't happened, the plague would kill even more. Do you think Merlin wants to...?"

I sighed. "This is so complicated." I thought about it for a minute. Then something came to me. "You didn't answer me, Gill. If he stops the fire, he alters history. Which means..."

"We have to make sure the fire goes on as planned."

"Gill...no. We can't do that. You said thousands would die."

He just looked at me. "History isn't pretty."

I shook my head. "There has to be another way."

He had already pulled out another silver coin and left it on the table. "First, we need to follow Thomas and find out where his bakery is. The fire starts on September sixth, so we have about two days to figure out what to do."

I nodded. "More importantly, first, how will we find my grandfather?"

"I don't suppose you know a locator... You know..."

Spell, I thought, but I didn't answer. "No, I don't."

"Well, then. Let's find someone who does."

Abruptly he stood and offered his hand, and I frowned but stood with him. We strolled out of the tavern, trying our best to look like a typical husband and wife on the streets of London. A couple who didn't, by any means, actually live in the twenty-first century.

"Where are we going?" I whispered.

"To find a witch, of course."

I bit my lip and felt my hand tremble. "Gill, remember what happened last time we..."

"I know. This time it will be different, though."

"But where, Gill? It's not like we can stop someone and ask..."

"You forget ... I'm a doctor." He smiled.

"Oh, no, what are you-"

I was cut off by a group of street urchins rushing around us. The tangle of boys, followed by a few girls, ran down the street hooping and hollering loudly. Gill pulled me aside as they stampeded through the alley.

"What meaneth this?" Gill reached out and grabbed one of the young girls who limped behind them.

"A young mistress has't breshew, m'lord" she answered, her eyes wide, "doctor sayeth she is a bedlam."

He released her immediately, and she hastened her gait to follow the children.

"Looks like a witch has come to us," he told me. I frowned. "Breshew? The plague? Here in London?"

He nodded.

"Are you ready to play nurse, wife?"

"What exactly do you have in mind?"

He grinned and opened his sleeve. I peered into it and saw a small plastic bag filled with white pills. "Gill, you didn't!"

"The hospital won't miss the streptomycin. Come on, let's follow the children."

We hurried after them, keeping our pace a few steps behind,

turning down several alleys as the dozen or so fled towards an even more peasant filled part of town. The smaller huts on this side of London were even more run down and many slanted to one side, as if they would topple at any moment. It started to rain, and as English rain often did, it quickly flew to a deluge, soaking us to the core. Up ahead, a group of men in black cloaks entered the narrow road, trailed by a much taller one holding a giant stick. I nearly gasped to see the elongated noses of their masks, but it was a familiar sight for me. *Plague doctors.*

Gill yanked me to the side and made a motion to cast a spell.

I shook my head and mouthed, "*Here?*"

"*Yes, now!*" He pointed to the one trailing behind.

I flicked my finger quickly, sending a quiet sleep spell. The figure slumped to the side of a wooden house. Gill rushed forward and dragged his body back to me, as the two others continued without their companion.

"Won't they notice?" I whispered urgently.

"Do they ever?"

I watched the terrifying figures, one of them swinging a lantern with burning herbs in front of him, as they continued without the third. *Sage and thyme*, my brain reminded me, ancient herbs that did little to banish the spirits. I knew full well the spirits didn't even mind and rather liked the savory sweet smell. The strange creatures didn't even look back. Making sure it was just them in the short alley, I cast a haze spell, cloaking the memories of their companion.

"Now they won't," I told Gill.

He didn't answer. He was busy tearing the mask, waxed leather cloak, and robe from our sleeping victim. As soon as he pulled off the man's hat, I could see under it he was so old it was amazing he could even walk anymore, let alone be doing any "doctoring." His shriveled skin revealed him to be about seventy, maybe eighty, years old, a remarkable age for this time period.

"Jesus, he's too old to be doing this," Gill murmured. "Thanks for the costume, anyway."

I grimaced at him. "He smells like he's nearly dead."

"This mask doesn't smell any better," Gill's muffled voice sounded behind the plaster. "Like rosemary and a hint of ... what's that? Probably shit."

"You sound spooky."

I wanted to giggle, but Gill was truly transformed into a terrifying doctor of the dead, even down the scratched and marred glass pieces set into the eyes of the mask. His green eyes blazed behind the foggy glass, sharp and piercing as he looked around.

"I think that's the point," he mumbled, his voice muffled by the mask. He ripped a piece of robe, which dragged behind him, and tossed it to me. "Now cover your head and face, you're my new nurse."

"Did plague doctors have those?" I did as he said, tucking the dingy cloth around my face and over my hair.

He picked up the stick from the alley where the old man had fallen under my spell. "They do now."

"There's one thing you're forgetting, Gill," I stopped him. "This medicine takes days to work, remember?"

"I know. The medicine is only an opportunity for you to heal the witch."

"I can't heal diseases. You know that! Minor wounds and stabbings, but not diseases!"

"Can you close a pustule?"

"A what?"

"Sore. From the plague."

"I suppose, but..."

"Okay, then that's the plan."

I groaned. "Your plans do not always go as planned."

"Yeah, that's why they are fun. Come on."

We hurried down the alley after the plague doctors. The one on the right turned and looked at Gill, then shook his head, pressed a black-gloved hand to it, and motioned us to follow them. The one on the right, I saw, held a cage of live toads to his chest. Their low croaks filled the silent alley.

Gill waved his cane in front of him as I stepped in line behind him, tucking my arms into my sleeves like the rest of them.

GILL

Marie wasn't wrong. My half-cocked plans hadn't worked out so well in the past. Even now I wasn't entirely sure if this one would work. I only had a vague idea of how to slip the medicine to the victim, somehow, without anyone figuring out who I was. The only problem I had was Marie needed to touch the sick person in order to set off her spell. And for that, no one could be around, lest she befall the same fate as the victim we were hurrying toward.

Pushing past the children crowding around, their faces pressed against the filthy windows, the four of us entered the house of sickness. The first plague doctor stopped and brushed sage across the door frame, marking the house with the deadly disease.

In the two years, I'd been a doctor. I'd seen my fair share of gruesome accidents, and even more as a paramedic in high school and college. By the time I completed my residency, very little shocked me. I'd stitched the wounded, prepped people for surgery, and reunited fingers, toes, and tongues. I saved patients and lost them. Multiple heart attacks came across my unit where it was too late to save them.

After all, I'd survived the plague in the middle ages, being drowned, and stabbed not once, but twice.

But this dingy one-room place of squalor had me staggering. I stifled a gag as we entered, though Marie wasn't so successful. I heard her turn and spill the contents of her stomach behind me, just outside the door, much to the odd delight of the children.

I wondered if the witch we had come to save was even worth this level of revulsion. Three dead, what I could only describe as once humans, lay piled in the corner. I shut my eyes tight to see one of them was a small child, no older than my five-year-old son, Richard, back home with my sister. I'd helped children, of course, but this one had a shock of red hair like him, and it took everything I had to stop my gloved hands from shaking violently. I felt Marie's hand on my shoulder, quick and light, and a surge of energy shot through me, filling me with a new resolve and vigor. If we had been alone, I would have yelled at her for using her magic on me in the open, but just now it was a welcome relief.

I scanned the room and spotted a young woman, no older than myself, lying on a thin straw pad against the left mud-wall. She was covered with a tattered blanket, and even from the doorway and in low light I could see her lymph nodes were swollen and blackened. The other two plague doctors with me knelt beside her, and Marie and I followed suit.

Before I could do anything, the doctor next to me produced a small dagger, and slit the inside of the women's arms from wrist to elbow. I resisted crying out at the brutality of a useless "treatment." The doctor across from us placed two toads on her arm, which defecated in the wound and then hopped off. They let them go.

Despite Marie's magic, I thought I was going to be sick.

Marie saved me at that moment. "Prithee, alloweth me prayeth for this mistress."

The doctors looked at her, one nodded, and they moved aside to stand by the door. Marie moved to the other side of me and pressed her leather-bound hands to the woman's chest. She glanced at me, pleading, I knew, to stop this. Once her magic released, the purple swirl of healing would expose her for what she was.

I didn't know what to do. Our plan wasn't going to work. I reached out to pull her away.

"Stand ho, wench!" One of the boys called from outside the building suddenly, and a scuffle ensued, with screaming and wailing erupting outside. The two doctors looked at each other, then stepped outside the building to pull them off each other.

"Go!" I whispered to Marie. She pushed hard into the woman's chest, the circle of magic exploding and spreading through her. Her chest cavity, barely moving, swelled as she sucked in a deep breath, her mouth opening wide. The doctors shuffled back in the room, and to hide the quickly subsiding magic, I flung myself over the body, tipping two pills into her mouth from my sleeve. As I did, the black pustules on her neck began to shrink and turned to red marks instead of black.

"What doth thou?" One of the doctors barked, his voice low and graveled. "M'lady is a bedlam!"

Marie stood, hiding her hands in the folds of her jacket, as I scrambled to stand. I didn't have time to check her pulse, but the wound in her arm had closed, and I didn't want the doctors to see it. I stood firmly in front of her, hiding her upper body from sight with the expanse of my cloak.

"The lady confesses she is not," Marie told them, her chin pointed outward.

The doctors turned their elongated nose masks to each other. "The tests must continueth according to law," the other said.

"Do you questioneth the will of our Lord?" Marie barked. I saw her hand wiggle in her jacket and wondered what she was casting.

The first doctor held up his hands, and they backed away from the door.

"What are we going to do?" Marie whispered to me.

"We have to get her out of here."

"Where?" she asked, then gasped. "Thea."

"It's worth a shot."

I reached down and cradled her on my arm. She was lighter than I thought, but even emaciated I groaned as I hoisted her off the floor. Her head lolled against my shoulder, but, even while unconscious, I could feel her steady breath against my neck.

"We cannot allow you to do this," the doctor said as we tried to exit.

"This is the will of God!" Marie focused on him, and her words sounded otherworldly, somehow. My vision swam, and I gripped the woman tighter in my arms.

"This is the will of God," the doctor repeated in the same monotone voice. He pushed the other doctor and a handful of the children behind him.

With Marie trailing behind me, we headed back to the Boar's Head and hoped Thea would offer the healed woman, as well as us, a place to stay.

We were one step closer to finding Merlin, but at what cost?

GILL

"Thee cannot bringeth her here!" Thea exclaimed as soon as Marie tried to explain why I was holding the sick woman. "She hast breshew! Doth thee seek to killeth us all?"

I hoisted the unconscious woman, who was beginning to stir and moaned into my shoulder. "Breshew brings the black mark," I tried to negotiate. "This woman doth hast a fever, 'tis all."

"She is mine own husband's kin," Marie lied. "Prithee, Thea, thee must give us a room!"

Thea rattled off something in French, and Marie answered urgently. Whatever Marie said, Thea's face softened, and she stepped aside, motioning to a narrow staircase just to the right of the back door.

"I cannot encave thee for long," Thea mumbled. "Two days, I doth not promiseth more. Last cubiculo on the right."

"Thanketh thee," Marie squeezed her hand and nodded for me to head up.

"Marie," I whispered as we narrowly slid through the door to the cramped room. "You realize in two days this place is going to go up in flames with the rest of London."

She was busy pulling the straw mat off the bed frame to the floor and throwing the worn cotton blanket back on the bed. I lay the woman on the mat. Her head turned left to right, and she moaned again but didn't stir.

"What's your point?" Marie asked.

"You might suggest to Thea to get out of town."

"How can I ask a barmaid to leave town without…"

I shook my coin purse at her.

"Of course. I will. Tomorrow. I'm exhausted."

"Sleep, I'll keep watch over her," I told her.

"No, you carried her all this way, I'll…"

"Marie." It wasn't a question.

She stared at me, defiant to the last.

"Doctor's orders."

Her face softened. "Okay, Gill." She lay down, and I sat against the wall in the far corner, watching our patient as she fought off the demons of the plague.

"Did I look like that?" I whispered to Marie. "You know...in Calais?"

Marie smiled softly, her eyes drooping shut. "You looked worse. I really thought you were going to die."

"Aren't you glad I didn't?"

She nodded, her eyes shutting. "Shouldn't I ask you the same question?"

Her carefully pinned hair had fallen at some point during our rush back to the Boar's Head, and her brown curls piled around her face, covering her eyes as she drifted off. I keenly remembered the day she died, at the Battle of the Druids. I found out later Merlin had preserved her soul in a bottle, to make me go back to the present. He had seen how Marie would die in the future and was trying to prevent it. Fortunately for us, the crazy wizard had never told her exactly how, so every day we had together was a gift. Unfortunately? Merlin had set off through time to prevent her death, and we still didn't know how. So far, all he had done was cause death and destruction wherever he went. Most of the time by accident.

I frowned. This time we would have to cause the death and destruction.

For the time being, traveling around time with Marie on my off days? That was a bonus. I'd do anything, go anywhere, to any time, for her, even if people had to die. The year I'd spent in 1156 had certainly changed me. Freshman Gill at Bay City University would have never thought this way. Dr. Gill, however, knew all too well what death looked like, and it wasn't pretty.

Drowsiness started to overtake me, so I shook my head to stay awake. I was just as exhausted as her, but used to thirty-hour shifts, so clarity came easier to me. I found my second wind and disrobed, tossing the horrid doctor costume into a corner and shook my arms and limbs, finally free of the heavy, waxed clothing. How they wore these things all day long, was beyond me. My chainmail armor back in the twelfth century had been lighter.

Hours passed, and the sun blanketed us in darkness. I lit the small lantern in the corner with a bit of flint, and it cast eerie shadows on the walls.

A few hours after full dark, I kissed Marie on the forehead and gently shook her awake. She blinked her eyes a few times and sat up. "Is it my turn, my love?"

"Yes, just for a couple hours so I can rest," I told her.

She reached out and yanked my collar towards her, pressing her lips to mine. I returned her kiss, pulling her into my arms. "I love you, Guillaume," she whispered.

"Where did that come from?" I asked, my hands running through her hair.

"I told you once I'd never let a day go by without saying it. I'm keeping my promise."

"I love you, too," I told her. "But now, let me get some rest before grumpy Gill comes out."

"Grumpy Gill is entertaining," she beamed at me as she knelt beside the woman. "She's still hot with fever," she told me. "But she's healing. Slowly."

I stretched out on the bed. "Let's hope the medicine works swiftly. We only have one more day to find Merlin."

MARIE

I watched Gill slip into dreamland, his arm tucked over him, and his short auburn hair shifted over his forehead. What did I do to deserve such a strong, intelligent, and irritating man? Even when he made me angry, I burned with love for him. I had ever since the day I met him. Four years without him had almost killed me, but I had finally found my way to him. My way home. As I sat on the floor, waiting for the sick woman to stir so finally we could tap into, what we hoped, was her witch skills, I circled my waist with my hands. *I must tell him soon,* I thought, *before it's too late.*

I wished I had the fortitude Gill had, and for all my experience as a traveler in my youth with Grandfather, I didn't know how he hopped time so easily and managed to stay sharp with such little sleep. Perhaps his long days at the hospital were an asset. The only quality time we spent together anymore was when we were chasing down my grandfather. I didn't know what we would do if I had to tell him the future was about to change. Pushing the thought aside, I dozed off.

"Wherest am I?"

I startled awake to see the woman's eyes had fluttered open and she turned and looked at me. Weakly, she tried to push to her elbows but ended up curling on her side. "What ... whoeth are thee?" She pushed her hands out in front of her, and I saw her hands glow as orange as my dress.

I hurried to my feet and backed up against the bed, kicking the frame to jar Gill awake. I put up my hands, circling my open palm with the finger of my other hand. "I'm just like you," I told the woman. A white flower blossomed in my palm, then withered and died with the snap of my finger. I couldn't remember the word the plague doctor had used. Then it finally came to me. "Bedlams."

"Bedlams?" Her already pale face went even whiter. She touched her hand to her neck, "How hast thee healed me?"

"What is going on?" Gill leapt up and stood between us, his back to me.

"I am Marie; I healed you, but it was mine husband, Gill, who gave you medicine."

"Medicine?" She said slowly, shaking her head, not understanding.

Gill nodded and pointed to the discarded plague doctor mask in the corner. "I'm a doctor," he said truthfully. Just not the kind she knew. "What is your name?"

"Charlotte."

"Charlotte, he is a doctor," I added. "We rescued you. We need your help to find another bedlam. A powerful one. My grandfather."

"What of my son? My daughter? My husband?"

Gill looked at me, and I shook my head.

"I'm sorry," he told her, his voice shifting to 'doctor mode' as he prepared to deliver the bad news. "The disease … it hath taken them."

Charlotte burst into tears, the orange fading from her hands as she covered her face with them. "No! Why hast the Lord forsaken me?"

I stepped beside Gill and could see his cheeks flamed red. He hated religious concepts, beliefs in any god, and people's frailty to depend on an "imaginary" ethereal being. He kept his anger well controlled as I knelt by the woman. She tried to pull away, but I hugged her to me, pulsing light into her as softly as I could. Her vision cleared, and she blinked at me. "I shall see mine folk in heaven," she muttered to me.

"And you have a chance to save thousands more," I told her softly.

She looked up at me. "How?"

"Help us find my grandfather. He's here, in London. He might hurt people, and we need to stop him."

She blinked. "I can findeth the bedlam, but only if't gent be closeth."

"Can you try now?" Gill urged.

"Thee must know I am weak, and needeth rest," she frowned at us, and I feared she wouldn't be able to help us at all. Gill had said we only had two days, and one had already got away from us. Time was of the essence.

"Prithee?" I added, enjoying the sound of that word now. "For mine husband and I?"

Shoulders slumping, she conceded. "I shall try thine hardest. Moveth, thee must."

I scooted away from her and Gill wrapped his arms around me, holding me tight. Charlotte sat with her legs crossed and her hands on her lap with her eyes closed. Her entire body began to glow with yellow and orange light, and the air in the room sparked with electricity. Fearful of her power, I spun a shield of vines around Gill and me.

I wanted to shut my eyes, but I couldn't. I watched everything.

Above Charlotte's head, a blur of faces, some I recognized, spun in dizzying circles. Some of them children, one I recognized from outside her house yesterday, and even the tailor from yesterday.

"Are those all…" Gill whispered in my ear.

"Witches? I think so," I told him.

Charlotte was humming softly now, a tune unfamiliar to me, but the glow around her increased. She lifted off the floor a few inches, still perfectly poised with her legs crossed in front of her. Then finally I saw him, my grandfather. I'd know that long gray beard anywhere. He flipped his cloak around him and vanished into thin air, but as he did, I saw a wooden sign behind him:

The baker.

I nudged Gill and could see he saw it, too.

Charlotte's eyes snapped open then, piercing orange that terrified me for a moment. The glow faded slowly, and she sank down to the floor where she collapsed onto her back, arms and legs spread out on the dingy floor.

Her chest wasn't moving.

I dropped our vine shield and rushed to her side. The black pustules had grown to the size of small onions now, even worse than when Gill and I had rescued her. I folded my hands over her chest as I tried to push my magic into her. I squeezed my eyes shut, feeling the familiar rush of my magic, as I pulled it like a fountain, urging the force forward. My hands heated, and I felt the sear of my healing when...

"Marie, don't."

Gill's hand was heavy on my shoulder as he reached around me and pushed two fingers to her neck. He slid her vacant eyes closed and looked at me, shaking his head.

"No!" I screamed, the purple tendrils of magic free flowing from my fingertips. "I have to bring her back."

Gill snatched my hands away and held them in front of him, wincing as my magic shocked into him. "Are you crazy? Mog said it was forbidden to bring back the dead."

"My grandfather, Merlin, he figured out how! Let me figure out. We didn't rescue her just to let her die."

"Marie." His jade eyes blazed into mine. "She's with her family now. She wouldn't have been happy on this earth."

I rocked back on my heels, scooting away from the dead woman.

My head in my hands, I forced myself to look at my beloved. "This isn't what we came to do, Gill, this isn't how it was supposed to be. We aren't supposed to lose people."

"I lose people all the time." He stood and ran a hand through his hair as he always did. He offered his other hand to me. "You saw the sign. Merlin may even be at the baker's shop right now. We have to hurry."

Knock, knock.

"Marie? Has't thee an issue? Mine own did hear yonder screaming."

Thea.

I took Gill's hand, and he pulled me to my feet. He mouthed to him, *I'll take care of this.* Opening the door a crack, I smiled at Thea. "We are well now," I told her in French. "Our companion is rife with fever."

"Shouldst I fetcheth foxglove?"

"Non," I answered, "My husband is a doctor."

"Oh!" Thea exclaimed. She backed away suddenly. "I shall leaveth thee alone."

I frowned then as I watched the fear envelope her features. In Gill's time, doctors were highly praised, and even from my travels I knew people were usually either relieved or scared of doctors, but Thea's face was more than fear - it was pure terror.

Gill tugged on the back of my dress, urging me to hurry.

"My husband and I will go fetch the herbs. Please do not disturb our companion."

Thea nodded quickly and raced back towards the stairs to the lower level.

Gill slipped out the door behind me and grabbed my hand. "She'll have a fright when she finds Charlotte's body," he whispered as he pulled me behind him.

"Let's just find Grandfather and get back to your time," I said softly. "We have a Netflix moving picture to finish."

Gill just chuckled.

GILL

I wasn't sure what our plan was when we burst through the back door of the inn and out into the alley. We had passed the baker's shop was down on the right, just before the Boar's head. It was barely dawn, and I just prayed we'd be there before the baker. Was Merlin already there? There was no way to tell if Charlotte's vision was the past, the present, or the future.

"Do you have a plan?" Marie asked behind me as she nearly collided with my back when I stopped at the end of the alley. The street was barren of people, a few beggars setting up against the wall of the opposite alley, and two flower vendors pulling their nearly empty carts to set up for the day.

I looked back at her and shrugged.

"Guillaume Lanval, we need to stop the world's most powerful wizard, and you have no idea how?"

"Spare me the lecture for burned roast and late arrivals," I smirked at her. "We don't know if Merlin will actually be there. Keep hold of your rosary, though. We may need to make a big fucking get away."

"Now that's the Gill I know." She smiled. "Come on, this way." As she pushed past me, I saw her hand was clasped around her neck. I followed her, knowing she was ready.

How hard could it be to capture an old man and bring him back to the present? Once we were there, I had no idea how to get him to Mog, but I knew it was better than him meddling with time.

The baker's shop was empty, the front locked, but we slipped around back and saw one single candle in the window. Instead of fresh baked breads and pastries, only the alley sewer smells greeted us. Peeking inside the open door, we found Thomas, his head down on the flour-caked counter.

From here I could smell the alcohol he had marinated in.

"Ugh," Marie said.

"Look, there!" I nudged her, as the flicker of another candle lit up the wall on the other side of the counter.

"There's someone else here," Marie whispered and edged forward.

I didn't like that she was going first, but I let her because I knew better than to try to stop her from doing what she wanted. I did, however, slide my arms under Thomas's passed out frame and slide him slowly to the floor, then dragged him outside the baker and into the alley.

At least you'll be safe here, I thought but didn't want to wake him. I took a deep breath and went to find Marie. No matter what happened tonight, that fire had to be started. I would see to that. But I didn't need Thomas's death on my hands as well.

Grabbing the candle out of the window, I ducked back into the baker's shop.

It wasn't hard to find Marie. She was shouting at someone, and as I rounded the corner, she stood face to face with her grandfather, the great and powerful Merlin.

"Surely you don't mean to let all those people die!" Marie was shouting.

Merlin smiled slowly at her, thumbing his beard as he did. "Die, lie, it makes no matter to me. As long as the fire is stopped."

"You can't stop the fire," I interrupted, standing just beside Marie, as I sidestepped the makeshift sawdust and pine shavings that surrounded one of the huge baking ovens. "I'll make sure it happens."

"Ah, you have brought young Gill. Not so young Gill, is he?" Merlin cackled.

"Listen to me," Marie argued. "You're coming with us. Mog wants you to…" She reached for him.

He swirled away, quick and agile despite looking his advanced age. There wasn't anywhere for him to go, besides out the front door, or the tiny slit of a window behind him, which wouldn't even fit a child. We had him pinned.

Marie's rosary hung loose from her neck, and she ripped a bead off. "Grandfather, you need help. You need to…"

"Save them all, I will! With the power of fire!"

I blew out my candle, drenching us only in the gray light of dawn. As I did, I grabbed the back upper hem of Marie's skirt. "No, no you won't." I smirked at Merlin. *Did he mean to start the fire, after all?*

"What did you come to do?" Marie pressed, stepping closer to him. I tightened my grip on Marie, advancing with her. "What will you gain by preventing the fire?"

If she can touch him, we can shift, and the fire will...

"Silly girl, silly boy. Thinking I would stop the fire. Why, why, why? The fire cleanses the plague. I came to make sure it was started." He smiled crazily at us.

"The great fire will start without you!"

"How do you know this?" he asked, tilting his head. "Do you have a memory of this?"

Marie gaped at him. "No, but..."

"Teehee!" Merlin clapped his hands. "It does not happen in your timeline, only his! Yes! Only his!" He pointed at me.

"Then why..." Marie started.

Merlin frowned at us for the first time. He looked at Marie, his face suddenly solemn. "Save you, I must. And your child."

"Richard is fine. He is at home, in Gill's time," Marie blinked at him, cocking her head to the side. "Where you can't get to him. You don't know when Gill is from."

"'Tis true, but silly girl, not his child. *Your child.*" He cackled loudly and pointed a long, bony finger to Marie's middle.

"What?" I asked, forgetting about the candle in my hand and letting it fall to the floor. "What is he talking about, Marie? I thought after he...you said you couldn't...." I choked my own words.

She stared at me over her shoulder, her mouth moving but no words coming out.

I felt weak, dizzy. My Marie was ... *pregnant*? I lost my grip on her dress and stepped back. She'd lost our child, back in 1156, on the eve after the Great Battle, where she had died. She had promised me children were not in our future, not after returning from the land of the dead. I'd accepted it - anything to be with her.

What a fool I'd been to believe her.

Merlin ignored me, oblivious to my inner turmoil. "Your timelines are twisted, like vines, but the child will be powerful. More powerful than me. Save it, I must. With the fire, England will be crippled and will let the colonies go. Without fire, they take over the world. Can't have that."

Marie lunged for him, her hand ready to drop the bead.

Before she could reach him, time slowed down around us as Merlin flicked his hand towards us. Both of us unable to move, or rather, moving at a much slower rate.

"Nooo," I tried to scream as I saw him lift his hands again. My words came out slow, sluggish, my lips forming around them as I struggled to bring them back. My entire body was frozen and just lifting my arm to reach out for Marie was taking a long fucking time.

We watched, helpless, as Merlin cackled again and lifted his hands, palms up, his fingers curled inward. He shot a bolt of lightning over our heads, right into the wood next to the open oven. It spitted and sparked to a fire immediately, spreading high into the oven before we could even turn around.

Merlin shifted into a crow, dropped his gray cloak to the ground, and he slipped through the window slit and flew away.

As time returned to normal, everything sped up quickly. I wrapped my hand around Marie's just in time as the time travel bead slipped to the floor and burst, sending us spiraling back to my time.

MARIE

"Jesus H. Christ!" Gill screamed as we landed hard in the dumpster behind his favorite diner. For some reason, when I used the bead and thought of home, it always dumped us here. Mog had said something about thin spaces, and this must have been one of them. Behind the diner, a fenced-off empty lot gave us the view of Bay City, that is, over the remains of an old apartment building long since destroyed, or so Gill had said.

Gill climbed out of the dumpster and helped me, his arms tugging my waist as I hopped to the ground.

He paced away from me, tugging his hair with both hands.

"Gill, I..."

"What the fuck was that, Marie?" he blurted as he spun to face me, his pale face burning as red as the crimson light of the dawn. He was lucky the diner wouldn't open for several more hours.

At least we traveled back at the same time, I thought. But there was more to focus on than that. "Grandfather can shift into a crow," I said, my voice flat. "I ... didn't know he could do that."

"Goddamn it, I'm not talking about that!" He paced back and forth. "What was all that nonsense about a child? Your child? Are you...?"

"Yes," I said, blinking at him.

"But I... you said..." He stopped, he hands out in front of him. "How, Marie?"

I turned away from him, to our garbage bag with the yellow tie that we'd left here before traveling. I ripped it open and tossed him his modern-day clothes while pulling mine out as well. "Get those rags in the dumpster before someone sees us," I barked.

"This conversation isn't over," he demanded, catching the jeans and shirt. "We need to talk about this, Marie."

I shrugged out of the itchy dress, stuffing it in the bag and slipped a blue sundress over my head. Gone were the horrible soft-sole shoes of the seventeenth century, replaced by my knee-high boots. I rather loved the comfortable and fashionable clothing of this time, I reminded myself. I turned back to see Gill had changed, and he disposed of his old clothing as well.

"There's no conversation *to* have," I told him plainly. "I'm having a baby. How hard is that to accept?"

"Merlin got away ... again! And now we are stuck here with you and this ..."

In two strides I stood toe to toe with him. I pulled the collar of his shirt down to my face, even though I was only two inches shorter. My hand glowed purple, and the magic had come unbidden this time. "This what, Gill? *This what?*"

He cleared his throat, his face turning purple. "Our miracle," he choked out.

"Fucking-A right." I let him go and dusted my hands on my dress. "Now, let's go home and get our son from your sister's. He has school in about two hours, and you have a shift at the hospital."

"So that's it? We just let Merlin go, into the fucking breeze, and we go back to life as normal?"

"We have before. You know how he works. We wait for Mog to make contact, and we tell him what happened." I turned away from him. "Besides, you act like this is the first time you've got a woman pregnant." I threw over my shoulder.

"I, uh…" he stumbled over his words as he jogged to catch up with me. "Marie, wait."

I felt his hand on mine, and I stopped, letting him turn me around.

He pulled me into his arms. "I'm sorry we couldn't stop him."

"Technically, nothing changed," I murmured into his shoulder. "All those people still died."

"But this time we didn't destroy history, so that's something." He kissed the top of my head. "And for what it's worth, I wouldn't mind being a father again. Richard is my pride and joy. You know that. I'm sorry, Marie, that I got so upset. I'm just worried for you. What if we travel again and it hurts the baby somehow?"

"I don't think that'll happen," I smiled up at him. "We'll be perfectly fine." Stretching on my tiptoes, I kissed him and then pushed him away.

"You say that now, but what will Merlin do next?"

"'Let every man be master of his time.'" I turned and headed towards the front of the diner.

Gill chased after me. "So, you do know Shakespeare after all!"

I just chuckled. He was often gone at the hospital, and what else was a poet sorceress to do, but read? Shakespeare held my attention for a time, but now I thought I would try a woman by the name of Rowling. I heard her tales of magic were a sight to behold, even more than mine.

ABOUT REBEKAH DODSON

Rebekah Dodson is a prolific word weaver of romance, fantasy, and science fiction novels. Her works include the series Postcards from Paris, The Surrogate, The Curse of Lanval series, several stand alone novels, and her upcoming YA novel, Clock City. She has been writing her whole life, with her first published work of historical fiction with 4H Clubs of America at the age of twelve, and poetry at the age of sixteen with the National Poetry Society. With an extensive academic background including education, history, psychology and English, she currently works as a college professor by day and a writer by night.

You can visit her website or follow her on social media for more info.
https://rebekahdodson.com/

 facebook.com/realrebekahdodson

twitter.com/AuthorRDodson

instagram.com/author_rdodson

WATCHMEN

BY DAMIAN CONNOLLY

Sly Stevens stood up, arching his back, wincing at every pop of his spine. The late afternoon was hot and humid, and he was stripped to the waist, his chest dripping with sweat and gore. He wiped an arm across his brow, leaving a sticky streak of blood on his forehead.

Sly regarded his work with a critical eye. At this point, it was less about the deed and more about the effect. All around him, the long grass and reeds were painted red and dripping with viscera. He repositioned an arm slightly with a nudge of his foot.

That was better.

A slight shift in the wind carried a faint whine to his ear implants. It was hard not to look up, but he allowed himself a small smile. *About time.*

Under the guise of a stretch, he cast a lazy eye around him. A ridge to the east was the most likely spot, so he used his augmented eye implants to zoom in until he could make out the faces of two grim-looking men watching him. Facial recognition kicked in, and soon the names and addresses of the two spectators flashed up on his retinas.

He focused on the youngest. *Officer Reece Conlon.*

He smiled and bent back to his work.

Frank Harding stood watch over the coffee machine as the morning sun bloomed over his neighbor's gable. Even this early in the morning, the sky was already a deep azure blue, without a cloud in sight.

A final bubble and a buzz announced that the percolating coffee was finished, and Frank took the pot and poured two large mugs, just as a pair of slim hands wrapped themselves around his waist.

"One of those better be for me," murmured Dee, as she kissed his shoulder. "I need it. Someone kept me up all night."

He turned and handed her one. "Describe the guy, and I'll put out an APB."

Dee took a sip and sighed with contentment. "Oh, he was tall," she said pecking him on the lips. "Hadn't shaved." Another kiss. "Snored really loudly." Her lips met empty air.

Frank rolled his eyes. "Don't start what you can't finish, dear. If you wanna talk about snoring, we can talk about snoring."

Their son Andy came barefoot into the kitchen, dragging a teddy bear, and rubbing his eyes. Frank picked him up and kissed him on the cheek. "Good morning, big man. Want some breakfast?"

"I'm tired."

"There's no school today, kiddo. You coulda stayed in bed."

"I didn't want you to go. Will you stay and play with me, Daddy?"

"I've gotta go to work now, kiddo. But I'll play with you when I get back tonight."

"Promise?"

"Promise."

Frank sat him at the dining table and set about preparing him a bowl of cereal. Then he buttered some toast and joined him.

Time passed languidly, and his son was coming into his usual cheeky self when his wife finally tapped him on the head. "You need to be getting to work. Otherwise, you'll be late."

"I have time this morning. I'm in no rush."

Still, he rose and, pulling two travel mugs out of his work bag, made two more cups of coffee, this time using capsules taken from his pocket. He kissed his wife, long enough that she finally pushed him off, laughing, before slapping his butt. A hug and a kiss from his son, and he was ready. He ignored the blinking red light over the oven.

On his way out, he grabbed the umbrella from where he'd left it by the door the previous night.

"Mr. Big Shot Detective," his wife called after him. "Have you done any detecting out the window lately? I doubt you'll need that today."

"You never know," he said with a smile.

"Bye bye Daddy," Andy said, already engrossed in his toys.

"Hey, big man?" His son looked up, curiosity written all over his face. "Made you look."

Andy beamed at him, and he took that look with him.

Half an hour later, he was letting his car weave its own way through traffic, while he studied the dossier he'd received on his new short-term partner. Outside, heavy rain drummed against the windshield, sleeting against the glass and making it look like he was driving underwater, despite the best efforts of the wipers. Frank didn't mind; he'd always found the sound of rain relaxing.

He flipped over a page to the psych report. It was meant to help new partners gel with each other, and while it left out a lot of the more intimate details, it helped paint a mental picture. *Protective. Impulsive tendencies. Morally conservative.* He'd memorized them all long ago. Until he got where he was going though, there was nothing better to do, so he reread them anyway.

Shortly afterward, his car pulled up to a small, two-story attached house, looking like it'd seen better days. In case he'd missed the obvious, the onboard GPS informed him that he'd arrived. It was still pelting down, so he flipped the siren on for a second; a short, offensive-sounding *blatt* echoing around the neighborhood. Something Frank was sure wasn't exactly unfamiliar around here.

He waited a few minutes, checking the mirrors out of habit before the front door opened and he was able to put flesh and bones to the picture in his dossier. A bit taller than he'd imagined, somewhat pudgier, and nowhere near the smiling demeanor from the photo. His new partner was arguing heatedly with someone inside. A final exchange, an exasperated wave of the hand, and the younger man slammed the door and ran to the car, hunched over against the rain.

He wrenched the car door open and threw himself in, shaking the rain off of his collar, and slicking his hair back with an angry flick of his hand.

"Trouble with the missus?" Frank asked mildly. The car purred to life and pulled out into traffic, slotting seamlessly into the flow.

His new partner blew out in a huff. "Ah, it's nothing. She don't like the area. She don't like the weather. *It's always raining here.* You get the picture."

"Going house-crazy."

He nodded. "I keep telling her. Give it time, give it time. But the only thing she's giving is an earache."

"Coffee?" Frank asked, holding up one of the travel mugs.

"My man! You shouldn't have." He accepted the cup and took a long drag. "No, really, you shouldn't have. This tastes like dirt."

"You got anything better? I can turn around."

"Ha, hell no. Dirt it is then." He took another long pull on the mug and managed to keep his shudder under control. "So where we going?" he asked, nodding to the car's dashboard, where the GPS wasn't showing any destination.

"Straight to the main office. It's somewhat of an unofficial black site."

His partner perked up. "Oh man, I can't believe I got picked for the expansion of the Watchmen program! I guess the training wheels are finally ready to come off, huh?"

Frank just nodded.

"Hey, thanks for picking me by the way. I know you're probably swamped in cases and offers."

Frank shrugged. "We were all fish once. It's not like there's a lot of us that do this."

"So is there anything I need to know before I get there?"

Frank leaned over him and popped the glovebox on his side. It fell open with a heavy thump. Inside was a folder about as thick as his fist, earmarked pages ready to spill out. "Read that."

His partner pulled out the folder with some trepidation, flipping from one text-filled page to another. "You're joking, right?"

Frank raised an eyebrow.

The younger man cleared his throat. "Right then," he said faintly. He turned to the front page. "Oh, hey, I never properly introduced myself." He stuck a hand out. "Reece Conlon."

Frank took his hand. He had a tight grip. "Frank Harding."

The rest of the trip passed in relative silence as Reece tried to cram as much info from the dossier as he could. Frank was pretty okay with this.

When they arrived at a nondescript building ringed by - in Frank's opinion - a ludicrous amount of security, his partner finally raised his head, a pained expression on his face.

"They didn't tell me there was gonna be so much math," he groaned.

"Honestly, you only need a very basic understanding of theoretical quantum physics," Frank said, as they were waved through by very serious looking men sporting very serious looking weaponry.

"I'm not sure if you're joking there."

"I know, right?" Perhaps he was taking a bit too much pleasure in this. More layers of security and scans followed before they could pull into a pristine parking lot without so much as a tire mark on the painted floors. He took the folder from Reece's unresisting hands and dumped it in the back seat. "Right. Enough of that. Let's go."

"But I've barely made it through the first section!" Reece sputtered. "What if I need what's in the rest of it?"

"No doubt you'll fail spectacularly then."

"But-"

"Listen, kid," Frank interrupted. There might have only been ten, fifteen years between them, but that meant he was permanently relegated to *kid* territory. "Stay close to me, don't let your head get carried away with all the special effects, and most of the rest is common sense. Worse case, you destroy the universe," he added with a shrug. "But then you ain't got a problem no more."

What more could he say to that?

To get into the Nest itself - Frank didn't know who originally came up with the nickname, but at this point, he couldn't even remember what the official name for the site was - they had to pass more security checkpoints. ID checks, biometric scanners, you name it. From the moment they passed through the doors, their every response was tracked, recorded, and matched with what was on the records. Frank led his partner deeper into the complex, pointing out useful areas and offices as he went. If Reece were able to remember a tenth of what he was telling him, he'd be all right.

Eventually, they came to a large set of double doors flanked by two policemen in riot gear that nodded to Frank as they passed. Beyond there was a small antechamber where an old white-haired cop sat reading a newspaper, his feet up on an expensive-looking console desk.

"One of these days, they're gonna fire you for that, Norm," Frank said with a smile.

"You gonna rat me out, Harding?" Norm said, eyeing them over the top of his paper. "Didn't think you'd be back so soon. Who's the fish?"

"Partner," Frank said, at the same time as Reece giving his name.

Norm gave Reece a long once-over. "Finally opening this puppy up, huh?"

"Maybe you'll have something to do, old man," Frank said. "Speaking of which, what do you have for me today?"

Norm sucked his teeth. "Not pretty," he said, grimacing and finally sitting up. "Body was found yesterday out in the badlands on the outskirts of town. Woman, early thirties. An auto-call from the victim's own chip. Some of the data is being flagged as possibles in other cases originally ruled suicide. So, possible serial, but pure whack job."

"So, let's get going to yesterday, then," Frank said.

Norm nodded and set to work with the intricate care and implicit distrust that all old people have for technology. Reece started walking towards the main chamber, where a dome light was slowly revolving over the door, throwing harsh amber shadows around the room. Frank grabbed him by the arm.

"Probably don't wanna go in there while it's warming up."

"Why not?"

"Well, I guess it depends on whether you like living or not?" Norm asked, looking between his mouse and the screen to make sure that whatever he was selecting hadn't jumped away in the meantime.

Frank went to a set of lockers running along the wall, pulled out a black rucksack and threw it to Reece, who nearly dropped it in surprise. "Here. I'm giving you the vital task of carrying all of my stuff."

Reece gave him a *look* but shouldered the rucksack without a word. He looked positively impatient to be on his way. Frank watched him with mild amusement. Had he ever been like this, way back when?

The light above the door finally turned green, and Frank hit the button that opened it. As always, it was like opening a door on a flying airplane. It slid up with a howling, sucking wind just on the threshold of bearable. His ears popped as the pressure equalized. The room beyond was mostly taken up by a long, shallow ramp, leading to a ring about ten feet across. It was covered with wires, magnets, and all manner of doohickeys that were beyond Frank's understanding. They twisted and ran across every free space, an ordered abomination of science and technology, before disappearing into the wall behind the ring. Frigid air rolled down the sides, fogging and pooling around their feet, making it look like they were standing on a cloud.

But the ring itself.

It took his breath away every time. A swirling vortex of color. A raging maelstrom of power. It drew the eye, pulled him towards it, promising salvation, promising oblivion.

Reece stood with his mouth open, his face pale. Frank put it even money that he'd throw up. "What the…" the rookie said, crossing himself.

"A wormhole. Or an Einstein-Rosen bridge if you wanna get technical," he shouted over the noise of the ring. "Gets us from here to then."

"Go if you're going," grumbled Norm, his hands stuffed into his armpits. "It's damn cold!"

Frank gave Reece a small push to get him moving. His partner shuffled up the ramp, unable to take his eyes away from the boiling rip in space-time in front of them. Frank could understand. "Now the first time, you might wanna keep your eyes closed. Keep your arms and elbows in, your tray table stowed, and your seat in the upright position."

They approached the wormhole, the sucking wind ripping at their clothes. Reece faltered. "Is it… Does it hurt?"

Frank looked him dead in the eye. "Like you wouldn't believe."

He shoved him through.

As Frank came out the other end, he had to throw up an arm against the blinding glare of the midday sun, beating down from a pristine blue sky. He took a moment to get his bearings. Time travel was always a little disorienting, no matter how often he did it. He opened a couple of buttons on his shirt. It was damned hot, and the air was heavy with humidity.

Reece was off to the side, throwing up. As Frank walked over to him, he stood, wiping his mouth with a shaky hand.

"You said it was gonna hurt," he said, spitting weakly to clear his mouth.

"Yeah, sue me," Frank replied absently, his mind only half on his partner. Wiry, knee-length grass, more yellow than green, grew in sporadic clumps as far as he could see. Twisted stumps of dead trees stood here and there, like morbid scarecrows, warning anyone with sense that here be dead things. A couple of vultures circled lazily overhead, and for a second, he thought they were too late. But no, Norm knew what he was doing.

He checked his watch, a model unlike anything found in a store. "All right. The timestamp from the vic's chip gives us about six hours. Let's get into position."

Reece pulled out his PDA, and looking quickly around to get his bearings, pointed off towards one of the tree skeletons. "Body was found over here."

"Then we probably don't wanna be there," Frank said dryly. He scanned the horizon. "That ridge over there should give us a good view of the show. Let's go."

It took a good forty minutes to get to the ridge, and they arrived dusty and sweaty, picking burrs out of their clothes where they'd brushed up against the shrubs. Reece shrugged out of the backpack with a sigh. His shirt was soaked through. "So what now?"

"Now we set up, and we wait. Perp could be here in two minutes, or two hours." He started pulling equipment out of the bag.

"Got any water in there?"

"What do you think?"

Reece kicked away a scorpion making its way across the cracked ground, then half-sat, half-collapsed. "So what's all this?" he said, after a few minutes.

"This," Frank replied, struggling to make everything click together, "is a camera probably worth more than both of us." He finally got everything in place, then set the camera up so it was facing the crime scene, consulting his own PDA until he was satisfied with the angle. A shotgun mic followed suit. When he was done, he checked his watch. Five hours.

"Okay," Frank said. "I'm gonna give you the five-minute explanation of what it means to be a Watchman. Everything anyone's told you about it, everything that you've read in that folder, it all boils down to this.

"Say Billy Bad-Guy lives up to his name and messes someone up. If they don't know who it is, they come to us. If they *do* know who it is, but can't prove it, they come to us. If they wanna see who ordered it, they come to us. We go back, get ourselves nice and cozy, then catch it all on video. Bing, bang, boom, nothing Billy says is getting him out of that."

"That's it?" Reece asked, somewhat incredulous.

"That's it."

"You mean we're not gonna stop the guy?"

"That comes after."

"But the vic...the woman. That was somebody's wife, or girlfriend, or mother, or daughter, or... That was somebody! We can stop it from happening. We can do something!"

Frank shook his head sadly. "What's done is done. We can't change that."

"Well, why the hell not?"

"We go down there and save this woman, we're heroes, right?" Reece nodded. "Except, then she's not dead, so we never get the case, so we never need to come here."

Reece started to say something, but stopped, trying to work it out in his head.

"Let's keep it going," Frank said. "Maybe she *is* a mother. Maybe she has a son, and that guy grows up and becomes an officer so he can stop bad guys, just like the one that killed his mother. How many does he stop? How many people does he save? If we save his mother, does he still do that? Maybe instead of joining the force, he sells mattresses, or second-hand cars, or just disappears into suburbia.

"Everything we do while we're here has an impact. *Everything.* Drive a car here, maybe the guy behind you gets a red light that he wouldn'ta got, and now he's late, and it changes his life. Tip a waitress, and maybe now she's got enough to buy a scratchcard on her way home. A butterfly flaps its wings and yada yada yada. When this tech first came on the scene, it didn't take a genius to figure out what it could be used for, so it got locked down. Hard.

"I was just like you, kid. I wanted to bust these guys, save lives, you name it. But everyone affected pays for it. Aside from what coulda been, turns out we're a bit sensitive to what they call *temporal disruption*," he said, tapping the side of his forehead. "Brain feels there's something *off*, gives you a headache trying to make sense of it. Change someone's life enough; you'll lay them out for a week with a migraine so bad, they'll wish they were dead."

"Better than actually *being* dead," Reece said, sullen.

Frank gave a tired smile. "Save one, kill a thousand. Who knows? You ain't God. You wanna be a Watchman? You're gonna see some dark stuff. Most people can't handle it, but only you can answer that question."

The next few hours passed in silence. Frank wished he'd brought a hat, for the sun was merciless. The camera stood ready, partially hidden in the scrub edging the ridge. Eventually, Reece nudged him and pointed with his head at a fast-approaching dust cloud.

"All right, remember what I said," Frank warned, the lack of water making his voice croak. He flipped the switch on the camera and mic, then dug through the backpack, pulling out a small case. Inside rested a small quadcopter drone. He unbuttoned the restraints and soon had it airborne, the faint whine of its motors quickly lost from hearing. They stretched out onto their stomachs, hiding behind the scant cover.

Down below, the dust cloud materialized into a battered van, which slid to a halt, momentarily hidden from view by the billowing dirt following behind. A man in a sleeveless vest jumped out. Reece streamed a still from the camera to his PDA and started running analysis. "Sly Stevens," he said after a moment. "Up until now, a low-level bagman. Nothing in his record like this."

Frank said nothing, his eyes on the scene below. Sly threw open the side of his van and dragged a struggling figure from inside. He stopped by the gnarled, white trunk of the tree that they'd flagged earlier.

At the first blow, Reece's hand dropped to his gun, and he started to scramble to his feet. Frank grabbed his arm, holding on to the rigid muscle. He shook his head. Reece stared at him, furious, but relaxed back down with a sour twist to his mouth.

The camera turned, and Frank kept his eyes on the scene below. Arcane laws meant that they needed to personally witness anything they may have to testify on later. It was easily the worst part of the job.

The sun was on its way down when Sly finally climbed back into his van and sped off. Frank made sure the plates were on record, then switched off the camera and started packing up.

"I take it we can't go down there," Reece said in a low voice, eerily calm.

"Can't contaminate the crime scene. Our part here is done."

"Then let's go back home." His partner climbed to his feet. There was no trace of the enthusiasm from this morning.

Frank watched him out of the corner of his eye. He hated to do this to him. He checked his watch. "Come on. The breach should be opening soon."

The return journey didn't affect Reece in the same way as the first one, though Frank put it down to being preoccupied. His partner clumped down the ramp, his face blank and unreadable. The thousand yard stare, as the head docs would put it.

They walked into a full antechamber and pulled up short. "Captain Perretta?" Frank asked, surprised.

The captain stood with his hands clasped in front of him, flanked by five other senior staff, and two men in suits that Frank didn't recognize. They all ignored him. Frank gave a questioning glance at

Norm, but the old man squirmed like he'd eaten something bad and avoided his eye.

"Officer Conlon," Perretta said. "You should come with us."

"What's that about?" Frank asked Norm as he watched everyone walk out.

Norm waited until he was sure they'd left, but even so, when he spoke, he kept his voice down. "Nothing good," he said, his mouth curling in distaste. "They're trying to keep it on the down low, but word is, while you guys were through the gate, his girlfriend got snatched and…" He trailed off, not wanting to say it.

"Wife," Frank said, looking at the door where his partner had gone through.

"Huh?"

"Not his girlfriend. His wife."

"Girlfriend. Wife. Don't make a bit of difference now." He shook his head, fidgeting at his console. "Some welcome to the city, am I right?"

Frank sighed. "Yeah."

It was nearly an hour before Perretta found him in the locker rooms, long out of the shower, but still not dressed.

"I take it you heard," the captain said. It wasn't a question.

"The gist anyway."

"I have some of the lab guys going over his house looking for anything that stands out. He can't be there, not yet anyway. I know you only met the kid this morning, but-"

"I got it, Captain," Frank interrupted.

Perretta looked at him for a moment, then nodded. "Keep him out of trouble."

Frank found Reece by the front desk. He gathered him up and took him to a bar a couple of minutes down the street. It was only when Frank placed the first glass of whiskey in front of him that he seemed to realize where he was. His gaze was fixed on his glass, as if he didn't want to meet Frank's eyes, then he drank it off in one, slow and deliberate.

Frank signaled the bartender again. "Leave the bottle this time," he said.

The barman took an experienced look at Reece. "Is he gonna be okay?" *Is he gonna wreck my bar?* being the unspoken question.

Frank flashed his badge. "Just leave the bottle." The barman shrugged and walked off. Frank topped up his partner's glass. Reece drank it off. Frank filled it again.

They sat side-by-side, not speaking. Frank was never good with this type of thing, and he figured the kid would talk if he wanted to. Sometimes all you needed to be was a silent ear.

"You know wha-" Reece began before his voice broke. His jaw worked, and he took another drink before trying again. "You know what I keep thinking about?"

Frank drank his own drink and said nothing.

"The last thing I said to her. The la-. The *last* thing. *Whatever.*"

Frank topped up their glasses again.

"Not, 'I love you.' Not, 'I'll see you tonight.' We were fighting, I didn't wanna listen, so I just said 'Whatever.' I just blew her off. Like she wasn't important." Reece stared at his glass. Stared *through* his glass. Then he screamed and hurled it into the wall.

Frank jumped up and restrained his partner with one arm and held up the other to stay the bartender, frozen in place with one hand under the counter.

Reece grabbed Frank's jacket and pulled him close, speaking urgently, breath stinking of alcohol. "We can go back! We can find out who did it. We can...we can *save* her!"

Frank looked into desperate eyes. He kept his voice low. Firm.

"There's already a team there. There's no way you'd - there's no way *we'd* - be let anywhere near it."

"I can't just do nothing," Reece hissed, trembling.

Frank called for his car to pull up outside the bar. "Except that's exactly what you're gonna do." He grabbed the bottle and threw down some notes on the counter. "Come on."

By the time they pulled up to Frank's house, Reece had worked his way through most of the whiskey and Frank had to help him out of the car. They staggered the short length to the door. There was no light from any of the windows, and it took a few curses before Frank was able to find the right key in the darkness. He kicked open the door, sliding the pile of mail behind it along with it, and dumped Reece into a chair in the living room. He flipped on a small table light so he wouldn't trip over anything.

"Damn," Reece slurred. "You're a slob."

Frank ignored him. "I'm gonna put on some coffee."

The coffee pot in the kitchen had maybe half a cup left in it, though it was spotted with mold. He rinsed it out, and after finding some out-of-date capsules in the cupboard, set it running. He took the two cleanest mugs that he could find, rinsed them, and dried them with his shirt. The coffee pot clicked off, he filled the mugs and brought them into the living room. "There's no milk or su-" He stopped. Reece was standing by the fireplace, holding a framed photo.

Frank walked over and replaced the photo in Reece's hand with one of the coffee mugs, then placed it carefully back where it had been. Reece looked at him, somewhat bleary-eyed, but steady. Then around him. At the stained carpet, the rubbish, the unwashed dishes strewn on the floor. The stale air.

"She leave you?" he asked finally.

Frank swallowed the lump in his throat. He smiled sadly. "You could say that, yeah."

Reece nodded slowly. "You coulda changed it."

Frank shook his head. "Watchmen didn't come in till years later. Too much history at that point."

"But you woulda?" Reece pressed.

Frank looked at him for a long time. "You should try to get some sleep."

Frank woke up to his phone ringing. He glanced at the clock. Half three. And not the good kind.

He answered. "Hel-"

"Frank? Frank! What are you? Dead? You don't answer your phone?"

It took a moment before his brain kicked into gear. "Norm?"

"You need to get your ass down here, ASAP! The kid came barging in with a gun! He's through the gate."

Sleep muddled with his thoughts. "Kid? What kid?" Andy was long gone.

"Your kid!" Norm snapped. "The fish."

Frank slid out his PDA. There'd been an update to Reece's case in the night. The Watchmen had come back with a name.

"I'm on my way."

Norm was pacing back and forth when Frank finally arrived. He practically jumped as the door opened.

"I swear you're slower'n I am," he griped.

Frank flapped at him like an annoying bug. "What do you have for me?"

"Your *partner*," Norm said, practically spitting the word, "threatened me with a gun. Me!"

"And I'm sure you live. Now, what do you have for me?"

Norm ground his teeth but walked around to his console. "I've kept the gate open so you'll be able to follow him, but he's got nearly an hour on you."

"It's fine. I know where he's going. How much time can you give me?"

"Not much. Pretty soon they're gonna be wondering why the gate's open this long."

"Do what you can, yeah? I'll owe you, big time."

"Next time I see him, Frank," Norm said, shaking a bony finger at him. "I'm gonna kick his ass."

"I'll try to warn him," he said, dryly.

When Frank arrived, rain was pouring down, and he was quickly soaked through. Popping his collar to try and stop it running down his neck, he flagged one of the passing autonomous cars. One immediately pulled out of the flow of traffic. He jumped in and gave his destination, passing his police override at the same time. The car pulled off, acceleration pressing him into his seat, while the traffic in front glided out of his way, alerted by the protocol his car was passing them.

He pulled up the case file on Reece's wife on his PDA. The timing would be tight, but he should make it.

With nothing to do in the meantime, the journey seemed to take absurdly long, though, in reality, it was nothing more than a few minutes. The car slid to a stop on the slick streets. Reece's house. Where he'd picked up his partner yesterday. Where he'd picked up his partner not an hour ago.

The door was open, light spilling out in the gloomy morning.

He jumped out, damp clothes sticking uncomfortably, unsheathed his gun, and made his way up. Through the pounding of the rain, he could make out shouting. Adrenaline coursed through him. It'd been a while since he'd done something like this, and his heart was thundering. Once he was under the porch door, he was able to make out what was going on inside.

"...coming home drunk of all things? How can you be drunk at nine in the morning?" That must be the wife.

"Baby, you're no-, you're not *listening* to me." Reece's voice was still somewhat slurred. "I just... I just... I love you."

"Reece, what are you doing? Why are you here? You're scaring me."

"Just know, no matter what - no matter *what* - I love you. I- I-"

"Reece, what happened? Why won't you tell me what happened?"

Frank made his way through the door, placing each foot with care.

"I c-can't." His partner sounded like he was crying. "I just..."

"Reece, please, talk to- Get off me, you're soaking wet! Oh my God, Reece, why do you have your gun out? Reece, you're scaring me. Talk to me, please!"

If Frank stuck his head out, he was liable to get a bullet for his troubles, so he stayed back beyond the door. "Hey, buddy," he called out, overly friendly.

There was a gunshot, and a chunk of wood exploded by his ear. Someone screamed. It might even have been him. "It's me, Reece, your partner. It's Frank."

Silence. Then, "What are you doing here?"

"I'm coming out now, all right? You're not gonna shoot me, are you? 'Cause I'd be pretty disappointed if you did, to be honest."

He stowed his gun, and came out slowly, hands first. Reece and his wife were in the kitchen, her cowering in the corner.

"What are you doing here?" Reece repeated.

"You wanna stow the pistol, kid? You're making me nervous." He couldn't read Reece's expression, but his partner eventually sheathed his gun. Frank looked at the man's wife, trying to make herself as small as possible in the corner. How much had he told her? "We, uh, we need to be going now. Big day, and all that. First day. Don't want to be late, am I right?"

"I'm right where I need to be, Frank." His voice was so *cold*.

"Yeah, I'm not so sure," Frank said, edging ever closer.

"You should go. There's no point in both of us going down for this."

"What are you talking about, Reece?" his wife asked. "Who is this?"

"Detective Frank Harding, mam. I'm your husband's partner. Reece is just a little...excited is all, isn't that right, kid? Sometimes the excitement just gets to you, and you go a little cuckoo. No harm, no foul. We'll go, and everything'll be just fine."

"I'm not leaving with you, Frank," Reece said. "Not yet."

"You can't change what's already happened, kid."

"Of course you can! Why else am I here? Now? Why did I get chosen for the program? Everything led to this point so that I *can* change it!"

"Reece?" his wife pleaded.

"They'll put you away," Frank said, softly.

"*And?* At least she'll still be... She'll be... It'll be worth it."

"Reece? I'll still be what, Reece?" His wife tugged on his arm, trying to get him to face her. "I'll still be what?"

"You'll still be right where I need you," said a thin voice by the door. She screamed, and Reece had his gun out and trained on the newcomer in a heartbeat. Frank's hand dropped to his pistol, but he stopped himself.

There, in the doorway, wearing the same bloody vest as they'd last seen him, stood Sly Stevens.

He walked in slowly. He wasn't armed and didn't seem fazed by the gun pointing at his head. "Detective Harding," he said, with a nod at Frank. "Officer Conlon. Mrs. Conlon." He said the last with distinct pleasure that Reece was sure to have heard. "If you don't mind," he said to Reece, "I've come to take your wife."

"What are you talking about?" she shrieked. "Reece, what is he talking about?"

Reece kept his gun trained on Sly, his arm trembling with the effort of not pulling the trigger. "Don't take another step."

Sly gave Frank a bemused smile as if to say, *Check this guy.* "I'd have thought you'd understand it by now. If you're here, then you know this has already happened. You know that this is *going* to happen. So what are you even doing here?"

"I said - don't - move," Reece seethed through clenched teeth.

Sly walked up until the gun was no more than an inch from his chest. "If you stop me here, then I don't kill your wife, but if I don't kill your wife, then why would you be here?" He prodded Reece with a finger. "You're a Watchman. Watch."

Reece's wife's face dropped in horror as Sly walked around her husband and she realized that he wasn't trying to stop him. "Reece? Reece! *Reece!* Get away from me! Get away-" The last word ended in a howl as Sly grabbed her hand and twisted it, sending her sprawling. Then he grabbed her hair in one hand, her belt with another, and started dragging her out.

"Reece! Help me!" she wailed, struggling against Sly's iron grip. "Do something! Why won't you do something? Pleeeease."

Reece stood, shoulders hunched, tears streaming down his face, and flinched with every word as if her voice were a whip flailing his soul. He shook his head, arguing with internal demons. When he looked at Frank, his eyes were dead.

"How often do you wish you could save your family?" Reece asked.

"Every day."

Reece raised his gun and pulled the trigger.

The debriefing lasted for hours. Half of the Nest were suffering the effects of the temporal disruption, and suffering them *hard*.

By the time Frank was released, it was edging into the evening. He was tired and hungry, and pretty soon was going to have one hell of a headache. He made his way through vacant halls and empty offices. The people he did meet were subdued; those in the know understandably shocked, the rest picking up on the mood.

He eventually found himself in front of a familiar set of double doors, though this time there were no guards. He pushed them open, weary to the bone.

"So they finally let you out?" Norm asked.

"Bigger fish to fry. Better things to do. Like trying to figure out what's changed."

"The kid?"

"His wife's alive, though he won't see her for a very long time."

Norm nodded sagely. The old man looked at him, a sharp glint in his eye. "Word on the grapevine is they're shutting down the expansion program."

"Seems like a good idea," he said, carefully.

Norm looked like he wanted to say more, struggling with how to put it. Then he changed the subject, to Frank's relief. "Same place?"

"Same place."

Norm bent to his console, and Frank waited for the light above the main door to turn green. When it did, he looked over at the old man. He was lost in his thoughts, a troubled look on his face.

"You have a good night now, Norm."

"You too, Frank, you too. Say hi to Dee for me."

"Will do."

The sun was just touching the rooftops when he walked up to his door and turned the key.

"Daddy!" Andy shouted as soon as he came in. The little boy bounced over to him, and Frank picked him up, hugging him tight.

Dee came over and gave him a warm kiss. "Didn't expect to see you home so soon."

"I snuck out early, don't tell anyone. Remember, snitches get stitches."

She batted him with the kitchen towel and rolled her eyes. "Want some coffee?"

"You read my mind."

He set Andy down, who promptly ran off to fetch him his latest drawing, kicked off his shoes, and fell into his favorite chair. He watched his wife move around the kitchen, golden beams of sun lancing through the window and giving everything a soft glow. This was a perfect moment. A *timeless* moment.

Something he'd no longer be able to come to if the Watchmen program had been expanded to general use. He'd been to the future.

Finding Stevens had been the hard part. Convincing him, less so. Given what the man was going to receive, what he'd gotten had been a small mercy.

Dee brought him a mug. "Oh babe, you look tired. Hard day?"

"The hardest," he said. "But worth it."

ABOUT DAMIAN CONNOLLY

Damian is a Science-Fiction and Fantasy author born in Ireland, but currently living in Bordeaux, France, where it's decidedly warmer.

His debut novel, Shepherds: Awakening, has won multiple awards, including the 2016 Lyra Fantasy Award.

You can find all his books on his website at
https://damianconnolly.com

 facebook.com/DamianConnollyAuthor

twitter.com/divillysausages

SCREWING WITH THE TIMELINE FOR FUN AND PROFIT

BY K. MATT

March 1992

"Care to explain yourselves?" the official barked, her steel gray eyes studying the trio of young women before her.

One of the ladies, a rather curvy one who seemed to be the group's leader, stepped forward. Feline ears poked up from her dark knee-length hair, a fluffy tail protruding from her back end.

"Yes. See, we call ourselves the Slaughter Angels, ma'am. We're a group of assassins, and you're sort of—no offense—in our way right now," she said, giving a surprisingly kind smile.

The official crossed her arms, staring down her long nose at the younger woman and her cohorts. One of the others stood at attention, hands behind her back and her pale red eyes studying her. The other one, however, showed no such respect, one hand on her cocked hip and the other holding an open flask of alcohol, the contents strong enough that it could be felt from yards away. The drunkard's turquoise eyes gazed upon the older woman in an almost teasing way, as if she was just looking for an opening to mess with her.

She narrowed her eyes, pulling out a small electronic device. She held it up, the assassins looking at it curiously. It reminded them of a mobile phone, but it was much smaller. Flatter, but not quite paper-thin.

"Beast Taylor…" she murmured, scanning the cat-woman with her device. "Genetic experiment, age nineteen."

The respectful one was scanned next, the official reading of her findings. "Yvette Sangre. Age fifteen. Witch. Hm…that's unusual…last I knew, magic was only a myth."

With a sigh, Yvette produced a ball of red light in the palm of her hand. "Not a myth, I promise."

"Right. And Ivy Sangre…age fifteen, psychic, and…I see a lot of question marks here."

Taking a quick swig from her flask, Ivy grinned. "Yeah, we're all still trying to figure out exactly what I am."

Beast put her hands on her hips, eying the stranger. "And just who the hell are you?" she asked.

The woman put her scanner on her belt, crossing her arms. "I am Officer Marjorie Payne, of the A.T.R."

The assassins looked to one another, Beast briefly wondering if this woman had misspelled "art." But Yvette was the one to raise her hand.

"Um…what is the A.T.R.?"

"Agency of Temporal Relations."

Ah. So, time cops, basically.

"And what's that thing?" Ivy asked, pointing to the scanner.

Payne rolled her eyes, arms crossed. "That's standard issue for my work. It does every required task, from scanning to transport." Officer Payne cleared her throat. "I've been asked to bring in a woman by the name of Darlena Williams. She's been attempting to disrupt the timeline."

With a twitch of her ears, Beast looked up at Officer Payne (who had a good eight inches on her).

"Yeah, we know all about what she's been up to," she said. "Why do you think we're after her?"

Payne poked a bony finger into Beast's sternum, eyes regarding her coldly. "For a quick buck, clearly. In the case of the Sangre degenerate," she pointed to Ivy, "booze money that she shouldn't really have in the first place. You're all children. This sort of mission is much too dangerous for three children, no matter how much they like to play at being assassins. Now go away and make some real plans for your future, girls."

The trio stared at her for a moment, unsure how to process what she'd just said to them. What they did know was that the verbal slap to their collective face could not be taken lightly. Was this woman utterly unaware of the hellish training they had endured to become assassins in the first place? There was at least one mock execution involved in said training! And Ivy's underage drinking was for medical reasons. That scan had indicated that she wasn't an ordinary human, after all. But they weren't going to argue. They'd just handle this on their own.

Ivy strode over toward Payne, putting an arm around her.

"Y'know what, officer? You're right. We should sit back, think about our futures, all that crap. Best of luck hunting this lady down!"

Payne gingerly pushed the teen's hand from her shoulder, before turning on a heel and walking away. And as soon as she was far enough away, Ivy held up the device that'd previously been used to scan them. Yvette gasped.

"Ivy, are you insane? You stole that!"

With a chuckle, Ivy started to tinker with the scanner, hoping to get some idea of how it worked. "Vette, we're professional killers. And yet theft is where you draw the line?"

"But you stole from a COP!"

"A **time** cop. Plus, you heard how condescending she was, calling us kids, right? She brought this on herself."

Yvette shook her head in disappointment. "No good can come of this, Ives...you should know better by now."

Before Ivy could retort, Officer Payne came storming back over, nostrils flared.

"Y'know, guys, I think she's mad..." Beast said, head tilted somewhat.

Yvette turned to the trio's eldest member, incredulous. "Are you kidding me right now?" she grumbled.

Officer Payne crossed her arms, glaring at the girls. How dare they even consider this course of action? She marched up to Ivy, holding out her hand for the device. Of course, Ivy knew what it was Payne really wanted from her...but that didn't stop her from bringing the palm of her own hand down on her palm.

"All right, now, up top!" she added, holding up her hand for a high five next.

"I demand that you hand over that device, Sangre, NOW!"

The teenager bit her lip for a moment, chewing on it in apparent thought. "Hm...nah, I don't think I will," she said finally, shrugging.

"And why is that?"

She smirked somewhat, before looking the device over. "Because I wanna see what it does!"

Payne growled and reached for it, but Ivy swiped it out of her grip, running to the other side of the room. The older woman charged after her. If looks could kill, her current glare would cause worldwide devastation. People would declare it the end times.

This damn kid was fast. But Payne was faster, as she dove to tackle Ivy. The girl fell, the device dropping from her hand. Yvette rushed over to retrieve it but stopped in her tracks upon hearing a beep.

"Is...is it supposed to do that?" she asked.

The beeps continued, becoming louder and higher pitched.

"No, it's not!" Payne shouted. "Duck and cover!"

Beast and Yvette didn't need to hear that twice, both of them rushing to hide behind a chair. Payne grabbed hold of Ivy, intent on getting the both of them to safety. They both ducked behind a different chair, as the device exploded. A wave of heat washed over the room before some force began to pull at the recliner Payne and Ivy tried to use as their refuge. Poking her head around the chair, Ivy could see a huge portal swirling in the center of the room.

"Aw, what the hell...?" she grumbled.

The girl wasn't exactly distressed, or even shocked.

"Ivy, what the hell did you do?" Yvette called from across the room, as she and Beast tried to hold onto something.

Unfortunately, the only thing they could really cling to was the chair they were hiding behind, and that wasn't exactly nailed down.

"How should I know? Hey, major pain, what's going on?"

The officer cleared her throat. "It's 'Marjorie,' and you just opened up a rift in time and space!"

Before anyone could get another word out, the chair Marjorie and Ivy used as the cover was torn away, disappearing into the portal. Rather than be appeased by the offering of a chair, like some other entities might be, the portal swirled even faster. Bolts of lightning emerged, one striking a wall just centimeters from Beast's ear. The oldest of the trio yelped. Yvette held onto Beast's waist, soon using a spell to try and anchor the both of them in place.

As for the other pair, Ivy tried to use her own abilities to keep herself and the officer from being sucked in. It required a bit more focus on her part than it did for Yvette, however.

Her focus went away within seconds, the portal tearing her and Officer Payne from their spot in the corner. The force with which they were pulled toward the swirling vortex was enough to knock the younger of the two out. Payne, being a time-based cop and all, had no such trouble with it.

"Dammit!" Yvette yelled, her own focus breaking as she saw her sister get sucked in.

That little lapse in focus was enough for the portal to take the two of them as well, the pair also losing consciousness as they entered the portal. The last thing on their mind, aside (of course) from concern for their friend, was uncertainty as to where—or when—they would land.

May 2018

The first thing Beast was aware of was the warm breeze against her neck. Second was the concrete below her, She groaned, her pale blue eyes working themselves open. Okay, so, time to get her bearings.

Yvette was a foot or so away from her, the witch pushing herself into a sitting position. She had a light scrape on her cheek, a scratch or two in her uniform, and her hair was a mess. Beast hoped there wasn't a mirror anywhere nearby, or Yvette would probably be aghast.

"Wait. Is Ivy anywhere nearby?" Yvette asked, looking around for the third member of their group.

Beast stood up, her legs shaking a bit. She grabbed hold of the nearest wall for support, frowning a bit at the scraped knee she'd sustained. Reaching down, she pulled a stocking back up to her thigh where it belonged, hiding the scrape effectively. She started looking around as well, taking a few moments to get her legs back in working order.

From an initial scan of their environment, Beast and Yvette could see that they were in an alley. Noticing a window nearby, they looked inside. People were walking along, all of whom wore lab coats. On a distant wall were various awards and certifications. The floor was comprised of alternating light and dark aqua-hued tiles.

"Hey, is that the lab?" Yvette asked.

"So, what, we ended up back home?" Beast replied. "We get pulled through a damn portal to who-knows-where…and we end up in our own freaking hometown. What a rip-off!"

Yvette pushed a bit of hair behind an ear. "Now, we don't know that, necessarily. There's a good chance we're not even in our home dimension. Who knows? This might be the Hell Bent where everything's run by a giant bird or one where the Nazis actually won…"

As Beast tried to formulate a response, she could hear something heavy landing on concrete. Her ear twitched, and she turned toward the mouth of the alley. That clang could be heard again, and again. Almost like footsteps, and they just got louder.

And that was when she saw her.

The woman walking by was short, though rather well-endowed. Her right eye was missing…or she just enjoyed wearing eyepatches. Either one of those would make sense to her, somehow. Her legs and arms were bulky and metal, painted red with pale blue streaks. Her arms were likewise bulky, red-painted metal, though her right hand ended in three long steel claws. But a good look at her long dark hair, fluffy black tail, and black feline ears got her thinking.

"Holy crap, I think that's me!"

Yvette gasped at the realization. "Do you think we're in the future, or a different dimension? What year is it, do you know?"

The cat-girl's ears flattened, and she turned back to her friend. "I know about as much about this place...time...whatever as you do. The hell makes you think I'd know what fucking year it is?"

"True."

Overwhelmed with curiosity, Beast began to walk toward her cybernetic counterpart, her tail twitching. Yvette followed.

"Are you sure this is a good idea?" she asked. "What if you and her are the same person, from the same timeline? I'm no expert, but doesn't that cause bad stuff to happen or whatever?"

Beast paused, considering this. "Maybe...only one way to find out, though."

'Don't you dare, Beast...' a familiar voice stated in her head.

"Ivy? Where are you right now?"

Her question was answered when the girl in question stood at the end of the alley, her slim arms crossed. Her turquoise eyes were narrowed, as she stared the two of them down. There was something slightly different about her. She didn't seem much older at all, but her hips were a bit wider. Her hair seemed to be more voluminous, as well. And she had started muttering to herself in a few different languages.

Yvette strode toward her, with every intention of hugging her sister. But this Ivy grabbed her wrist as soon as she was close.

"Um, Ivy, what year is this?" Beast asked as Yvette pulled her wrist from her sister's grip.

The psychic took the flask from her hip, taking a long drink from it. "Well, guys. The year's 2018. Yes, you're in the timeline you know, but it's, like, the future. And you're here because younger me screwed something up. Beast, avoid talking to future you, all right? Because that will mess things up. Badly. Like, you two touch each other, one of you explodes, it takes out an entire city block, and I'm pretty sure that's something we'd all like to avoid, y'know?"

The pair from the past blinked, perplexed. "Is that what happened to past you?" Yvette asked.

A chuckle. "Really, 'Vette, what makes you think that happened? Does it look like any part of the city's a wreck?"

"To be fair, there are other blocks…"

"No. No, I didn't meet past-me. I'm…" She paused. "I landed somewhere back in the 1950s. With that damn time cop."

Yvette's eyes widened, and she sprang forward, gripping Ivy's shoulders. "Can you tell us everything? Please? Like how you got out of that time period and back to the present? Would this even count as the present to you? It feels weird calling our future the present. Wait, would it still be our future if we don't get this resolved?"

Ivy pushed her away. "Damn, 'Vette…calm the hell down, would you? I don't have a full picture of the situation. And I can't really communicate with past me. I'm just going off of what I'd have to remember from then, if that makes sense."

Beast nodded. "So…any idea what to do, here?" she asked. "I mean, you clearly had to get out of that situation, or else we wouldn't be having this conversation. But we also wouldn't be in this situation if it weren't for y—"

"That is beside the point!" Ivy snapped. "Anyway, our best lead would be to poke around some of the labs. I know Serena's messed with time travel before, but she's kinda sworn that off…"

Before Beast could utter another word, Ivy started leading the pair out of that alley. She hoped that they would be able to avoid that timeline's Beast. She still had no idea if some disaster would, in fact, occur if the past and future versions of her were to meet. It wasn't like she was an expert in quantum physics or anything like that. The only thing she really considered herself an expert in was murder (well, that and booze).

But they would go to Dr. Serena Taylor's lab and see what she could tell them of her brief dabble into the tricky realm of time travel.

Beast looked forward to seeing how her sister was doing in this time, whereas Yvette couldn't help but imagine the doctor having a good old-fashioned freak-out over the entire situation.

May 1953

The feeling of her arms being pulled behind her brought Ivy back into reality. Sniffing a bit, she could tell that she was outside somewhere and that the grass had been cut recently. Her eyes wrenched themselves open, and she tried to get a good look behind her.

Great...

The time cop was there and was putting her in handcuffs. Her semi-conscious state jumped straight to full wakefulness, and she nearly leaped to her feet. Her turquoise eyes narrowed at Officer Payne.

"What gives?" the assassin demanded.

Marjorie hoisted her to her feet, a hand on her shoulder. She was grumbling to herself.

"You're under arrest, is what gives," she told her. "You can't expect to steal from an agent of the ATR and destroy ATR property without repercussions, you realize."

The officer started pushing her along, storming toward the sidewalk. Ivy tried to focus on pushing her away with her powers. But there was one slight issue...her abilities weren't working. Period. She took a few breaths, trying to wrap her head around this. Officer Payne's thoughts didn't reach her mind at all, an eerie silence replacing it.

Marjorie chuckled a bit as she saw Ivy focusing on her.

"You trying to use those powers of yours, Sangre?"

Ivy scoffed. "And what if I am?"

"Those cuffs were specifically designed to inhibit the powers of anyone they're placed on. See, people like you? Those with super-human abilities can't always be trusted. We've had issues with them escaping in the past."

She blinked. "...But what if we're in the past now? Wouldn't those be issues in the future?"

"I don't believe I asked for your input, Sangre," Officer Payne muttered, giving her a light slap to the back of the head.

"Ow, child abuse!" Ivy shot back.

"Let's just find out which era we're in and get ourselves back to our proper era."

Officer Payne led her crook around. They passed through a suburb, past the white picket fences and pristine homes of Hell Bent's residential area. In a backyard, the two saw a woman with a sizable belly, hanging laundry on a clothesline. Her soft purple short-sleeved dress looked like something right out of the 40s or 50s. Ivy couldn't be sure; Yvette was more of an expert with stuff like fashion. The woman's brown and black hair was styled in curls, pinned to her head. She didn't even notice the two newcomers.

"Excuse me! Ma'am?" Marjorie called, striding confidently toward the yard.

The woman jumped slightly, before turning toward the pair. Her pale red eyes looked over the slim time cop and the annoyed-looking teenager beside her. And then she focused right on the officer.

"...Care to explain what's going on here?" she asked. "Who are you, why are you here, and why do you have a kid in handcuffs?"

It took everything Ivy had not to make a smartass remark. But in the end, that wasn't good enough.

"This lady's insane and thinks she's a cop," she said. "But to be honest, she's kind of a—"

Marjorie cleared her throat, a firm hand on Ivy's shoulder. "I assure you, ma'am, I am an actual officer of the Agency of Temporal Relations."

"Still sounds made up to me..." Ivy muttered.

"I would like to know where we are, and what year it is. If you wouldn't mind, of course."

The woman narrowed her eyes, pulling a flask from the pocket of her apron and taking a drink. Her eyes flared a light red color for a moment, causing Ivy to blink. She studied the two of them for a moment, before nodding somewhat.

"My husband won't be home for a couple hours," she said. "So, if you would come with me, Officer Payne, I might be able to help you out."

Marjorie stepped back, eying this woman with suspicion. Ivy, on the other hand, was intrigued.

"Are you a mind-reader, outta curiosity?" she asked.

The woman didn't answer, instead ushering the pair into her house. The house itself was practically spotless, with the living room's pristine white carpet and light gray walls. The red sofa and chairs looked as though they were fresh from the showroom, and a small TV set with a wooden casing and a pair of antennae.

She gestured for the pair to sit on the sofa, before settling on one of the chairs, herself. Folding her hands on her lap, she looked at the two.

"To answer your question, Ivy, yes, I am a mind-reader. And given that your last name is Sangre as opposed to Smith, I'd say that I'm having a girl and that you're my granddaughter."

Ivy blinked. "Huh...cool. But wait...do you have that weird blood thing?"

"Alcohol?"

"Yeah."

"Yes, I do. And I'm not the first in the family," the woman replied. "Anyhow, you're in 1953, in Hell Bent. My name, by the way, is Lucille."

As Ivy thought about the fact that they had just met her grandmother, Officer Payne stood, clearing her throat. She looked at Lucille, giving her the most no-nonsense expression, she could muster.

"You see, Mrs. Smith, I am Officer Marjorie Payne of the Agency of Temporal Relations. Your granddaughter is in deep trouble. She stole from an officer of the law, broke that officer's property, and has single-handedly sent the two of us back in time. We came in from 1992."

Lucille nodded, before looking to Ivy. "Is this true?"

The teen scoffed. "She's the one that said my friends and me—"

"My friends and *I*," Marjorie corrected. "Even your grammar, child..."

A roll of the eyes. "Look, the point here is, Major Pain here said that we were too young to be out assassinating someone. Like we hadn't gone through a few years of extensive training. I dunno about you, but I really don't like when someone talks down to me like that, y'know?"

Lucille nodded again. "I do, however, agree that fifteen is a bit young to be a murderess."

Marjorie gave a triumphant smirk.

"But you shouldn't discount their training. They might be more competent than you realize."

The smirk faded back into a scowl, Ivy grinning at her. Marjorie cleared her throat, looking at Lucille once more.

"Would you happen to know of anyone working with time travel around here? The ATR was, after all, founded in 1954, in this very city, and that technology doesn't simply pop up out of nowhere. It needs to be developed over time."

Lucille smoothed out the skirt of her dress, thinking on that one. She didn't exactly know about which labs in that city did what, but she figured that this officer could figure it out.

"If you look around for a bit, you may find the right lab. I wish I could be more help."

Marjorie nodded, smoothing any wrinkles from her uniform. "One way you can help is to keep an eye on the kid. I'd rather she didn't get in the way. Now, would you happen to know where I could find a lab that specializes in quantum physics?"

Ivy could have sworn she heard crickets chirping somewhere nearby. Or perhaps it was just her own imagination filling in the silence. Lucille merely shook her head, as Marjorie shrugged.

"No matter. I'll be back as soon as I find what I'm looking for."

Officer Payne strode toward the door, leaving the teen and her grandmother alone. They watched her go, unsure about where to find what Marjorie wanted, themselves.

May 2018

Serena's ears twitched as the trio entered her lab. She looked almost identical to Beast, save for the fact that she still had glasses. Her hair was a bit shorter, extending only to mid-back, and her tail considerably less fluffy. She pushed up her blue-lensed glasses, looking at them with some amount of surprise.

"Yvette..." she murmured. "Didn't expect to see you again. I'd ask if you managed to escape, but that doesn't explain Beast...Feels weird to see her without my enhancements."

Beast rubbed the back of her neck, her tail flicking idly behind her. Yvette tilted her head to the side, wondering just what Serena was talking about. Ivy cleared her throat. Time to explain things here, then.

"Well, Serena..." she began. "Time travel's sort of involved, here. Someone—or rather, I—managed to mess something up."

"Ivy, what the hell did you do?" Serena sighed, her pale blue eyes narrowing at the psychic.

Beast went on to describe what had occurred between them and Officer Marjorie Payne: the time travel device, the argument, the theft, and the fallout. The scientist listened intently, before muttering under her breath.

"So, you mean to tell me that someone's successfully figured out this whole time travel thing?" she asked. "Any idea who it is? I want to compare notes. See where I screwed up last time..."

Ivy leaned against one of the smooth steel walls, pulling out her flask again. "Yeah, I've got no idea, either. But it probably wouldn't hurt to ask if you'd know where to start looking. What do you remember about your last experience with time travel?"

A chuckle. "Aside from that portal ripping open, bringing forth a monster, and the neighbors' house being demolished? Nothing much.

I haven't destroyed the notes, but I'm not exactly inclined to hunt them down again just yet, either."

Beast crossed her arms, looking at her now much-older twin sister. Her eyes narrowed a bit. "Serena, please, help us out with this? It's a matter of life and death. Seriously. See, we were on a job. After this woman named Darlena Williams. She's been trying to get her hands on some sort of doomsday weapon or whatever, so she could go through to different periods of time and start committing genocide. Her bid to make sure there're enough resources for everyone, apparently."

Serena scoffed, shaking her head. Beast's ears flattened, and she growled for a second.

"What, you don't believe me?"

"Oh, no, I believe you. It's just that there's no way that sort of plan would work out. It makes no sense. I'm not sure which labs around here would've perfected time travel...but what I do know is that there was a lab around here in the early 50s that dealt with all things nuclear. For that entire decade, the city of Hell Bent was a hub for that sort of thing."

Ivy nearly dropped her flask in response, and she walked over to Serena. A grin crossed her face, and she just started laughing a bit. Yvette wondered if her own much-older twin had cracked.

"Would it have been around in 1953, by any chance?" she asked.

"Yes. Why?"

"That's where 1992 me is!"

Yvette smiled. "In that case, and since you seem to have memories of that time and all...you remembered to split the pay with Beast and me, right?"

To that, Ivy was unresponsive. Her eyes rolled back in her head before she collapsed right there on the floor. Yvette rushed to her, sighing in relief as she found a pulse. She didn't hear the dull thud just outside of the door. Beast, on the other hand, did, and rushed to the door, Serena in tow. And both of them gasped in shock at what sat before them.

It was Yvette, albeit an older version of her. Her heart had been removed, and decomposition had already started to kick in. Beast was generally accustomed to death. It was what she was trained in, and most bodies had absolutely no effect on her.

But Yvette was one of her closest friends, and she held a hand to her mouth, trying everything she could not to vomit. Her legs were shaking, and a few tears were starting to stream down her cheeks. Serena pulled her sister back inside, likewise shaken over this whole thing.

"What just happened...?" Beast asked. "What...what's going on?"

Serena pushed up her glasses with a sigh. "I really don't know, Beast..."

They had to wonder...did this mean that Darlena had succeeded in her goal?

1953

Officer Payne explored the many laboratories in Hell Bent. There were a few on each street. She passed by one that had a large sculpture of a hydrogen atom on its roof, and that caught her attention for a bit. But she would have to check that out later. Her first priority was to find a way to get through time. She knew that the ATR wouldn't be founded for another year or so, but that research still had to be to a certain point by then. They had, after all, spent several months trying to figure out what to do with their findings.

As she started walking past the building with the atom on top, she could see someone walking in like she owned the place. The woman looked a bit out of place for 1953. She was wearing leg warmers, for one thing. And the flowing bell sleeves of her off-the-shoulder blouse were likewise not very 1950s-ish. Marjorie's eyes narrowed.

Darlena.

The time cop began to follow her inside, pulling out her sidearm as she entered. Said sidearm was a non-lethal sort of thing, meant to stun its target. She would track Darlena down, subdue her, and then find a way to travel to her rightful timeline with both of her detainees.

She needed to solve this. She needed to bring Williams in, herself. That woman had murdered her partner in cold blood when she broke into the ATR's headquarters in the first place. Marjorie's partner was young, a rookie of no more than seventeen. The girl had tried to stop her but was quickly taken out. Her own time travel multi-tool had been taken when she fell, thus giving Darlena Williams what she wanted.

And so, Officer Marjorie Payne had to be the one to bring this monster to justice. The target walked ahead of her by a few yards, which soon became a few feet, which eventually became inches.

"Attention, Darlena Williams. I'm Officer Payne of the Agency of Temporal Relations. Stand down, and I can bring you in without any pain for either of us. Deal?"

The strawberry blonde woman with genocidal designs turned, arching an eyebrow at this woman. She pulled her firearm from the waistband of her pants, pointing it at Payne. Her eyes narrowed.

"No deal, officer. What I'm doing here is right, and you'd do well to step off and let me complete my goal. If I take out enough of the population over generations, that should help keep the future population under control. It's a culling that needs to happen."

"It's *madness*, Williams! Don't you realize this?" Payne demanded.

Darlena shrugged, firing the pistol at her confronter's face. The round entered right between the eyes, killing her instantly. The other woman walked away, intent on finding just the perfect weaponry to take through time with her. She would start with the Roman Empire, then move on to each major empire from there. Who knew? Maybe she could make a name for herself through the eras...become some sort of supreme empress of the world. Though that may have been a bit ambitious for her liking... She wasn't entirely sure on that, but she wouldn't rule it out.

Back with Ivy and Lucille, the latter had decided to let her granddaughter out of the handcuffs. It felt strange to have her future grandchild there with her, particularly when her own child hadn't been born yet. But to have that same grandchild handcuffed in her parlor? She wouldn't hear of it.

The woman poured a glass of brandy for her, figuring she could use her strength. Ivy was more partial to vodka, but she wasn't one to turn down a good drink. And as she downed the contents of the glass, she blinked.

"Does something feel weird to you?" the teen asked.

Lucille's eyes glowed for a few moments, and she nodded. "That officer's in trouble...you might want to go to her. She might appreciate the help."

"Where?" Ivy asked.

"One of the labs downtown. I imagine you'd have an easier time tracking them when you get closer."

She finished off the drink, bolting out of the door without another word. Lucille watched her go, huffing with some level of indignation. That may have been her future granddaughter, and she might have been going off to hopefully prevent a disaster...but did she really have to be so rude about leaving? Really, leaving without so much as a 'Thank you'?

As Darlena Williams strode through the lab, she considered her options. She would have to find some way to transport her weapons to the intended eras, so she wished to avoid anything massive. But locating anything small enough that she could carry four at a time? That was proving to be difficult. Perhaps she'd miscalculated. Maybe she should have picked a different time period.

She took a few more steps before something made her stop in her tracks. An invisible force had snagged a hold of her, and she gasped in surprise. That same force slammed her into the floor, and she looked up to see Ivy approaching her. The younger of the two glared down at her, eyes glowing.

When Ivy showed up, it was a minute or so after Officer Payne was gunned down. She'd cursed herself for being a bit too late but didn't take time to dwell on that. While Payne might have been...well, a pain, she didn't deserve that. Not like the monster she was here to take out.

Darlena tried to move, but Ivy wasn't about to allow that. She pulled a sword from a sheath on her back, wasting no time in running

Williams through with it. Once her opponent lay dead on the floor, she wiped off her blade on the leg of her uniform, then re-sheathed it. She rummaged through the woman's pockets, found a device identical to the one she'd stolen earlier, and walked away. Maybe she could find a way to get back to her time or find where the others had disappeared to.

Yes, she wanted to find where Beast and Yvette ended up. That felt important to her. As she walked through the streets, she scrolled through some of the options on the device. She decided on the year 2020, figuring that if she went for a time in the future, someone might know how to look for specific people through time. And 2020 Hell Bent was probably her best bet, anyway, given the city's emphasis on science.

She activated the device, a portal appearing before her. It felt odd, creating this thing intentionally. But she stepped through it, hoping that the landing would be quite a bit smoother than the one that had dumped her into the 50s.

June 2020

Ivy's hopes of a smoother landing were dashed as she landed flat on her face. She stood up shakily, trying not to lose the contents of her stomach. And she was trying to get a good look at where she was.

It was blurry, but she could see concrete below her. She was…was it in a parking lot? Where, exactly, was she, anyway? And why did it feel like someone was poking her in the arm?

Turning, she saw a man standing behind her, his green eyes wide with curiosity and…shock, it seemed like. He had extremely long red hair, which had to be at least twenty feet in length. A monkey-like tail protruded from his back end, and he had to have at least twenty piercings.

"Ivy? Is…is that really you?"

She blinked. Who was this monkey man, and why did he know her name? Ivy backed away. "I have no idea who you are…"

His tail drooped. "But...but we were together for five years. You died a week ago...did that make you forget? Is there any way I can help you jog your memory?"

She slammed him against the brick wall of a nearby pizza restaurant with her powers. This man was freaking her out a bit.

"I'm fifteen, creep! What's going on here, anyway?"

The redhead backed off. "I'm so sorry...I take it you went through time?"

She nodded, going for her flask. She wondered just what was going on, though.

"So, you know about time travel, huh?"

"Yeah. I know about you killing some genocidal maniac. We met when I was twenty, hit it off well, got into a relationship...and then the explosion happened. I took a few days to recover, but you never did. You became sort of despondent after your sister died but managed to hold on for a couple years. We got closer during those years."

Well, this was a lot to take in...she had a half-monkey boyfriend for a while, died in an explosion, lost Yvette...

But she completed the job, at least. So that was a plus, right?

The girl patted her apparent future boyfriend on the shoulder. He was honestly sort of attractive, she had to admit. But she wasn't here for him. She wanted to figure out where in the timeline her sister and Beast were.

"Would you know where I could find the ATR's headquarters or whatever?" she asked, looking up at the monkey man.

He scratched the back of his head, his tail flicking a little. "That time travel thingy?"

"Yes."

The monkey man started walking. "That'd be this way, Ivy."

She followed his lead, looking around at how the region had changed. And to be honest, not much had changed in the area. There were still labs on every street, the tall towers of the schools still loomed over everything...the sidewalk looked new, but it was almost always that way.

Well, that was a disappointment.

Eventually, he had led her to a building she actually had never seen before. Fuchsia lights crisscrossed the windows, standing out against the darkness of the rest of the building. Ivy looked for the door, thanked the monkey man for his help, and walked in. He considered going in with her, but she turned him away. He figured it was best not to go in, in retrospect. He never knew when they might find a way to experiment on him there.

Ivy walked into the lobby of the ATR's offices, striding across the glowing fuchsia tiles and up to the desk. A receptionist, her hair pulled into a neat bun, popped her gum at the girl.

"Whaddya need?" she asked.

"I was wondering who I might talk to about finding someone that's been taken through time?" Ivy replied. "There was an accident, you see..."

"Third floor."

The teen walked through the building, making her way to the stairs and up to the floor in question. As she reached the third floor, she noticed a wall with a number of names. Upon further inspection, she noticed that she remembered one of those names. Marjorie Payne. Killed In Action, 1953. With a sigh, she continued down the hallway. Room after room lined the hall.

Eventually, she stopped by one of the rooms. Room number 616 was devoted to Location of Individuals. Perfect. She opened the door, not bothering to knock as she sauntered her way in there. The scientists at work jumped, a few glaring as she entered.

One rose from a chair, striding toward the girl. "What is it you want?" she asked.

"Hey...I was hoping to locate my sister and our friend, and this felt like the place to go about it."

The scientist pulled one of those time travel devices from her lab coat, using it to scan Ivy for her identity. "Hm...this seems wrong somehow..."

"What?"

"This says that you're from 1992."

Ivy chuckled. "Yeah, time travel does that…"

"But that doesn't match up to your birth records at all, Ms. Sangre. You're from 1992, born in 1975. But if we cross-reference that with your birth records, it says that you were born in 1972."

She blinked in confusion. Well, this was, indeed, weird.

"I bet you're not even in the right timeline."

Okay, now this was really weird. Alternate timeline? So, how was she to get to her own timeline if she was, in fact, in the wrong one? She definitely needed a freaking drink, now.

"If you go down the hall, you'll find a room devoted to alternate timelines. Try going there, and you may find what you're looking for."

Huh. Well, then. It seemed that time travel had advanced quite a bit since 1992. Walking through the hall, she found a door at the very end. Once more, she opened said door and strode inside without a care in the world (much to the consternation of those inside). She could sense that they weren't pleased with that, but she didn't entirely care, either. All she cared about was finding her friends.

There were five scientists glaring at her, and one with their back turned. She turned around to look at her and performed a scan on Ivy right away. The teen had gotten somewhat accustomed to that by now and waited for the doc's assessment. She typed on a keyboard, her fingers flying across the letters. On the large screen ahead of her, a long list of numbers and words scrolled through. It nearly made Ivy dizzy to watch it.

"You're in an entirely different timeline from the friends you know, Sangre. After you killed Darlena Williams, things shifted."

She raised an eyebrow. "But…but I did my job, right? That shouldn't, y'know, screw the timeline too badly, right?"

"Thanks to that, you were all able to retire early."

"And the downside?"

"Other reprehensible types got out there. Tons of casualties."

She groaned. "Well, you know what would've happened if I didn't kill her, right?"

The scientist typed something else, and a scene was displayed of Darlena obtaining what she had come for. Ivy saw herself there as well, dead at Williams' feet. And then the real fun began, as Williams got to ancient Rome and set off one of her mini nukes there. Then again in India, Russia, China, Western Europe... She had succeeded in her goals of reducing the population. But the radiation had also demolished many of the resources, thus rendering her whole plan pointless.

Ivy was mildly unnerved about part of that. "But you see, that's why I needed to kill her! It's not like 'Vette could've done it. Who the hell knows where she ended up, anyway?"

The scientist typed something up. "There is another timeline out there, where your sister does, indeed, kill her."

And then that scene started to play out. A portal opened as Ivy was confronting Darlena. Darlena nearly shot Ivy, but Yvette managed to shoot her just in time to avoid this fate. Things flashed forward a few years, to the year 2016. In that one, the Nazis came to power in the US. And the new mayor of Hell Bent was not only in that party, but he also seemed to be an angry bird.

She blinked. "...Okay, so how in the hell is that better than me managing to do my job? Because from the sound of it, it feels like that's the best option."

"We've found no timeline in which she doesn't manage to kill Officer Payne," the scientist said. "There is, however, one more timeline..."

More typing and another scene started up, text scrolling quickly along the side. This one had both Yvette and Beast in that lab with Ivy, with Beast slaughtering the target horribly. Yvette cleaned up the mess, as usual. And then they saw how things played out in the future. The three worked together until 2017 or so when Yvette was taken from them.

"So, I'm guessing that's the best possible timeline to go with, then?" she asked.

"It would appear so," the scientist began.

"And which one are they in now?"

More typing again. They were in 2018, looking extremely confused with a dead older Yvette outside and an unconscious older

Ivy on the floor. An older Beast had walked into the lab, shocked upon seeing a younger version of herself. Rubbing the back of her neck, Ivy sighed.

"Could anyone send me to some time before that happened?" she asked.

"Search for May 13, 2018, just outside of the HBPD labs, 2:19 in the afternoon."

Ivy nodded, taking the device she'd retrieved from Darlena and typing a bit. Though she decided it might be best to go back to March 1992, before they encountered Officer Payne in the first place. After thinking about it, though, she went to the time mentioned to her by the scientist. The other way might further screw up the timeline, and to be honest, she didn't want to bring about a zombie apocalypse inadvertently. Chances were that if she had done that, she wouldn't be around to enjoy slaughtering the zombies, anyway.

May 13, 2018, 2:19 PM

The portal opened, as Ivy stumbled through and landed near another portal. That other portal spat Beast and Yvette out onto the sidewalk, the pair somewhat out of sorts. Yvette was the first to notice Ivy rising to her feet, rushing over and hugging her tightly.

Ivy returned the hug, having a hard time breathing as Beast got to her.

"We thought we'd lost you when those portals opened up! Are you okay?" Yvette asked.

"Yep, I'm good. But we kinda need to get to 1953, so Beast can kill Williams. It can't be me, 'cause the future doesn't look good from there. And it can't be Yvette, because things get *really* bleak from there. You don't wanna know how bad."

Before either of them could argue, Ivy ran a search on the device for the day that she killed Darlena Williams. May 21, 1953, 4:11pm. The three got sucked through one more portal. Ivy looked forward to when this whole affair was over with. She was getting sick of going through portal after portal.

May 21, 1953 4:11 PM

The trio appeared in the lab. They saw the younger Ivy facing off with Williams, focused on her. Beast looked at the Ivy that was there with them, eyebrow cocked.

"You look like you've got it under control…"

"I shouldn't, though," Ivy replied. "Now go!"

She shoved Beast toward Darlena, pouncing at her other self right after. Ivy shoved Other Ivy to the floor, breaking the girl's concentration. Other Ivy yelped in shock, blinking as the one version of herself punched her in the face, over and over. Yvette watched in almost horrified amazement, still trying to wrap her head around the whole time travel thing.

As for Beast, she clawed at Darlena's back when she turned away from the scene. A bad idea, turning one's back on a trained assassin. As she turned to face Beast, the cat-girl plunged the claws on her gloves through the target's chest. The tips got right to her heart, puncturing it right away. It took some effort to push her off of her claws, but she'd managed. She wiped the blades off on her skirt, watching as Other Ivy faded from beneath the one she'd traveled with.

"So…did that fix things?" Beast asked.

She noticed that a bit of blood was still on one of her claws, licking that off. A red light washed over the room, removing all evidence that they were there. That was a spell of Yvette's own creation and something of which she was rather proud.

"Yeah, all good now," said Ivy. "Should be, anyway. All right, let's get back home."

March 1992, Five Minutes After The Portal Incident

Ivy, Beast, and Yvette emerged from what they sincerely hoped would be the last time-related portal any of them would have to deal with for a while. They were back in the room from which they'd started, though it was now missing two of the three chairs that used to be in there. Papers had been strewn about, and Beast could see claw marks in the floor, likely from where she'd tried to grab onto something to anchor herself. Yvette collapsed into the remaining chair. Ivy lay on her back, ready to fall asleep. Beast sat on the floor beside them, knees drawn up to her chest. She looked down at her friend, curious.

"So...what kinds of things did you see, going through time?" she asked.

Ivy shrugged. "Saw grandma, I guess. Still no idea who our mom is, and don't exactly care."

"You saw yourself fade away...you okay?" Beast's tail flicked next to Ivy's head.

She reached out and gripped the fluffy tail in question, chuckling somewhat. "I'm fine, Beasty. It's honestly not the most traumatic thing ever. Not after...y'know, childhood in the lab."

Beast cringed. "Ugh, yeah, I hear that..."

Ivy dozed off, for the time being, Beast following suit. She would have to ask later about those other futures. But for now, it was time to rest. Yvette reported their success to their client, and their $30,000 would be wired to them overnight. The witch relaxed after that, joining her sisters in arms in their rest.

THE END

ABOUT K. MATT

K. Matt is both an author and an illustrator, with an affinity for animation, horror, sci-fi, and B-movies. She resides in Upstate New York, and writes as a way to escape that. Or vent her frustrations. It all depends on the day, really. Her main work is the Hell Bent series of graphic novel/prose novella hybrids.

 facebook.com/HellBentBookSeries

twitter.com/MarieTwixie

instagram.com/kmatt666

COFFEE

BY BOB JAMES

Steam rose from my mug as I looked out my office window at the Pacific Ocean. The gray fog blanketed the ocean, swirling in the ocean breezes. The fog calmed me, and I took a sip of my coffee. I looked down at the traffic. Most of the people of Los Angeles still used land cars, so the city was a giant parking lot during the early morning rush hour. Those who had the flying cars enjoyed a lot of freedom.

I drained the last drops of coffee from my mug and frowned. "Coffee time's about over." I turned and took one last wistful glance out the window and headed back to my desk.

I was about to sit down when my aide walked in carrying a coffee pot. "Commander Friday, you may need more coffee. There's a call for you on line one. The Time Managers." He looked worried. "It's Angus."

I exhaled deeply. "First things first, Harry. We've worked together long enough that you can call me Jack. That promotion didn't end our friendship or our partnership." I shook my head as I thought about how many times Sargent Gannon had pulled me out of trouble on the field even before we joined the Time Protection Division. "Second, you're right. I do need more coffee. You've gotten so much better at making coffee than when you were a rookie."

"That ain't saying much, but thanks Com...er...Jack." Then he laughed as he looked at my mug. "That mug still cracks me up."

I lifted it up in salute. "It was a nice promotion gift, especially so, given all the coffee I drink. It's true that for me, 'There's always time for coffee.'" Harry was proud of his little joke. I held the mug out for him to fill it. "Any info on what Angus wants to talk about?"

"No, sir. He seemed to be a bit anxious. He probably won't be too happy about how long you've taken to answer the phone." Harry finished pouring the coffee and went toward the front part of the office. "He never calls just to pass the time of day, though." He closed the door behind him as he left.

He's right. None of them do, I thought as I sat down and put the phone on speaker. "Friday. What can I do for you, Angus?"

"We've got a situation, Commander. I need to talk with you in person. I'll be there in a minute."

Must be important if he's coming down, I thought. I looked at my conference table. I still had boxes from moving into my new office sitting on the chairs. Those boxes! I panicked. I ran to the table and picked up the box on the chair next to my usual seat. I took it back to my desk and put it in the kneehole. I scurried back and forth with box after box, wanting to be sure that Angus didn't catch me with souvenirs of my cases. He frowned upon his agents keeping relics from the past.

I was securing the last box when the knock reverberated throughout the room. Before I could answer, the door swung open. "Hey! You can't just barge in like that." Harry still tried to protect me.

"I'm sure Commander Friday doesn't mind. He's expecting us."

"Thanks, Harry," I said, trying to smooth things over. "For future reference, the Commissioner and his chiefs are always welcome to come in." I made a mental note to put the artifacts in a much safer place. "Come and sit down, gentlemen," I said, noting the presence of Chief Bradford also. "Harry, could I ask you to get some coffee for the Commissioner and the chief?"

"Yes, sir, Commander." No one followed protocol like Harry. "Cream and/or sugar?" he asked them.

I shuddered when they both nodded. They may be my bosses, but coffee should be drunk black. I was glad that they missed my shudder while they were looking back at Harry.

When I set my coffee mug down, Angus laughed. "'There's Always Time for Coffee.' Cute. Where'd you find it?"

"Harry. He thought it was a good way to celebrate my promotion."

"Might be a good gift for my chiefs." He looked at Bradford. "Not a word."

Bradford's response was to pull the invisible zipper across his lips without cracking a smile. I don't think Bradford ever told or got a joke in his life. I would have had a hard time looking at him wearing those orange board shorts with a yellow Hawaiian shirt and believing that if I hadn't worked with him over the years.

––––––––

Harry came in with the tea tray and set it down on the table. "I don't know how much milk or sugar you like, so I thought you'd want to fix your own," he said as he pointed to the milk pitcher and sugar bowl. "And the lemons are in this bowl here." He took the cover off another bowl to show the lemons. "Commander, you'll use your regular cup, I presume?"

I lifted my teacup in salute. Harry always found the funniest cups.

Angus lifted an eyebrow. I could tell he was amused. "'Time begins with Tea.' Quite clever. Did you find this cup, Harry?"

"Yes, sir," Harry smiled at the compliment and stepped away from the table, staying close enough to be available if we needed him.

Bradford cocked his head. "Angus?" he pointed his chin at Harry.

Angus looked at me. "Do you have any reason to doubt Harry's integrity?"

"No, sir. I'd trust him with my life. I bounce ideas off him all the time."

Angus shrugged. "I'm guessing Jack would discuss plans with Harry after we left." When I nodded, he turned to Bradford. "He can stay. Commander Friday will need someone to talk to. Best he have all the information."

We'd discussed my teacup, but I still hadn't filled my cup. I remedied the situation while waiting on Angus to begin, adding milk and sugar. I watched Angus because I'd forgotten how he liked his tea. When neither Angus nor Bradford started fixing their tea, I jumped in. "The tea's going to get cold, gentlemen."

Bradford almost burst out laughing, ok, he stopped frowning for a half a second, but that's close to laughing for him. "I'd prefer coffee."

Angus rolled his eyes. "Wait five minutes for once, will ya?" he griped at Bradford.

Before Angus could explain it to me, I jumped in. "A joke Bradford. Well done. Next trip back in time, I'll pick up some coffee for you." I snort-laughed and added, "That's if I go back to 2036 or before." I'd heard that the last gasp of coffee in 2037 was too bitter to drink.

"You could do that," Angus said. "Or, you could solve the Time Fluctuation."

"I'm guessing that's what you came to talk with me about?"

Bradford nodded. "Right now, time is fluctuating every five or ten minutes. We need you to figure out why we have the fluctuations and fix it."

"Why do you need me when you have such specific information?" I've been told that my sarcasm would keep me from ever being a Time Manager. That didn't bother me.

Angus rubbed his chin. "It seems to me that someone who loves coffee as much as you do would be anxious to figure out what's happening?"

I bit my lower lip and stared at him. He didn't seem to be joking. When I tried to protest, he held up his hand to stop me.

"In the fluctuation, the major change is that this time drinks tea because coffee isn't available. The coffee blight you alluded to earlier comes to mind. The fluctuation began three days ago. While time's still fluctuating right now, you only have about 6 days and 13 hours before this time becomes permanent."

I screwed my face up and tried to stop myself, but I blurted it out.

"So, we need to stop tea time to save coffee time? Is that what you're saying?"

Bradford groaned and rolled his eyes. "Give me a break. This is no joking matter."

"Yes, sir," I saluted him, wondering if he realized that he'd made his own joke. *Nah, he doesn't have the kind of perception.* "Something stopped the coffee blight from happening in 2037 in standard time that didn't happen in flux time. I need to figure out what happened to create the time flux and keep that from happening."

Angus nodded. "You have an amazing grasp of the obvious. Get busy." He and Bradford got up to walk back to their office. "Come, Bradford. We'll take the stairs it may be coffee time when we get back to the office." He shouted back at me. "Email coming so that both yous know what's going on." He banged the door shut behind him.

I watched them leave and shook my head. "Acting like one flight of stairs is a big deal," I said. "'It may be coffee time…' What a crock." I shook my head and walked back to my desk. "Think those two will last if tough times come, Harry?" I asked Gannon, who stood off to the side, so he'd be out of the way.

"I don't know, Jack. Maybe they need a cup of coffee." We both laughed.

We laughed for a while. I forgot what we were laughing about. The computer dinged to let me know that I had an email. "The Time Managers said something about sending me an important email!" I exclaimed as I jumped up and trotted to my desk. I opened the email and put my hand over my mouth to keep from laughing.

"Was that the Time Managers' email?" Harry asked.

"Do any of them disguise themselves as 'hot, Russian girls?'"

Harry cocked his head as if thinking about it.

"Don't think too hard." I pointed at the table. "We probably need to clean off the table. Those coffee cups won't get to the sink on their own." I walked toward the table.

"Commander!" Harry's voice rang out. "You do not clear tables or wash dishes. That's my job."

"Whoa!" I was shocked. "Hadn't heard that kind of authority from you before, Harry." I laughed. "But if you insist..." I swept my arm across my chest, motioning Harry toward the dishes. When the email alert chimed again I called out to Harry, "Hey, if it's an offer for those 'magic pills,' do you want me to forward it to you?"

"Keep it up, Jack, keep it up. I can find some other detail where I can work."

I couldn't contain my laughter, so I started coughing to cover it up. I was sure that Harry had no idea what kind of joke he'd just made.

"You ok, Jack?"

"Yeah, sorry. I must have swallowed my coffee wrong," I said as I pointed at the mug.

"You had me worried," he paused and looked me in the eyes without blinking. "You were coughing pretty hard."

I stared into Harry's face. Nope, he was innocent. Those two lines were purely accidental. It was hard to keep myself from laughing, but I did the best I could as I checked the email again. This time, it was the Time Managers. "Harry, forget the coffee cups for now and get over here. This is serious."

The crash of coffee cups on the table, let me know that Harry was on his way. I pointed at the screen, my hand trembling. "There."

Harry whistled. He kept reading. Then he turned to me. "Six days, huh?" He stared into my eyes, waiting for an answer.

I shrugged. "I can't imagine why anyone would want to destroy the coffee crop. God have mercy on their soul."

"Wondering won't get us anywhere, boss. We need to do some research."

I nodded. "Yeah. We probably need to check out news stories from 2037 and before. See if there's anything about problems with the coffee crop." My coffee must have heard that comment as it's wonderful aroma reached out to me as if looking for comfort. I protected it the best I could and looked at my now empty cup. "I can only imagine..."

"If we don't get busy, all you'll be able to do is imagine stories about coffee." Harry prodded me into action. "We've got about eight minutes before the time fluctuation. We need to get some information quickly."

A sigh escaped my lips. "You're right. Let's start looking." Harry headed toward his desk, and I opened my search engine. "I'm searching 'Coffee Blight 2037.' You search 'coffee problems 2037.'"

"Got it, Jack," he yelled back. The silence fell across the office as we both searched and read, and read, and searched. After a couple of minutes, I stood up to stretch and refill my coffee mug. I thought I'd found something. Not much was left in the pot, so I got about three-quarters of a cup and gulped it down as I went back to my desk. I found the article that confirmed my hunch and pasted the text into a document. News and memories would change with the fluctuation, but what we typed and saved would pass across any time anomalies. I pressed "save" and breathed a sigh of relief.

"I got it, Jack!" Harry yelled. He came running into my part of the office. "Randall Stevenson. He saved the coffee crop."

I nodded. "Maybe the most important man the world has ever known." I grinned so that Harry knew I was exaggerating, but it wasn't much of an exaggeration. "I got the same name." We had something, or someone to go on."

Harry gave me a blank stare. He scratched his head as he thought. "Unless I'm hallucinating, the Time Managers said something about a time fluctuation."

"Right." I looked at my monitor. "According to them, this is the flux time. The coffee blight we experienced in 2037 didn't happen in standard time." I searched my files. "There." I pointed. "An unnamed file saved two minutes ago. I wonder if…" I opened the file. "Apparently, a guy named Randall Stevenson prevented the coffee blight. He worked in the Department of Agriculture. He was a deputy secretary or something like that."

"Any chance he's still around?" Harry asked. The blight struck only thirty-seven years ago.

"I'll look." I entered Randall's name and any information I could find in the search engine. "Lots of Randall Stevensons," I said, "but no one with that name and the same type of job description." That wasn't definitive since many things changed in a time fluctuation, but it was a start.

"So, what do we do now?" Harry scratched his head as if he were trying to make direct contact with his brain.

I shrugged and walked over to the windows. The smog swirled around the window, making it difficult to look down on the traffic from this height. The wind created windows in the smog that allowed me to see that traffic was still moving, but just barely. "Ever see old cartoon reruns, Harry?" The reflection in the window revealed that he was shaking his head. I turned to look at him. "They had some great ones back in the day. One of them was called 'The Jetsons.' From back in the 1960s." My eyes searched the skies again. "It portrayed a future time. They had the flying cars, but they didn't show the smog we have now." I snort laughed. "They left out a few other things too."

Harry chuckled. "No smog, eh?" His shoes clicked as he walked across the wooden floor toward me. He pointed outside. "As much smog as flying cars put out, I can only laugh."

"Good point." I nodded and smiled. Then, a light bulb went off in my head. "If the Department of Agriculture caught the problems with the coffee crop in the other timeline, maybe they caught it in this timeline and just didn't know how to stop it."

"What good would it do to have that information?" Harry asked.

"Did Stevenson just put the pieces together and gain credit for someone else's work or did he actually do the work? Maybe someone else discovered the problem and Stevenson got credit for it because he was higher up."

Harry stared at me, and a wry smile played on his lips. "I can see that happening. Higher-ups tend to get all the credit for the work the people underneath them do." He puckered his lips and nodded. When he saw my expression, he played innocent. "Oh, not you, Jack. I wasn't saying anything about you."

As my eyes burned a hole in him, I thought back through the history of our partnership. *Did I take credit that should have gone to Harry?* I couldn't remember anything like that. "I'm glad to hear that you think I've been fair, Harry. We need to search articles about the coffee blight and see what the Department of Agriculture did during this time period."

Harry nodded. "Nope, not you," he said under his breath. Then he added. "Will do, Jack. Will do." He headed back to his desk to begin his search.

Harry could be loyal and a great help. At other times, he was like a paper cut on a raw nerve. I took a deep breath and then counted to ten as I exhaled. Then I did it again. This was a two-tenner irritation. I had direct access to government databases since my promotion. I'd probably get the information before Harry did. But he didn't need to know how I got the information before he did.

There wasn't a lot of confidential information in this database, so I expected an easy retrieval of the data. Using the keywords "Coffee Production" and "2030-2037" I expected instant coffee results. I'd never gotten a message that told me my access level was too low. Until now.

"Crap!" *Great. Harry will hear that.*

I began a search of my computer looking for my password file just as Harry called out, "What's wrong, Jack?"

"Paywalls," I called out. "Hate 'em!"

"Pay the money, Jack. There's enough money in the budget." I could see Harry shaking his head and "tsk-tsking" me in my mind's eye.

"It's the principle of things, Harry." I didn't lie to Harry often, but this was a necessary lie. *What was taking my computer so long to search?*

"Those aren't principles worth dying for, Jack. We've got an important case to solve. Pay the money."

"Sure, Harry, sure. Easy for you to say," I shouted back. I clicked the icon for the administrative password file that showed up in the search engine and then copied and pasted the password into the box. The folder title made me whistle.

"What'd you find?" I could hear Harry roll his seat into his desk as he walked back. "I haven't seen anything."

"Found a backdoor into the records." I pursed my lips and pointed at the monitor as Harry came over.

"CB Investigation: Demotions and Terminations" Harry read. He looked at me. "I think they know they screwed up. Whatta you think?"

"Let's take a look," I said as I clicked it open. I chose the file named "Overview" and opened it. I glanced back at Harry, who was breathing in my ear as he looked over my shoulder while he tried to read the file. "Hey, Harry. You get much closer, and you're gonna have to take me out for dinner."

"Sorry Jack," Harry said as he straightened up. "I just don't get to read top-secret files very often. I got excited."

"Just give me some space," I snarled. Then I read the first line of the report. "The Coffee Blight of 2037 was caused by incompetence and negligence at all levels of the Department of Agriculture." I continued skimming, my eyes opening wide. I turned and looked at Harry. "Are you catching this?" I copied and pasted the information into the unnamed file while Harry read the information. I saved it as "coffee blight."

"You mean the part about the Chinese and the English orchestrating the destruction of the coffee growing areas?" Harry asked in his monotone voice. "Yeah. I guess it wasn't worth going to war over coffee."

I looked back at Harry. "There you have it." I pointed back at the monitor and read. "Randall Stevenson noticed coffee production dropping in key areas. Investigation initiated because of that observation led to diplomatic efforts that caused the Anglo-Sino alliance to cease operations to poison the coffee producing lands."

"Got him a major promotion, too," Harry added as he read down the page. "Deputy Secretary of Agriculture."

"Apparently Chinese and the British didn't think it was worth going to war over," I said as I saw that part of the action report. "So how and why did Randall Stevenson fail to exist?"

"Ok, I got it. I'll run the genealogy," Harry said just before he let out a sigh. "You'd think these guys would learn that they can't change history." He walked back to the front and began working.

Have the British or the Chinese discovered the secret to Time Travel? I wondered. I sent an email off to the Angus asking him that. If they did, that would make life much more difficult.

"How far back should I go?" Harry shouted through the doorway.

I thought. The farther back we went, the more resources it would take. Angus could probably justify a request to cover expenses for coffee in front of any congressional committee. Then I laughed. *If it was whiskey that I saved, they'd triple our budget.* "Take it back to '39," I answered. "This is coffee we're talking about." We hadn't been able to break the 1939 barrier up to now.

Harry laughed. "Yep, Congress will pay for coffee. They'd be even more willing to pay if this investigation saved whiskey."

Great minds, I thought. "Good point," I yelled. It didn't hurt me to let him think that he came up with that thought. My email alert dinged. *Angus must be concerned about this case.* I read the email. That was one potential problem taken care of. I could begin checking logs.

Military use was restricted after their forays, well-meaning of course, into fixing past events back in 2054 when we discovered time travel. They'd gone as far back as possible, that year hasn't changed since the beginning and had taken out Hitler. Our records weren't as detailed back in the independent cowboy era of time travel, but apparently, this upended history. Admiral Dönitz knew how to conduct a war from the political side, and Field Marshall Rommel led the Germans on the battlefield. The result was German occupation in England, Europe, and all of Russia until the early 1970s. Not that I told people that I saved Hitler's life. Most wouldn't understand that.

Harry came in while the computer was checking the genealogy. "While we're waiting, have you thought about checking the logs?"

"On it, Harry! I sent an email to the tourist agencies." Once news about Time Travel had leaked out, we were forced to make accommodations for public use of Time Travel. In spite of the strict restrictions on such travel, every once in a while, someone broke the rules. "I asked them to send a list of passengers for the last ten days. We only need seven, but I thought ten would be a good round number."

Harry rubbed his chin, deep in thought. "What about internal travel? Who from the agency has traveled in the last seven days?"

"Oh wow! Thanks. I forgot about that. I'll check those logs myself."

"You'd better, that's above my pay grade." Harry laughed as he said that. "I'll go check on the genealogy run."

I nodded, then turned back to the computer so I could enter my password in the program that kept our internal Time Travel logs. I entered our time range and got two names. I whistled as I read them. Then I copied and pasted them into the continuing file knowing that the time flux would be happening soon. It would be interesting to see if the time fluctuations changed those visits. Then, I waited for responses from the agencies and for Harry to bring in the genealogy report.

"Here it is, Jack!" Harry called out. I could hear the printer spitting out the pages.

"Send the file to me also," I yelled back." And put a copy in the 'coffee blight' folder."

Harry walked back to my desk. "What's the latest on the investigation?"

I opened the Coffee Blight folder and raised an eyebrow. "You apparently finished loading a genealogy file. I'm guessing we're in flux time now, but it looks like you saved it just before the change."

"Have we checked with anyone about recent time travel escapades?"

"Let me see." I opened the log file that allowed us to keep track between the time fluctuations. "I sent requests to all seventeen sanctioned tourist agencies for the last ten days." I stopped. "I need to rerun the agency logs in this fluctuation. I want to see if we get the same results." I shielded the earlier results so that Harry couldn't see Julia's name as one of the Travelers.

"You do that, and I'll check the genealogy against this fluctuation. What's the name of our target again?" It was hard to tell if Harry knew I was hiding that from him.

I looked at the file. "Randall Stevenson's the guy," I said. "Keep going back until we find how he got dropped from history."

Harry left to go back to the front office and run the program. I ran a search on recent travel events from our office. Julia still showed up. Frank, the other Commander in the unit, had a trip back to 2013. Julia had gone back to 1980. I prayed that I wouldn't have to talk with her about anything but our upcoming date.

My phone rang. I looked at it and sighed. "Yes Angus," I said when I clicked it on.

I listened as he reminded me of the importance of this case. Then he asked how things were going.

"Faster computers would help," I said. "We're running a genealogy trace and comparison going all the way back to 1939 and the computer's running slow."

I held the phone away from my ear after the first few shouted words. "...know how expensive that is? How'm I gonna justify that kind of expense before Congress?"

"Congressmen love coffee, right? Just remind them of the stakes."

I listened and did a facepalm when he reminded me that we couldn't give details on our cases. "How did I forget that?" I muttered under my breath. I racked my brain searching for a response. Then it hit me. "You can say that it involved saving a beverage that we all know and love. They'll think you're talking about Scotch Whiskey and double the appropriation."

Angus chuckled at the other end, then let me know that I was wrong. "OK. Bourbon. Any other suggestions?" As soon as I said that,

I bit my lip, hoping he wouldn't answer. He did tend to give me long drawn out answers that never helped. I breathed a sigh of relief when he told me "no" and then hung up. *He must really be worried about this case!*

I walked out toward Harry's area and stuck my head out my door. "To quote the amazing Angus, 'how's it going?'"

Harry chuckled. "Angus does like to practice his "hands-on approach" to supervising. He misses the job."

I hadn't thought about it that way. "Good observation, Harry. I hadn't thought about it that way." then I looked him straight in the eyes. "On a serious note. How is it going? How much longer before we get some data?"

Harry shrugged. "No idea. The computer will sound an alert when she finds any discrepancy. Since it's focused on the Randall Stevenson family, we should be able to run with that data."

"It's taking a long time," I said as I shook my head in worry, I didn't want to talk to Julia about business until we cleared up our other issues. I was hoping to do that on our date. If this analysis came back with a date that put her within five years of the event horizon, I'd have to talk with her, and she'd take it as an accusation.

"I think I've got it, Jack!" Harry called out.

I heard the printer whirring, so I knew that he'd be bringing me his findings. I got up and walked over to the window, hoping that the swirling winds of the city might blow some of the clouds and smog away so I could look out at the ocean. I waited for a few minutes, then gave up hope and went back to my desk just as Harry walked in.

"I saved a copy of both reports in the folder, Jack. In the coffee timeline, Walt Stevenson married Jane Rothland in 1985. Their children included Russell Stevenson, Randall's dad. In the tea timeline, Walt Stevenson was single and died in a one-car accident in 1986." Harry put the paper on the desk before me.

I groaned inwardly. I was going to need to talk to Julia before we had a chance to clear the air privately. I hung my head in my hands. "I guess I'll have to talk to Julia."

Harry looked over my shoulder while I looked at the folder. "Looks like Julia from Accounting made a trip back in 1980. You gonna go talk to her?"

I smiled. "Yep. Sweet girl. If I didn't have a policy about dating girls from work..." I let that hang.

Harry laughed. "Maybe you oughta give up that policy. That way when work gets bad, you could talk with someone about it."

"Good point," I said as I nodded. Restricting my opportunities hadn't helped my love life much. "Let me send her an email and see how soon she can meet." I opened up my email program, but before I started to write, I saw that I had gotten numerous responses to my request from the travel agencies. "Hey, Harry. While I get this off to Julia, would you check these responses to see if we have any possibles?"

"Sure thing, Jack. Just send them to me." He went back to his desk.

There were times I wish Angus and the chiefs would let Harry work in my office with me. Maybe they could get him a laptop or something. "You'll get too familiar with your aide, then." The fact that we'd worked together for fifteen years didn't matter to Angus. He demanded that separation.

I rolled my eyes as I thought about how ridiculous that was and forwarded those emails to Harry. Then I sent Julia an email asking for an immediate meeting. Even though it was getting late in the day, I needed to maintain my edge, so I poured another cup of coffee and walked over to the window.

The view from the window was fantastic with the sun hitting the waves and reflecting like they were sparkling diamonds. The ocean always calmed me, and today I needed some of that peace. With a sigh, I turned back from my one-minute break, knowing how important every second was, and walked back to my desk. The idea that if I failed meant that I'd never be able to drink this amazing brew ever again made me appreciate my coffee that much more.

I set my cup down beside my keyboard and looked at the

computer, willing the response from Julia to come. It didn't. "Time's a wastin," I said as I glared at my computer monitor. "Stupid thing about technology is that it never does what you want it to do, only what you tell it to do," I grumbled. Then I laughed at myself.

"Harry!" I yelled. "Anything interesting?"

"Double checking a couple of possible leads," he yelled back. "There are only thirteen responses here. How much longer do they have to answer?"

"Let me check," I answered. Usually, timing didn't matter. For certain situations, they did. That's when I invoked "rule thirty-nine." Travel Agencies had twenty minutes to respond to requests for records. They were supposed to keep personnel on duty twenty-four hours a day as part of their licenses. I looked at the computer timer. "Two more minutes. Let me check the email again."

No response yet from Julia. I was getting worried. "I got one more for you, Harry," I called out. I sent him the mail. When the forwarding window closed, I saw Julia's response. I forwarded it to my phone and started running. "Julia responded," I said between breaths. "I gotta head there now."

I didn't hear Harry's response. I wanted to talk with her now because I didn't know how things would play out in the fluctuation. I hoped that the email I forwarded would remind me what I needed to say if...

One thing that you could smell at any police station at any time of the day was coffee. Cops lived on coffee. That was true of time cops and beat cops. The long hours made that extra jolt of energy necessary. So, the aroma of coffee brewing wafted through the hallways all hours of the day, was like music to my nose.

I ran down the stairs to the Accounting Office and toward Julia's office. She was standing at the door, waiting for me. "Come on in," she said as she turned into her office. "Have a seat. This looks important."

I sat down and took a few breaths. Then I responded. "It is, I've got a very important matter to discuss."

"You bet it's important, mister," she said. "How dare you stand me up on my birthday."

I looked around, finally realizing that I was in Julia's office. I groaned. "No excuses, Jules."

The glare she gave me when I used my pet nickname for her, let me know I was really in trouble. "There are no good excuses, but let me hear the one you're going to try on me."

"Can we discuss it tomorrow night on our date?" I pleaded. "I've got a work issue I'm dealing with."

"It's always work with you, isn't it," she said with a sneer. "Is that your way of chickening out on this discussion?"

"No, I promise. We have a time fluctuation, and we're on a deadline to fix it, that's approaching way too fast."

She rolled her eyes. "And how does that involve me, 'Mr. Forgets His Date and Leaves Her Stranded at the Restaurant?'"

If this were a problem that demanded logic, I could have explained things. This was a far deeper hurt. "Julia, words can't express how sorry I am that I didn't show up on your birthday. I want to make things up to you. We have a worldwide crisis that will become permanent if we don't fix it. You traveled during the window."

Julia perked up when I said that. Nobody in the Time Management Division wanted to change history. "Being in the window," was a fear that every time traveling employee lived with. "What happened? When?"

"A man by the name of Walt Stevenson married a woman by the name of Jane Rothland in June of 1985 in standard time. Their grandson, Randall Stevenson, made a discovery that helped the world. In the time fluctuation, Walt and Jane never married. Randall was never born, and ..."

Julia nodded. "I know you can't say too much." She stopped to ponder the situation. "Which time is the wrong time?"

I shrugged my shoulders and looked at the floor.

"Oh, I get it. And us? In standard time?"

I looked at the notes on my phone. "My aide wrote that I should break my rule about dating co-workers and go out with you." I paused. Then I asked the question I didn't really want to ask, "You went back in December of 1980. What were you doing? Any chance you influenced either of those two?"

"I doubt I could have been an influence," she said. "I went back on company business." When I raised an eyebrow, she continued. "I buy stocks for our retirement plan. It's easy to pick winners after looking at fifty or more years of history. A certain tech company had their IPO that month."

"That doesn't sound legal," I said.

"But now you know why you don't get much taken out of your check for your retirement," she said while trying to look innocent.

"Do people in your office listen to your conversations in here?" I asked in a low voice. When she shook her head, I continued. "How many shares did you buy?"

"When we do this, we usually buy one hundred shares. It doesn't attract notice that way."

"Who authorizes you to go back in time and buy stocks like that?"

"The investment committee."

I shook my head. "How many times have you done that?"

Julia shrugged. "I don't know. Less than ten. It doesn't take many big buys like that to create a huge pension fund."

"Have you ever used that time you were back to buy stock for your personal portfolio?"

She bit her lower lip and looked at the lights while blinking her eyelashes quickly. "It's possible I might have thought about ways to provide for our family in the future."

I bowed my head and rubbed my eyes. "I'm thinking that I'd better not ask you any more questions because the less I know, the better. Is that a good assumption?"

It looked like she was trying to keep from smiling as she clenched her jaw and nodded. "Let me ask a question," she said. "If you and I aren't together in the standard timeline, why would I want to help you turn the world back to that timeline? I like what we have together."

"Nice way to change the subject," I said with a chuckle. "Perhaps we ought to fix things because man shouldn't tamper with the natural order of things."

She hung her head, not wanting to say a thing.

"I'm not planning to report you unless there's a compelling reason to related to this case." I could see the relief on her face. "I just hope nothing you did led to this problem." I sighed. "Does this mean you forgive me for standing you up on your birthday?"

She laughed and swatted me on the arm playfully as I turned to leave.

I turned back at her and gave her a look. "I love you, but if this ever happens again, I'll have to do something." She nodded as I left the room. She wasn't looking very playful as I left.

I didn't say much while I walked back to my office. If anybody overheard me talking to myself right then, I'd be in big trouble, and so would Julia. *Blackmail probably isn't the best foundation for a good relationship, but it'll have to do for now.* My thoughts turned back to the case. I hoped Harry had found something we could use.

———

"We're expecting three more responses, right Jack?" Harry asked as I entered the door.

I looked and saw the coffee cup on his desk, The trip to Julia's office and back and been a little over ten minutes. "Does that mean those leads you thought you had didn't work out?"

Harry shook his head. "Nope. It looked good. Frank Stevenson is a nephew of Randall Stevenson. He went back to 1985 to watch the wedding. That was," he pulled out a notebook and checked his notes, "about a week before the anomaly began. According to Temporal Travel Services, he was in tears by the time the wedding was over. He took notes for his own upcoming wedding."

"Great idea," I said as I nodded my head. "I've never heard of that idea before. Nice way to carry on family traditions."

"Save the coffee, save the wedding," Harry said as if repeating the advice of the ancient sages.

I nodded. "C'mon back with me and let's check the email." I waved him on with my hand as I walked back to my desk without turning around to look. A thought hit me, and I stopped suddenly. Harry couldn't stop in time and ran into me.

"Sorry Jack," he said as he grabbed me by the shoulders to keep me from falling.

"No brake lights, I can't blame you," I said with a laugh. "We've focused on Randall Stevenson. What if he's collateral damage? What if someone wanted to stop the wedding for other reasons: A jealous lover spurned wanting to get back at the person who jilted them, for example. Did any of the names of the tourist time travelers relate to other people in the genealogy?"

"Let's see what the emails show first. I can run a matching program in just a few minutes when I get back to my desk," Harry said.

"Sounds good." I resumed walking to my computer. The program was open to the email from Julia that had made me go check her out. I closed it and looked at the list of received emails. Two more companies had responded. I snarled that one of the companies hadn't as I checked the last two emails for information. No one had gone back in that time frame.

I scowled. This wasn't good. "We got the two emails, leaving one left, but they're ten minutes late now."

"Which one didn't respond?" Harry asked.

"I'm working on that now," I said. I realized that I'd sounded irritated. "Sorry Harry. Didn't mean to take my frustration out on you."

"I understand, Jack. No harm, no foul." Harry turned back toward his desk. "I'm gonna start that program now. I want to see if we can find some other way to look at this problem." I watched as he went to his desk and started typing.

I checked my sent mail. One of the recipients hadn't even opened the email. I whistled, because "Just in Time Travel Agency" usually was the first to answer these calls, then I took a screenshot and saved the picture in the folder. *They're in for a world of hurt.* I sniffed and looked up their address. It was time to pay them a visit.

"Harry, you got that program running? We need to take a field trip."

"Give me two minutes," he yelled back at me.

"You got it," I said, trying to hide my frustration at two more minutes of delay. I drummed my fingers on the desk, trying to skim through my emails wondering if I'd missed something about the Agency or if there was any news about them on the wires. The drumming echoed around the room, intensifying as no news showed up on the screen. I know that people say that "no news is good news," but when you're trying to get information, no news isn't good news. It's mind-numbing.

I loaded for battle as Harry's two minutes drew closer to an end. I carried a .5 Amp Taser on my right hip. I kept it on the lowest setting to avoid killing but could dial it up quickly if need be. On the left hip, I kept a tracking gun. When fired, it tagged my suspect genetically and broadcast his or her position when they tried to escape. My electro-static vest, police issue only, of course, could protect me from 1.2 million volts and 1.5 Amps. "Let's go, Harry," I said as I trotted past him. "Time's a-wastin'."

Harry stared intently at the monitor as he said "Two more lines of code. Just two."

I exhaled deeply. "Timing's important, Harry. We need to see them in this timeline. If Stevenson's really the center of this time fluctuation, whoever changed the timeline did so from this one."

"Do you enjoy nagging me, Jack?" Harry asked. "Let me grab my gear and head out to the car. I'll meet you there."

"Quickly," was my only response. I trotted toward the garage. My vehicle was on the second level, so I ran down the stairs instead of waiting for Harry to respond.

When they renovated the garage recently, they'd added lighting, so it was easy to see my flyers, parked side by side. I headed toward the marked flyer since this was wasn't a secret visit. Once I got in, I started it up to get the AC started.

The light from the building backlit Harry and cast a long shadow in the garage. I flashed my lights to let Harry know where the flyer was. I could hear the clicking of his heels as he picked up his pace heading to the door.

"They need some light in here," Harry said as he shook his head in disgust. "The Police Commissioner got his suite redone, and we can't even get decent lighting in the garage."

I nodded, then it hit me. "I think we had another time fluctuation. Do you remember what we were going to do?"

Harry looked at me and shrugged. "I just remember you telling me to meet you in the flyer."

I exhaled loudly. "Let me check the notes." I shifted in the seat to pull my phone out of its holster and checked the folder. "We're headed to 'Just in Time Travel Agency' on Collis Avenue. Apparently, they didn't answer the email in 20 minutes, nor did they respond when I called."

"Why not call again, before we get out into that?" He shuddered as he pointed out into the brownish smog.

"Based on what the notes say and my intuition, we need to contact them in the other time fluctuation." I shoved my phone toward Harry so he could read for himself.

"Are you wanting to drop in unannounced, or can if I call?" Harry asked.

I thought about that as I pulled my phone back and put it in its holster. I turned on the magnetic flight mode, and we lifted about three feet. After turning on the floodlights, we pulled her out of the space and slowly navigated the garage pathways to head onto the street. The brown, pea soup fog had never lifted today, making navigation much more difficult.

"Well?" Harry challenged my silence.

"Let's drop in unannounced," I said. "If there's anything going on, we won't give people advance warning to get away."

"Makes sense, I guess," Harry said. He watched as I maneuvered out of the garage and set the flight path for twenty yards above the ground - the standard police altitude. I put the directions into the onboard navigator, and we took off with lights flashing, but no siren.

I looked at Harry. "I hope anyone who might be straying in altitude will notice the lights," I said with a wry smile. "The fog will eat those lights up."

"Not exactly Jack. The only thing that will eat light up is a Black Hole. In a Black Hole, the gravitational pull is so strong that even light gets pulled in." Harry nodded as if he's just scored points in the Useless Knowledge category of the "Super-Genius" television show.

"It was a figure of speech. This fog is so dense that light won't penetrate the darkness." I might have come across a bit too harshly based on Harry's response.

"Oh. Sorry," was all he said. Then he stared straight ahead, not saying a word for about 30 seconds. That may have been a new record for him. "Then why are you turning on the flyer's lights?"

It took me a second to realize that Harry was actually making a joke. He and Bradford could probably sit around talking all day and only crack one joke between them...if that many.

"Whether people can see them or not, it's the law, Harry," I turned and smiled at him, so he could tell that I was joking. "It would be a good idea if we followed the law."

He smiled. Laughing wasn't his style unless the joke was just plain stupid. "What's causing the time fluctuation, Jack? Have you seen one in the past?"

"We've had a couple in the past before you came over, I think. That or you were on vacation." I screwed my face up in thought. "In both cases, a person went back in time to fix something they thought was wrong. A grandparent who died in an accident, once. In another case, a young man heard tales of the love of his mother's life being murdered, and he went back to fix things. In both cases, that led to the young men involved never having been born - which meant they couldn't go back in time to fix the wrong. The time fluctuations were minor though. These are the most severe I've ever seen."

"Why do you think that is?"

"I think this 'fix' caused more ripples in the time continuum.

Perhaps Father Time likes coffee more than tea, and he's giving us longer to find a way to save coffee."

Harry nodded as if this was profound advice. "I can see Father Time drinking coffee," he said.

Harry looked smug when I turned to him. *Did he have a sense of humor in this timeline?* "We should get there in a few minutes." I looked at the directions on the navigation system. They said three minutes. If we arrive before the next fluctuation, we'll stop about half a block short on Collis Avenue - somewhere around Burr. Then, we'll head to the corner at Pullman until we get to Just in Time."

"Collis is pretty busy, won't we be noticed?"

"What? Cops don't drive on Collis Avenue?" I laughed.

"Let's just say they're not always welcome," Harry said. "The unmarked flyer would have been better, although a flyer might still be more than the rest of the neighborhood has."

Collis Avenue had once been in the elite neighborhoods of the city. Now, driving down the street reminded people that it had seen better days. "Not much choice, Harry. We gotta check this place out."

Harry nodded. "Just be ready."

"Ready for what?" Harry didn't respond to my question. He just put a smug smile on his face and looked out the window. He couldn't see much because of the smog that swirled around even though it was late in the day for that.

Harry sighed, drawing my attention. "What's wrong, Harry?"

"Since we've been in Time Management, we haven't spent much time in these neighborhoods. They used to be beautiful. Now I don't recognize the place."

The place had changed so much that I forgot that Harry and I had worked a beat in this neighborhood a few years before the Time Management Division was created. From what I could see through the windows, once proud mansions were decrepit shells of their former selves. The elegance of former years had been sliced and diced into duplexes and quadruplexes housing families that barely scraped a living out of the Los Angeles community. Once green lawns had become bare patches of dirt, dotted by weeds. I began to wonder if Harry might have been right about the possible danger.

The flyer positioned itself close to the curb just past Burr Street. Then, the auto-pilot finished the parking job by letting the wheels down and settling on the land. The winds had whipped most of the fog out of the area here, so I had a clear view of the land ahead of us. I looked to the right, and people sitting on their stoops started looking and pointing. A flyer was a rarity in this neighborhood. I looked across the street and noticed that not only were they pointing and staring, but a few groups had also gotten together and had begun walking toward us.

"I hope the time flips back soon," Harry said. "The people on the right have decided to walk over and investigate us."

"So have the people on the left," I said. I tried not to let the rising fear show in my voice.

"You got plans to deal with this?" he asked.

I did, but I didn't want to use them unless I absolutely had to. "You know cop cars," I said. The nervous laugh gave me away. "I've got contingency plans that I don't want to have to use." I slid my hand down below the seat, ready to react if necessary.

I looked at my watch on the other hand. Then I looked back at the crowd that was coalescing. I licked my lips, but there wasn't much moisture anywhere around my mouth.

"Jack?" Harry asked.

I knew what he was asking. "Any second now." My voice trembled. "Any second." I looked out, and the crowd seemed angry. The flyer was mostly soundproof so I couldn't hear them, but the raised fists and contorted faces let me know that they meant business.

I closed my eyes as a flash of light burst around the car, and then I heard pounding on the door. No, not pounding. Knocking. I opened my eyes and blinked away the light. I realized that time had flipped again. Knowing that the time fluctuations were happening might be making it easier to remember across fluctuations. I shook my head. The knocking continued. I looked at my window and saw a face there.

"I say, officer, could I ask a favor? We have a delivery coming in, and you're in the way. Could you please move your vehicle?"

"Of course, sir," I said after rolling down the window. "We've got an appointment in the next five minutes anyway." I rolled the window back up and looked over at Harry. "Entitled rich snobs," I grunted as I fired up the flyer.

Harry laughed. Then he pointed toward the front of the flyer. "Looks like trouble," he said.

The flashing lights that prompted Harry's remark were close to the area where the Just in Time Travel Agency had offices. "Let's check it out," I said as I moved the flyer forward on the ground. I heard a siren behind me, and after checking the rearview mirror, I waited for the ambulance to fly past me as it joined the crowd of vehicles around the building.

"It looks like..." Harry began.

"Yeah, I know," I answered before he could finish. "Life just got even more complicated." A street cop stopped us outside the yellow tape. I let out a deep breath before I turned the flyer off and got out of the vehicle. I stood up with my knee still on the seat and watched my brothers in blue walk in and out of the Just in Time Travel Agency.

Before I could go any further, that street cop yelled at me. "Sir, please get back in the vehicle and drive away. This is now a restricted area."

I slammed the door a little too hard as I pulled out my shield. "Think I can join the party, Officer," I peered at his badge, "Webb?"

"Commander Friday!" he exclaimed as he looked at my credentials. "We just called Time Protection about five minutes ago. How did you...?" He stopped, and a knowing smile spread across his face. "I get it. You went back in time so that you could be on the scene quicker."

Harry laughed. "We don't work that way, son. Time travel is only used in extreme cases."

"Why'd ya call us?" I asked, trying to get the investigation back on track.

"Sergeant Morgan found evidence that this travel agency was one of the time travel agencies. He thought you'd need to secure any evidence related to time travel." He paused, then a puzzled look passed across his face. "So, how'd you get here so fast if you didn't go back in time?"

"We're investigating a time travel anomaly. When we contacted the agencies with time travel capability, this place didn't answer," I said. "We were on our way here.".

"Do you think your case and what happened here are related?" Officer Webb said. Then he hit himself on the forehead. "Of course they are!" He laughed. "I'm not always this dumb." Then he smiled as he swept his arm out to invite us into the building. "If you'll follow me."

Harry saw the look on my face. "Whatcha thinking, Jack?"

"I'm thinking I may never get to taste coffee again," I said as I shook my head. Then I nodded toward Officer Webb. "That guy's a complete doofus. If the rest of his team is like that, they may have screwed up the time travel evidence."

"Be optimistic, Jack, the guy who tore up the place, may have destroyed the evidence." He chuckled as we walked past Officer Webb and into the scene of destruction. When he caught my sour look, the smile disappeared.

I looked around at the destruction and whistled. I hadn't seen destruction like this since I'd saved Hitler in 1939. Smashed windows and furniture made it hard to walk without stepping on potential evidence.

I looked to my right as I scanned the front room. A few pictures hung on for dear life on the bland walls. A computer monitor was smashed on the desk next to the wall. Shattered glass pieces adorned the desk. As I looked at the floor, I noted a few drops of blood. That brought out a sigh. Someone was hurt. I saw two other desks that had gotten the same treatment in the room as I slowly moved my field of vision toward the left. The wall in the back of the room was indented as if someone had swung a bat or a pipe trying to break through the wall. There was more blood splatter on the wall, but still, nothing to indicate the source. Just past the desks was a carpeted hallway leading to a doorway protected by a shattered door hanging onto its hinges for life. As I scanned to the right, that's when I saw the body of an older man, his thinning gray-haired head soaked with blood from a bashed-in head.

"That's the owner," a voice to the left said. I jerked my head over to see a uniformed officer at the doorway to what looked like a control room. "Preliminary thought is that he fought to keep the perp from getting his keys and going in." The officer shook his head, sadly. Then he looked at me. "You time protection division?"

"Commander Friday," I said as I walked over to shake the sergeant's hand. "You call the coroner yet?"

"Sergeant Morgan, sir. I wanted to wait for you before I called the coroner." He pointed at the door to the control center. "He got in but must have been scared off by the alarms. He was gone when we got here. When I saw the control room, I called you guys."

He moved to the right as I walked in and looked around the control room. The control panel had been smashed so badly the chip jewelers would have slim pickings. Computers, monitors, meters...anything that was necessary to send people back in time had been destroyed beyond repair.

"All gone?" Harry asked while I stood there gaping.

After I nodded, I said, "That's what I'd say for public consumption."

"Between you and me?" he asked.

I turned, so my back was to the other sergeant. "He didn't get the auxiliary backup drive.

"That means we should be able to track him down, right? Why the secrecy?" I had to give Harry credit for keeping his voice low. He usually had two volumes: loud and louder.

"If the perp's still in the area, we don't want to let him know we're on to him.." Then I looked back to make sure Morgan was at his station. "That and the auxiliary hard drives are top secret - for occasions like this."

Harry nodded, and I called Sergeant Morgan. "Sergeant! Do you have your radio? We didn't bring ours. We don't normally need to contact dispatch on these cases."

"Sure thing, Commander." He seemed eager to help. "Why do you need dispatch this time?" And curious.

"He wrecked the control room pretty bad," I said. "We got some great techs who might be able to reconstruct the computers. If so, we can check out the last few travelers and, perhaps, find the killer."

While I contacted dispatch, who patched me through to Angus, Sergeant Morgan's face suddenly got serious. He'd been so caught up in working with the thrill of Time Protection that he'd forgotten about the dead guy. "I hope we can find him, sir." He was much more subdued.

"Angus, this is Friday."

"I know it's Friday. The weekend's coming!"

I rolled my eyes at the joke he'd only used about a hundred times. "We need the techs out here. Just In Time travel agency has been destroyed. The control room computers and circuit boards were smashed to pieces. We need to gather the evidence."

He developed the protocol, so he knew not to say anything about the auxiliary drive. "Understood loud and clear. Tech guys are on their way. We'll talk when you get back to the station."

"Roger," I said as I clicked off the radio. As I handed the radio back to the wide-eyed sergeant, I said, "Why don't you secure the area while you wait for homicide. Now would also be a good time to call the coroner. Please don't come by the control room, or go through that door," I pointed at the door that led to the Time Travel capsule and launching area. "It's top secret."

"Not even a peek into either?" he asked hopefully.

"I guess you could," I said, and then paused, "but then I'd have to kill you."

He laughed. I didn't. "Gotcha sir," he said as he threw a salute at me before backing away slowly.

Harry kept a straight face until Morgan walked away. "You were pretty blunt, Jack. He probably thinks you'd actually shoot him."

"I would."

Harry searched my face. "You really would?" When I nodded, he continued. "Would you shoot me?"

"Nah, you're family."

"But he's family too. We're all cops."

"You're family-er," I said and then smiled a bit before getting serious again. "When you joined the Time Protection Unit, you agreed to keep anything you learned about time travel secret. You're not allowed to write a tell-all book. You can't give interviews about any of your missions."

"Really?" Harry said. "Was that part of all that paperwork I signed?" He chuckled. "I never read them. Just signed and forgot them."

I shook my head. "Harry," was all I could say. Then I nodded toward Sergeant Morgan. "He didn't sign anything. He and that pipsqueak officer will have to be questioned. We can't take a chance on letting this technology get out to other nations."

Harry pondered that for a moment. "Maybe we could improve on history a little bit. What if we went back and..." I hid my eyes. *Don't go there.* "...killed Hitler, or ..."

"Stop," I said in a loud whisper. "Don't even think about it. Our job is to restore history, not change it."

"But wouldn't stopping Hitler be a good thing?"

"No, it wasn't."

Harry realized what I was saying. He looked like he was about to ask me another question, but I glared at him, warning him to stop. "So how bad is the interrogation my brothers in blue will endure?"

I could tell Harry was miffed. I couldn't help that. "Not sure. We've never had a situation like this before."

"Never before?" he lifted his eyebrows.

"Public time travel's only been around for about five years." I looked around at the damage in the control room. "Not many people have taken this trip. It's too expensive for most people, especially the criminal element."

"Good point," Harry said. "So, what do you make of this?"

"Whoever changed history did this, perhaps to keep us from finding out about him."

"But the auxiliary backup?" Harry glanced at the area where the backup drive would be. "He didn't touch that."

"You didn't know about it until now, did you?" I smiled as I asked the question.

Harry nodded. "How much time until the techs get here?"

I shrugged and lifted my hands in exasperation. "Ya never know with those guys."

The coroner came in and began his odious task. The cop who'd been taking care of the body walked over to us. "Sergeant Morgan, gentlemen. You are?"

I rolled my eyes. I knew about and was used to the time fluctuations, but Morgan didn't know what was going on. He didn't need to. "Jack Friday, Sergeant. Time Protection division. This is my partner Harry Gannon. Looks brutal here." I stood so that I blocked the entrance to the control room.

"Nice to meet you. Never worked with Time Protection guys before. What brings you...," realization dawned in his eyes, "this crime has something to do with time travel. Wow! I've never worked with anyone from Time Protection before."

There's a reason for that. "We don't usually work out in the public eye." I glanced around the room as I responded. The lights were dimmer and were having a difficult time fighting back against the darkness. I sensed Morgan edging his way to get a look in the control room. "Harry," I said as I turned to look at him. "Can you compare notes with Sergeant Morgan so that we can get on the same page."

He realized what was going on and walked past me to grab Morgan's elbow and lead him out of the area as he asked questions. "So, when did you get the call about this?" He fanned his arm out, ending up pointing at the victim.

I laughed as Harry walked out of earshot, chatting with the

Sergeant. When he needed to, he could talk your ear off. I turned and saw the guys from the lab walking over. Except these were the regular police lab guys, not the Time Protection ones. I stood my ground and called out, "Hey guys, what's going on?"

"We need to check that room out, detective. The sergeant told us that it had been tossed pretty bad." This guy was obviously the leader of the crew. The others stayed silent, although they nodded in agreement.

"I think not," I said. "I need to protect this room until the tech crew comes." I smiled, somewhat bemused by being called detective.

"You may not have noticed, detective," he was overly polite, to the point of sarcasm, "but we're the tech crew. See the white jumpsuits?"

I pulled my shield from my breast pocket and opened it up and held it out ... "Detective?" I asked. "Care to examine this shield?" Then I asked in the most casual, threatening way I could, "And if I could have your name for my report, I'd appreciate it."

I'd read a lot of stories where someone heard the guilty person "gulp." This was the first time I experienced it myself. "Uhm...sorry, Commander. I had no idea." He began backing away.

"Your name?" For some perverse reason, I was enjoying scaring this young whippersnapper.

"Oh yeah, sorry, sir. I'm Jackson Foster, sir," he turned to leave.

"One more thing, Mr. Foster."

"What's that?" He was entirely subdued now.

"You and your whole crew may need to be interrogated, so don't leave the premises until either me or Detective Gannon releases you." I pointed to Harry, who was busy with Sergeant Morgan. "Do you understand that?"

"Yes, sir." Foster was thoroughly cowed by now.

I began pacing, looking at my watch. The Time Tech Crew should be here soon. I wanted that information, and I wanted to get this anomaly fixed!

"Jack!" I jumped. I'd been so lost in thought that I'd missed the Tech Crew's arrival. "Jack, wake up."

That was Angus's voice. I turned to look at him. "What're you doing here?" I asked. "Isn't this the first time you've left the building since you became a time manager?"

"First time we've ever had a murder related to the case in our time. This is the first time a control panel's been ruined. Lots of firsts, here." He turned to the tech crew. "If Commander Friday will move, the controls are in there. We need the information as soon as possible." He beckoned me to him.

"What's the situation? Who do I need to talk to?"

I jerked my head around. "You're doing the interrogations? Wow."

Angus shrugged. "This is another first. If I'm going to write the protocols for investigating incidental contact with the Time Controllers, I need to experience the investigation."

I shook my head, trying to clear it. "And all this time I thought your job was sitting around in your comfy office all day drinking coffee...er...tea and ordering us around."

Angus chuckled. "You ever done parking meter duty, funny guy?" He read my silence and continued. "So, who do I need to talk with? Who knows anything about this situation?"

I told Angus about the Sergeant, the patrolman, and the tech crew. As I explained what I knew about their contact with the controller, he absorbed the information and then said, "If all these stories are true, it shouldn't take much time to clear them."

"If only we had a 'flashy-thingy,'" I said with the faint hint of a smile.

"A what?" Angus asked. Then I remembered.

"Sorry, boss. That's a joke from a movie I saw back in the late 20th century. Forgot where I'd seen it." I wondered if Angus heard my gulp. Going out to a movie during time travel was not normally acceptable.

Angus glared at me. "That kind of move might just get you moved to parking lot duty," he said with a growl. "I don't remember any movie from previous debriefings. We'll talk about that."

I gulped again. "Yes, sir." Angus strained to hear me. "I should note, sir, that I gave Jackson Foster on the tech crew a bad time. He was trying to be diligent in his duties when I kept him from going into the control room. If you could let him know I said good things about him, I'd appreciate it."

Angus snorted. Then, he reached for his phone. He looked at the phone and gave a thumbs up to the tech crew in the control room. I looked back and saw the tech smiling and returning the gesture. "Get a good night's sleep, Commander. We have a name and a date for you. You go back in time tomorrow morning."

"Alone or with Harry?"

Angus scratched his chin and looked off into the distance. "We don't want too many people back at one time. Ya think he can run logistics from the capsule computer?"

"Harry's a whiz at that," I said. "He could run it from his phone. The capsule computer, even limited as it is, would be a luxury for him." I looked over at him talking with Sergeant Morgan and smiled. "Besides, this is so important that he'd be good to have as backup if anything goes wrong."

Angus scowled. "Don't think about anything going wrong. Harry can go with you, but he can only leave the capsule if you die or become incapacitated. Now, go home and get some sleep!"

"Sounds fair. Send me the info."

"Just get Harry and take him back to the station so you two can be ready for tomorrow."

With a nod and a salute, I turned on my heels and went to get Harry. He saw me coming and broke off his conversation with Sergeant Morgan."

"What's up, Jack?"

"Chief Angus has ordered us back to headquarters to file reports," I told him, knowing that Sergeant Morgan was within listening distance. "Oh, Sergeant Morgan," I pointed to Angus, "that's the man you need to talk to. Head on over there while I take Detective Gannon back the station." I shook my head in mock disgust. "I hate paperwork, don't you?"

Sergeant Morgan laughed. No cop liked the paperwork. "Is he the 'grand inquisitor?'"

Harry laughed. "Worse. He's the boss."

We all laughed, and I slapped the sergeant on the back and directed him toward Angus. Then I looked at Harry. "We leave early tomorrow morning. Angus is going to send us the info,"

"I'm going with?"

"Logistics and backup. You stay in the capsule coordinating things unless something lethal happens to me. Security ya know." I began walking toward the flyer.

Harry was smiling. "First time we get to go back together in a long time. I won't let you down, Jack."

I looked back over my shoulder. "C'mon, enough with the chit-chat. We need to get home and get some sleep. You know how much time travel takes out of you."

"What's the plan again?" Harry asked. He kept working on the programming for the time capsule.

I stifled my smart-aleck remark as I backed away from stooping down to make sure all the wires and hoses were connected. Harry needed time to mull the plan over in his head and hearing it three or four times helped him get it down. Once he understood, though, no one carried out a plan better than him. I took a sip of coffee. The fluctuations were about eight minutes apart now, and I wanted to be sure to drink as much as I could.

"Based on what Angus told us, the last person to use the "Just in Time" capsule was Ronald Stevenson, Randall's son. His application to observe included watching the moment in time when his great-grandparents met." I pulled out my phone and looked at the data Angus had sent. "It seems that they met in a coffee shop in Swarthmore, Pennsylvania."

Harry looked up from the monitor. "Where in the world is Swarthmore, Pennsylvania?"

I laughed. "Yeah, I had to look it up too. It's in the southeastern corner of Pennsylvania, just west of Philadelphia and north of New Jersey. I'll send the coordinates to your phone." I copied and pasted the coordinates for the college where Ronald had begun his search. "That's where Ronald landed. We need to be about thirty feet to the east of him. I'm sending the time he landed also. I want to be there about five minutes before he lands."

"Got the info," Harry said, and he turned back to his programming while I worked on making sure all the hoses, tubes, and wires were connected.

"How much longer on the programming?" We had people on staff who did that all the time. Harry insisted on doing the programming himself if he was taking this trip. He was slower.

Harry looked at the manual. "I've still got the shielding and the electronics to program. It should be about ten minutes."

Ten minutes. That'll throw us into tea time. "Got it. I'm going to get changed so I can be ready. Connections are all made."

"I'll check them just before I head back to change," he said without looking up.

That figures. I went back to wardrobe so that I'd look like I belonged in 1983. "Sarah, I'm here for my fitting," I yelled in case she was lost in the closets.

"No need to yell, Jack," she said from the desk behind the door. "Angus gave me a heads up, so I've got the perfect set of clothes for you in dressing room two."

I chuckled. "So now I get dressing room number two? How did I get demoted?"

Sarah swooned. She nodded her head toward the time capsule area. "Harry's a dreamboat."

I rolled my eyes, which caused Sarah to giggle. "Really? Is this official? How long?"

She shrugged her shoulders. "We're only flirting - it's been a couple of months. Harry doesn't seem to know how to take the next step."

"Need me to encourage him?" I shifted my eyes from side to side as if I was making sure that Harry wasn't around.

"Just go get dressed," she said as she threw the dressing room key at me.

I locked the door behind me before I turned around to check out the vintage duds she'd picked out for me. I picked up the light blue shirt. Long sleeves. I was worried until I remembered that Pennsylvania was cooler in the spring than Los Angeles. I put it on and grabbed the tan pants. *Tan pants. You have to be kidding me!* Sarah knew her clothing, so I didn't question her. Then I pulled out a diagonally striped pastel tie. People had stopped wearing ties back in 2029. I inhaled and then exhaled loudly as I tried to remember how to tie one. When I finished, I looked myself in the mirror.

"Hey Sarah, did I make you mad or something?" I yelled out the door as I shook my head. I looked around for the belt and found a weird yellow contraption with two bands converging into one with clips on each of the ends. I unlocked the door and slammed it open. "Seriously Sarah, what is this garbage?" I indicated my clothes by running my right hand down my body since the left one was holding that yellow contraption.

She beamed at her handiwork. "That, my handsome friend, is vintage 1980s clothing." Then she frowned. "But the tie needs some adjustments and," she closed her eyes and took a deep breath, "you're not wearing the suspenders."

I held the yellow thing up. "This thing? Is that what you call suspenders?" I asked, trying to understand the 1980s.

"Yes, silly, come here," she said. When I came up to her, she straightened my tie and tightened the knot. "Give me that," she demanded with her hand held out toward the suspenders. I handed them over and followed her instructions as she told me to turn around. She fiddled with the waistband of my pants and threw something over my shoulders. "Use the clips to attach these things to your pants. You don't want them to fall down, do you?"

I grabbed one strand and started to tug at the end. I was about to try attaching them when she interrupted me. "You want these straight," she said as she untwisted them. I hitched the clip to my waist and then tried the other, trying to make sure they were straight also.

"How'd I do?" I asked as I threw out jazz hands.

She laughed. "Not too bad," she said as she unclipped both bands and straightened them out. "You need to keep them equal distances apart from the buttons," she said as she re-attached the clips. "One more thing to complete the outfit," she said as she went back to her counter. She came back with a pair of tortoiseshell glasses. "Here, put these on." She handed the glasses to me.

"They still used glasses in 1983?" I asked.

She glared at me until I put the glasses on. "Now, look at yourself," she said as she indicated the full-length mirror on the wall.

I turned and looked. My jaw dropped, and I shook my head. "People actually wore this...stuff?" I asked as I turned first to the right, and then to the left to check out the back of the outfit. "Seriously?" I saw her holding a camera in the mirror and said, "No! You aren't going to..." The flash interrupted my protest.

"For research purposes only," she said with the most innocent eyes I've ever seen.

I shook my head in disgust. "Did Harry find his costume yet?"

He hasn't come back here yet," she said.

I grimaced. We didn't have much time. "You got any tea here while I'm waiting?"

"Of course! Go ahead and sit down." She indicated a break table on the other wall from the mirror. It was obvious Sarah wanted to get back in my good graces. "Do you take it with milk and sugar?"

I nodded. "And a little lemon, too."

She brought the tea set over, and I started steeping the tea. "Can you check on Harry for me?" I asked, growing impatient.

"He's particular, that Harry is," Sarah said. "I'll be happy to check on him." She left the tea with me and went out into the time capsule area.

They talked in hushed tones, so I couldn't tell what they were saying. I think that was their plan, though. I plunged my tea bag up and down. Seeing that it was finally the right strength, I added my fixings and sipped tea while I waited.

They were laughing as they came in the room, walking very close together. Harry pulled away a little when he saw me looking. I said nothing, but the smile that escaped from my mouth, let him know that I'd seen.

"Dressing Room One, Detective," she said as she handed him the key. Her hands seemed to linger a little before she pulled them away.

Harry blushed a little as he headed into the dressing room.

I took another sip of my tea and smiled. "That looks like a little bit more than innocent flirtation," I said.

"Perhaps," Sarah said, but she blushed a bit also. She turned away and tended to some paperwork that had suddenly become important.

The table had a text reader, so I dialed up the news site and looked for anything unusual that had happened. All right, I looked for information on the "Just in Time" murder. If Angus did his job, the worst we'd see would be an account of a murder-robbery. Time Protection Division cops didn't like to be in the spotlight. *Nothing.* I sipped my tea and smiled. Angus, well, actually Carlotta, had done the job. Carlotta was the Time Manager who dealt with the media.

"What are these things?" Harry yelled from his dressing room.

"Suspenders," I called back. "Come on out and I'll...er...Sarah will help you." I'd caught her eye just before I finished my sentence.

He stepped out with suspenders dangling from one hand and the other hand holding a light blue suit coat slung over his shoulder. He had on a black shirt that had a white collar and a white tie. His blue pants, a little lighter than my shirt, matched his coat. I turned my head so he couldn't see me laugh. I'd won the costume contest this time.

Sarah fussed over him, helping to fix the suspenders and then she pulled out some kind of silver bar and attached it to the collar of his shirt underneath his tie. God only knew what that accomplished.

When Sarah finished, he put his jacket on and asked, "How do I look?"

"Like a million bucks," I said with a laugh.

He frowned. Sarah looked at him and said, "Harry, remember that a million bucks was a lot of money back in 1983."

I put my teacup down. "Let's go. It's time to party like it's 1983." We walked out to the time capsule area to get ready for our journey.

Angus had come by to give us some last-minute wisdom. He was sitting down outside the control room gulping coffee from an earthenware mug. "Ah, the 1980s fashion show." He lifted his mug with a smile. "Here's to you two. You look rad to the max."

I rolled my eyes in disgust. Harry just looked puzzled. "Angus, you've got to stop trying to talk like the times we're going to. You sound grody."

Angus narrowed his eyes and looked at me suspiciously. Then it dawned on him, and he laughed. "That was fresh, Jack. Fresh."

"Do you two want to speak English?" Harry stood with his hands on his hips, gawking at us.

"We do this a lot," I explained. "You just heard some 1980s slang."

"When did you learn that?" He asked as an accusation.

"I didn't go to sleep right away last night."

"If you two fashion models are finished, d'ya think we could get this show on the road?" Angus was clearly having too much fun.

"You ready, Detective?"

"Any time, Commander."

Angus got serious. "This may be our only shot, so don't fail."

I saluted, while Harry looked puzzled again. "I'll explain later," I whispered.

We walked into the time capsule and sealed the door behind us before strapping ourselves into our seats. Then Harry began the final check-downs before launching. "Ready, Jack?" He asked. When I nodded, he started us on our journey.

I wish I could describe time travel. I've tried many times and haven't ever been able to approach its beauty in my attempts. At first, it's total blackness. But not that smothering blackness that leaves you feeling like nothing will ever be right again. This blackness is alive. It embraces you as you enter and pass through. It warms your heart and your soul. It energizes every part of your body and your spirit. I've never felt more alive than when I go through that blackness.

Then, as you approach terminal velocity, lightning starts crackling all around - inside and outside the capsule. At first, it's just a few streaks. Then it multiplies until it's flashing all around. In the end, there's an explosion of white that washes out everything. If you didn't have the headgear, you'd be blinded. Then, before you have time to get used to the white, you're there.

And just like that and we were sitting in my time capsule in Swarthmore, Pennsylvania in late April of 1983 at 10:30 in the morning. Students were walking back and forth going to their classes, utterly oblivious to the visitor in their midst. As it should be.

I yawned. Time travel, as exhilarating as it is, exhausted me. I rechecked my clothes and shook my head. "Sarah," I muttered a little too loud.

"This is it," Harry said. "1983, and Sarah, no matter what you may say, picked the perfect clothes for us." He started pointing out the students and faculty members who wore similar attire.

I had to agree that Sarah hadn't done as badly as I wanted to complain about, but I still would have preferred faded blue jeans and a burgundy, no, a gray polo. "The 'Just in Time' capsule should be here in about ten minutes. Do what you can to stay awake." I went to the cupboard and pulled out some roasted coffee beans, hoping that the raw caffeine would help keep me awake.

It was time to get to work. Harry double-checked the cloaking device and the coordinates where the Just in Time capsule would land. I checked the electronic intercepts. We'd be able to see and hear everything aboard the incoming time capsule.

"How much longer?" Harry's question broke my concentration, but it was easy to get over-fixated on the details.

"We've got about five minutes until touchdown," I said. "How close are you to finishing?"

"Two minutes. You?"

I made two last connections on the circuit board. "Finished."

"Enjoy history, then," Harry said while pointing at the view screen.

I watched the viewscreen while I waited with that sense of awe I never lost seeing history in action. This was mundane, everyday life. The kind of stuff you'd never see in a history book. Young lovers holding hands walked past, completely oblivious to our presence. A couple of guys throwing a football on the green in front of me. "Some things never change," I said quietly. I'd seen similar scenes in every time period I'd ever traveled to, including that trip in 1939.

"Doesn't look like anything important's happening out there, does it?" Harry was looking over my shoulder. "If people only knew."

I chuckled. "The most important thing that happens today is that Walt Stevenson and Jane Rothland will meet, and their progeny will save the coffee crop in 2037. Nothing really important."

Harry snorted. "We'd better get this issue cleared up. A world without coffee seems to be a dreary place." He paused. "Why do we only get one shot at this problem, by the way?"

"Fixed Time Point Conundrum," I said while watching a couple of guys harassing a girl who was trying to walk to class. "Jerks." I spat the word out.

Harry shook his head. "This kind of stuff went on until about 2030. You can't change that. We can only fix history, not change it."

I nodded. "Still…"

"Tell me about this 'Fixed Time Point Conundrum,'" Harry asked while making the air quotes around the new phrase.

"Angus explained it. Apparently, there are times when people change time; they create a fixed point in time. Any time you have time fluctuations, you get a fixed time point conundrum, for instance. There's some mathematical formula to determine how long you have to fix the change before it becomes unfixable."

"How did they discover that?" Harry asked.

I looked out the viewscreen, still people watching. "I never thought to ask that question, Harry." That was hard to admit. "I guess I'll ask when we get back to our time."

Harry didn't have a chance to berate me because a notice showed up letting us know that the communications intercept was getting input. "Incoming," was all Harry said as he went back to his control panel and pushed buttons and moved dials until we had visual and audio information from the incoming module projected on the view screen. Ronald was already arguing with the pilot just after the bright stage, just before landing.

"How much can it hurt if I just leave the capsule and visit the gallery where my great-grandfather showed his paintings?"

The pilot was patient but firm. "You didn't ask for an exfiltration excursion. Those have different equipment requirements that we don't bring along except by request."

"And a lot of extra money too, I bet," Stevenson seemed to be trying to shame the pilot into letting him walk free in 1983.

"Yup. That it does. And since you didn't pay the money upfront, we don't have the equipment available. Now hush. I've got to land this contraption."

I was amazed at how calmly the pilot finished the landing sequence in spite of the distractions. When I looked at the instruments, I saw that he'd landed about ten yards to the east of our capsule.

Once the landing process was complete, Ronald began again. "C'mon man. Give a guy a break. I didn't know I needed to pay upfront. Just let me out for five minutes, and I'll make it worth your while."

The pilot slammed his fist down on his armrest and unstrapped angrily. He turned toward Stevenson, and I saw his face. He was flushed and scary looking. "You have no idea with the forces of nature that you'd be playin with," he said through clenched teeth. "Changing the air currents could cause a fly to go off course in a way that would change history, and you might cease to exist."

Ronald's shoulders clenched up in a shrug. "Don't take this so seriously, man. This is fun. Come join me."

The pilot shook his head. "Strap back in. We're headed back."

I nodded my approval. Ronald had crossed over the line. But Ronald jumped out of his seat instead and pushed the pilot back. The pilot hit the corner of his seat and spun around, landing face-first on the floor of the capsule. Without looking back, he bolted for the exit door, and before I could react, he'd left the capsule and headed toward the east.

"Genetic tracker, Harry!" I yelled as I jumped out of my chair to switch the view on the screen. I checked carefully to make sure no one was looking at the capsule. Cloaking devices couldn't stop the appearance of a man from out of nowhere from being strange.

The way seemed clear, so I slipped out of the capsule after telling Harry to check on the other pilot. I pulled out my cell phone and was about to call Harry to transfer the data on Stevenson to me. Then it hit me. The first cell service was months away. Not only would it take Harry a while to activate the mobile cellular service device, I'd look pretty strange talking on a cell phone here and now.

I chuckled as I realized that all these kids were looking at each other and talking instead of burying their faces in their phones. I hoped Harry established communications quickly. In the meanwhile, the chase was on. Stevenson didn't have much of a head start, but he was young and may not have been affected by the time travel as much as me. I headed east and looked for unusual motion ahead.

The folks walking on the paths made it hard to see anyone in particular, but as I reached a street called Swarthmore Street, I saw him. He was dodging vehicles as he crossed. The clothes he was wearing were the giveaway. He hadn't even bothered to find something from the 80s. People who watched might have thought the billowing purple fabric on the purple polka dotted shirt was somewhat eccentric, but this was vintage 2050s clothing. The orange balloon pants made him stand out even from a block away.

"He's a block in front of you, Jack," Harry's voice broke my concentration on Stevenson. "He's on a street called Swarthmore."

"Yeah, I got a visual. He stands out like a ..." the analogy failed me.

"...sore thumb?" Harry asked carefully.

I stopped and looked around as I thought about the saying. If I stayed on the phone much more, I'd stand out like a sore whatever myself. "Don't think so." I scratched my head. "I'll get it eventually. Anyway, I'm sticking out myself with this call. Let's be circumspect about using it."

"Gotcha," Harry said. But it was too late.

"Wow! Is that the new handheld CB Radio?" I think it was a student at the college who came up to me and asked.

I jumped and yelled "Oh!" Then I calmed down. "Sorry, you startled me," I said, hoping Harry was searching for information. "What'd you ask?"

"Is that the new handheld CB radio?"

I looked back and forth as if trying to spot anyone listening in. My eyes kept glancing down at my phone. If Harry hadn't left to care for the other pilot, he oughtta be feeding me information. Nothing came. "Listen, dude. This isn't the new CB radio. It's the newest CB radio. It's a prototype version that I'm testing."

"Can I hold it?" He was actually trembling.

I wonder what he'll do when new cell phones get released. "Let you hold it. I could lose my job," I hesitated for effect, "or worse if anyone knew that you saw it." I hissed the words out in as low a voice as I could.

He caught on. "Who's making this. Who do you work for?"

I looked at him, forgetting the names of the tech companies of the 80s. Then, I exhaled slowly, through the nose for effect and asked him, "Who do you think could make a mobile CB radio this advanced?"

"I knew it!" he exclaimed, drawing looks from others around. Then, he bent down and whispered. "It's Motorola, right?" He shook his head and smiled. "They're the only company that could come up with something like this."

My face dropped. "Please don't tell anyone you saw me or the Motorola 2055." I clasped my hand to my mouth as if I'd made a mistake. "You didn't hear that number," I spoke firmly.

"Got it. I never heard about the top-secret Motorola 2055 prototype." He was grinning from ear to ear.

I closed my eyes and shook my head. "I am so screwed." Then I looked him in the eye. "Truth? We need this launch to be successful, or else things will go bad quickly. If our competition gets wind of what we're working on, it could ruin everything. Don't say a word." I put my finger to my lips as a warning.

It was hard to hold back my laughter as I watched him run off after nodding agreement. He wasn't going to tell anyone, of course, except for a few of his best friends and anyone else he knew. "Good thing they don't have social media," I said to myself with a chuckle.

"Breaker 1-9 Good buddy," Harry's voice came out of the phone.

"There are no smokies in sight," I responded, wondering if I'd gotten the CB lingo right.

"Neither is your friend. I'm having trouble keeping up with him. It's like he's ghosting."

"Whadda ya mean?" I resumed walking toward the end of the block.

Harry's deep breath was loud enough for the phone. "Bear with me. I'm having to look at my readout and a map so I can get the street names. I think he turned on Yale Street. Hmm." Harry paused. "Yeah, I think it's Yale street. It's the next major intersection. Anyway, there's another major street to the south, southeast." There was another pause. "Sorry, had to check the map again. I can't imagine how people got around with paper maps! That street's Morton Street if I'm reading it right."

"What about Morton Street?" I was rushing down Swarthmore with the next major intersection about one hundred feet in front of me and biting my lip as he delayed giving me the information.

"Every couple of seconds or so, I get a blip from the DNA scanner, as if he jumped over to Morton and then back to Yale."

I scratched my head as I picked up the pace. I had a feeling that we were getting closer to a moment that would change time forever.

"You there?" Harry's voice interrupted my reverie.

"Yeah, just trying to figure things out." We'd used the genetic tracker before with nary a glitch. It didn't make sense. "Harry, send me a screenshot if you see the ghosting again. Maybe I need to see it."

I dodged the traffic and crossed the street at Yale. Yale ran toward the northeast, so I chose the shady side of the street and kept pushing forward. My phone dinged to let me know that I was needed. I looked. Harry had sent me two screenshots. The further I got from the capsule and the network source, the slower things worked, and it seemed to take forever to download the pictures.

"Not sure what to make of them," I said as I glanced down at the pictures. I wiped my brow. Even with the cooler temperatures, my haste made me sweat. Maybe it was the tension and the thought of never having coffee again. "Have we ever seen a glitch like this?" I stopped to rest in some shade.

"It's hard to research databases through time," he responded. "But so far, nothing exactly like this."

I was about to respond when I glimpsed a patrol car crawl to a stop in the street right next to me. "No transmissions for a short time." I slipped the phone into my pocket. Pretending to take no notice of the cop, I started heading up Yale Street.

The siren gave one whoop as the cop made sure I realized he wanted to talk with me. He rolled down the window and yelled at me to stop. I stopped and turned to look at him. "Sir?" I raised my eyebrows and lowered my forehead as I acknowledged his command.

The door to the old cruiser squeaked as the cop opened it. He put his arm on top of the open door and pulled himself up. He started talking over the car as he turned to look at me. "We gotta report about someone acting strangely around here."

I knew where he was going, but I couldn't help myself. "Goodness officer. That's bad. I haven't seen anyone acting strangely around here."

He looked at me, not sure how to respond to that. Finally, he nodded his head and laughed as he slammed the door and began walking around to talk with me. "The reports described you, funny guy."

"I'm just walking here, officer. I don't know anything strange about that."

He ambled over and looked at me. "People say you been looking at something in your hand and talking as you walked. You got something to look at? Why you looking at your hand? Why you talking to yourself?"

I stared at him, without blinking. Then, I burst out in laughter. I could tell he didn't expect that. "I'm new in town and had a list of coffee shops," I said. "I'm looking for a place that serves decent coffee. You know any good places?"

He scratched his head. Then, he rubbed the side of his face until he ended up in contemplation while stroking his jaw. After a pause, he responded. "You're not too far from a new place called the Coffee Station. Just opened earlier this year."

"Well, I'm game to try something new. How do I get there?" I said, hoping that my deflection would get me out of the mess. No such luck.

"Keep following Yale until it joins with and becomes Morton. That'll run into a major street. If you turn left, you'll find yourself on Woodland Avenue. You don't want Woodland, so turn right and get on Kedron. Oh, be sure you cross Kedron first. About half a block down, you'll turn left into the coffee shop. You can't miss it." He paused as if to catch his breath. You got any other spots on that list?" he asked. "Can I see it?" He wasn't demanding to search me. He seemed to be trying to be helpful. Perhaps he realized that I didn't have any paper in my hand.

"Of course, officer." I reached into my pocket and pulled out what looked like a business card case. "It should be in ..." I frowned and shook my head as I opened it. "Blast it all!"

"What's wrong?"

"I musta dropped it back there when I thought I put it back in my pocket."

He eyed me in disbelief. "Well, there's always the yellow pages," he said just before he looked at my "business card case." "Nice case. Mind if I have a look at it?"

"Most other people would have a fight on their hands if they tried to take it off me, it was a gift from my Uncle John Locke." I hoped he hadn't noticed the emphases on the words "off" and "lock." "I figure if you can't trust a cop, who can you trust?" I extended my arm with the case to him.

He laughed. "It's gettin' so we don't get that respect no more, son. Thanks." He took the case from my hands and examined it. He opened it up. "Not many cards here," he said.

"Starting new in a new town, sir," I laid the respect on heavy, He looked like he appreciated the gesture.

He tapped the area where the cards would go. I held my breath, hoping the lock wouldn't get jarred open. After thirty seconds that lasted for years, he handed the case back to me. "Nice case. I haven't seen one like that before. Where'd ya get it?"

I tried to avoid sounding relieved. "A little shop down in Sausalito. There's an old guy who runs a one of a kind trinket shop on the oceanfront who got it for me when I lived there."

"Coming from Cali, eh? We get a bit cooler here." Then he looked serious. "Be careful how you comport yourself, son. A lotta people here are nervous since the break-ins started. They'll be watching you, and I'm willing to bet a few might shoot if you get too close to their place, or their neighbors."

"Thanks, officer. I'll be careful," I said as I watched him climb back in the car. He pulled away with a wave, and I finally let out a sigh of relief. I started walking faster, trying to make up some of the time I'd wasted with the cop. I pulled out my card case and said, "Unlock." OK, it wasn't much of a code, but it matched my voiceprint. I opened it and looked at the screen.

"Whatta we got, Harry?" I asked.

"Oh, welcome back, Jack," Harry said.

"How much did you hear?"

"Enough to tell you to be careful."

"Any changes in the situation?" Sometimes Harry was insufferable.

"Based on what the cop said, the coffee shop could be the destination. He seems to be pretty...What was that?" I had to pull the phone away from my ear, Harry shouted so loud.

"You tell me. And if you ever lose your voice, I got an extra pound of it here." I rubbed my ear.

"The tracker's really going crazy now. We've got the main signal. The ghost signal on Morton Avenue's still there. There's a new ghost somewhere around where that coffee shop is."

It sounded like he was going to add something to what he was saying, but I interrupted. "I've got it. The key is the Morton Avenue ghost. Let me know about Stevenson and let me know about the ghost signal on Morton Avenue. How close is it to the coffee shop?"

"The ghost signal on Morton's been stopped for a few minutes. I've got your signal on a separate display, and it looks like you're a minute or two ahead of the ghost, for now. Ronald is almost at the shop if my calculations are correct." I took a breath. "Let me know the minute the Morton Avenue Ghost starts moving again." If my hunch was correct, I wasn't too late, but I had to keep moving.

I walked toward the coffee shop for what seemed a couple of years. The trees thinned out as I got closer to a five-way intersection with a row of train tracks. I stopped a few houses away from the intersection and wiped my brow. Even though the day had started out cool, the close to noonday sun added to my exertion left me sweating. "Am I at the right intersection?" I asked Harry as I shaded my eyes and looked due east hoping that I was close. Not only did I hope that I was nearing the end of the mission, I figured I could use a cup about now. Yes, I like hot coffee when it's hot. Don't judge me!

"Yeah," he replied. "Be sure to cross Kedron street, turn right and go half a block. You can't miss it." I listened carefully. Yep, Harry was chuckling.

"If I didn't know better, Harry, I'd say you were quoting that cop."

"Not word for word," he said, still laughing, "I could play the file for you."

I growled. "Never mind about that. What about the Morton Avenue Ghost?"

"If that thing were any closer to you, I'd think you were holding hands."

"That wouldn't do," I muttered quietly and looked around as I started out again. *There.* I was a little ahead of the situation, but not enough to waste any time. The light and the traffic were both against me, and I had to wait.

I was so intent on my mission that I didn't notice her until I heard the voice. "A penny for your thought."

I turned around and saw Jane Stevenson ... er ... Rothland now, who was smiling at me. "Uh, hello, miss." I was stuttering. "I do seem to have a lot on my mind."

"Like what?"

"Er...coffee, for instance," I said. It wasn't exactly a lie, but she might run away screaming if I'd said something like, "I'm trying to make your love life happen."

The light changed, and we crossed the street. "I'm headed to a new coffee shop right now! It' right over there." She pointed, and I could see the sign for the Coffee Station.

"I'd heard about that place and was headed over there myself," I said.

We walked together, not saying much. She put her hand on my arm as we turned toward the shop. "I hope I haven't led you on, but I really have another reason for going to the coffee shop." She paused. "There's a guy I admire who works there. I'm trying to get to know him better."

I nodded my head. "I never had any thoughts about that honey. I don't think I'm the right age for you anyway."

She breathed a sigh of relief. "Would you mind going in ahead of me, then. I don't want him to see us together." She blushed. "Just because."

"Happy to do that. Would I be out of line if I told you I hoped everything worked out?"

"Thank you." She let go of my arm and waited for me to move ahead of her.

I opened the door and looked around the shop. I had to blink a few times to let my eyes adjust to the lower light level. Harry's voice came over the phone. "The main dot and the ghosts are together."

"I can see that," I said before I shut the sound off. Now was not the time to spook anyone with voices coming from a box in my hand. I wished I'd brought the earbuds. He was sitting to the left in the corner by the display case with the pastries. He seemed to be looking at the door, but he looked straight past me.

I snuck up on him in plain sight by walking over to the pastry case. He was staring at the door as if he knew the exact time she'd appear. I couldn't help but wonder how many times he'd heard the story of them meeting. I glanced at the counter where Walt Stevenson and another clerk fixed the coffee orders. I looked back at the table where

Ronald was seated and almost laughed. The plan was so simple that it might work.

When she walked through the door, he jumped a little in his seat and swung his left arm back. He looked puzzled and then turned to look for his coffee cup.

"Cheers," I said as I saluted him with the cup he'd been trying to knock off the table. Then, my face turned innocent as I saw his anger. "Sorry, Ronald. I didn't think you'd mind since you were planning to dump it over anyway."

It took a few seconds, but the look of anger morphed into a look of fear. "How'd you…" He stopped when I showed him my badge.

"You were fixin' to be a naughty boy, Ronald. Your great-grandparents were very much in love. Why would you try to keep them from getting to know each other?" He slumped in his seat as if he hoped he could hide from me. "I'd love to sit with you. Thanks." I sat down next to him at the table.

I looked up at the counter as I sat down. Jane Rothland was making her play for Walt Stevenson. They seemed to be getting along very well. "Ah, young love. Isn't it beautiful?"

"Do you mean to tell me that you spent millions of taxpayer dollars to go back in time so that young lovers could get together?"

"Your father was an important man on the natural timeline. He saved the coffee crop in 2037."

"Yeah, wonderful." His noted lack of enthusiasm made me want to dig deeper.

"So, what happened?" I asked. "Why did you hate your father so much you'd deny your great-grandparents happiness?"

"He was so important; he didn't have time for us. He had time for his bimbos, but he couldn't find time for us and left my mom crying too many nights. They stayed married, but she had to raise me like a single mother. He destroyed my mom's confidence in herself. She was a broken woman."

"You not only destroyed their relationship," I nodded toward the register, "you destroyed yourself too. If your father wasn't born, then neither were you." I paused, letting that sink in. "You created a time fluctuation loop. Your great-grandparents never met, so you weren't born. Because you weren't born, your great-grandparents met and had your dad, and you were born, allowing you to go back in time and keep your great-grandparents from meeting."

Ronald looked at me with a smirk. "That's sort of cool!"

I didn't want to repeat my anger management class, so I didn't lose my cool. "'Cool' that you destroy your own existence?" Then I narrowed my eyes. "'Cool' that you doom the world to an existence without coffee?"

"You said the timeline would go back and forth. That sounds interesting."

I shook my head. "What I didn't tell you is that the timelines were converging. They won't keep shifting back and forth forever. Time fluctuations resolve in unchangeable positions. You would be gone forever."

"Worth it to get back at my father," he muttered.

"He'd never be born, and he'd never know," I said. "You'd have accomplished nothing."

He cocked his head as if in thought. "Hadn't thought about that," he said after he let it run through his mind.

I nodded, pulled out my cuffs and slapped them on his wrists. "Now it's time to pay," I said. People took notice when the cuffs clicked. I held up my badge. "No worries, folks. Police business." Then I turned the phone on and sent a message to Harry to bring the time capsule by and pick us up. All I wanted to do now was to drop this character off and have a cup of coffee.

Our missions were supposed to be secret, but the grapevine gossip spread. I accepted congratulations and well wishes, many saluting me with their coffee cups as I headed to the break room to meet Julia. I saw her sitting at a table drinking a cup of coffee. I'd brought my own cup, the one my coworkers gave me as a present for my promotion. I filled it full of coffee and invited myself to sit down, not like I needed to ask.

"I like that cup," she said to me. "It's simple and has an inside joke: 'It's always coffee time.' I need to get one like that."

I smiled. "You just like the idea of his and hers cups."

She laughed and moved her chair closer to mine. She watched me as I poured two or three teaspoons worth of sugar into my cup and a couple of dollops of cream for good measure. "Sometimes I think you drink coffee just to have an excuse for drinking cream and sugar."

I lifted my cup to salute her and took a long swig of coffee.

Then she asked a serious question. "I've heard rumors that even when we fix the timeline like you just did," she frowned at my "who me" face and continued, "there can still be permanent changes to people and events. Know anything about that?"

"Speaking in general." I winked. "I've heard the Time Managers talk about that, but I've never seen any evidence of it." I took another drink of my creamy sweetness. "Let's stop with the speculation, though. Let's talk about something more important, like our wedding plans."

ABOUT BOB JAMES

Bob James is a native of the Chicago area, growing up in Oak Park, Ill. He currently lives in Corpus Christi, TX. He retired after twenty-five years in the education business – one year as a sign language interpreter followed by twenty-four years as a teacher in the fields of Special Education and Technology. All of his unpublished work can be accessed through his new site, Bob James – The Author. He writes daily devotionals, Science Fiction and Thrillers, and is also working on a book about the journey that he and his wife went through during her battle with breast cancer. Bob has been married to his wife Lucy since 1979. They have two sons, one daughter, one granddaughter, and one grandson.

facebook.com/BobJamesauthor

twitter.com/rockyfort

DEEP ECHOES

BY R.M. ALEXANDER WRITING AS MELODY ASH

The French Chateau rose into view, first with its vibrant blue slate rooftop, then the limestone exterior, a graceful contrast of color breaking through the vibrant green of the South Carolina forests. A hidden treasure now exposed for world review. Caitlin Benoit's pace slowed, her long legs basking in the rays of the warm southern sun. Other visitors hurried past her, more concerned with getting inside the house than enjoying the view or understanding the history of a Gilded Age estate. She tussled the thick curls she'd inherited from her father—dark brown like his, highlighted by her mother's gold, Caucasian coloring. Anyone's quick glance would see a woman with a healthy, year-round tan, a good mix of her mother's European and her father's African roots. And she was equally proud of both sides of her heritage. A heritage that defined a passion for understanding the past through research and exploration.

But, she reminded herself, visiting the Biltmore Estate wasn't work. This was a vacation. A break from exploring a history in slave trade around the world in all its ugly incarnations. This was a break, and she thought with a sigh, one much needed.

She rejoined the foot traffic to the front of the chateau, the size and grandeur more impressive the closer she got. The vastness of an estate that seemed to stretch in every direction surrounded by gardens, forests, and fountains.

Her phone rang as she stood in line to enter the house, and Caitlin rolled her eyes. Just an afternoon to herself—it couldn't be that much to ask. Should have left it in the car. She pulled the phone from a pocket and glanced at the name, the exasperation replaced with a soft smile playing across her lips.

"Hey, Sean. You're lucky I like you."

He chuckled. "I knew that, but why?'

She pressed a finger against one ear to drown out the surrounding voices and laughter. "I'm getting ready to go inside the Biltmore Estate. When the phone rang, I was ready to wring the neck of whoever was interrupting my vacation." Caitlin smiled sweetly at a man who'd turned around with a raised brow and met her eyes. As he turned and returned his attention to his family, she shook her head with a roll of her eyes. People could be so nosey.

"Biltmore, huh?" Sean asked. "How do you feel about a side trip?"

Caitlin stepped out of line, nodded to the people behind her. "Side trip? Why would I do that?"

"I found something you might be interested in."

Her stomach did a familiar flip it did with any new discovery. Even after ten years of working in the field, new sites made her blood race. "Oh?"

And to make matters worse, she could hear the smile through the phone. Sean knew he had her undivided attention.

"A local builder was clearing ground for a new factory, found the remains of what appears to be slave shacks."

The flips erupted into a full-on explosion. "Has an archaeological team been called in yet?"

"Yeah. You."

She laughed. They'd graduated college at the same time and, along with another friend, Jenny, formed a team quickly respected by the archaeological community. "I like that. Where are you?"

"Just north of Charleston. Should be about a four-hour drive from where you are."

She nodded, glanced at the Biltmore Estate with a passing shade of disappointment, then turned and headed back down the driveway. The vacation didn't have to be canceled, just postponed. Besides, Sean knew she'd never turn down the chance to explore a new find. It's why he called her. "I'm far too predictable. You knew I'd come running."

"Predictable is not a word I'd use to describe Caitlin Benoit, but in this case, I had a pretty good hunch. But just in case you need further incentive, the shacks aren't all that was found."

"I'm already on my way. You don't have to play dirty."

He laughed. "I found a stone. Looks like Hoodoo symbols are carved into it."

She trotted the rest of the way to the car. A stone with writing meant a gold mine to treasure seekers. If word got out, she'd never make it on time. "Was it pulled from the site already?"

"No, it's waiting for you."

"Has it been made public yet?"

"You know me better than that, Caitlin. Don't worry. The whole site has been taped off. You have first dibs, so don't kill yourself getting here."

As he finished the sentence, Caitlin's foot was already stomping against the pedal, tires screeching from the parking space as other visitors to Biltmore stared at her in wonder. "You take all the fun out of everything."

"Someone has to. I'll see you in a couple hours."

"You said it would take about four to get to you."

"Right. And the way you drive, it'll be two."

Caitlin said goodbye and ended the call, cranked up the volume on a favorite mix of songs spanning three decades, and turned onto I-26 East. She settled in the seat, ready for a beautiful ride through the Carolina mountains and forests beneath clear blue skies. Her mind raced over the possibilities. A carved stone found at the site of slave shack remains. Hoodoo and Voodoo were both widely practiced religions among early slaves, both faiths a thick blend of Christian beliefs blended with African rituals. The stone wasn't a big surprise. Simple tools of their faith, like a rock, would have been easy to hide from the plantation masters who didn't want their workforce dabbling in what would have been seen as witchcraft. A rock in the corner of a house? Who would look twice at that?

"But every find tells a bigger story." Caitlin pressed further on the pedal, the Jeep barely twitching in response to the acceleration. What remained of the Antebellum South had been romanticized, the best of the slave quarters far less characteristic of what many were forced to live in. Brick houses with well-constructed walls and fireplaces were not commonplace, but the far more common wooden structures weren't easy to find. Most had been destroyed over the past century and a half, even most of the plantation mansions were nothing more than a long-forgotten memory.

Studying this period of American history always placed Caitlin in an odd juxtaposition between the two separate histories that coursed through her veins and shared her heart. Maybe that was why it captivated her so much.

To travel back in time, to see the histories merge into one clumsy choreographed dance.

"I'd have to be invisible, but it'd be interesting." She looked across the rich jade forests lining either side of the highway. "But since that's not a possibility, I'll keep digging."

After all, digging was what she was meant to do.

A four-hour trip into Charleston was an extreme over-estimation. Caitlin chuckled as she pulled into a parking lot where Sean told her to meet him. As promised, he stood against the car, arms crossed, a smirk playing on his lips beneath a thick beard, his long, black hair pulled into one of those man-buns she didn't quite understand. She climbed from the car and worked her long brown hair into a ponytail.

"Any tickets?"

Caitlin scoffed. "Of course not. The police love me."

"I'm afraid to ask what that means."

She waved a hand in the air. "It means I don't drive fast enough for them to care enough to catch me."

Sean guffawed as he crossed his thick arms and leaned against the car. "When you cut the trip in nearly half, I have a hard time believing that."

"Well, when they aren't looking," Caitlin said, "it's a completely different matter. But now you're just trying to distract me. Where is this site?"

"About ten minutes up the road."

She nodded, pleased the site was so far removed from public eyes. "And the legalities of the dig?"

"Permits obtained, we are clear with the South Carolina's archaeological department."

"Oh, that's good news." With the paperwork in hand, a tremendous amount of time would be saved, and no waiting. That's what made her happiest—no red tape, no wait, just digging in and exploring. "Is this Federal or state land?"

"State."

She nodded. Good, that made it even easier. "No signs of being a burial site?"

"None. I've covered all the territory, so don't worry. Like I said, we are in the clear."

And that was why she loved working with Sean. They made a good team, one of the best in the field. "Then don't keep me waiting any longer."

"I don't know," Sean chuckled. "It's fun to see you squirm like this. Let's talk some more."

Caitlin gave him a light punch on the shoulder. "I'll go without you."

"All right, all right. Want to ride along or follow?"

"I'll follow. Is Jenny going to meet us here?"

Sean shook his head. "She's at another site in Florida and can't get away. It's just you and me for now."

"Good enough. I'm sure it's nothing we can't handle."

"That's what I'm thinking. From what I can tell, the site is a small one. We'll section it off, explore a little further out, but I think the big find is the stone."

"Well, let's see. Lead the way. And don't take every back road on the way."

Sean smiled the mischievous grin Caitlin loved so much. He was a good friend, always had been, and his wife the sweetest woman in the world. Now with a baby on the way, Caitlin guessed Sean would be stepping away from the job for a while, at least until the family grew settled into a new lifestyle filled with dirty diapers and three a.m. feedings.

"Would I do that?" he asked, green eyes twinkling.

"In a heartbeat."

He laughed. "You're right. Okay. I'll be nice. Keep your britches on. We'll be there in ten."

"No one says that anymore, you know."

"I do. I'm someone."

Caitlin laughed as she got in the car. Yeah, she loved him. But she'd kick him in the shins if he made her wait a second longer than necessary.

Caitlin grabbed her backpack from the trunk as she scanned across an empty field bordered by a thick state forest. Mostly undisturbed grass grew hip-high, and Caitlin guessed the area was the kind of place where few people did more than pass quickly by on their way into the woods where they could hike or bird watch, search for waterfalls or go for a picnic beneath cover from the sun.

Caitlin liked nature as much as anyone, had a soft spot for animals of every size and shape, but her captivation remained locked on what was hidden in the ground, what was left behind by the people who came before her, and before them, and before them. A giant jigsaw puzzle that explained why people were who they were, breadcrumbs that led the way into the human psyche, the ones people preferred to forget until something appeared to capture their imagination and sparked emotions.

A puzzle far more important than the kind hobbyists glued together and hung in frames along the walls.

Now, the only living humans were herself and Sean. No cars, no audience outside the songbirds hiding within trees draped in brown moss.

Sean stopped at the base of a thigh-high pile of stone barely visible in the grasses. Though weathered, the angles and edges still resembled the craftsmanship of the carver. She stooped beside the collection, finger tracing the quarter-circle of stones still half-buried among the surrounding grass and dirt.

"Like you said, not much left of the structure."

"No, probably destroyed after the Civil War, and then forgotten."

She nodded. "Happened to most slave quarters." She scanned the inner circle of the remains, a circular stone catching her eye. Caitlin glanced at Sean. "That's it?"

He nodded, his smile wide. "It's what you drove a hundred miles an hour down the interstate for."

Caitlin rolled her eyes and turned her attention back to the stone. Unlike all the surrounding stonework, this one was a clear circle, the carvings a series of swirls and lines contained within an outer ring. "It's phenomenal. Those swirls, they don't look random, do they?"

"I admit, I didn't study it closely, I left that for you. But no, not random at all."

Caitlin picked up a stone slightly larger than her hand, stared at the carving, eyes following lines she imagined had once been traced in white paint. "This is a gold mine, just with this rock alone."

"That's what I thought, too."

"We'll have to study it, see if there's a special significance," Caitlin hovered a hand above the rock, gently waved over the carving.

The air around her grew stuffy in the late afternoon heat, an elastic feeling of plastic wrap filling her lungs. Caitlin cleared her throat, tried to speak, but her voice was lost.

Then, with a shallow cough, she found her voice once more. "I hate swallowing down the wrong pipe."

Sean's voice called out from the distance and then disappeared altogether. Caitlin lifted her eyes and stifled a scream. The open field was gone, replaced by a row of wooden houses. The air smelled different, more natural, the trees shorter. It looked right, and horribly, terrifyingly wrong.

Caitlin dropped the stone at her feet, missed her toes by a fraction of an inch. But she didn't notice. Instead, she stared at the nearest cabin. Somehow, the ruins had blossomed into a full-sized slave cabin. She covered her nose, the sickening smell of human waste trickling through open windows.

"That's impossible. How…"

Voices in the distance grew louder, and Caitlin desperately searched for a hiding place. Only slave cabins provided cover, and she dashed behind one, breath held as the voices drew closer.

"Henry, you go near the main house again, and you be whipped fo' sure."

The master? Caitlin's head rang, and mind raced to make sense of the images and words.

A woman and a child—Caitlin guess he was around eight years old —walked in front of the house next to the one she hid behind. The woman, dressed in a long, tattered dress and a head wrap knotted at the top of her head, gently pushed the child along a path that didn't exist any more than the houses did a few minutes ago.

"Mawmaw!"

"You hush, boy. You lucky to be with your momma and poppa, you know that. Now you mind and get inside a'fore you cause more troubles."

The dust from the path took to the air and tickled Caitlin's nose. The sneeze happened before she could stop it, and even as she pressed hard against the wall of the cabin, Caitlin knew she'd been discovered.

"Who out there? I hear'd ya. Who there?'

Caitlin searched the field, calculated the distance to the trees. If the woman didn't come around to the back of the cabin, she might be able to make it to the forest, and they'd be thick enough to conceal her for a little while. Might buy some time to figure out what happened, where she was.

"Who there?" the woman demanded, but the footsteps didn't sound any closer.

With a deep breath, Caitlin pushed off the back wall and sprinted for the trees.

The woman's voice faded as Caitlin headed further into the cover of the South Carolinian trees. She leaped over a fallen tree, lost her footing and stumbled, sharp pain rocketing through her right ankle. Caitlin fell to the ground, grimaced as she glanced down at the ankle already swelling. She lay against the forest floor, stared at the blue sky above the reach of the trees. Great. Just great.

Closing her eyes, she circled through her thoughts. Any other time, she'd be more than equipped to deal with the sprain. But the backpack carried only a brush and tiny shovel, nothing to stabilize a weakened ankle. And right now, she had no idea where that was, or where Sean was. She didn't know where she was.

If she were to venture a guess, Caitlin'd guess she had jetted right into Gone with the Wind.

The stone. Her brows furrowed as she sketched the symbols onto the forest floor, searching for a memory of their meaning, then shook her head. Impossible. A rock doesn't have any real power.

Caitlin took a broken branch and flattened out the dirt, listened for footsteps. Content she was alone, she scanned the property beyond the trees. Worker houses that appeared out of mid-air. The dirt path, the woman, and her child. The air.

The clues were everywhere, impossible or not.

But time travel was a bedtime story, a corny romance story on a lonely Friday night. It wasn't real.

The throbbing in her ankle cut short the thoughts. Caitlin grimaced as she pulled the ankle closer, examined the blue tint shadowing the balloon filling her ankle. Caitlin shook her head. She'd never run, and hardly be able to walk, until the ankle healed. "Five to ten days stuck here."

Even though she still wasn't altogether sure where here was.

Caitlin reached for a nearby tree and used the trunk to steady herself while standing up with the one good leg. Leaning against the tree with one shoulder, she stared through the trees at the cabins. If she was indeed in pre-Civil War days, that meant her parentage would cause an uproar in the Caucasian population, and African American population may only be fractionally more welcoming. And then, there would be the issue of the plantation master discovering a strange woman harbored on the property. Complications didn't begin to define the situation that would create. But then, if she got her hands back on the stone, wouldn't be as easy as simply doing another wave across the symbols and go home? Healing in the twenty-first century would be far easier than here among strangers and potential enemies.

Caitlin reached for a thick, fallen limb, trimmed the leaves and thin limbs from it, pressed the branch into the sodden earth and tested her weight. A rough cane, but it would do the job until she reached the stone. Then a simple wave, a zap back through the plastic air, and she'd be home. No one would know, no one would be put in danger because she was there.

A warm southern breeze eased across the forest as she moved to the tree line and carefully listened. No more voices. Maybe the woman returned to wherever she was supposed to be, the child locked in a cabin. Although, the child should be working as well, which meant someone would be looking for him. She'd have to be careful.

Caitlin hobbled across the long blades of grass, eased next to the cabin and rested for a minute. When the cabins materialized, she'd dropped the rock on the ground, and Caitlin doubted it moved. Her brows furrowed. Unless it went back home. If it were possible, that would mean she was stuck. A shiver ran down her spine.

With one last test of her weight against the limb, Caitlin hobbled to the front of the cabin, smiled to see the rock still where she thought it would be. Clumsily, she bent over and picked up the rock, gave a glance up and down the dirt path and breathed a sigh of relief to see she was still alone.

"Now, just a quick wave, and home I go." Grimacing as she put her foot down, Caitlin waved a hand over the symbols, closed her eyes and waited.

Nothing.

Opening her eyes, Caitlin scanned the world around her. Nothing changed. "That doesn't make sense." Another wave, eyes open, she waited for a white spark or a jolt of electricity or anything. No plastic wrap around her lungs, no Sean, nor the wonderful twenty-first-century world. "Oh, come on. This can't be happening."

She waved her hand over the symbols again and again, faster, more frantic. And her heart dropped when time and again, nothing changed.

"Okay," she whispered. "Obviously, I'm doing something wrong, or different, from the first go around. Maybe this thing needs to be recharged or something."

Her thoughts shifted through all she'd learned about the practice of hoodoo. There was no recharging the stone, but if it were, in fact, a hoodoo artifact, from all she remembered, everything about the conditions would have to be identical for the thing to work again.

Caitlin looked at the sun. The weather was identical to back home, but maybe the sun was hitting the stone from a different angle. Painfully, she circled, angled the stone beneath the sun, tried again. Then raked a hand through her thick curls.

"Okay. For whatever reason, I'm stuck. So, figure out exactly where here is, learn what I can, and figure out how to get home." Caitlin took a step and stumbled to the ground, gritting her teeth against the pain.

"O' chil'. What you doin' back here? If the masta catch you, it be whippin' for sho."

The woman hurried to her side, eased Caitlin to her feet. "Oh, lawdy chil'. That bad there. Come inside," the woman looked around, her face panicked. "We can't stay out here, we be seen for sure. Come. Come."

The woman helped Caitlin into a cabin under a roof riddled with thin holes. Little furniture existed save a small, crudely built table, piles of thin material piled in two of the corners, and a stone fireplace with a well-dented pot sitting on the hearth. A single bed built of weathered wood stood in the corner, the blankets pockmarked with holes and frayed at the ends. The space was pitiful, depressing, and yet love hung from the walls in an invisible film of retreat.

Caitlin looked at the woman at her side.

She smiled. "'Tis the best house I ever lived in."

Caitlin nodded, forced a smile. "It's very nice," she said in a whisper. The risk of someone hearing a conversation through the thin walls too great.

"You are kind," she replied with a nod. "It'll do. Rest where the grandchil'en sleep." She rested Caitlin on the floor in a corner furthest from the bed, which wasn't saying much. "I'm Mitilda."

Caitlin had to wonder, as she inched closer to the wall, how so many people lived in such a tiny place. "It's nice to meet you, Mitilda. I'm Caitlin. I don't want to impose."

"Impose?"

"Um, be a problem."

Mitilda shook her head with brows furrowed as she studied Caitlin for the first time. "You not dressed like a slave."

"I'm not a slave."

"Underground Railroad?" Mitilda nodded as she whispered with some urgency.

There was no sense in correcting the error, Caitlin wasn't sure how to explain a truth she didn't quite understand herself. Aside from passing through the plastic wrap-like space and shortness of breath, there was no hint that anything actually happened during the few short seconds it took to shift from decimated cabins to standing, living history. A dream only shattered by the reality of an injured ankle and the woman standing in front of her. Mitilda was real enough, Caitlin thought, and how that made sense still tickled every nerve.

"I'll be back. Rest here," Mitilda said, breaking through Caitlin's thoughts. She hurried out of the cabin and quickly returned with two small sticks, sat on the floor next to Caitlin with the sticks resting next to one leg. "It is bad, but it will heal. With these here sticks and scraps of material. You will have to rest a day or two. "

Caitlin nodded as she observed Mitilda wrap strips that looked as though they'd been torn from clothing. Two or three days trapped in the eighteen-hundreds—an endless opportunity to study lives first-hand. And countless opportunities to cause irreparable damage to history. Or, she wondered, was that just something that happened in the movies and fiction?

"That there should help."

Caitlin examined the make-shift bandage, smiled. "You did a good job. Thank you."

Mitilda grinned. "I's old. Spend 'nough time in this here life, and you learn how to do a lot."

"I'm sure. Forgive me, but you don't work in the fields?"

Mitilda shook her head. "I's too old to pick cotton. I would have been sold during the last auction but masta' decided to keep me so as I can fix cuts and help the sick to keep my people in the field. If they's come in hurt at the end of the night, I fix 'em so they can go back out the next day, or they be punished. I be punished. The smile was gone now, replaced with a sadness brought on by years of captivity. "I take care of the child'en too young to work. Sometimes go to the masta's house when they have a dinner party. They make use of me."

Caitlin reached out and gently put rested on hand on top of the older woman's weathered skin. Sadness, yes, broken, no, and Caitlin couldn't help admire the slave. "I'm glad you were here today."

Mitilda smiled. "You talk funny. Like the masta's family only different. Are you learned?"

Caitlin nodded. "Actually, I'm not from around here. I was wondering if you can help me with something?"

A bell rang in the distance and Mitilda jumped to her feet. "'Twill have to wait. You stay here and hide. Do not come out of the cabin. If the masta finds you, 'twill be trouble for sure."

Caitlin nodded again as Mitilda hurried out of the cabin. The woman talked much better than Caitlin expected. From all the history she'd studied, slaves weren't allowed to read or write which created a sense of dependency for the slaves to their owners. Plantation owners also felt, however misguided, that the dumbing down of a people prevented revolts.

But Mitilda had a better understanding of English than a kinder-gartner, which was the accepted level for a typical slave. Caitlin wondered if the master, whoever he was, accepted it, or if he knew. People could find a way to play dumb when needed or wanted, and maybe that's what Mitilda did for survival.

Caitlin brought the stone from the backpack and looked at it again, ran a hand over the markings, not expecting the cabin to disap-pear. When nothing happened, Caitlin rolled her eyes. "Of course not." She traced the markings with one finger, remembering seeing some-thing like them in a book once. Caitlin stared hard at the image, her finger going over it once, twice, three times. A ritual marking, she remembered. "Obviously time travel, that much is clear, I think." Caitlin chuckled. "But why isn't it working now?"

She pinched two fingers across her forehead. Nothing she had ever seen gave a step-by-step account of how to perform hoodoo rituals, and certainly nothing about time travel. "If the plantation masters knew about this," she ran a hand through her hair. "Oh, what they would have said." With a passing glance at the now bandaged ankle, Caitlin struggled to stand, hand on the weak cabin wall. She glanced upward at the slits of the sun shining through the roof. On nice days, the light must be welcome. During storms, it must be horrific—not a dry spot anywhere. Caitlin shook her head. Shelter from the elements, but not much. It was already hot and stuffy. She could imagine what late July might feel like inside. Or should a hurricane come through… Caitlin's chest tightened at the thought. How many must have lost their lives in storms, those lives and deaths left unrecorded and lost to history?

Leaning on the wall for support, Caitlin hobbled her way through the tiny space. The table held only a couple of crude spoons that looked as though they'd been hammered with rocks or some other equally crude instrument. She turned, scanned the rest of the space. A single change of clothes, she noticed as she counted, one for each member of the family. No shoes, no books, no paper, no writing tools. What they did have looked like it was brought in from a dumpster, and Caitlin guessed that wasn't too far off the mark. The master probably didn't give them more than a few rags once a year, from everything she read, and she guessed dinner was scarce too.

But none of these details answered the single question on her mind. How did she get home? First-hand knowledge to bring back to the table, but that knowledge was useless until she got back home.

Her ankle hollered in protest as she attempted to walk. Finally, Caitlin sunk back down to the floor. One day in the cabin was probably safe enough. Give the ankle a chance to heal and then she'd be back around tomorrow.

Caitlin gritted her teeth. She'd had a sprained ankle a time or two in the past and knew how unlikely it would improve dramatically overnight. But staying longer was out of the question. When Mitlida came back, she'd talk to the woman about the rock. Chances were, she'd know a thing or two about the Hoodoo symbols. The rock was found among these ruined cabins. It must belong to this family.

Then she'd go home and leave the past to figure out the future.

Footsteps against the wood slat flooring on the outside porch startled Caitlin awake, and she bolted upright, surprised she'd fallen asleep. She braced for whoever would come into the cabin, recalling her college studies. Plantation masters and their overseers performed random cabin checks for anything they considered contraband, and in a room so thinly dressed, hiding places were scarce. And in a place where the landowner prevented an uprising at all costs would mean no weapons.

Caitlin readied herself. A weapon would help but wasn't necessary. If needed, she'd fight fist-to-fist. Self-defense had been a helpful field skill in the past, and now, being in the past, she thought with a chuckle, it might come in handy again.

She balled up both fists as the door opened, then relaxed as Mitilda walked in followed by a man and woman who looked ready to fall over and a couple of children who were scantily dressed.

Caitlin sat up, ready to move, or leave, to make room for the family.

Mitilda waved a hand. "Sit, sit. This is my daughter, Etta, and her husband, James. I tells them about you. There is no reason to get up. 'Sides, you shouldn't be on your ankle lessen you want it to be worse."

Caitlin shook her head as her eyes locked on the two children as they sat on the floor, bare bottoms on the rough floor. "I can't intrude like that. I'll camp in the forest, allow you your privacy."

Etta raised a brow while Mitilda nodded. "I tells you she is learned."

"You no slave, are you?"

Caitlin shook her head as she returned her eyes to the hosts. "No, I'm not."

More steps on the front porch caused an exchange of worried glances that were impossible to miss.

"Come here, chil'ren," Mitilda herded the kids into a corner behind the table as the door opened and a man with light brown hair brushed back in a wave and dressed in a fancy red coat. There was little doubt in Caitlin's mind he was someone important on the plantation, but his face was kind, and Mitilda and her family relaxed instantly. Not the master, then.

"Good evening, Mitilda. I understand I'm a night early, but ..." his eyes fell on Caitlin, and a warm grin spread across his face.

Caitlin instantly decided that she liked him.

"Well, who do we have here?" he asked as he took another step into the cabin.

Mitilda smiled. "Ev'ning, Mr. John. This poor woman twisted her ankle. She be stayin' with us 'til she c'n leave."

Mr. John held out a hand. Caitlin reached to shake it, but instead held the hand gently in one palm and kissed the top of her hand. "A pleasure to meet you, m'lady."

"A pleasure to meet you, Mr. John." Caitlin pulled her hand back, surprised to find her heart fluttering in a way she'd never experienced before. Must be the jet lag, she thought with a short smile.

"Please, not Mr. John. M'lady is most welcome to call me by my given name. Dare I ask how you injured your ankle?"

"I'm afraid I wasn't watching where I was going and twisted it. The sprain isn't too bad."

John's cherry wood eyes studied her, drank her in. "I am pleased to hear as much. I'm sure Miltida is able to help you heal quickly. I'm sorry, I don't remember seeing you before. I most certainly would remember if I had. Where did you say you're from?"

"Up north."

"And what brings you here?"

Her mind raced, searching for a story that would fit, fighting to recall her history. "My father recently became a professor at the University of South Carolina."

"I hear that's a growing educational institution."

"Indeed, it is."

"Yes. Is your mother in the area as well?"

"Yes. In a home near the university."

John nodded, eyes still locked hard on hers. Friendly eyes, but also wise enough to recognize the lie. John studied her silently, but instead of testing her further, he only smiled. "Welcome to Shady Oak. May I send someone for your father? Surely he would like to hear of your injury."

"No, no," Caitlin's mind raced for an explanation. "He returned north to retrieve the rest of our belongings. I'm sure one night will make a big difference, and I'll be able to leave."

John nodded. "You are most welcome to stay in the main house."

She shook her head and smiled. "That's very kind of you, but I'm sure your family would prefer that I not."

John cocked his head to one side, clearly surprised by the bluntness. And why wouldn't he be? In his time, this time, women were trained to be demure, quiet, obedient. Caitlin suppressed a grin. She wouldn't fit in well at all, and not just because of the color of her skin.

"Is there anything I can get for you then, to make your stay more comfortable?" he asked.

"No, I'm fine, thank you."

"Very well." He turned his attention back to the family. "Perhaps we should postpone our lessons for another night, Mitilda?"

"As you would like, Mr. John."

"Please," Caitlin sat upright. "Don't let me stop you. I don't want to be in anyone's way."

"Well, I think that settles it, then. Shall we, James?"

"Yes, sir."

The two men settled at the table, with the little boy comfortable on James' lap. Etta sat next to Caitlin on the floor. "Mr. John teaches James and Henry to read. Momma and me are even picking up a little."

The heir to the plantation, teaching slaves to read and write. That was something she didn't expect. John was breaking the law by doing so, and the family breaking the law for learning. His punishment would be minor, theirs, likely death. "Does his father know?"

"The masta? Oh, heavens no. We'd be thrashed for sho, and Mr. John might be disowned for helping us."

"And he continues to take that kind of chance?"

"Oh, he a good man, Miss Caitlin. We are lucky to have him to help us."

John turned around in the makeshift chair, meeting Caitlin's eyes once more. "With a father as a professor, I assume you know how to read?"

Caitlin bit the inside of her lip to keep from laughing. "Yes. I do. And arithmetic."

John raised a brow and grinned. "That's more than most women know."

"He felt it important, believes times are changing."

"That they are," John agreed. "And they're going to change more if that Republican Lincoln wins the Presidential run. My father says if he does, the South will leave the Union."

James eased Henry off his knee and patted the boy's bottom, sent him to play with his sister on the other side of the room. "Does you thinks it will?"

John smiled and patted the man's arm, something Caitlin guessed typically didn't happen between the white and black of the time. But neither seemed uncomfortable or surprised by the gesture. "Do you think it will, James. But you're getting there." The man nodded, and John continued. "I don't rightly know. Men are in my father's office arguing it out as we speak. I think Lincoln has a good chance, and if the South does secede, I'll move north." He turned to Caitlin. "Your father might have moved his family at a bad time."

"There's never a good time when you have a family like mine."

John smiled and nodded again. "Yes, I suppose that is true." He stood, hands clapped together. "I better return to the main house before my father begins looking for me. Mitilda, James, Etta, I'll be down again later this week when my parents leave for a couple days. Caitlin, it was an honor to meet you. I hope to see you again before you leave."

"I would like that," she replied, surprised to find it true.

"Very well. Good night."

John stepped out of the cabin and Caitlin turned to the family harboring her. "Isn't it dangerous for him to be coming here like that?"

"Dangerous? His father will surely be mad, but the masta not like to harm his son."

"Not for him, for you. The law is clear."

"Yes, 'spose it is. But Mr. John has a special feelin's 'bout James."

"Why is that?"

"Child'n, go lie down, go to sleep," Etta ordered, then continued. "Mr. John was in the field one night with a lady friend. James just finished working. Sumthing caught his eye and James stood up, sees sumthing moving right for Mr. John. He ran to warn Mr. John but was a'most too late. A large tiger was creep'n for Mr. John. Mr. John would be dead now if James hadn't acted so fast."

Tiger? Caitlin's brows furrowed. There were never tigers in North America, so the orange and black striped cats didn't complete the picture correctly. Shifting through history, she realized Etta was referring to the Eastern Cougar, whose territory stretched across the entire expanse of Eastern North America. Early settlers first referred to the animal as the tiger, a term that stuck for many years.

Caitlin nodded. "Is that why he comes here a couple times a week?"

Etta nodded. "He say the masta knows. He don't like it but won't stop Mr. John. Long as we do what we told and don't cause no trouble, the masta doesn't say nothin'. That's why Momma hasn't been sold off, why my chil'n are still here and not sold to 'nother masta."

Mitilda bent down and examined Caitlin's ankle. "The masta not a terrible man. I owned by men worse'n than him. But we still slaves, and we have to mind our place 'til them changes Mr. John keeps talkin' 'bout happen."

Caitlin glanced at the ankle, which was much less swollen than it was earlier that afternoon. "I'm putting you all in danger by being here."

Mitilda shook her head. "Mr. John won't say anything, and you can go be with your father soon."

"My father isn't anywhere near here. Or my mother."

"I know," Mitilda rewrapped the ankle.

"You know?"

"Of course. If your daddy was near, you wouldn't be with us. And you wouldn't be half-dressed in man's clothes.

"I've never seen a man dressed like that," James said.

Caitlin reached for the backpack she shoved behind her back when she had heard the first footsteps. "You're right. I was wondering if you could help me with that." She pulled the stone from the bag. "I found this, and it's how I came here. Do you know anything about it?"

Mitilda took the stone, showed the stone to both Etta and James, who exchanged looks with the older woman before turning away. Mitilda shook her head. "Nothin'. We don't know nothin'."

Caitlin took the rock, glanced at the symbols. She hadn't missed the exchange between the family. They knew something they were unwilling to share. "Are you sure? I think this can help me get back home. You must realize I didn't come with my father."

"It ain't none of our business. And what will get you back to your father is healing that ankle, not a painted rock."

Caitlin nodded. "Well, it was worth asking."

"It be best we all go to sleep. We wake early."

As it turned out, early meant long before the sun came up. After a breakfast consisting of only a small ration of cornmeal mush, Mitilda, Henry and Caitlin stayed behind while everyone else left for the fields. Caitlin's stomach still growled in protest, the meager offerings not near enough. She laid an arm over it, ignored the hunger pain. The rations were more than the family could afford to share, and she doubted they had enough for themselves, much less share with a stranger from another time.

Caitlin scrambled to her feet, helped Mitilda wipe down the dishes in a bucket of rainwater as the two women swatted away mosquitos and flies, unable to wipe the images of the breakfast gathering from her mind. How anyone spent twelve to fifteen hours without passing out from malnutrition under a beating sun surpassed her under-standing.

Mitilda took the last bowl from Caitlin, wiped it against a dirty apron, and rested it on the table. Then she settled at Caitlin's feet, unwrapped the ankle. "It be bruised, but the swelling is better. You might right to bear some weight on it by tomorrow or day after."

Caitlin watched the woman's hands wrap the rags with more skill than she'd ever wrap an elastic bandage. As Mitilda backed away and asked for Caitlin to try out the ankle, Caitlin grinned. "I'm impressed. Whenever I wrap a sprain, the bandage slips right off."

"Bandage?"

"A brown elastic ... It's something made to make sprains feel better."

Mitilda stopped, looked up at Caitlin with strange eyes, glanced at the shorts and t-shirt now filthy from the forest and cabin floor. Then, she focused again on the ankle. "Thank you. No one says that very much." She stood up. "I best see to my chores for the day. Rest. You'll be able to go home soon."

She left the cabin with Henry at her side. Caitlin moved around the cabin once more. This time, she ignored the living conditions, searching instead for items tied to the Hoodoo culture. In the northeast corner of the house, Caitlin discovered a small bundle of cloth. Though it looked like a discarded ball of scrap material, she carefully retrieved it and unrolled the torn fabric. Inside, a small treasure of Hoodoo-reminiscent items rested in the palm of her hand: brass pins, rock crystal, a small brass bell, and a tiny bone.

Bingo. Exactly the proof she was looking for that the family practiced the religion tied to the stone that brought her to this time.

A gentle knock on the door made Caitlin jump, and she folded the items back into a ball and rested them against the corner where they were, then hobbled across toward the center of the cabin in time for the door to open.

John walked in, a single tulip and a book in hand. Caitlin began to limp toward him, but he shook his head and held up a hand. "Please. You must rest your foot." He hurried to the table and picked up a chair, set it in the middle of the room. "Sit."

She obliged, as much to get off the foot as to satisfy him. "James and Mitilda are ... in the fields. But surely, you must know that."

He nodded. "I do. I came to see you." He glanced at the closed door behind him. "I know it is not considered appropriate for us to be alone, but I mean you no harm."

Caitlin smiled, recalling what was considered appropriate etiquette of the nineteenth century. A woman and a man who were not married in a private room were considered far from appropriate. "I'm not worried about us being alone."

"I did not think you would be. You are different from other women I have held the acquaintance of. Why is that?"

If I told you, you'd never believe me, she thought. "Maybe because I'm not from around here, or from Georgia."

John took a careful step forward and stooped, handed her the flower and book. Caitlin took them, laid the tulip to one side and examined the book. Charles Dickens' *David Copperfield*. Caitlin grinned. More appropriate than he could know.

"I hope the tokens are acceptable. While James and Mitilda only read simple words, I suspected you know how to read as well as I."

"It's perfect. Thank you."

"You are most welcome. May I?" John motioned to the other chair. Caitlin nodded, and he pulled the other chair over to sit in front of her. "I thought perhaps the book would help pass the time while you wait for the healing of your ankle."

"It will. Thank you."

John's eyes dropped to Caitlin's legs, following them down to the ankle. "How is the sprain?"

Caitlin shifted in the chair, absently wondered if the man had ever seen a woman's legs from beneath all the petticoats, crinolines, and gowns. "Tender, but the swelling is down, so I'm hoping to be able to return home soon."

"I am happy for your quick healing, though sorry to hear you will be leaving so quickly."

"Oh?"

He seemed briefly embarrassed before recovering quickly. "As I said, you are different from other women I have come to know. I would have liked to spend more time getting to know you."

Caitlin turned her attention back to the book, opened to the first page of a story she remembered from her days in college. Second year, maybe?

John's head tilted to one side, eyes trained on her. Caitlin didn't mind the way he studied her. She did enough of that on her own. But the way the look went through her...

She carefully held the gaze as he asked, "Have you read it already?"

"A few years ago. It's a story I really enjoyed."

"Good, I am pleased to hear that."

They sat for a minute in silence and Caitlin smiled as John shifted uncomfortably. The man looked to be in his early twenties with a sharp chin and gentle eyes. Though she imagined the families who lived in the cabins did most of the work on the plantation, John looked like he knew his way around manual labor with the thick muscles that defined his shoulders, biceps, and chest.

"Tell me, Caitlin, about where you come from."

She nearly choked, cleared her throat. Of all the questions he could ask...

"You have never been to the north?"

"No. I haven't the opportunity to travel. Father's work on the plantation keeps my family here. I intend to move north, especially should Lincoln win the run for the presidency and the South secedes from the Union."

"Even though this is all you've ever known?"

"It may be all I've known, but don't suppose I agree with the way of life."

Caitlin raised a brow, dropped her eyes to the book on her lap. Easy for him to say now, while he still had his Daddy's money and favor.

"You don't agree." It wasn't a question. He must have seen the doubt all over her face, and Caitlin learned something more about him. John was observant. "You think I can't leave my father's wealth."

"I think you are used to a certain way of life, and if you were to leave it, you'd have a hard time adjusting to less."

He tilted his head in consideration and Caitlin readied for an argument. Instead, he only said, "You make many assumptions of my character for one I just met."

"I guess I do, but that doesn't change the fact. Losing wealth and social position is a challenge most can't get past."

"And how is it you know so much on the subject?"

She bent, rubbed the ankle to buy time for her head to think. The answer came quicker than she's expected. "My father is a professor of socioeconomics."

"I have never heard of such a study."

"It's the study economics plays on social classes."

John guffawed. "You don't need a professor for that. All you have to do is take a look around Shady Oak Plantation."

Caitlin grinned. To his mind, he had a point. The plantation was the perfect study of the great divide between the rich and poor, the socially ranked and the socially discarded. "His studies go deeper than plantation owners and slaves." She pulled in a deep breath. Careful, she thought. She had to be careful. "You don't agree with slavery?"

With a heavy sigh, John glanced around the cabin. "James and his family are good people. He saved my life once."

Despite hearing James' version, Caitlin thought it best to allow John to tell his version. He might be hurt, or worse, angry if he knew Etta had said something. "Did he?"

"Yes, about five years ago. A tiger came out of the grass, didn't even know he was there. The cat could have killed me, easily, but James saw it. I don't know how. Maybe he's just used to watching for them in the fields. But he threw the sickle and hit the animal. That's why my parents turn a blind eye to my visits with James and his family."

"They know?"

"My parents suspect. If Father knew, he would surely stop it, especially should he know I help the family learn to read and write."

"They would be killed."

He looked at her again with the same studying gaze, but she didn't flinch. And he relaxed. "They could be. But I hope one day James and his family will be free. That all of them will be. And, if they are, I want to help James have the best opportunity available to them. They can't have that if they don't read or write. As long as they don't cause any trouble on the plantation, or start rallying the other slaves, my father doesn't say much."

"But if your father found an excuse?"

"I just help ensure he doesn't. Like I said, they are good people, and I owe James everything. My parents are not made to forget that."

Caitlin's heart softened towards John. Yes, James and his family were good people, but so was this man before her. A product of his times, for sure, but wasn't everyone?

"You are smiling. You have a most captivating smile."

"Thank you."

"Well, I better get back to the main house. I hope the book helps you pass the time today, and the flower cheers you up."

"They will. Both."

"Good. And, Caitlin, please, don't leave the cabin. I'll try to keep the overseer from coming here, but if anyone sees you, I won't be able to do so."

She nodded, all too sure of what was at stake, not just for herself, but for John, Mitilda, James, Etta, and the children. "I will."

He nodded. "I'll return tonight and try to bring something more to eat. Until then."

Two days later, Caitlin tentatively stood on the sprained ankle. Still sore, still swollen, but with the rags and thin pieces of wood flanking each side of the leg, Caitlin was sure she could get around enough to figure out the stone and go home. She'd stayed too long as it was.

She pulled the rock out from beneath the ragged blankets, studied the etching. Three circles connected to a larger circle by thin lines. A central figure—two half boxes facing opposite directions and meeting on the center lines, stood between two of the lines. Caitlin sighed. She'd seen something similar once before in a book, but still couldn't remember where or when. More importantly, the meaning behind it. Caitlin waved a hand over the images, not unsurprised when nothing happened.

"Okay. The first time, I was outside next to the remains of this cabin." She glanced around the single room. Everything in the cabin was made of wood, mostly poorly constructed. It was no wonder very little of the cabin remained by the twenty-first century. The only part of the cabin with brick was the fireplace, and in contrast to the rest of the building, was very well constructed. "The remains Sean discovered are from the fireplace. So, if I was standing next to the remains in the twenty-first century, I would have to be standing about," she took a couple of painful steps closer to the fireplace, "about here."

She studied the fireplace, fingers running over the precisely lain bricks, shook her head. Nothing close to anything she saw on the stone. No etchings at all. "What am I missing?" With a single sidestep,

Caitlin moved along the hearth. "This might be about right, might have been where I was standing. Can't hurt to try again." A quick motion over the stone. "This isn't making sense. If it's connected to this site, it should work."

The door squeaked open behind her and Caitlin whirled around, tucking the stone in a back pocket, and breathing a little easier to see John.

"Good afternoon. You can walk."

She laughed. "Sort of. Better than I could."

He glanced at her ankle. "It still appears to be swollen."

"It is. But I need to leave as soon as I can. I don't want to see Mitilda and her family get into trouble because of me."

He nodded. "Here. I know you must be tired of eating cornmeal mush and bread." John handed her an apple and a small box of chocolate. "I hope they are both to your liking."

"Thank you. You didn't have to."

"You do not like them?"

"No, that's not it at all. I just...your family."

"I think you are more than worth the risk of angering my father."

"That's a nice thing to say, but I can't stay, so that's not—"

John took another step forward. "I know this is uncommon and inappropriate. But if you are to leave soon..." his voice trailed off as he reached for her hand, carefully brought it closer to his lips until his breath tickled Caitlin's fingertips and teased her pulse. "May I have the honor?" he asked, eyes fixed on hers.

Caitlin nodded and breathlessly watched as John softly kissed her fingers. "It is my wish to see you again."

She smiled. "I wish that were possible, but I'm afraid it won't be once I leave."

"Then I shall have to make an effort to see you before you leave."

"I would like that."

Caitlin settled at the table, pulled in a deep breath. Judging from the fading light through the cracks in the roof, Mitilda, James, and Etta would be back soon from the fields. She pushed the rock gently in a circle on the table's surface. No more time to waste. After John's visit that afternoon, and a couple nights on the floor, it was time to figure out what she was doing wrong with the rock and leave the nineteenth century before she was discovered. She couldn't risk hurting this family who'd taken her in despite all danger of doing so and didn't want to complicate John's life more than he already had by befriending the slaves. Mitilda knew more than what she was saying, and one way or the other, Caitlin was going to find out what it was.

When they came in, the family looked more exhausted than usual. James looked as though he could barely crawl, much less walk as he trudged to the nearest chair, and Caitlin immediately relinquished the other chair to Etta.

Mitilda carried first Henry, then Rosie, to the opposite corner and laid them down, each covered with an old shirt as they snored with thumbs securely stuck in their mouths. Children settled, Mitilda moved to the fireplace and started a flame under a badly bruised kettle. Then she knelt on the floor next to a stool and began splitting green beans. Caitlin made her way to Mitilda's side. "Here. Let me help. You look like you could fall over."

"Please, honey. We do this every night. I be fine."

Caitlin shook her head. "Well, then, tonight is your night off. I've been staying here for a couple days. It's the least I can do."

"No, that is not the way we do things. Have a rest, and I'll have dinner ready soon."

"If you won't allow me to do it for you, at least allow me to help." Caitlin settled next to Mitilda on the floor. She picked up a green bean, snapped off each end, and tossed it into the pot.

"You a sweet chil'."

"It's nothing. You've helped me out, took good care of my ankle. This is the least I can do."

"Where did this come from?" James asked, his voice husky as he picked up the rock.

Caitlin glanced around at the people in the room, the looks all the confirmation she needed. "That's mine."

James looked to Mitilda. "Did you give this to her, Momma?"

"No, and don't question your Momma."

"I brought it with me from home," Caitlin said. "But I don't know for sure what it is."

"Momma, you know if the masta catches us with this, it will be a whippin' for sure."

"If they find Caitlin here, there'll be bigger trouble than that there rock."

"But using it would mean..."

"Tsk tsk, don't argue with your momma, James." Mitilda shifted her attention to Caitlin. "I know about the rock, but we do not use it."

"So," Caitlin dropped a green bean in the kettle and sat back, careful not to turn her ankle, "are you telling me you know it travels through time?"

James stood. "We shouldn't be talkin' 'bout this."

Mitilda shook her head. "Look at her, James. Do you 'pose she came from north like she say to Mister John? Look at her clothes."

Etta nodded. "She right."

James shook his head, glared hard at Caitlin, mistrust replacing kindness for the first time. "Maybe she is, but we talk about this, and someone's bound to hear us. I have to take care of my family."

"And the best way to do that," Caitlin said gently, "is for me to go home. I can't stay here much longer without being discovered."

James shook his head. "I'll be on the porch, take in the fresh air. I don't want to hear none of this."

Etta shook her head as her husband left the cabin. "I's sorry, Caitlin. He a good man, but fear rules his heart."

"I can't blame him. The lives that you have here, the dangers you live under... that's why I can't stay any longer. I like your family. I don't want to cause more trouble for you."

"Momma?"

Mitilda stood and hovered over the kettle, stirred the beans, dropped a beef bone into the water, rested the spoon on the side of the kettle and turned to face Caitlin.

"I like you, honey. But what you are talkin' 'bout is powerful hoodoo."

Caitlin nodded as she retrieved the stone from the table and sat in front of Mitilda as she rested the stone on her lap. "I'm aware of that. If this wasn't powerful, I don't think I would be sitting in your cabin. But you knew this stone allows for time travel?"

"I knew only of the symbols. I know what they mean, but I never used the stone."

"Can I ask why not? Why not try to escape all this?"

"I have a family. A son, daughter, grandchild'n. Life is hard, but we knows it. What happens whe'ver you from? It might be worse'n for us. We can't trust that."

Caitlin nodded. "I guess I can understand. It is better there, I can tell you that, but I understand not being able to take the chance.

"My home is back there, though, and I can't figure how this works. I keep waving my hand over the rock, nothing happens. I tried it outside where I appeared when I first got here. Nothing happens. I tried next to the fireplace because I stood near the ruins of that fireplace in my time, and nothing happens. I know I'm doing something wrong, I just don't know what it is."

"You needs be in the sunlight, inside a circle," Mitilda said matter-of-factly before turning back to the kettle.

Caitlin stared at her back. "In the circle, in the sunlight." Her thoughts circled back a couple days earlier, while tracing the symbol with a single finger. "Of course. I don't know why I didn't think of it. I've tried the sunlight, and I've tried the circle, but I haven't tried both together." She glanced upward to the roof, where a thin moonbeam shined through the cracks. "Tomorrow mid-day, the sun should shine right through the roof there."

Etta nodded.

"I'll go home then."

The last night on the plantation was more fun than Caitlin would have ever expected. Some of the slaves in neighboring cabins gathered on the front porches, playing spoons, a discarded fiddle, singing, dancing, the children running circles around one another. Caitlin stayed in the cabin, away from other slaves and eyes that may report her presence to the master. But Mitilda left the door open, and Caitlin watched the festivities from around the corner beneath the moon and stars. The songs were ones she remembered from studying the history of slavery in America. The smiles were something more. As she sat back and watched them all through the open door, she wondered how often they were able to enjoy moments like these. Marveled at their strength, their tenacity. Admiration filled her heart, consumed every part of her being.

The music and the laughter filled the night air until the potluck-style meal ended and everyone faded into their own cabins. Caitlin settled on the hard, cold floor, curled in a ball, counting down to the following day and going home.

Gasps, angry voices, and a hard jolt woke Caitlin. She opened her eyes to find a man dressed in a black tail overcoat and top hat standing over her, face twisted with anger and a sharp hatred.

"Get up, thief!" he yelled as he yanked hard at her arm. "Get up now."

Caitlin ripped her arm from his grip, glared hard as she stood. "I haven't stolen a thing."

"You're stealing our food and the roof over your head. Thief. Do you know what we do to thieves around here?"

"I'm just traveling through, twisted my ankle. I'm leaving today."

"You bet you are, but not until you pay what you owe us. And James, if you have enough food to share with runaways, you'll find your ration decreased. Now everyone outside."

Mitilda, James, Etta, and the children were pushed out the door in rotating shoves, and as they stumbled to the earthy ground, the man pushed Caitlin off the porch to her knees next to them. She turned to look at him, and then saw the whip she hadn't noticed inside the cabin.

Her eyes grew wide as she turned to the family who had become her friends. She expected fear and panic but found only strength and resolution etched on their faces. Even little Henry, who stood in front of his mother, eyes on the ground as were everyone else's, but he didn't shake, he didn't cry, as he huddled behind the safety of his mother's arms.

Movement from the corner of one eye made Caitlin turn her head. The man pulled James aside among quiet gasps, arm raised, whip readied behind his back.

She rushed forward, kneed the man in the groin. As he dropped to the ground, Caitlin took James hand and struggled to pull him from the courtyard as he shook his head, eyes pleading.

"You make it worse," he whispered.

"You and your family can come with me. People are free in my time. You'll be safe."

Her whispers ended in time for her arm to be pulled backward and she gritted her teeth to silence a scream. "You'll pay for that insolence with your life," the man growled.

Despite the painful ankle, Caitlin kicked and struggled from his grip as he pulled her towards a tree with weeping branches. A rope hung ominously, ready, from the saddest branch. Caitlin kicked harder, pushing dirt around her feet into a trail of mounds as the man dragged her towards the waiting oak.

"Edward! Unhand her!" Caitlin glanced over a shoulder to see John riding through the crowd of slaves. He slid off the horse before the animal came to a full stop. "You will not harm that woman."

Edward turned but didn't let go, his fingers digging further into her bicep. "Your softness for these animals is disturbing."

"Be that as it may, you will unhand her now or will pay the consequences for disobeying an order."

Edward narrowed his eyes, pushed Caitlin into him. "Take your Negro slut. But I'll be talking to your father about this, and you won't be able to protect them any longer."

John gently nudged Caitlin to stand behind him as she seethed. If only she could get her hands on Edward, he'd know what a twenty-first-century woman did to a man who thought he could manhandle her. Instead, John's arm restrained her gently, and the reminder caused her to bite her lip. Charging at Edward would only worsen the situation, not teach the idiot a lesson.

John laughed. "I urge you to take it up with my father. You may be the overseer, but I am still his son."

"A son who has a soft spot for these slave trash. How long do you think he'll keep looking the other way?"

"As long as I continue to be his son, which will be a whole lot longer than you'll find employment here if you press this matter further."

Edward's hand tightened around the handle of the whip and John took a step forward. "Should you follow through with what you are thinking, not only will you find yourself unemployed with my family, but you'll be staying the night with the Sheriff. I urge you to consider the decision with the utmost of care."

"Your father will hear of this."

Edward stomped off, and John ordered everyone back into the cabins. As the crowd dispersed, he took Caitlin's hand gently into his own. He walked with her into James' home with the family following closely behind.

"Edward is a bad egg, but he does follow the rules set forth by my father. I fear my father will not be dissuaded as easily. You must leave today."

Caitlin nodded. "I plan to. What about Mitilda and James and..."

"Do not worry yourself about them. I can protect them. But you attacked Edward, and I cannot protect you from my father's wrath."

"I fought back."

"Yes, be that as it may, my father will see that you attacked him, and there will be no alternative to death. I will not see a rope around your neck."

Caitlin nodded. "Okay, as long as they are safe."

"They will be. You have my word."

John's word was enough. She looked up at the roof, sunbeams

278

shining through the cracks in the bright, late morning. "Mitilda? Is there enough sun?"

"There should be, sugar."

"Sun? What do you need sun for?"

Caitlin smiled at the kind face she'd miss as John stared at her, brows furrowed, jaw locked.

"You can go, I'll be safe now."

But instead of walking out the door, John took stepped closer. "Before you leave, can I ask something of you?"

"After what you just did, you can ask anything."

"It is inappropriate, but maybe … may I kiss you?"

Caitlin raised a brow, searching his eyes. Then, slowly, she nodded. As he drew closer, all the rush and demand of twenty-first-century men was clearly absent. Instead, he eased close, her breath hitching as he hovered a breath from her lips. Then, carefully, he pressed his mouth against hers. Slowly, she wrapped both arms around his neck, his arms natural around her waist.

Then, it was over.

"I wish this were another time, another place," he said as they parted.

"Me, too."

Shouts in the distance caused the family to turn their heads to the door.

"My father. You must go, now."

Caitlin nodded as Mitilda handed her the rock. "Now, sugar. Before it's too late."

Taking the rock in hand, Caitlin looked around the family one last time. "I'll miss you all. Thank you."

"Now, Caitlin."

She stepped next to the fireplace, the sunbeams shining onto the symbols of the rock. Locking eyes with John, she waved a hand over the rock.

Plastic wrap constricted her lungs, the air growing stale.

And slowly, the feeling faded. Caitlin opened her eyes and looked around.

Then her heart dropped.

A European mansion loomed before her, one she'd seen in movies and in pictures.

Chatling Hall.

She wasn't home. She was further from twenty-first century United States than before.

A horse clogged up the dirt path as she watched a man dressed in black pants and a long overcoat. Rock in hand, she stared at the ground, then lifted her eyes to search the sky. Clouds concealed the sun, blocking a quick escape.

"Madame?" She turned and stared into the face of a man's face. Based on his dress, he fit the title of Duke or Earl. "Can I help you?"

Caitlin shook her head. "I think I'm lost."

Note from Author:

Deep Echoes is a prequel novella to the upcoming time travel series, *Web of Echoes*. Caitlin will find herself pushed deeper and deeper into a web of mystery and adventure where danger and romance await as she searches for the way back to her time. Check out my website, newsletter, or Facebook for upcoming news on this exciting new series.

ABOUT R.M. ALEXANDER

WRITING AS MELODY ASH

From a young age, RM Alexander surrounded herself with books, loving the escape into worlds of all kinds, staying up until way past bed time to finish a good read. It didn't take long for that love of reading to grow into a captivation with writing. As an adult, RM lived in the real world in office jobs and a career in travel before taking her writing more seriously.

The first release, Matter of Choice, was published in 2014. Since the release of this first book, her books have been nominated for several awards, including a Reader's Choice award and an Author's Academy Award.

As RM's list of romantic suspense novels grew, RM decided to begin writing fantasy under the name Melody Ash.

When she's not writing, RM spends time with her husband and

two children. She loves to travel, especially to Walt Disney World, and is addicted to orange juice and Ghiradelli chocolate. She is often found on Twitter and Facebook chatting with other authors and readers.

 facebook.com/rmalexanderauthor

twitter.com/rmalexanderauth

instagram.com/rmalexanderauthor

ABOUT NANEA KNOTT

Nanea Knott is a romance author who hopes to one day have name recognition for being famous, not infamous. She's determined to find the readers who like a good story with a little humor, some romance, and of course, sex. She has two naughty cats and is the proud owner of the title "crazy cat lady." She reads faster than she writes, has a mad obsession for arts and crafts, and has way more coffee mugs a person who doesn't drink coffee ought to own. Willow is nothing like what she usually writes, but every once in awhile, she likes to mix it up.

 facebook.com/NaneaKnott

twitter.com/authornaneak

instagram.com/authornaneak

WILLOW

BY NANEA KNOTT

GLOSSARY OF TERMS

Aikido - Japanese Martial art.

Dojo - A place where martial arts are learned and practiced.

Geiko - A geisha that has completed her training.

Geta - Distinctive sandals made of wood.

Gi - Clothing worn by those learning/practicing martial arts.

Hai - A form of "yes" in Japan.

Hakama skirt -Traditional Japanese clothing that splits like pants.

Hana Kanzashi - Hair ornament worn by first-year apprentice geisha.

Katami wake - "Keepsake gifts" - When belongings of the deceased are given away.

Kimono- Traditional Japanese clothing for both men and women.

Konnichiwa - "Good afternoon" in Japanese.

Maiko - An apprentice geisha.

Miso - A fermented paste that is the base of a popular Japanese soup.

Obaasan – Grandmother.

Obake - Ghost or another supernatural being.

Obi - Part of the kimono that wraps around the middle.

Okiya - Places where geishas train and live.

Okobo - Tall wooden sandals.

Oni - A demon.

Sakura - Cherry Blossom.

Sensei - Teacher/instructor.

Shamisen - Traditional Japanese three-stringed instrument.

Spam musubi - A rectangular ball of rice, with soy sauce, fried spam and nori.

Sumimasen - "Excuse me" in Japanese.

Tabi - Toe socks that separate the big toe from the others.

Tai no Henko - Aikido training that uses the opponent's momentum against them.

Takamakura - Tall pillows on stands used by maikos to avoid messing up their elaborate hairstyles.

Tofu - Fermented bean curd, usually cubed and put into miso soup

Wakarimasen - "I don't understand" in Japanese.

Startled awake from a nightmare, Emi kicked the covers off and rolled to a sitting position. The same dream had haunted her for the third night in a row, and this time had been more vivid than the last. Before the nightmare, images had rolled through her consciousness. She'd experienced a moment of peace, existing in a space between the ordinary and the bizarre. It was the place where the mind struggles to understand, and instinct has yet to take over.

Floating freely in the state of bliss, she was abruptly torn from it when she experienced the sensation of someone grabbing her arm and throwing her to the ground. The weight of him covering her with his body. Her own clothing kept her pinned down while his large hand covered her mouth to prevent her from giving away their location. His dark eyes stared into hers with a burning hatred deep enough to sear her soul. Once her spirit left this life, she would carry the trauma of it into her next one.

Upon waking, Emi shook her head, trying to dislodge the images still playing in her mind, but she could still see them. A beam of light reflecting off honed steel. A flashing snapshot of silk fabric dragged through the dirt. A spreading crimson stain and staring eyes in a beautiful face painted white.

With spring came the hope of new life and possibilities, but it didn't always. April in Hawaii is a beautiful time of year. The humidity isn't as high as it would be during the summer, and the rain of winter had stopped. From now on, they would only have the occasional showers and brief thunderstorms that would water the islands for the rest of the year.

On Oahu, Emiko Takai stood on the porch of their crappy apartment. She leaned on the wooden railing, staring across the street at a cement wall topped with chain-link fencing. She and her family lived behind a business that took up most of a city block. Their street was a dead end in more ways than one. Her mother, Yuki, had given in to the depressing state of their lives by choosing to become bedridden. Emi's older sister Mariko was kept busy with her two jobs. Emi had been doing her best while taking classes at the community college, but she was barely passing.

The one-bedroom apartment the three people in their family shared was one section of a large house. Smaller apartments resulted when the house had been sectioned off. Next door to them lived a man who was fooling around with a married woman. Almost every night, the philandering wife parked her car so it was partially blocking Emi's parking space. The ones who lived under them seemed to spend more money on drugs than food. The couple in the apartment behind them fought daily, usually before dawn. Police dispatch would answer the call with, "Yes, we know where that is."

Life was miserable.

Emi got in her car that morning and went to pay the rent. Once that was done, she drove to her grandmother's condo about a half hour away in Salt Lake. It used to take only ten minutes to get there from their house. Honolulu traffic had gotten so bad; it now took twice as long to get anywhere.

The Salt Lake neighborhood consisted mostly of high rise apartments and condos, although there were still some single-family homes and low-rise apartments on the perimeter. Her grandmother was fortunate to get a unit with an unobstructed view from her patio. It overlooked a golf course while giving her a front row seat to beautiful sunsets every evening. The condo was high enough to get cool breezes coming in through the sliding screen door all year long. Parking in one of the visitor spots, Emi took the elevator to the eighth floor. Knocking on the door, her grandmother's next-door neighbor, Jane, opened it.

"Emiko, how are you?" Jane asked.

"I'm well Jane and glad to see you," Emi replied hugging her.

Emi smiled at the older woman with her wrinkled skin and kind eyes. As usual, the older woman had too much perfume on, but her smile was joyful, and her hugs were genuine. Jane grew up in a time in Hawaii when most people were kind, and she had continued to live her life that way. Bitterness seemed to color everything in Emi's life, and she wished she could live without it. She was eighteen, and her faith in humanity was already faltering.

Looking past Jane, Emi saw her grandmother sitting at her dining table scrutinizing the playing cards in her hand. Her grandmother tilted her head down to look at Emi above her glasses.

"Poker again, Baba?" Emi asked. Her grandmother's face crinkled into a smile.

"I'm old, what else am I going to do?" Her grandmother answered.

"Kumi," Jane said, "I'll let you two spend time together. I'll call you later."

Jane let herself out, and Emi closed and locked the door behind her. Emi's grandmother, Kumi, was dressed in shorts and a top with tabi on her feet. She was always saying that her toes were cold, and socks were a modern convention that she refused to wear. Emi didn't like wearing tabis, it felt weird to wear the foot covering and have her big toe separated from the other toes, but it was part of traditional Japanese footwear. It was one of the few things her grandmother had clung to with ferocity.

Her grandmother was the first generation to come to the United States, having left Japan shortly after World War II. Emigration had seemed the only option if she wanted a new life and to let go of bad memories. Shortly after moving to Hawaii, she met and married an American businessman.

Her grandmother put the cards away and watched Emi carefully. Emi knew there was very little those sharp, dark eyes missed. "What's wrong Emiko? Is everything all right?"

Shaking her head, Emi replied, "Yes and no. I mean everything is the same, nothing is different, except the rent is going up, and the landlord refuses to do anything about the rats in our ceiling. The lights flicker constantly, and you can hear them running overhead at night."

Kumi shuddered. "I don't know why your mother refuses to move all of you out of there to come live with me."

Emi shrugged, it was an old argument between mother and daughter that wouldn't be remedied today. Emi gazed around the room, taking in her grandmother's spacious apartment. Even on the hottest days, this place was comfortable. There was more than enough room for the four of them here, but her mother wouldn't even talk about it. Things had been difficult for their family since Kumi lost her husband, and Emi lost her father, one after the other. The three generations of women were grief-stricken and struggling.

"I'm not here to talk about mom, Baba. I need to talk to you about something else. Thank you for paying for more Aikido classes."

Her grandmother nodded. "You're welcome. Do you want water or something?" Kumi stood from the table and went to the cabinet to take out a glass. Glancing back at her granddaughter, she waited for an answer. Emi nodded, and Kumi took out another. "How are your martial arts class going?"

Emi watched her grandmother put ice into the glasses from the freezer.

"It's going great," Emi answered. "My sensei says I'm doing well and that I'm one of his best students."

Hearing the water splashing over the ice made Emi thirstier. Putting the glasses on the table, her grandmother smiled, and then made herself comfortable in her chair. "I'm glad to hear it. Your mother told me you're struggling in school, though."

Emi drummed her fingers on the table next to her glass. "I'm trying, but I can't seem to get it right."

Her grandmother reached across the table and gripped her hand. "You will. I know you will. Now, why did you come to see me? I'm not complaining, but I saw you three days ago."

Emi took a sip of her water. "I've been having weird dreams of walking down a path with another woman. We're both dressed in kimonos wearing those high wooden Japanese sandals, geta?"

Emi had never worn the traditional Japanese garment and would have no idea how to move around in it. She would have broken an ankle in those shoes.

"The shoes are called okobo," her grandmother corrected her. "If you were dreaming that you were a geisha, you would still be a maiko, an apprentice. The apprentices wear the higher okobo shoes. Geta sandals are lower in height and are only worn by geiko, the geisha that are considered accomplished."

Emi nodded, unsure of what it meant, but she trusted her grandmother's knowledge. At one time she had trained to be a geisha while she was still in Japan, but it was something she rarely discussed. The only time Emi would see evidence of it was when they attended Japanese festivals. It was the rare occasion when her grandmother allowed herself to speak Japanese.

"OK, well, whatever they are," Emi said, "I was walking in them, and so was she. It was at night, and we were both excited, but I don't know why."

Her grandmother's expression was thoughtful, but her eyes were filled with worry. She folded her hands on the table and sighed. "I don't know why you're dreaming what you are Emiko-chan, but dreams tell us things, and we need to listen."

"It was probably because of the hair ornament you gave me," Emi said, noting her grandmother's term of endearment at the end of her name.

Her grandmother had given her something a few days ago, a Japanese hair ornament. She told her it was something that only a maiko would wear during their first year of training. The ornament was called a hana kanzashi; it was a waterfall of silk long enough to go all the way to the chin. This one symbolized the leaning branches of the willow tree and represented the season of summer. Emi wasn't sure why her grandmother had given it to her, only that she wanted her to have it. She took it home and put it on the table next to her bed.

Her grandmother's answer about the dreams didn't surprise her; it was just like Baba to say something cryptic. They talked until Emi could tell her grandmother was tired, and then she left promising to call and check on her in a couple of days.

"Tell me if you have any more dreams," her grandmother instructed.

Emi agreed.

It was only four-thirty on a Tuesday afternoon, and instead of going home, Emi chose to visit the dojo, the place where she took her martial arts classes. It was housed next to a family owned pizza place in a strip mall. From the outside, it looked small, but the inside was spacious; the locker rooms were equal in size to the training space. The front of the dojo had glass windows allowing others to observe the precise movements of the training from outside. Classes were held all day, every day except Sunday. Different instructors taught different classes, and she was welcome to watch or participate as she chose. Today she decided to observe.

Carrying her white gi and black hakama skirt, the traditional uniform for learning Aikido, Emi walked in and went to the back to change. She could watch all the classes she wanted, but she had to dress for it in case an instructor called on her to participate in a demonstration. She pulled her dark hair into a ponytail and went to observe.

A class was already in session, and Emi crept to sit at the back of the room. The mirrored wall behind the instructor reflected her movements, but no one would pay her much attention. This was a beginner's class not unlike the first one she had taken last year. The instructor was not her sensei, her primary instructor, but another man named Jason, who had been with the dojo since he was seven years old. He'd achieved black belt status last year and was offered a position to teach.

Jason was now nineteen and was quickly becoming a favorite dojo instructor. With brown eyes and black hair; he was also good-looking, and Emi had tried not to stare. His Asian eyes crinkled when he smiled, and he was patient with his students. Emi hoped one day to be more like him.

He took the class through the various stretches of the wrist and elbows before moving on to the next lesson. He wanted them to practice the techniques of Tai No Henko, which were basic defense maneuvers. It allowed for the fluidity of movement and could equal the playing field when dealing with a larger, heavier opponent.

Emi had been practicing it for several months and felt confident. Watching others practice the motions of it gave her a sense of peace. There was beauty in it, like watching water flow over rocks. There was no clash of energy, but a redistribution of it. The students of the class were seated at the edges of the mat preparing to watch the demonstration. When Jason performed one of the positions for the class with one of the students, he was beautiful to watch as he made it seem effortless. His sparring partner was down on the mat in about a minute, but a real-life response would have been even faster. He could have his opponent neutralized before his attacker knew what was happening.

"Emiko?" Jason called.

"Hai," Emi answered, saying yes in Japanese while standing and bowing.

"Please," Jason said, gesturing with his hand to the area in front of him. Emi moved to where he indicated and bowed when he did.

"Class, this is Emiko, she is also a student here, and often comes to observe. I know she has studied this technique. Let's see what she's learned," Jason said.

Emi felt her heart start racing. She'd often watched classes here, but was rarely called upon. Most of the time she kept quiet, and the instructors let her be.

She looked at Jason, and they bowed to signify they were ready. He struck out and grabbed her arm. Instead of turning her body the way she was taught, Emi froze then panicked pulling away. Jason released her, and she fell to the mat suppressing the urge to scream. She looked up at the students closest to her and saw the confusion on their faces.

What the hell is wrong with me?

"Emi?" Jason's voice made her turn her head to look at him. She was lying on her stomach on the mat. Getting to her feet, she bowed. "Forgive me, may I try again?"

Jason nodded and then they stood in the starting position to bow again. This time when Jason grabbed her arm, Emi's training took over. Turning her body, she twisted Jason's wrist, making it impossible for him to do anything other than follow the motion of it, forcing him down on the mat. Getting to his feet, he insisted on another demonstration. The second time, Emi moved faster with more precision.

Jason took a step back. "Thank you, Emi, you may return to your seat." They bowed, and Emi walked off the mat. "That, ladies and gentlemen, is how you do Tai No Henko. I'm a big guy; it's not hard for you to imagine that I can put someone down. Emi is around five feet three, and if I had to guess, weighs about a hundred fifteen pounds soaking wet. I wanted you to see that no matter who you are, if you use the techniques correctly, you'll be able to do the same. Let's partner up to practice."

The students broke into pairs and spread out on the mat. Some of them looked at her with awe, others with looks of aggression as if she wasn't so tough, Emi ignored them all. Her body had learned a discipline her mind had yet to grasp. True mastery took years, but it wasn't due to training the body, it was training the mind.

When the class was over, she let the students use the changing rooms first. Jason came over to speak to her.

"I'm sorry if I startled you the first time during the demonstration," he said.

Emi smiled. "Don't worry about it. It wasn't you."

Jason made a face. "Then what was it?"

She and Jason were friends, and he would listen if she wanted to talk about it, but she couldn't explain it. She thought she was ready, but the moment his hand connected with her wrist, fear ran through her body. Her mind flashed the image of being dressed in a kimono again. In her imagination, she felt her arm being grabbed at the same time Jason's hand circled her arm, and terror stole her breath. It felt like she was stuck somewhere between the dojo and the dream. She couldn't tell which was real and the moment of confusion had paralyzed her.

Emi made the decision not to say anything about it. Instead, she told him it had been a long day, and she was tired. He nodded, told her that if she needed anything to let him know, then went to change. Glancing up, she caught sight of herself in the mirrored wall. At first, she thought she saw someone else, but there was no one there. The others had already left or were still changing.

Walking up to the mirror, she looked into her eyes and blinked a few times. She recognized her own reflection, but there was something different. Emi felt like she was looking at someone who looked like her but wasn't her. Moving in closer to the mirror, she scrutinized herself. Something was off, and she tried to determine what was different.

Laughter shook her from her thoughts and made her glance behind her in the mirror. There stood a woman wearing a green kimono with a red and white collar. With a pleasant smile, she bowed and disappeared. Spinning around, Emi found no one.

On her way home from the dojo, night was falling quickly. She had the windows open instead of turning on the air conditioning as it was cooling down and the breeze through the car felt good. Emi needed to go home and cook dinner as there were no leftovers from last night. She drove home and parked the car as best she could. Her neighbor's girlfriend was blocking her space again. Emi had a vindictive thought and considered finding the woman's husband to tell him his wife was fooling around and then thought better of it. For all the time the woman spent here with her lover, the husband probably already knew and didn't care.

Walking into the house, she put her bag down and checked with her mother to see what she wanted for dinner. Once that was figured out, Emi started cooking. Her sister, Mariko, wouldn't be home for several hours. By now, she had already left one job and was on her way to the other. She wouldn't be home until after everyone had gone to bed.

"Dinner is served, Madame." Emi handed her mother the warm plate.

Yuki sat up and smiled. "Thank you."

"Mom, when are you going to get out of this bed? After the tests, the doctor told you there was nothing wrong with you. You're perfectly fine. If you continue to lie here day after day, you're going to create problems where there are none," Emi remarked.

Yuki frowned. "Are you trying to spoil my appetite? I don't feel well. I don't care what the doctor says. I'm going to rest until I feel better. If you don't want to take care of me, say so. I'm sure Mariko would be more than happy to do it," she scolded.

Emi huffed. "Mariko is already working two jobs, she hardly sleeps. She can't take care of you too."

"I've already said I don't want to talk about it. Thank you for dinner, now leave me alone," Yuki snapped.

Emi left the bedroom and went into the living room. It had been turned into a bedroom that she shared with her older sister. She watched TV while eating her dinner, flipping channels looking for something interesting. There was a movie on that was set in Los Angeles. Something inside her wished she was there instead.

The desire for something better lived with her every second of every day. Getting out of there would require money, but she couldn't get a job. It would be too hard trying to fit it around her class schedule and take care of her mother at the same time. It was all she could do to make the Aikido class sometimes. If it weren't for her grandmother's birthday gift, she wouldn't have been able to pay for the classes.

The temperature had started dropping as soon as the sun set, and the humidity was comfortable. Emi went into her mother's room to clear away the dishes and clean up. With rats and cockroaches in the building, leaving dirty dishes wasn't an option.

Her mother watched TV in her room and would do so for the rest of the night. Emi turned off the TV in the living room with the intention of reading her assignment and studying for the upcoming test.

Sitting on top of the book was the hana kanzashi. Emi took it in her hand and looked closely at it, knowing it was handmade in Japan. The flowers were made of silk, formed into the shape of the bending bows of the willow tree with delicate green leaves. Fingering the fine work gently, she saw images in her head of hands folding the tiny squares of cloth. It was like they were her hands. The perfectly folded squares were placed on a board that had been slathered with glue to hold them in shape. They would stay in the desired position until the final design could be completed. She felt the care and precision of the person creating the masterpiece that she now held in her hands. A scent wafted to her nose. It was a combination of wood smoke and green tea.

Emi closed her eyes and let those images become fluid enough to submerge herself in them. She felt content; observing work that produced a feeling of joy. The person she watched put in a lot of effort for something that on the surface seemed trivial. Then she felt the dedication to their craft. What they did was a small part of a greater whole that contributed to a tradition that dated back centuries. Geisha had been entertaining Japan since the Shogun ruled the land. Hair ornaments were as important as anything else they wore.

The shouting of Emi's neighbor broke her from the reverie and brought her back into the present. Putting the kanzashi aside, she picked up her textbook and began studying. A few minutes later her phone rang.

"Hello Baba," Emi answered, seeing her name pop up on the screen.

"Emiko," her grandmother paused, "please come over, now."

Emi stood, dropping the book in her lap to the floor. "I'm on my way."

Hanging up the phone, she stuck her head into her mother's room to let her know where she was going. "I'm going to grandma's house."

"No, I want you to stay home," Yuki declared.

Emi stared at her mother. "I'm going," Emi stated. She turned from the room and grabbed her purse and keys. The key to Baba's front door was on a hook in the kitchen, Emi snatched it in case she needed it. Her mother shouted for her to stay, but Emi ignored her. There was something off about her mother's behavior, but Emi was too concerned with the reason for her grandmother's call to think about it now. Emi locked the front door and drove away.

Her grandmother rarely called at this time of night. Something was definitely wrong. Emi was nervous as she drove, gripping the steering wheel and worrying about it. She forced her fingers to relax. Her first instinct when she got the call was to ask, but Baba didn't talk over the phone, she liked to speak face to face.

The traffic made her anxiety worse, but she felt it ease the closer she got to the building. There were no open visitor spaces when she arrived. Pulling out of the parking lot, she drove around to find parking on the street a couple of blocks away. Running toward the building, she was grateful she had memorized the security code to get inside.

Taking the elevator to her grandmother's floor, she felt a sense of unease creeping up the back of her neck. By the time she reached the front door, she had the key in her hand. She inserted it into the lock, but noticed something odd. It was quiet. Her grandmother kept the TV or radio on almost all the time. She needed background noise. Hearing nothing but silence made Emi even more anxious.

Opening the door, she was conscious of not disturbing the quiet. Emi wanted to know the reason for the silence before she disrupted it. She stepped inside and locked it behind her. The lights were on, which wasn't unusual; her grandmother wasn't fond of the dark either.

"Emiko?"

Emi released a breath of relief hearing her grandmother's voice.

"Where are you, Baba?" Emiko took off her shoes and walked toward the hallway.

"I'm in my bedroom."

Moving to the end of the hall, Emi turned right to enter the master bedroom. The TV sitting on the dresser was on, but the sound was muted. Her grandmother was seated in her easy chair, dressed in her pajamas with a knitted blanket over her legs. In her lap, was a brightly colored journal decorated with sakura flowers, blooms from the cherry blossom tree.

"Good, you're here," her grandmother said. "I think it's time."

"Time for what?" Emi asked.

Smiling, her grandmother patted the edge of the bed, indicating where she wanted her to sit. Lit only by the single lamp next to the bed, the light in the room was dim. This room had always been Emi's favorite because it made her feel as if she was somewhere else in time. Japanese prints her grandmother had gathered over the years decorated the walls. They were depictions of life in Japan when honor meant everything, and the geisha were considered as precious as sparkling jewels.

One of the prints was of a shamisen, a traditional three-stringed instrument. Inevitably, at festivals, they would run into someone who had one, and her grandmother would always ask if she could play.

Years of training as a geisha reflected in her performance. The grace and skill she displayed with the instrument amazed Emi and easily enthralled others.

Kumi smiled sadly while drumming her fingers on the small, brightly colored notebook she held. "I've been praying for her soul a long time. I hoped she was strong enough to come back to this world to complete her journey."

Emi pulled her legs up and sat cross-legged on the bed. "Who are you talking about?"

"My friend Mitsuko," her grandmother answered. "I dreamt that when she was taken, she was trapped and not able to reincarnate."

Emi wiggled to make herself more comfortable. "Who is that? You've never mentioned her before."

Kumi nodded and looked down for a few minutes. Emi could tell she was gearing up to tell a story. Sometimes her storytelling took a while; it was best to be patient.

"You know I was a maiko," Kumi said. "I had just started my training when the Emperor ordered the attack on Pearl Harbor." Raising a hand, her grandmother gestured to the window because Pearl Harbor was only about ten minutes away from where they sat.

"I remember," Emi replied. "What about it?"

"I left, after the war, and came to Hawaii. After the surrender, it was very hard in Japan, so much suffering. I wanted to leave it behind and start again."

Her grandmother spoke carefully. For a first-generation Japanese immigrant, her English was impeccable. She'd worked very hard when she arrived to lose her Japanese accent and spoke English perfectly. The only exception was when she talked about her memories of Japan, and then her accent would surface. She would also pepper her sentences with Japanese words without realizing it.

"I was happy as a maiko. I was excited to learn how to be like those beautiful, graceful women I would see from time to time. It was an honor to spend time with them. Then the war started, and we thought all would be fine. We carried on as if nothing was happening. Men were going off to fight the war, and the women were expected to continue as we always had. It was hard sometimes, but we did our best."

Emi's grandmother's eyes filled with tears and she brought a wrinkled hand to her cheek to catch one that had fallen. Folding her hands in her lap, Emi kept quiet. Her grandmother wasn't a crier. This was something that had left her deeply disturbed, something she would probably never speak of again if Emi interrupted.

"It was in 1944, while the war dragged on, that we geisha began to be afraid. We were working very hard to keep the spirits of our patrons high during this time. The war was taking its toll on everyone. It was the summer of that year when it happened. They found her a short time later," Kumi admitted.

Emi made a face. "Found who?"

"Mitsuko," Kumi blurted.

Emi's eyes widened. "I still don't understand, Baba."

"A week or so before, Mitsuko and I were walking back to our okiya, the house we lived in while we were training. It was late; we had two appointments that evening. We were tired, but happy. Our patrons were pleased, and we left both teahouses with promises of more appointments."

A glass of water Emi hadn't noticed before sat on the nightstand. Her grandmother reached over and took a sip from it.

"We needed to hurry," Kumi continued. "It was almost past our curfew. If we were late, we would have been in trouble. A path through the park was a faster way to get home, and we took it to cut down on time. As we were walking, a pebble lodged in my okobo, and I stopped to shake it out. Mitsuko got ahead of me a few steps and..."

Stopping to take a breath, her grandmother's hands shook. Emi kept quiet and continued to be patient. The story would be revealed in its own time, in its own way.

"A man jumped from the trees, snarling and pushed me away. Grabbing Mitsuko, he pulled her into the woods. I tried to follow, but I was tangled in my kimono, and I fell. I was shouting..."

Her grandmother struggled to get the rest of the story out.

"Take your time, Baba," Emi encouraged. "Tell me what happened next."

Her grandmother's shoulders were hunched. She dipped her chin, taking a deep shuddering breath. "She was gone. The only thing I had left of her was the kanzashi I gave you."

Emi made a sour face. "You gave me the hair ornament of a dead woman? Eww."

Her grandmother smiled and waved a hand at her. "Silly. I was invited to the katami wake, and it was the only thing of hers I wanted. She was wearing it when she was abducted, and it was what I carried with me to the okiya to tell them what happened."

"Why did you take something so sad, Baba?" Emi asked watching her grandmother cry again.

Katami wake translates as keepsake gifts. Emi knew it was when the personal belongings of the deceased were given away. For family and friends, it was a way to have something to remember the departed. It bothered Emi that her grandmother would take something that would forever remind her of the terrible incident.

"It was her favorite thing. I wanted to remember the evening from before we walked home. Mitsuko had the most beautiful voice; our patrons were so happy that night." Kumi looked down at the notebook in her lap before holding it out to Emi who took it from her and looked at it. The entire book was written in Japanese.

"I can't read this, Baba. What does it say?"

"Check the paper inside."

Emi flipped open the cover and found a handwritten note in her grandmother's writing.

We have two appointments tonight. The older geisha will meet us at the first appointment. Mitsuko and I are to leave on time to be sure we're not late. Unless it begins to rain, we're walking to the teahouses. Mitsuko wanted to take an umbrella, but our housemistress said no. The rain would ruin our kimono and would cost a lot of money to replace. I must go now, it's time to leave, and our patrons are paying for the time it takes us to get to the teahouse. I will write more when I return.

How can one night be wonderful and terrible at the same time? My heart is broken. Mitsuko, where are you? Where has he taken you? Please forgive me. I tried to reach you, but the obi on the back of my kimono snagged on the bushes. I struggled against the long cloth, but by the time I pulled myself free, you were gone. I could still hear your cries, but I couldn't tell which direction they were coming from. I tried to follow the sound of your voice until I could hear nothing but the silence. I called for you. Did you hear me? Could you hear me calling your name? I ran to the okiya as fast as I could. They scolded me when I returned until I told them what had happened. I wanted to change and look for you again, but they forbade me from leaving. Where are you? Please come home.

The other side of the note told the story of what happened a few days after the katami wake.

I'm finally back from the teahouse. I'm tired. It was hard for me to concentrate during my appointment with the other geisha. I was too distracted thinking about the Buddhist monk I saw before I left the okiya.
He was dressed in gray, and I had never seen him before. He asked to speak to me, but I was allowed only to see him for a few minutes, as I needed to get ready to leave. He told me that the man who attacked Mitsuko was possessed by an oni - a demon. The monk had been hunting it for a long time. By the time he arrived here, the demon had already moved to another body, and the man had no knowledge of what he'd done.
The monk warned me that my family and I would be cursed with bad luck unless the demon could be stopped. He told me to be careful. I didn't believe him; I told him he was crazy. He ordered me to get Mitsuko's kanzashi for him. I was so afraid of him; I gave it to him. He held it in his hands while he prayed over it for a moment. He gave it back to me saying it now had the power to help me fight the demon.
The monk promised to continue to hunt for it, but he knew the final battle would occur long after he was dead. He blessed me and told me I would have a good life away from Japan. He handed the kanzashi back to me, and I looked at it. It felt alive in my hand; it was warm and seemed to tingle

against my palm. When I looked up to ask him why it was like that, he was gone.

"This is weird, but I still don't understand," Emi said.

"You have been dreaming about Mitsuko," her grandmother whispered. "She and I were on the path walking home when she was abducted. I have been dreaming that you are the one to fight the demon."

The shock of what she heard must have registered on her face, it made her grandmother laugh, but it was without joy. "I had that same look on my face when the monk came to see me," she said. "I was afraid that I would be expected to do something. I had begun dreaming about Mitsuko crying and thought it might be time for me to fight the demon. Then the dreams stopped, and a few months later I left Japan and emigrated to Hawaii. I met your grandfather, and we had your mother. When she was nineteen, the dreams started again, but they stopped, and I was happy. I began to believe that what the monk said wasn't true."

"What happened when Mariko was born?" Emi asked.

Her grandmother smiled sadly again. "Nothing, no dreams. I thought when she turned nineteen that the dreams would start again, but they didn't. I thought we were safe."

"Until me, you mean?" Emi asked.

Kumi nodded. "After your birthday a few months ago, I had the dreams again. I was surprised knowing you were only eighteen. I was shown that I needed to give you the willow kanzashi. You will be the one to fight the demon that plagues us even now. You must prevent us from being cursed and save Mitsuko."

Emi made a face. "How do I do that? Mitsuko died before I was born."

Her grandmother shrugged. "There must be a way, but I don't know how. If I could take this away from you, I would, but this journey is yours. Look to your dreams. They will show you the way. Once you are given instructions, do not hesitate," her grandmother said.

Emi stood and leaned over to kiss her grandmother's soft cheek. "Are you sure about this?" She asked.

"There are many things between Heaven and Earth that I do not understand, but this I believe. Be careful," her grandmother said. "Go now. It's late."

Glancing at her watch, Emi realized that two hours had gone by. It was now after ten. Her grandmother was usually in bed by eight. She left to allow her grandmother to rest.

Driving home, Emi felt odd. Thankfully, there wasn't much traffic on the road. Emi rolled down the window and allowed the warm night air to flow through the car. She wasn't sure she believed what her grandmother told her. Emi had heard the story of her grandmother's friend's abduction, but Emi didn't know any of the details. Thoughts of curses, demons, and mysterious monks made her wonder if mental illness ran in her family. Considering what had been happening, it could be a viable explanation, and the reason her mother wouldn't get out of bed.

When she arrived, her sister's car was there. Looking at the time, she realized it was too early for her to be home. Emi parked the car and went in. Mariko's purse was on her bed, and Emi noticed the bathroom door was closed. The walls of the apartment were thin, and she could hear Mariko throwing up. It wasn't often that her sister got sick. Emi thought to boil hot water for tea. It might help settle Mariko's stomach.

With a greenish cast to her skin, her sister left the bathroom.

"Do you want some tea?" Emi asked.

Mariko shook her head and lay down on her bed. Turning onto her side, she curled into the fetal position and hugged her pillow. Emi went to turn off the water knowing it would stay hot for a while; it was possible that her sister might change her mind later. Emi was tired and ready to go to bed. Leaving her sister to rest, she checked on her mother who was still awake.

"Baba wasn't feeling well," Emi insisted.

Her mother frowned at her. "I told you not to go over there," she scolded.

"Yeah, why did you say that? She could have called because she needed a doctor or something," Emi commented.

"You need to be careful," her mother warned. "You don't want to make him angry."

"Make who angry?" Emi asked.

Her mother had a strange, faraway expression on her face that Emi found disturbing. The thought that her family had a streak of mental illness was gaining ground in her mind again. Her family could absolutely have a crack in their psychological makeup, which left her wondering if she were next.

"The powerful man who lives across the street."

Frowning, Emi looked out the bedroom window. All she could see was the cement wall.

"No one lives there, Mom," Emi responded. "Does he live in the apartments up the street?"

Her mother frowned. "No, he told me he lives right across from us and can see everything we do. He said not to listen to your grandmother because we have a curse on us. To break it, we have to do what he says. I have to stay in bed, Mariko has to work, and you need to go to school. Ignore everything your Baba says about the past; she's old and doesn't know what she's talking about." Her mother became insistent as she spoke, so much so that Emi stepped back.

"Who is this man?" Emi asked.

"He whispers to me from outside, can't you hear him?" Her mother asked.

Emi watched her mother turn to look out the window. "I don't hear anything," Emi said.

Her mother nodded as if listening. "Hai. He says it's because your grandmother has been stopping you from hearing the truth. From now on you will stay away from her. Let the old woman have her fantasies. We have our own lives to live."

Emi pointed to where her mother lay in bed. "You call this living?

You refuse to get out of bed. Mariko and I are forced to serve you hand and foot. What happens when you can't get out of bed because your muscles have atrophied? Do you expect us to change your diapers and bathe you too?"

Yuki grabbed a book off her nightstand and threw it at Emi who caught it. "Don't you talk to me like that, I'm your mother. It's your responsibility to take care of your elders."

"Baba is my elder," Emi reminded her. "Yours too."

"Stop being disrespectful and do what I say! Get out of here," her mother shouted.

Emi spun on her heel and left the room.

Mariko was still lying on her side, and despite the warmth of the night, she was shivering. Emi pulled up the blanket from the end of the bed, draped it over her sister and in a few moments, the shivering abated. Emi wondered if she needed to drive Mariko to the emergency room. She asked her if she needed anything, or wanted to go to the doctor, Mariko said no. Deciding to leave her be for the moment, Emi went to take a shower.

Tiredness was taking its toll and the test she had tomorrow worried her. She hadn't done as much studying as she planned to do tonight. She would find a way to make time to study tomorrow before class.

Taking a shower, washing her hair, she let the cool water run over her head and closed her eyes. As soon as she did, images from the dreams played on the inside of her eyelids. They were vivid, alive with movement. Varying shades of green and warm gold played before her eyes. Emi heard the whispering of the wind through the trees even though she knew there were no trees outside the bathroom window. She even felt the breeze on her face.

Opening her eyes, she blinked to clear her vision. While her eyes were open, she could see still the dream images superimposed on the walls of the shower. Finishing up, she grabbed two towels, one for her hair, and the other for her body. Stepping out, she felt strange; the images in her mind were only now beginning to fade.

Looking around, she realized she had forgotten to bring clean clothes with her. She left the bathroom wearing the towel to pull clothes from her dresser. Swinging the bathroom door wide, she found Mariko sitting up on her bed with the willow kanzashi in her hand.

"Where did you get this?" Mariko asked.

"Baba gave it to me, why?" Emi answered, walking over to her dresser. She began digging through the various drawers looking for what she wanted. Emi went back into the bathroom to put on her clothes, but she kept the door cracked to hear her sister's response.

"You shouldn't have this, you know," Mariko said. "You should give it back to Baba and tell her you don't want it."

Emi came back into the room and looked at her sister staring at the hair ornament in her hand. Strangely, the palms of Mariko's hands were turning red.

"What is wrong with you, do I need to take you to the doctor?" Emi asked.

Mariko looked at her. "No, I feel fine," she said.

"Then why were you sick earlier?"

"Ow," Mariko yelped, dropping the kanzashi on her bed and shaking her hands as if burned. "What are you talking about?"

Emi snatched the kanzashi off Mariko's bed and held it. It didn't feel different, but her sister's hands were still red.

"You came home early from work, and you were throwing up when I walked in, what was that?" Emi asked.

"No, I wasn't," Mariko insisted. "And so what if I left work a little early?"

Mariko turned to look at the bathroom door, then back at her as if trying to remember something. Emi knew something was wrong with both her mother and her sister. She was about to ask Mariko if she could take her temperature when her cell phone rang. It was her grandmother again.

"Where are you?" her grandmother asked when she answered. Emi thought she sounded exhausted.

"At home," Emi answered. "Are you okay?"

"No, I need you to come over now," her grandmother insisted.

"Baba, I was just there," Emi complained. "I'll come over after school tomorrow. I'm tired, and I have a test tomorrow."

As she talked on the phone, her sister watched her intently. It was uncomfortable, but not unusual. Unless she went outside to sit in her car, there was no such thing as privacy. Emi turned away to look out the window.

"Did you hear me? Come now," her grandmother ordered. "It's not safe there. I had a dream that something happened to your mother and Mariko. Don't sleep there. Leave now."

Her grandmother hung up. The conversation was over, and there would be no arguments. Being the matriarch of the family, whenever she gave an order, she expected to be obeyed. Emi stared at the blank screen on her phone for a moment before making a sound of frustration. She wouldn't bother changing back into her street clothes; she was already wearing her pajamas. Emi searched and found her other bag to pack the things she'd need for tonight and tomorrow.

"You can't go."

Emi turned at the sound of her mother's voice.

"What?" She was surprised to see her out of bed and standing in the doorway to her room.

"I said you can't go," her mother repeated in a strange tone of voice. It caused the hair on Emi's neck to stand up and made her pack her things faster.

"Did you hear what mom said?" Mariko asked, standing and getting in her way when Emi headed for the bathroom to get her toothbrush.

By this time, the hair on Emi's arms had joined the hair on her neck by pulling away from her skin. Her family's behavior had rolled right past strange and was swiftly approaching creepy. She expected them soon to start grabbing her, but thankfully they kept their distance while trying to persuade her to stay. Ignoring their protests, Emi got her things together and put on her socks and sneakers. Pulling her hoodie over her head, she walked out, taking the kanzashi and the bag containing her books with her.

Emi unlocked her car and tossed her bags over to the passenger side, remembering that she would have to park in the building's garage. Mariko and her mother parked there when they went to visit because they had the remotes to open the gates. At this hour of the night, the visitor spots would be taken, and it was unlikely she would find space on the street.

Sorting through the keys on her keychain, she found the one for her mother's car. As it hardly moved these days, there was no reason to keep the remote in that car. Emi unlocked the driver's side door and pulled the remote off the visor. Her mother called her name from the front door, telling her to put it back. Emi locked the car and looked up; both her mother and sister were standing at the screen door watching her. Getting back in her car, Emi locked the door and started it up. She drove away feeling something cold and slimy sweep across the back of her neck.

The clock on her dashboard showed it was now past midnight. Confusion mixed with tiredness in her brain. She should be in bed by now with her head full of places, names, and dates of the Great Depression. Instead, she was driving away from her bizarre family.

Traffic was light, and it wouldn't take long to get there. The night air was cool, and she kept the windows rolled up to keep warm. She pulled into the parking lot and let the car idle while she waited for the gate to roll up. The garage was well lit and regularly patrolled by the security staff. It was one of the reasons her grandmother had chosen this building, and now that Emi thought about it, she thought it odd. There were other places she could have chosen, but her grandmother was adamant about living here. Baba had also insisted on living on the eighth floor. Emi assumed it was for good luck. Getting into the elevator, Emi noticed something she never gave any thought to before. The building was tall, at least twenty floors, but the elevator was missing the buttons for floors four, thirteen, and fourteen. Four is considered bad luck in Japan. Emi thought it interesting that superstition was still alive and well, even in the most modern of cities.

Carrying both bags, she walked down the hall. Emi was hoping that whatever her grandmother wanted with her wouldn't take much time; she wanted to go to bed. Using her key, she opened the door and found her grandmother pacing the living room; she rushed to her as Emi closed and locked the door. Toeing off her shoes, Emi left them near the front door while her grandmother asked her a question.

"Are you all right?" she asked.

Emi made a face. "Yes, why wouldn't I be?"

"Good, good. I wanted to make sure you got here all right."

"What is going on?" Emi asked allowing her backpacks to fall to the floor.

Breathing out a deep breath, her grandmother said, "Go to bed. You'll go to school tomorrow, then come right back here."

Her grandmother's tone implied there would be no argument about it, and Emi was too tired to fight with her. Emi picked up her bags, went into the second of the three bedrooms, put her bags in the closet, and took off her jacket. The kanzashi fell out of her pocket, and she put that on the nightstand. Standing at the door, preparing to close it, she saw her grandmother watching her from further down the hall. She said goodnight, closed the door, turned the light off, and flopped into bed. She pulled the covers up and curled onto her side. The dream began as soon as she was asleep.

Overlooking a large pond, she stood on a sturdy wooden bridge while colorful koi fish created ripples in the water as they swam under the bridge. The late afternoon air carried a chill that settled on her skin. The sun stretched shadows all around her. Her hands rested on the cool railing as her eyes scanned as far as she could see. Wherever she was, there were no buildings tall enough to create a discernible skyline. She could see nothing but beautiful green trees and blooming flowers.

The breeze brushed Emi's neck, and she shivered. Instinctively, she reached to pull up the hood on her jacket when she noticed she wasn't wearing one. Looking at her arm, she quickly figured out she was wearing a kimono. It was blue and white made of a soft, sturdy fabric, the kind of clothing someone would wear every day. Wiggling her toes, she found tabis on her feet and the pressure of the strap of the low woven sandal between her big and second toes on each foot. In front of her on the railing was a cloth bag. She had no idea what was inside but assumed it was hers.

Emi got the feeling that she needed to be somewhere and the general direction that she should go. Taking her cloth bag, she hurried off the bridge. Passing others, she bowed slightly as she walked. She kept going, not knowing where she would end up, but certain she needed to be there. Leaving the bridge, she walked on a path that cut through some trees. She walked around a corner and there on a stone bench was a Buddhist monk dressed in gray robes. The monk's hair was cut very close to his head, and he had a kind smile. He stood when she approached, and they bowed to one another.

"Please sit," he said in Japanese.

She didn't feel any sort of unease around him, only curiosity. Emi sat on the hard stone and waited with the knowledge that she was dreaming, and nothing could hurt her.

"Emiko, I have been waiting for you a long time," he confessed.

"Waiting for what?" Emi asked. She made a face, realizing she'd answered him in Japanese. She understood some Japanese but couldn't speak it.

"I am Kinsei; my task is to banish an oni that is destroying history. His interference is creating an imbalance in the universe. I must stop him now to prevent the things that will happen in the future."

Emi watched him speak. It was obvious that he was passionate about his work, but she wasn't certain how she could help and said as much.

"The oni is running loose," Kinsei announced. "He's possessing people and making them do terrible things. I've been chasing him for a long time and have been unable to banish him. This demon is smart, he knows me. As soon as I get close to him, he vanishes. I need someone to help me capture him; someone he will assume is too weak to assist me."

Emi shuffled her feet as she sat there. Others continued to pass by bowing in acknowledgment.

"I don't know anything about oni demons or balancing the universe. I'm eighteen years old. I can barely get myself out of bed in the morning. I don't see how I can help you."

Kinsei nodded and his lips curved into a smile. "I see there is something your grandmother has not told you. The man who abducted Mitsuko took the wrong woman. He was sent for your grandmother. Someone in the okiya must have told the oni what color kimono she was supposed to wear that night. At the last minute, the kimonos were switched."

"Why would the demon want my grandmother?" Emi asked. "She was just one of many maikos in the city. There were also plenty of geikos. Why her?"

Kinsei turned at the sound of a shrub rustling nearby. He turned back after determining it was only the wind. "The abducted women were maiko-still in training. They were all regarded as exceptionally beautiful and talented. The oni sought to destroy the most promising artisans. Your grandmother impressed many with her ability to play the shamisen."

"Is that why she was cursed?" Emi asked.

The day was beautiful, and despite the peacefulness of her surroundings, Emi felt anxious.

Kinsei ran a hand down his face before answering. "Yes, the demon had already affected many lives, but he follows yours. He's determined not only to destroy the woman he missed, but also her family. None in your family has been strong enough to resist his influence. The only exceptions are you and your grandmother."

Emi's eyes widened wondering if that was the reason her mother and sister had been so weird of late. Adjusting his robes and clearing his throat, Kinsei seemed to be waiting for Emi to speak.

"What do I do?" she asked.

"Rest now, speak to your grandmother later. She will explain more," Kinsei promised. Emi watched as he faded from her sight. She reached for him, intending to ask more questions. Her hand landed on the spot where he sat. It was still warm.

Waking up to a knock on the door, Emi remembered she wasn't at home. She opened the door to find her grandmother standing there with a smile on her face.

"Good morning, I made you breakfast and lunch. I didn't want you to be late for school."

Emi nodded bleary-eyed and headed toward the bathroom. Then she remembered her backpacks were in the closet. She turned around, and her grandmother handed her the one with her clothes. Emi took it and went to wash up. By the time she was done, she was dressed in jeans, a t-shirt, and her favorite hoodie. Socks were on her feet, and her shoes were by the door.

Her grandmother had bacon and eggs on a plate with a cup of tea and toast waiting for her. Two spam musubi sat beside the plate, bound in plastic wrap ready to go. It was one of Emi's favorite things to dig into, this compact lunch made of rectangular shaped rice, flavored with soy sauce, topped with a piece of spam fried until crispy and wrapped in dried seaweed called nori. They would go into the other backpack that was waiting on the chair next to her. Emi had her breakfast, packed her lunch, and left.

On her way to school, the traffic was brutal, but she made it in time for biology class, and it went as well as she had hoped. History was the class she was most worried about, and as she took her seat, having gotten there early, she felt anxiety rising in the pit of her stomach. Trying not to think about it, she smiled at Michelle, the woman who normally took the seat next to her.

"Hi, how's it going?" Michelle asked. "Are you ready for the test?"

Emi made a face. "Not really, I didn't have time to study. I'm going to wing it," she answered.

The instructor handed out the exam. Emi took hers and wrote her name at the top. It was four pages long; questions were both multiple choice and essay. She flipped back and forth to the multiple-choice ones first to answer those quickly and get them out of the way. Emi wanted more time to try to write something coherent and logical for the essays. She was already struggling in most of her classes. Despite her best intentions, a failing grade on this exam could drag down her G.P.A. even more.

Looking up to give her eyes a break, she saw something colorful out of the corner of her eye. Near the door, stood a woman dressed in a green kimono. Her face was painted white, and only her bottom lip had lipstick. She tilted her head and her lips lifted in a little smile that crinkled her eyes. In her dark hair, she wore the willow kanzashi Emi recognized.

"Konnichiwa," the woman said. Emi looked around the room. No else seemed to notice the visitor say, 'good afternoon.'

"My name is Mitsuko."

Even those staring off in her direction seemed not to notice her, but, Emi dared not speak in the quiet classroom.

"You don't have to say anything," Mitsuko continued in Japanese. "Your obaasan, your grandmother, my friend Kumi, says you are strong and believes you can help me. I am trapped and cannot reincarnate. Now that I see you, I think she is right. No matter what happens, I wish you good fortune and many blessings."

The apparition faded, and Emi steadied her breathing to try to calm her thundering heart.

"Time's up class, please hand in your exam." The instructor's voice seemed too loud for the quiet room. Emi frantically looked at her paper. She knew she hadn't finished. Staring at it, she saw that every question had been answered.

Leaving the classroom, Emi went to a convenience store near campus and bought a bottle of water. A park wasn't far, and she walked there to sit under a tree to eat her lunch. Other students were there enjoying the day. Some were talking, eating, or studying. Others were throwing a football. Sitting on the grass in the shade of a tree, Emi opened her backpack. She took out one of the musubi and peeled back the wrapper to take a bite. Sitting cross-legged, she watched the others run on the grass. It was nice to listen to them laugh and tease one another.

Emi never really had time for friends. She'd had a few over the years, but things happen. Friendships, like all things that are not maintained, fall apart. With the way her life was structured, it made it difficult to take time to spend with other people, but she had a feeling that things would soon be different.

Taking a sip of water, she ate her musubi in peace. The warm breeze was comforting on such a hot day. It rustled the leaves over-head causing flickering shadows on the ground. She watched them closely, appreciating the coordinated movement of them. Each leaf on the tree took the precise steps in the dance the wind played. The sounds of the others around her faded away.

She saw herself in the clothes she now wore, walking along a lighted path at night. The temperature was cool, but she was comfortable. There were no overhead lamps; paper lanterns lighted the path with flickering flames. The dim lamps cast light and shadow in equal measure. She was in the same area she'd been in, during the dream with Kinsei, and the bench she sat on earlier was just ahead. Next to that was a thick clump of bushes. Standing there for a moment not knowing what to do, she looked around trying to decide. Turning at the sound of voices, she could hear two women speaking, and saw them drawing closer. Emi heard one of them telling the other to hurry, or they would be scolded.

Unable to think what else to do, Emi chose to step off the path and hide behind the bushes to let the women pass. When they got closer, she realized who they were. One was her grandmother, the other, Mitsuko, the woman who had visited her less than an hour ago. The two women walked past giggling and moving as fast as their tall okobo would allow. Kumi stopped to shake her right foot in an attempt to dislodge a pebble from her shoe. Emi stood to tell Mitsuko to stop, but it was too late.

The vision changed, and Emi was not herself. When she felt someone grab her arm and drag her off the path, she realized she was Mitsuko. She shrieked. A heavy hand hit her on the side of the head. Dazed, she could no longer fight him as he grabbed her around the waist. He pulled her up against his body. His clothes smelled of sweat, fried food, and the alcohol scent of spilled sake. He began carrying her uphill through the trees. The bottom of her kimono dragged in the dirt. He lost his grip on the fabric. She tumbled to the ground hitting her head. Darkness soon enveloped her.

The vision changed again. Emi was now Kumi, pulling free of the bush that held fast to her obi. She kicked off her okobo and tried to run between the trees where she had seen the man take her friend. She stepped on the hem of her kimono and went down. Digging in her fingers, she pushed up from the dirt, flung the hem of the kimono aside, and tried to run again. The pain of stepping on a rock threw her off balance, sending her careening into a tree. Mitsuko's bright kimono was almost out of sight. There was no way she would be able to keep up. She had to go for help. Emi as Kumi gathered the end of her kimono to carry it and went back to the path leaving her shoes behind. She picked up Mitsuko's kanzashi and ran to the okiya screaming for help the whole way.

The sound of a car horn blaring on the street startled Emi reminding her she was still sitting beneath a tree on a sunny day. Her grandmother's story had just come to life in her head.

What the hell is happening to me?

The last class of the day was music appreciation, and it went well. Emi got through it and then walked to where she parked her car. Dropping her bag on the passenger's seat, her cell phone started ringing. Looking at the screen, she answered, "Hello Baba."

"Come straight here, don't go home," her grandmother demanded.

The timing of her grandmother's call was so perfect it was eerie. "But I need clothes, I only have my pajamas," Emi whined.

"Never mind that, come here as soon as you can," her grandmother ordered.

Emi sighed putting the key in the ignition. "OK. I'm leaving school now. I'll be there as soon as I can."

"I mean it Emi; this is very important, don't go home. Not yet. I'll explain when you get here."

Emi promised she would drive there with no stops. To do that, the easiest thing would be to get on the H1 freeway. Opening the windows to let the heat out before turning on the air conditioning, Emi started the car and drove away from the campus. She made her way to the nearest on-ramp to go in the Ewa bound direction to head for Salt Lake.

Emi parked in the garage and used the code to enter the building to take the elevator. Opening the front door of the condo with her key, Emi could see her grandmother standing in the kitchen. From the sound of something boiling on the stove, Emi assumed she had started to cook dinner. Her grandmother put down the spoon she was using to look at her. Baba was wearing her favorite apron. It was made from fabric printed with different kinds of sushi on it.

"I'm glad you're here," Kumi said.

Emi stopped to take off her shoes by the door and put her bag down on the couch before walking into the kitchen. Her grandmother had dinner ingredients spread out all over the counter. The cabinetry was white, but Baba had insisted on a dark, marble-like countertop. Emi had always been fascinated with it. It was a deep blue with a smattering of gold and silver under the clear top. Emi thought they had captured a piece of the universe and looking at it was a chance to gaze into infinity.

"Now that I am here," Emi observed. "What is this about?"

Her grandmother turned away to stir what was in the pot. The miso paste and tofu on the counter told Emi it was miso soup and it made her mouth water.

"Until this is finished one way or another, you can't go home. I went to your house today and got clothes for you. I have a feeling that if we don't succeed, it won't matter," her grandmother said.

"What are you talking about? None of this is making sense to me. I feel like I'm losing my mind. The three people I'm closest to are acting weird. I hallucinated today with a waking dream. If you can't explain this to me, then at least take me to the doctor. I think I might need medication," Emi commented.

Her grandmother laughed. "There's nothing wrong with you. Come sit down."

She gestured for Emi to sit at the table before taking off her apron, folding it, and putting it on the counter. Emi patiently waited for an explanation.

"I know you don't understand," her grandmother said. "I don't either. All I know is that for years, I've been dreaming about a monk, the same one I met years ago. He kept telling me over and over in the dreams that one day there will be justice for Mitsuko. He told me someone I knew would help her. I think that person is you, but of course, I don't know for certain. I'm only going by what my dreams have told me."

Emi sighed. "I don't know what I'm supposed to do or if I can do anything at all," she said. She then described the dream from last night and the waking dream during lunch.

The older lady shook her head. "The monk told me someone would find a way to save Mitsuko, and I can't help thinking that you're involved."

Emi leaned back in her chair and looked out the glass of the sliding door. The sunset began to turn the sky all the colors she associated with paradise. Pink, purple, gold and orange painted the top of the world. She took a breath in appreciation for the beauty she often took for granted.

Her grandmother stood and reached for something on the counter. Emi saw it was the kanzashi. She thought it was weird to be there as the last time that she'd seen it, it was still in her backpack.

"Go study until it's time for dinner," her grandmother said, holding the ornament out to her.

Emi stood and took the kanzashi from her.

"Put your shoes on," her grandmother insisted.

"Huh?" It was a strange request as they never wore shoes in the house. Her grandmother nodded, giving her a stern look warning her not to argue, and Emi went to put her shoes back on. She reached for her backpack to get her books.

"You won't need that," her grandmother said.

Emi's face scrunched up. "How can I study without my books?"

Her grandmother pointed a finger toward the hallway. "Take the kanzashi and go," she ordered.

Emi rolled her eyes and headed for her bedroom. Right before she stepped through the doorway, she dropped the kanzashi. Leaning forward to pick it up, she lost her balance and fell forward. Instead of landing on the carpet in her bedroom, she ended up sprawling face down in the dirt behind a bush. Clearing the dirt from her face, she rolled over. Even in the dark, she recognized where she was and more importantly, *when* she was.

Flickering lanterns on the side of the path cast just enough light to see by. The light was too dim to see anyone who might be hiding. The smell of cooking food and incense wafted through the air. It was quiet and peaceful. Emi was near the path where she had seen the two maikos walking.

Emi's heart was racing even though this couldn't be real. Reaching out, she touched a leaf on the bush in front of her feeling the firm veins and traced the smooth edge of it. Putting it up to her nose and smelling it, Emi knew this was real. The leaf in her hand confirmed that she'd traveled back in time to the moments right before the women were attacked.

Knowing about the attack didn't help Emi know how to stop it. The attack would happen at a blind corner further up the path from where she stood. She ducked down when the women came into view. Emi could see that one of them wore a light green kimono and the other wore pink. Even in the murky light, the satin fabric shimmered as they moved. They were enjoying themselves, huddled together, giggling, and speaking in low voices.

Drawing closer to where Emi hunkered down, they seemed to have no idea she was there. It was late at night, but they were not as vigilant as Emi expected them to be. Then she remembered that this was a time when violence was unlikely. Most could walk late at night with little fear of being accosted. The sound of their wooden shoes striking the paving stones echoed in the silence. Little steps moved them forward, their tightly wrapped kimonos restricting the movement of their legs.

The only sounds were of the women and the whisper of the wind through the trees. From the security of the bushes, Emi's heart thundered in her chest as she watched them pass. When they were far enough away not to notice, she crept out to walk silently behind them, grateful for her modern shoes. They were coming to the blind bend in the path where Mitsuko would be taken. Emi decided to walk up into the trees and see if the kidnapper was there. She made her way between the trunks and saw the man waiting for them.

Emi saw him hunched over next to a tree at the edge of the path. He was nothing more than a dark shadow until he turned his head to watch them approach. Emi saw his eyes reflecting light in the darkness. They had a strange reddish glow. It was then that she believed she was fighting a demon. Emi moved closer waiting for inspiration to strike to tell her what to do next.

The women came to the curve, and her grandmother stopped. Mitsuko kept walking. The sound of an okobo striking the path reverberated. The demon pounced. Emi watched him leap from his hiding place, the scant light reflecting off a knife in his hand. He grabbed Mitsuko, and she screamed. Kumi scrabbled to hold onto Mitsuko's kimono. The demon reached over and shoved her back, throwing her off balance. It sent her careening into the plants on the other side of the path. He dropped the knife and used two hands to drag Mitsuko between the trees.

"Let her go," Emi shouted stepping forward. The demon turned to her. The light from his eyes was not a reflection. They were glowing red. He snarled at her, threw Mitsuko to the ground, and stalked toward Emi. The ground she stood on was uneven, but Emi secured her footing as best she could. Refusing to think about how much larger her opponent was as he approached. Emi could hear his harsh breathing filtering through his grimaced teeth. His eyes still emanated the ghostly red light. Her instincts told her run and never look back. As she stood there shaking, she almost did. The sounds of fear coming from the other two women kept her glued to the spot.

Mitsuko whimpered. Kumi had scrambled into the trees toward her friend and had begun trying to get Mitsuko to her feet. Emi watched them work to escape but couldn't spare them any further attention. The demon was now within arm's reach. Emi allowed her thoughts and feelings to fall away and let her Tai No Henko training take over. He swung a heavy arm toward her. She stepped to the side to avoid it while clamping her fingers around his wrist. Emi used his own momentum to twist his hand and throw him to the ground, then stepped out of reach again. Roaring, he stood. Emi positioned herself, being conscious of where the trees were to have enough room to maneuver.

He came at her again. Turning her body once more, she rolled her back along his arm throwing him off balance again. Emi planned to run as soon as she was clear of his weight, but his hand struck out grabbing her ponytail. As he fell, he pulled her off her feet, releasing her when they hit the ground. Emi rolled out of reach, using a tree to scramble to her feet.

She thought of running again, but the man the demon occupied was fit and tall. He would catch her with the length of his stride, and she had nowhere to run. He stood and came at her once more. Emi used her smaller stature and faster reflexes to avoid and deflect his blows over and over. Sweat dripped into her eyes. Her muscles ached from the strain. He seized her arm and flung her against a tree, knocking the breath from her, and leaving her dazed. She dropped to the dirt on her hands and knees, gasping for breath. Her head cleared enough for her to reach toward the base of the tree to help her stand.

Grabbing her around the middle, the demon hiked her up on his side.

"I'll take you instead." Her attacker chuckled. Suspended and dangling from his side, he carried Emi without effort. Her head hurt, and she was only partially aware of what was happening. She thrashed in his grip, and he hit her with a solid hand, leaving her senses reeling again. The only thought in her mind was that she was being dragged away by the demon who had murdered Mitsuko.

With her head spinning and her vision blurred, she dared not struggle. He might hit her harder the next time, making her pass out. To survive, she had to stay conscious. He was moving swiftly now, taking her further away from the only part of Japan she knew. Panic started in the pit of her stomach, and the jostling she endured as he carried her made her nauseous. They were still in the trees, but the forest was thinning out. The tree trunks were spaced wider apart, and she could see light coming from somewhere ahead of them.

An idea surfaced in her addled mind, but she wasn't sure it would work. She only had one chance to do something, and she had to act, or she would die. Emi let her weight go slack. He was now carrying her as dead weight. He shook her trying to wake her, and she continued to hold herself motionless.

He stopped and put her down to look at her. When he turned her over, Emi positioned her arm to land on her chest. Her eyes were open and staring, being careful not to blink or move. As he leaned closer, she remained still and held her breath. When he was close enough, she stiffened her wrist, flung out her elbow, and struck. The firm edge of her hand landed on the side of his throat. Her abductor squeaked out a strangled sound and moved away, clutching his neck. Emi rolled to a crouch and spun, extending a leg to sweep his feet out from under him, then standing to her full height. He went down with a hard grunt. As he rose, Emi kneed him in the chest, sending him sprawling on his side, his weight and momentum turned him onto his back, landing face up. She positioned herself to fight again. He lay still in the dirt. She couldn't even tell if he was breathing. Emi thought she saw blood near his temple, but she stayed where she was and waited, not willing to take the chance he was only pretending to be unconscious.

Movement from her left made her back up and pivot her body to prepare for an attack from that direction while keeping her eyes on the man on the ground.

"Emiko, it's Kinsei."

Emi heard the voice and saw him approach in his monk's robes.

Holding her position, adrenaline coursed through Emi's veins. Still on edge and mistrustful of everything around her, she remained watchful. Her head hurt, and her body ached while she balanced somewhere between wanting to scream or cry.

To Emi's relief, Kinsei didn't get close. He moved to the man on the ground. Emi moved a step closer to observe. Kinsei held up his hand.

"Keep your distance."

Emi took a few steps back. Kinsei chanted softly, and the man's body began to glow with the same red light that before had only been in his eyes. Emi's mouth dropped open as the light separated from the man's body and floated above it. Red tinted smoke swirled in the air until it coalesced into a hunched translucent creature made of crimson light. It was nearly half the size of the man it hovered over. It opened its mouth showing its fangs and flexed leathery wings. Emi stepped back again, and the creature turned and hissed at her. She leaned against a tree and suddenly felt faint. It was only the firmness of the wood beneath her hand that kept her steady on her feet.

Emi watched as Kinsei raised his left hand and the creature was unable to move. It struggled against an invisible barrier. With his other hand, Kinsei drew a circular shape in the air, and a ring of white light appeared to the right of the monster. The perimeter of the sphere flashed brightly when it was completed, and the creature flinched. Kinsei moved the hand that had drawn the circle swiftly from right to left. The circle moved, passing over the creature making it disappear. As soon as Emi could no longer see it, Kinsei closed his left hand as if crushing a piece of paper. The circle closed to a pinpoint of light. Kinsei turned his fist, palm up, opened his hand, and blew on it. The point of light flew away on the wind. Emi watched all of this with awe. She'd never seen anything like it before and doubted she would again.

Kinsei smiled at her and faded from her vision.

"Wait, how do I get back?" She shouted.

Emi looked around disoriented. She could return to the path but had no idea where to go from there.

"Sumimasen." A voice saying 'excuse me' from behind her made Emi jump. It was Kumi dressed in a casual kimono, with her makeup still on her face.

Emi turned to look at her. "Hai," Emi answered bowing.

Laughter creased the face of her grandmother's younger self. "Your bowing is terrible," she said.

"I can't pour tea either," Emi replied in English noting that it came out in Japanese.

Her grandmother laughed. "My name is Kumi, come with me. You can stay with us until the monk returns for you," she said.

"Wakarimasen," Emi answered, admitting that she didn't understand. Kumi waved her hand encouraging her to follow. Not having any other options, Emi trailed her grandmother out of the trees.

"What are you doing here?" Emi asked, amazed that she was speaking Japanese fluently.

Kumi answered. "I saw you fight off the man. When we went to our okiya, they didn't believe that another woman had fought him off and allowed us to get away. I climbed out the window to come back here. I needed to make sure you were all right. I saw you defeat him like the monk said you would."

"Wait, you knew?" Emi asked, stopping on the path to look at Kumi who looked at the ground for a moment before speaking.

"I wasn't sure. I saw the monk one day in town. He stopped me to say that soon I would be in danger and there would be a woman dressed strangely that would come to help. To return the favor, I needed to take care of her for a few hours, and by morning she would be gone. I didn't believe him, but now I see that he was right."

Kumi walked forward again, and Emi followed. Not knowing

where she was, following her was Emi's best chance for staying out of trouble. Emi was dressed, in jeans, sneakers, and a hoodie, along with her mannerisms, there was no way she would fool anyone into thinking that she belonged here.

The path split a little further down as they walked, and Kumi bore to the left. Shortly after that, buildings came into view. Kumi led her past four of them. Each was painted black with sliding screens. Lanterns hung from the eaves of the buildings, and all was quiet. Kumi turned between two buildings on the left, and their feet soon walked on soft grass. Walking up to the side of a much larger building, Kumi climbed in an open window and then waited for Emi to do the same. Once inside, Kumi took her into another room and sat on the floor next to a low table. Another moment later, Mitsuko came in carrying a tray with tea and cookies.

"I thought you might be hungry," Mitsuko said. "What is your name?"

Emi took a cookie and ate it wondering what to do next. "Emi, um, Emiko," she answered.

"Thank you for saving us, Emiko-san," Mitsuko said. Emi nodded with her mouth full. Glancing at the woman who would be her grandmother, she found her staring.

"What?" Emi asked.

"The monk told me you would look like me and you do. He wouldn't tell me why. Are we related? Are you a cousin of mine?" Kumi asked.

Emi didn't know what to say. She wasn't sure how her actions in the past would affect the future. It was possible that by giving her that information, it could change whether or not Emi was even born. She decided to keep it simple. "You do look familiar, but I know all of my cousins," Emi replied.

Kumi nodded. The three girls sat in silence for the most part. Emi drank the slightly bitter green tea offered to her. She answered their questions as vaguely as she could. The three of them then moved into the room where the women slept.

The room held very little aside from the sleeping pallets with the takamakura, the raised pillows used by maikos. It was to prevent them from crushing the elaborate hairstyles comprised of their own hair. Emi knew that once they were older and became geikos, they could use wigs. Due to the attack, both of them would have to have their hair restyled in the morning. They could sleep however they wanted tonight.

Sunlight was beginning to light the house, and Emi couldn't stifle a yawn any longer. Kumi made up a sleeping pallet for her and gave her a heavy blanket. Both geisha took the time to remove their make-up carefully, then made themselves comfortable and quickly fell asleep. Emi laid awake flat on her back with her bunched-up hoodie under her head for a pillow. She turned onto her side and fell asleep knowing she was alive and well in Japan during World War II.

It seemed only a few moments had passed when a sound woke Emi. When she opened her eyes, she was on her side looking at the younger version of her grandmother. The sound was ruffling cloth. She looked down near her feet and saw Kinsei sitting there drinking a cup of tea. Rolling to a sitting position, she looked at the monk who smiled at her.

"Forgive me for leaving you. I had to make sure I completed my duty with the demon before coming back for you," Kinsei apologized.

Kumi and Mitsuko were still asleep, undisturbed with having a man in their room. Emi also thought it was odd that no one had noticed she was here. Her grandmother had once told her that the okiya was a busy place. Everyone was always checking up on her to make sure she was following her training.

"How much longer do I need to be here?" Emi asked.

"Not long now, a few more minutes," Kinsei said. "Why don't you stand, stretch, and have a cup of tea?"

Emi stretched as he suggested, then sat and drank tea while the young geisha slept on. Soon she could hear sounds in the rest of the building. Others were waking up. Someone stood at the door to the room, and then Emi watched that person crouch down to open the door. An older woman came into the room. Emi stood expecting to be asked who she was and what she was doing, but the woman didn't notice her or the monk.

"She can't see us," Kinsei said. "We are in the space between."

"What does that mean?" Emi asked before pulling the hoodie on over her head.

"It means that we are in a pocket of time. To get you here, we needed to wait for the right moment. To get you back, we need to do the same. There is a flow to things that happen in time. When powerful forces like demons attempt to corrupt those things, it causes a fold. A kind of loop that generates ripples throughout time like a pebble dropped in the water. Sometimes we have an opportunity to stop the pebble from being thrown."

"So that's what this is, an attempt to stop the ripples?" Emi asked.

Kinsei nodded and got to his feet. "The demon has greatly affected time and must be stopped. From last to first, the disturbances must be corrected in order, and I need help to do it, but not today. For today, the job is done." He closed his eyes and took a breath. When he opened them again, he smiled. Emi watched him reach into his robes and pull something out of his pocket.

"Emiko, catch," Kinsei said.

He tossed something small and round into the air, out of reflex, she snatched it as it descended. A piece of cloth had been rolled tightly together. As she felt the texture of the woven fabric, it began to unravel in her hand. It looked like a handkerchief. Emi looked up to ask him what it was for and found herself standing in a room she didn't recognize.

Facing a set of French doors, Emi stood in the living room of a house. Sunlight streamed through the doors casting blocks of light onto the plush carpet beneath her feet. Moving closer to the glass, she glanced outside, taking in a sweeping view of the city of Honolulu. A noise behind her made her turn. It was her grandmother.

"I wondered when you would be back," Kumi said.

"How long have I been gone?" Emi asked.

"Two days, but in the timeline, it's only been a few hours. Come sit down and eat," her grandmother said. Emi followed her through a large kitchen and kept moving as her grandmother gestured for her to have a seat at the breakfast nook near a bay window that overlooked a pool.

"Where are we?" Emi asked, sliding onto the bench surrounding the table.

Pulling things out of the refrigerator, her grandmother then took out a frying pan and started making breakfast. "This is my house. I'm sorry your grandfather isn't here to greet you, he's off golfing with his buddies," Kumi said smiling.

"What?"

Her grandmother chuckled. "When you saved Mitsuko, you also saved us by breaking the curse on our family. The next morning, everything had changed. I was here, and your grandfather was making me breakfast. When I woke up, I had memories of the old life along with the new ones."

Emi watched her grandmother put down a plate of scrambled eggs and sausages on the table.

"What else?" Emi asked, digging into the food.

Her grandmother sat down on the other side of the table. "Your father is also alive. He and your mother are having a great time gambling in Las Vegas right now. Your sister called me yesterday to ask if I could help her choose her wedding dress. She plans to shop for it when your mother comes home."

Emi's mouth dropped open. "This can't be real."

Her grandmother nodded. "It is. The curse the demon placed on us is gone. I couldn't believe it myself. I almost screamed when I saw your grandfather, I thought he was an obake."

Emi laughed imagining her grandmother thinking her husband was a ghost.

"Once I got used to that, my phone rang," Kumi said. "A friend called to ask when I was free to go to lunch. It was Mitsuko. I cried when I heard her voice. She thought I was crazy."

Emi laughed again, continuing to eat. She was hungry but didn't notice it until she smelled the food. Looking at her grandmother's face, Emi knew it was all true. Baba was happy. Emi could feel and see the joy radiating from her.

"Hurry and eat," her grandmother said. "I told Jason that I would have you call when you woke up. I told him that you spent the night because you weren't feeling well. He's concerned."

Emi's eyes widened. "Jason who?" she asked.

"Jason from Aikido class. You and he are good friends and have been spending a lot of time together. He let it slip while he was talking to me that he was planning to ask you out." Her grandmother narrowed her eyes and wiggled her eyebrows. Emi choked on her sausage and felt her face get hot.

"Baba!"

Kumi chuckled. "The day after the attack, I woke up remembering you in the okiya and I was sad that you were gone. I wanted to know more about you. Then I had a vision of you right after you were born, and I knew who you were, and why you looked like me. Years later, when we were in the hospital after your mother had you, she was about to tell me your name. I said it, Emiko, and she asked me how I knew. I told her it was because I had already met you."

Emi finished her breakfast and leaned back against the bench. "Thank you, Baba, that was delicious," she remarked. Slipping her hands into the pocket of her hoodie, she felt what was in there. She pulled it out to show it to her grandmother and told her where she got it.

Handing it to her, the older woman opened it all the way. The handkerchief had delicate embroidery of green willow tree branches in one corner. It looked similar to Mitsuko's kanzashi. As Emi watched, Kumi stood from the table and went to a cabinet next to the kitchen to pull out a small box. Bringing it back to the table, Emi could see it was lacquered black and painted with a Sakura tree in full bloom. Opening it, her grandmother revealed twelve black velvet covered sections, each containing a hair ornament.

Emi watched her grandmother smooth the handkerchief and fold it in a precise manner to display the willow design. It fit in the last square on the bottom right side. "I bought this box years ago, and Mitsuko's kanzashi was stored in it before I gave it to you. Now that the ornament has been returned to its owner, things have been set right. We have a handkerchief to fill that spot, but there are others."

"What do you mean?" Emi asked.

"Do you remember when I showed you the journal?"

Emi nodded, and her grandmother turned the box allowing her to take a closer look at everything inside. "The pages I translated for you were only the first few pages. The ones I wrote after, were everything I could discover about the other women who were found like Mitsuko. What you see here is the last thing each was wearing in her hair when she disappeared."

Emi counted eleven other objects in the box. "All of these?" Emi asked, reaching out to touch the delicate silk flowers and fans.

"Emi, Mitsuko was the last of many. I gathered all the information I could to try to track the demon. I didn't want him to win."

Something Kinsei mentioned surfaced in Emi's memory. He talked about other ripples in time, ones that had to be reversed from last to first.

"We have to help them, Emi," her grandmother said, watching her carefully.

Emi looked at the shimmering ornaments knowing each represented a life cut short. She also considered who else might have been cursed for generations like them. Emi wasn't sure how, but she would do what she could to restore the lives of every woman listed in the sakura notebook.

The End

THANK YOU

We hope you have enjoyed our anthology. It would mean the world to us if you had the time to leave a review! Reviews are what keep us writing!

FOLLOW FICTION-ATLAS PRESS FOR INFORMATION ON FUTURE PUBLICATIONS.

FICTION-ATLAS
PRESS LLC

http://fiction-atlas.com

facebook.com/fictionatlas

twitter.com/fabookbargains

instagram.com/cl_cannon

youtube.com/cl_cannonauthor